THE LONE RANGER CARD

To: Lindy

THE LONE RANGER CARD

Wishing You A Soft Pillow,

Allen Smyth

A NOVEL

ALLEN SMYTH

First Edition

Manufactured in the United States

Paperback Edition ISBN: 978-0-578-47819-7

Cover Art: Bogdan Maksimovic
Cover and Interior Design: Creative Publishing Book Design

To Marilynn, for everything

Whither should I fly?
I have done no harm. But I remember now
I am in this earthly world, where to do harm
Is often laudable, to do good sometime
Accounted dangerous folly. Why then, alas,
.... To say I have done no harm?

Macbeth by William Shakespeare

TABLE OF CONTENTS

PART I

PART II

PART III

PART I

CHAPTER 1

LESTER

Wednesday, September 13, 2000. Lester Rumsfeld pulled his car into a spot on the far right of the student lot away from the hubbub of the school's main entrance. Too many sets of eyes over there.

Michelle's car would be in the teacher's lot around back. Taking his car back there also might arouse curiosity, so he opted to park out here and wait. When it was time, he could walk around.

The big clock on the huge building showed 1:40. The architects of the new red brick high school with its little brick chimneys had tried to emulate a traditional schoolhouse. Somehow it got away from them. The finished product was a huge, sprawling warehouse-like structure with a vast greenish metal roof. More an institution than a schoolhouse. Lester was intimidated by it. He was glad he'd decided to do it outside.

The weather helped. Perfect Fall day. Temp in the high 70s with a light breeze. People in Michigan lived for days like this. Still, it was a little warm inside the car. He lowered both front windows and looked at the big clock. 2:00. He expected her to come out about 3:30. Plan was to go back and crouch behind her car at 3:15 and wait till she walked up. Already he was getting restless; 20 minutes was a long time for Lester to sit still. He shouldn't have gotten there so early.

He was average size, just under six feet, maybe a little tall for his 150 lbs. He never gained back most of what he lost in the hospital. Despite his slight frame nobody was going to mistake him for a student. He was 37 years old and looked 50. He felt even older than that. The lingering symptoms took a toll.

More than anything, he was angry. Not a new feeling for Lester. He'd been angry a lot in the last couple years, ever since the accident, but never like this. This time she'd crossed the line. Now he was jacked to a whole new level. So much so that ten days ago he drove down to Ohio, just outside of Toledo, for the last day of a gun show.

Lester didn't know much about guns. He walked around the rented hall not sure what he was looking for. All he knew was he didn't have much money. His disability claim had not yet been approved. The cheapest gun he saw was on a table near the periphery of the hall, a hundred and seventy five bucks. Seemed like a lot of money for a one-time use, but it was all he could afford. The table was sort of a makeshift setup along the wall; hand printed sign, like at a flea market. Turned out the guy sitting there was not even a licensed gun dealer, but still legal. He was allowed to sell guns at the show. His transactions were called "private sales." Private sales were where you could get a gun without all the bullshit. No hassle about a waiting period or background check or any kinda red tape to slow you down.

The seller said the gun was a snub-nosed, six-cylinder, .38 revolver. Sub-nosed meant it had a very short barrel – about three inches – which, he told Lester, "might make it easier to carry and conceal, but it could affect the accuracy." He tried to sell Lester one with a big long, eight-inch barrel that went for $400. Lester refused. He didn't care about accuracy; he was going to be real close. Didn't have $400 anyway.

Now the big clock showed 2:15. Lester's was getting serious jitters. Sitting for a long time, like more than five minutes, was hard, made harder by his paranoia about being watched. People might be looking out the big windows at this end of the building, focusing on him, wondering what he was doing out here. One of them might call the cops, thinking he was going to grab a kid or something. That would sure screw up his plan.

Maybe I should just improvise a little bit and go in the school now, somehow find her, and get it done. Better than sitting out here forever.

The gun was in the glove compartment. At 2:20 he took it out, stuffed it in his belt, got out of the car, and walked toward the door on the east side of the building. Kids had been coming out of that door every few minutes. Maybe it wasn't locked from the inside, or if it was, he might be able to slip past one of the kids coming out.

He walked along the open traffic lane that went around the east end of the building till he got even with the east door, then turned and walked up to it. The gun was hidden underneath his denim vest jacket, which he didn't otherwise need, seeing how warm it was. He hoped nobody picked up on that.

No one started walking toward him, or yelled, "Hey you," or nothing. He tried the door. It opened from the outside. The Columbine school massacre had happened the year before, but there'd been no school shooting incidents since, so in most schools security was still a low priority. Lester had watched some of the Columbine TV coverage, which at the time lit up a little bulb in his head about Michelle, but like all his other bright ideas, he soon forgot about it. The arrival of the divorce papers last month turned that little bulb back on.

Once inside he entered a long, wide hallway with doors on each side about 30 yards apart. He assumed most of the doors led into classrooms, which was confirmed as he walked down the hallway. Staying in the center so as not to be easily visible from inside the rooms, he walked past each door, taking only a glance through its glass, looking for Michelle. He thought she'd be up in the front of the class.

After what seemed like a lot of doors, he saw her, standing near the front but on the opposite wall, facing the door. Her eyes were directed at a tall brunette, likely one of the students, standing next to the teacher's desk in front of the class. The girl was reading aloud from a paper in her hand. Michelle was focusing on the girl. She didn't see Lester.

The rest was simple. He walked to the door, opened it, took two steps into the class, pulled the gun from the belt of his pants, and as Michelle yelled, "LESTER!" he emptied the six chambers at her. He wasn't as close as he'd planned, but as he turned to run out, he saw Michelle fall. He didn't remember seeing anything else.

Back in the car, turning left onto Six Mile Road toward Sheldon, he smiled, proud of how he'd pulled it off without a hitch.

CHAPTER 2

THE WHITE CASTLE LUNCH

Friday, December, 12, 2014. Pete was nervous. This would be the first time he said the words out loud. He didn't know how to start.

"I, uh...this is going to sound a bit strange, I suppose."

Sitting across the table from Pete, Dylan arched his left eyebrow, creating a facial question mark.

Pete went on, barely above a whisper. "I have something to tell you, to ask you, I mean. I've been planning this...uh...*thing* for some time now, and it's...it's about ready to go." Another pause, trying to find the right words. "As I said, this is going to sound strange, but it's..." He stopped, aware he was rambling, stalling the big reveal.

Dylan, still quizzical, tilted his head as if trying to hear more clearly.

Pete took a deep breath, maintained his muted tone, and spewed it out, "I'm going to assassinate a Supreme Court justice, and I need your help."

It was Friday afternoon. They were having a late lunch in the White Castle on Ford Road. Pete had ordered two double cheeseburgers with fries and Diet Coke. Dylan had two of the regular little burgers, the original sliders, and water. White Castle was Pete's suggestion, not Dylan's. It wouldn't occur to Dylan to eat here. To him, White Castle was at the bottom of the fast food universe, the home of the little three-bite burgers featuring small portions of scary, mystery meat best devoured while holding one's nose with a roll of Tums at the ready. Pete, on the other hand, did White Castle almost once a week, usually alone. He discovered the place over fifty years ago as a twelve-year-old paper boy in Detroit and found the cheap little morsels – 15 cents apiece back then – to be a simple taste pleasure. He'd been eating them long enough to be assured they weren't poison, and he didn't care about their nutritional value.

Arriving before Dylan, he chose a table by the far wall, away from the service counter, where they could talk without entertaining eavesdroppers. The drive-in window kept the staff busy and provided enough clatter to cover their conversation. Only two other customers were eating inside; both sat at tables near the counter. To the casual observer Pete and Dylan were two businessmen slumming it. Pete, the elder, average in every way, including his casual attire; Dylan, bigger, better looking, physically fit, in a suit and tie.

After the stunning pronouncement, Dylan stayed quiet, waiting for the punch line or maybe a "Gotcha!" Pete said nothing, instead reaching into his carton of fries. Both of Dylan's eyebrows were up now, making his eyes bigger and causing them to blink. He held that expression, still waiting for a "just kidding" to confirm he'd heard wrong.

In asking Dylan to lunch, Pete told him only that he had a proposition to discuss. Nothing more. Understandably, his good friend Dylan wouldn't be prepared for the enormity of it. What the hell, it had taken Pete years to get used to the idea himself.

Dylan decided it was a joke. "Maybe we could do a couple Senators while we're at it. Hear some of them are real assholes, too." He muffled his voice, mimicking Pete, lest their strange, dark humor be overheard.

Again silence. Confirmation crept into Dylan's face. It wasn't a prank or a joke or a test. Pete was serious. Dylan's eyebrows retreated down his forehead and narrowed to a pinched position. *WTF? How does a person respond to such an outrageous statement?*

Their table was next to a window wall with wide vertical metal panels separating even wider panes of glass. Dylan turned his head and took in the bleak winter scene outside. Two days before, the season's first big snowfall created an idyllic winter wonderland across southeast Michigan. As of this afternoon the virginal white had aged into dismal brown and gray. It reflected Dylan's mood. He'd been down for some time. Unbeknownst to Pete, Dylan had a plateful of problems. He didn't need another.

He turned back to face Pete. Dylan's body spoke weariness. He set his little burger on its carton, still not having taken a bite, put his elbows on the table, touched his fingers together in that childhood church steeple formation with his thumbs under his chin and his index fingers touching his nose, and took a deep breath, then another. Finally lowering his hands to the table, he spoke in a measured tone, like a parent counseling an adolescent child about the perils of drugs or sex.

"Pete, yes I…I have killed people." He glanced over his shoulder to scan the room for uninvited listeners. "But clearly that was different. I was in the military. I was serving our country."

He leaned back. "I know," holding his hands up with his palms facing Pete, "some of those people were not uniformed combatants. But Pete, it was never like this. They were enemies of our country, for God's sake…like terrorists. This guy isn't a terrorist. Why would we…?" His voice trailed off.

Pete wanted to say, "*Define terrorist,*" but held his tongue, rechecking the counter to see if anyone was reacting to their words.

Like most people, and unlike Dylan, Pete had never killed anyone. Even in Vietnam. In fact, in his whole life he'd hardly ever broken the law, other than minor traffic violations. That's just the way he was, or had been. He knew some of his recent prep activities may have crossed the line, but none involved violence or larceny. In any case, he decided those transgressions didn't count; they were in service of the plan. He had mostly gotten past *that* moral dilemma. And he knew he would soon be breaking the law at a level of magnitude not previously imagined.

Still, Pete did have moments where his conscience intruded a bit. One example being how it bothered him to use the word "kill" in referring to the plan. "Assassinate" sounded a little better, maybe even noble. And he convinced himself it wasn't just a euphemism, because the guy was a big kahuna. Some people certainly would call it an assassination.

What upset him was knowing the pundits and prosecutors and the like would call it "murder." That was the worst. He didn't like that word at all. He wasn't a murderer. Was he? In his most clear-headed moments he knew he'd have to get over the linguistics of it. He'd come too far to be distracted by terminology. He needed to focus on the mission. Nothing else counted.

In the silence, Pete could sense his friend was thinking hard. Had he connected it to Keenie yet?

Dylan was trying to calm himself with deep breathing as he formed a response. Finally, his body tensed forward, and the words slowly accelerated, like a semi pulling away from a traffic light.

"Pete, just picture the media circus. They'll play it like a crime of the century." Picking up speed, "It'll be Judge Crater all over again. Completely out of control, a fucking tsunami."

Pete had no idea who Judge Crater was. Later on, when he got home, he Googled the name and found that back in the 1920s, almost a hundred years ago, a prominent judge named Crater walked out of a New York City restaurant after dinner and disappeared. They never found him. It became a huge national crisis. The crime story of the era. In time Judge Crater became a punch line for comedians, a metaphor for a missing person. It went on for 25 years. Once again Pete was reminded that Dylan knew a lot of stuff, surprising for a guy who never went to college.

Still lecturing, Dylan shifted into higher gear, "Not only the media, but it'll be a law enforcement shitstorm. Cops will be everywhere. And the FBI? They'll never let it go. We'll be looking over our shoulders the rest of our lives." He managed to keep his voice down, if not his blood pressure.

Pete knew Dylan was right; assassinating a Supreme Court justice would attract a lot of attention. But it didn't matter. It had to be this guy. He wondered if Dylan was taking it seriously or just pretending, humoring him because of Keenie.

They both lost interest in the food. Most of it sat untouched on the table. Finally Pete said, "I understand it's bizarre. You can't just go out there and do something that seems so crazy. Right now you're kind of in the dark. By the way, it's Ramirez, the justice, that's his name. Not a random choice. Obviously, you have to know the whole story, see the whole picture, how everything comes together, whether it makes sense.

"As it happens, I have something in the works that'll help you make a decision. I'm putting everything in writing, the whole thing, the history, the rationale, the method, everything. It'll be a first hand account. All there for posterity to judge. The world needs to know why I'm doing this. I can't just do it and walk away. That wouldn't make any sense. Be no purpose in it, if people don't understand why. And it can do double duty to have you read it. Bring you on board with the whole story.

"It'll take me a couple weeks to get it all down. Should be ready first of the year latest. When I'm done, you can read it all and make your decision."

Dylan gave no verbal response, but his body language showed relief. He was going to be able to get out of there without either committing to an outrageously stupid task or refusing his friend. He said he'd read the write-up.

Pete knew Dylan was a reader. He hoped, when Dylan saw the complete story on paper, he'd go along. If he knew everything, he'd understand. He'd have the full picture. He could even critique it, to make sure they got it right.

Pete also offered Dylan one million dollars, which made Dylan's eyebrows go up again. Pete was pretty sure Dylan needed the money.

They agreed to get back together when Pete's write-up was ready. They shook hands and parted in the parking lot.

Getting into his car, Dylan muttered under his breath, "What the fuck just happened?" His very close friend had sprung a leak. The whole thing was so preposterous. This was not the Pete Rossi he knew. Pete was not someone who would be planning a murder, an assassination of a top government official. He was a law abiding, do-the-right-thing kind of guy, a good man. He treated people well. He was the kindest, gentlest, most considerate person Dylan had ever known. People said that Pete was so nice he didn't even hang up on telemarketers.

Turning onto the freeway, Dylan made an easy decision *not* to go back to the office. It was 2:30, Friday afternoon. A new dusting of snow was falling, exacerbating the road conditions, which had not yet recovered completely from Wednesday's storm, and he was in no mood to deal with work shit. On the car's voice-activated system he instructed his cell phone to call the office. He got Tanya, the office manager, and told her not to expect him back and to send the others home at 3:30. It was only fair.

His most compelling need at the moment was a drink, and the best place for that was home. Henry would be gone to the restaurant, having left in mid-morning, and with Friday the busiest restaurant day of the week, he wouldn't be back before midnight. Dylan could sit alone quietly, have his drink, and think without interruption about how to deal with Pete.

CHAPTER 3

JOURNAL – THE WHOLE TRUTH

3pm, Friday, 12-12-2014

My name is Pete Rossi, and this is the complete story of the assassination of U.S. Supreme Court Justice Jesse David Ramirez, which is scheduled to take place on February 13, 2015, exactly nine weeks from today.

This event in February will no doubt create a great deal of media attention, not only on a national scope, but possibly even worldwide; and this attention will garner intense speculation about what happened, why it happened, and who did it. So, the purpose here is to provide an accurate record of everything leading up to that event plus the details of the event itself – all of it – from the inside. This is the whole truth by the one person who was there through it all.

I had lunch with Dylan Armstrong today, and I asked him to be my accomplice. If he agrees, he'll likely be called that – my accomplice – as soon as they figure out there were two of us. I'd rather not expose him to the risk, but I'm not convinced I can pull it off by myself, being 64 and sometimes a bit less resourceful than I once was. I chose Dylan because I trust him, he's a friend, my closest friend; and because he has experience in this sort of thing, having served as a Navy SEAL and Special Ops Team Leader. He'll be invaluable when it comes to performing under pressure – especially the physical part – or making a mid-course correction, if we have to. He said he'd consider it, and I'm hopeful he'll come around. Of course, he'll be well compensated.

Why am I writing this document? There are several reasons.

First, and most importantly, for posterity. For the assassination to be meaningful and worthwhile, it must be understood by everyone. The "whys" have to be laid out and appreciated, not just by Dylan and me, but by journalists and the general public, and by investigators and lawyers, even historians.

Second, putting the whole thing in writing will bring organization to the project; help assure the plan is foolproof and doable. I'll be able to look at it on paper (actually on a computer monitor) rather than only seeing it in my mind as I lie awake. I've always been a stickler for being organized.

Third, it will help Dylan better understand. Otherwise I can't expect him to help.

Finally (and for my benefit only), it'll get me through the holidays; give me something to do other than busy work and volunteering. Everybody says being alone for the holidays, especially Christmas, can bring you down. I say amen to that. It's been 14 years now, and the holidays are still a downer.

Obviously, this journal, this first hand account, won't be read by anyone other than Dylan (and me, of course) until we're both dead and gone. I have no intention of turning myself in once the objective is achieved. Nor do I intend to compromise Dylan. To that end, this computer will remain offline, never connected to the Internet, thereby assuring it doesn't get hacked. When it's complete, I'll transfer everything to a thumb drive, destroy the computer hard drive, and store the thumb drive in a safety deposit box. Finally, a letter will be given to a trusted law firm, instructing them not to open the box until both of us are deceased, and on that occasion, to open it and forward the thumb drive to a designated law enforcement official. I'm confident these precautions will be sufficient to protect us.

I have considerable ground to cover here in a short time. All the background info and the plan itself has to be done by the first of the year for Dylan, which means I'll be writing pretty much every day between now and then. To keep track of my progress the entries will all be dated. There'll also be a wrap-up section after we've completed our task, that is, after February 13. Then I'll put it to bed, so to speak, in the safety deposit box.

One codicil, some of this write-up is about events and conversations that happened years ago, some of it more recent. In either case it's all from memory, and as an ex-cop I know memories can be imperfect. I'll do my best to be accurate. This is the way I remember it. I'm not intentionally making any of it up.

Probably the best way to tell the whole story is to go back to the beginning, the real beginning – my youth. If I were seeing a shrink again (no, there's no way I'll be seeing a shrink again, but if I were) the shrink would start with my childhood, looking for clues as to why I've decided this is the right way to go.

I'll be writing this document in indeterminate chunks starting early in the morning each day. I have sleep issues which affect my lucidity as the day goes on. Hence the early starts. On occasion, I will take a break for lunch and resume in the afternoon, assuming I'm clearheaded enough to do so. I also volunteer at the soup kitchen downtown on Sundays and holidays. I might not write on those days. Otherwise my lucid time will pretty much be given to this activity.

Tomorrow morning we'll start with how Grampa plays into all this.

CHAPTER 4

DYLAN – AFTER THE LUNCH

F*riday, December, 12, 2014.* Leaving the White Castle, Dylan pointed the white Lincoln MKZ north on I-275 to I-96, then headed east toward downtown Detroit. Careful not to speed, which was his tendency when excited or provoked, he blended into the moderate eastbound traffic flow. Once in the city itself, he passed miles of decaying neighborhoods. The freeway gave drivers a below ground-level vantage point, partially obscuring much of Detroit's squalor and shame from freeway travelers. Dylan was grateful for the cover. Every weekday he drove out of the city in the morning and back in at night. He didn't want to be reminded of the city's desperation over and over again on his reverse commute.

After I-96 dipped down toward the Ambassador Bridge, he merged east onto I-75 past the old Tiger Stadium site, then south onto I-375 to Jefferson Avenue with the venerable Christ's Church and its stone masonry on the southeast corner. He turned east onto Jefferson, now on the same sight level as the confirming evidence of the broken city.

To distract himself from the lunch conversation, he pondered the city's dilemma. It was 2014. Detroit was emerging from bankruptcy, the largest municipal bankruptcy in history. The city had evolved in the last sixty years into a black ghetto. The current population was less than 700,000, down from almost 2,000,000 back in the 1950s, the escapees, mostly white, now paying their municipal taxes elsewhere. The city government had become a cesspool of civic incompetence. At night the dangerous streets were dark, because many of the street lights didn't work, having been shot out by kids with guns and unexplainably *not* repaired by the Lighting Department. If you had an emergency and called 911, the cops or rescue vehicles might not show up for a couple hours. Retail stores, including grocery stores, had disappeared. Public transportation was a joke, and the school system was downright scary. They were talking about turning large tracts of city land into farms. The new farm land once had houses on it, houses people lived in and paid property taxes on. The newspapers treated the story like it was a positive development, trying to turn lemons into lemonade.

Every decade or so a new savior appeared signaling indications of a turnaround after which conditions only got worse. Today was no different except that more than one savior seemed to be in play: a businessman buying up and restoring commercial buildings, companies moving their facilities back into the city, a business turnaround specialist elected mayor, hotels and restaurants opening up, retail coming back. Perhaps this was it. Glimpses of the long promised renaissance jumped out from the side streets as Dylan drove the short distance from downtown past the Belle Isle bridge. But the dissonance of the neat new row houses on one street alongside war-zone like squalor on the next street invited skepticism.

Dylan turned north onto Iroquois Street into Indian Village, a little reverse socio-economic ghetto of its own. The name Indian Village, he assumed, came from the two streets, Iroquois and Seminole, running through its center. Indian Village is a small, very quaint, often elegant enclave, surrounded by some of Detroit's worst slums. Relatively few suburbanites even know it exists. About 100 years ago, as many of the automotive industry's founding families discovered the early stages of wealth, they settled in Indian Village. They built beautiful homes – the original mini-mansions – and lived in them until they got crazy rich, at which point they moved to Grosse Pointe and other points outside the city limits, where they built real mansions. How Indian Village survived in such good condition into the 21st century, while most of the rest of the city was decaying so badly, is a monument to community organization. Henry, with his affinity for "old tasteful things", found the place and lobbied hard for them to live there. Dylan gave in, but if it had been up to him they'd be out in the burbs, where the drives to his office and the restaurant were more manageable.

He drove up Iroquois almost to Kercheval, turned into the driveway of their Tudor-style house, negotiated the narrow passage to the secluded backyard, and nosed into the two-car detached garage.

As he pushed on the car door to get out, he was perspiring, still stressed from the lunch conversation. The 35-minute drive had failed to diminish his tension. The cold Detroit winter air delivered some relief. He strode through the light snow shower to the back porch and up the steps, unlocked the back door, stepped into the kitchen, pressed the button to close the automatic garage door, then hurried across the kitchen to the old walnut cabinet where the drink glasses were kept. He opened the cabinet door, grabbed a rocks glass, and took two steps sideways to the refrigerator for ice cubes. After scooping ice cubes into the glass, he set it on the counter next to the refrigerator, grabbed the big liter and a half bottle of Hendricks gin from the liquor cabinet and pulled the cork-like stopper. The urgency of the moment precluded the need for vermouth or olives or other ingredients. Rushing to fill the glass, he splashed some of the gin from the heavy black bottle onto the granite counter. The portion making it into the glass caused a crackling sound in the ice, adding to his craving.

He raised the glass and gulped down two mouthfuls, smelling the juniper bouquet he'd come to savor, feeling a slight burn in the back of his throat followed by the first inkling of a soothing sensation throughout his nervous system, the early comfortable feeling when his body and mind would start to ease into a cruising mode. He dismissed the thought that maybe he liked it too much, that maybe he was headed into long term trouble. Clearly, this was a special situation, if ever he had one. The Pete Rossi crisis he thought had been avoided years ago was assuming proportions he never would have imagined. It may not yet be out of control, but it was picking up speed. Could he stop it?

He had to.

He took another generous mouthful of the tranquilizing liquid, replaced it in the glass with an equally generous pour from the big, black bottle and checked to confirm the ice cubes still held their volume.

Drink in hand; careful not to spill, he walked out of the kitchen down the hall to the little den, his sitting room. He put the glass on the side table, and half fell into the recliner, his favorite piece of furniture. A good place to drink and think. He rolled it all through his mind.

Pete is planning to assassinate Supreme Court Justice Ramirez. Frigging unbelievable. Pete, our own Mr. Rogers.

Why'd he pick this guy? Ramirez was easily the least consequential of all the Supreme Court justices. You never heard anything about him. He didn't seem to do anything. How'd he get on Pete's radar? What has he done?

What about security? Aren't justices protected? Personal security? Secret Service or trained bodyguards or something? If we tried to take Ramirez down, we'd have to take the security guys with him. How does Pete think we could pull that off? Be like killing our own.

Says he's got a real tight plan. Been working on it for years. Foolproof. No such thing. Shit happens. Real bad shit. Especially in an op like this.

What sane reason could possibly justify it? How would it make up for Keenie & Donna? Says I'll understand once I see the whole picture. Thought we'd gotten past that. All this time he never said a word.

Gonna pay me a million bucks. Got money he doesn't know what to do with. For a million bucks I become one of the world's most wanted criminals. Still, a million would certainly take a lotta pressure off. Man, oh fucking man.

Made me promise not to tell Henry. I don't lie to Henry. I don't keep secrets from him. Not much, anyway. Shit. It would hurt him or make him furious or both. How long can I go without telling him? Not long. Jesus, what a mess. Fucking, cockamamie bullshit.

No one else knows. Two months. I gotta do something. Can't let this happen.

He had to calm himself again. He needed to think now, to think clearly. So many questions. He looked at the empty glass on the side table. Maybe the gin was taking him in reverse, riling rather than calming. Should he stop now? No more gin? Just that one? Or two? He remembered it'd been a generous double.

But he needed something. He retraced his steps into the kitchen and opened the fridge. *How about a Gibson? Where the hell were the cocktail onions? Never mind, just use olives and make a martini. Only one. Have to keep a clear head. Get back to the den recliner, sit down, think.*

The promise not to tell Henry bugged him. He regretted agreeing to it. He said out loud. "How the fuck can I do that?" After a few seconds he told himself to quiet down and try to figure out what to do. He picked up the glass, took a sip, set it back on the side table.

He had to get organized, like Pete. The controlling factor was two months…two months to bring Pete to his senses. He took another sip. His mind wandered…the old days, the excitement. Hadn't done a real op in almost 25 years. He felt a positive tug of nostalgia. Those days were fun…some of them. He reached down for the martini. Empty. Didn't remember emptying it. Just one more.

Back in the kitchen, mixing another martini, he vowed, once again, it would be the last for the day. He wanted to think about how to deal with Pete. *Where to start? What to say? Pete was a rational person. Solid. No nonsense. But this is not rational. Is it too late? If he's beyond reason, what can be done? Have to assume I can get through to him.*

Dylan returned to the den and the recliner. He pushed back to almost horizontal and put his feet up on the soft, dark-brown leather. *Slow down. Don't get too comfortable; might nod off, spill the drink.* He pulled himself and the chair to a more upright position, and double-sipped. The very mellow euphoria of early intoxication – just before deciding "that's enough" or "what the hell, let's go over Niagara Falls," – was sneaking up on him. He'd been pretty good at stopping himself, usually. He told himself the exceptions were infrequent. Maybe more now than when he was younger, but that was probably just age. No, couldn't be age. He was only fifty-two.

Whatever. Maybe he needed to watch it. Henry made a comment a few weeks ago. Certainly he'd have to watch it around Henry. And he'd have to hold off on telling Henry about the Pete thing; time's not right yet. His thoughts wandered.

What the fuck is Pete thinking? He stopped and scolded himself for being flippant. *The man deserves consideration and respect. He's counting on me. How can I let him down after all he's done for me?*

No matter, I can't let him do this.

CHAPTER 5

JOURNAL – THE LONE RANGER SPEECH

5am, Saturday, 12-13-2014

My grandfather's influence on my life is central to my being and a critical factor in this plan, making it essential to the record.

One particular incident is paramount. I was seven-years old the first time it happened. That was 1957, a long time ago, but still clear in my mind. Not something you'd forget. I was sitting on his lap in front of the TV, probably a sixteen-inch, black and white. We were watching The Lone Ranger Show. It came on at 7:30 on Thursday night, my folks' night out. They'd go to a movie or to the K of C hall for Bingo or card games, and Grampa and Lucille would watch me and my little brother, Nicky. (He was four. My little sister, Annie, wasn't born yet.) I'd be with Grampa and Lucille would get little Nicky. For reasons I don't remember, we called her Lucille, instead of Gramma.

Grampa picked The Lone Ranger show. He'd sit in his big chair in the living room and pull me up on his lap. He was a big man. Not just tall but thick too, well over 200 lbs. He smelled of pipe tobacco and maybe once in a while beer. His arms were big and hairy and he usually needed a shave. His moustache was thick, and it covered most of the space between his nose and his mouth. Sometimes it had a little reddish-brown stain from the nicotine in the pipe smoke.

Facing the TV, I straddled his left leg, sort of propped between his big left bicep and left side of his chest. The top of my head barely cleared his shoulder. At the start of the show, when the theme music came on, and then at intervals throughout, his right leg would bounce to the music, but gently, so as not to disturb me perched on his other leg, and his right hand and wrist moved side to side to direct the invisible orchestra.

The music was Rossini's "William Tell Overture." He was a big fan of Rossini. For years after I assumed it was why he chose The Lone Ranger as our TV show.

We watched The Lone Ranger and his "faithful Indian companion, Tonto" come riding to the rescue of the helpless and innocent towns-people as they were about to be victimized by the villains. The Lone Ranger, with some help from Tonto, would save the day and then ride off into the sunset with that exciting theme music playing, leaving only a silver bullet as a calling card.

To Grampa, the Lone Ranger became the best of all heroes, resolving the problem of the little people by vanquishing the bad guys and expecting nothing in the way of gratitude or recognition, just riding off. Not to mention he was handsome and rode a beautiful white horse and wore a white hat.

Now here's the weird part, the part that stuck with me. Grampa said it at the end of one of the shows in the second year and repeated it to me numerous times thereafter. He lifted and turned me in his lap to face him. All of a sudden he was very serious.

He said, "Petey, some day you're gonna be a Lone Ranger. You're gonna be in a situation where you have to do something, something very difficult, so difficult nobody else'll do it. But you will, 'cause it has to be done, and it'll be the right thing to do."

Now that's *not* something a little boy forgets real fast, like maybe never. I'm sure he'd been thinking about it for awhile. I don't remember how I responded, but as one might expect, for a long time after I didn't really understand what the heck he was talking about. As I said, that happened in our second season, when I was seven. We started watching when I was six, and we stayed with it for two seasons. I think the program went off the air after that.

Although I didn't understand it, I never forgot it. During that second season, he repeated it at least three times. And at key points in my life, like when I graduated from high school and college and the police academy, he would bring it back up.

I called it "Grampa's Lone Ranger speech." His intensity and the periodic reminders seared the words into my mind. It's one of the keys to his influence on me, the Lone Ranger connection, and it plays a major role in what we're going to do. Now to fully understand how and why it's so critical requires some background. One needs to know a bit more about Grampa and me, our history together.

Tomorrow we'll get to that.

CHAPTER 6

JOURNAL – THAT'S NOT EXACTLY WHAT HAPPENED

5am, Sunday, 12-14-2014

Right after I was born, my parents bought the house next door to my grandparents. It wasn't uncommon then for married kids to live near their parents, especially immigrant families. So, when I was small, with Dad working two jobs and Mom working part-time, I had a lot of exposure to my grandparents.

The two small frame houses were in a blue-collar, almost middle-class neighborhood in Northwest Detroit. This was in the '50s, before white flight and Dutch elm disease and a wave of racial, cultural and economic collisions. Most of the modest homes were surrounded by small lawns and trimmed shrubs and well-kept flower beds. The streets were tree-lined, lots of mature elms and maples and oaks. In the spring and summer it was green – a bright, intense green, like the fields of Ireland. In the fall you didn't have to go up north to see the color; the yellows and oranges and reds were there, right out your front door. And in the winter you saw an occasional white landscape that reminded you of those idyllic painted scenes on Christmas cards. Age has made me a lot grumpier about northern winters now, but when I was a kid, they didn't seem so bad. Everything I can remember about that environment made it a nice place for a little boy to grow up.

We were in that place, at that time, because of Grampa.

He was born in Italy, Pietro Antonio Rossini, and he came to America in 1912 at the age of twenty. Right off the boat he went to Fredonia, New York, near Buffalo, to do farm work along with other Italian immigrants.

Then in 1914 Henry Ford set up an advanced assembly-line approach for making cars, and his company recruited workers by offering the princely sum of five dollars a day. Five bucks a day was a big deal. It was national news, the first step in Detroit ultimately becoming the manufacturing capital of the world. People, including Grampa, relocated to Detroit from all over the country in hopes of cashing in.

He came alone, his relatives still back in Italy. He got one of the jobs and found a rooming situation with an Italian family in nearby southwest Detroit. Within a few years he got married, bought a house in the city and started raising a family of his own. He lived in Detroit until he died in 1975.

My dad, Grampa's youngest child, was born in 1923, named Giacomo and always called Jack, even though Giacomo translates to James in English. His older brother and sister were my Uncle Phil (Filipe) and Aunt Irene (Irenea). As he learned English, Grampa gave up on the Italian versions of those names.

In the late 1920s, my grandmother, Grampa's first wife, Katrina, died. Nobody ever told me exactly what she died of. Within 15 months of her passing, Grampa remarried. The new wife was Lucille. According to Uncle Phil, the reason for this quickie second marriage was more pragmatic than romantic. He said Grampa was anxious to have someone around to take care of the kids while he was at work, so he had to have a wife, because that's what wives did, mostly. That's how it was in those days. Times were different and harder, or so I'm told.

Well, maybe he wasn't initially in love, but for what it's worth, Grampa and Lucille were good to each other, and their marriage lasted until he died.

The details of his immigration to America were always a bit vague, because he wouldn't talk about it, except in generalities. At that time most Italian immigrants came to this country because of the stark poverty in the old country, and because America was the land of opportunity. But that never made sense in Grampa's case. He said he had a job over there, and his uncle, who he lived with, had a very good job.

His kids – my dad and aunt and uncle – suspected it might be something else, something he was hiding. For one thing, why was he so clammed up about it? They speculated that maybe he got into some difficulty, something that expedited his departure from the homeland, something he wouldn't want to talk about.

Years later, out of curiosity, when Uncle Phil was in Italy at the end of the war, he did a little investigating. He went up to Carrara, where Grampa lived before coming to the States. It's a town in the Tuscany region near the west coast of Italy about 75 miles southeast of Genoa. The area is known for fine Italian marble, the marble of choice for centuries in the most opulent cathedrals, palaces, museums, commercial buildings and mansions around the world. It's also called statuario marble because it's favored by sculptors. Michelangelo used it to sculpt "David" and "The Pieta."

Grampa was actually born on the other side of the Italian boot near Padua. His parents both died when he was a boy, and he had no siblings. After their deaths, he was sent to Carrara to live with his father's brother, Giacomo, (my father's namesake) and Giacomo's wife, Chiara, who were childless. So, Grampa was, in a sense, still an only child. He said they always treated him well, as if he were their own.

Grampa said his Uncle Giacomo worked in the quarries as a carver. Carvers were the upper class of quarry workers, skilled tradesmen. They polished and otherwise finished the marble after it was extracted from the walls of the quarry.

At the age of 16, Grampa himself got a job in one of the quarries. He assisted in transporting the raw marble blocks down from the walls of the quarry to the carving shacks, where the carvers prepared them for shipment to sculptors and builders around the world. "Transporting" sounds a bit technically advanced for the method they used. There were no cranes or fork lifts. They literally dragged the blocks and slabs of marble, with teams of oxen, often sixteen deep, down steep, narrow, harrowing cliff-side trails with a wall on one side and a perilous, straight drop down on the other. Grampa used a long whip to control the oxen. He told me he got real good with it, like Indiana Jones and Zorro. From a short distance he could hit boulders or wrap the whip around a fence post.

When Uncle Phil went to Carrara, he was on a short leave from his Army Base near Rome. All of Italy, including Carrara, was war-torn and struggling to recover. Church and city records had been removed to various secure locations in the mountains and not yet retrieved. Trying to get information, he talked to priests and local officials, none of whom seemed to know anything about Grampa. No one even remembered the family, which was puzzling. Granted it had been almost 35 years since Grampa left, and there was a worldwide depression and two world wars in between. But still.

In talking to people, Uncle Phil learned about the labor strife in the quarries at the turn of the century. Quarry work, particularly the removal of the blocks of marble from the walls, was hard and dangerous. If a quarry worker had all his fingers and thumbs intact, he was considered lucky. Serious accidents and even fatalities were not uncommon. In 1911, the year before Grampa left, one accident occurred in which ten men were killed.

Conditions were such that the quarries were in a constant state of labor unrest. Labor organizers and political reformers went to Carrara to encourage quarry workers to organize. And, of course, the owners resisted. They beefed up security. Remember this was 1912. The quarry owners in those days were not exactly progressive thinkers. (Come to think of it, the quarry owners today may not be very progressive thinkers.)

Anyway there was a great deal of conflict between workers and security forces. Sometimes workers were beaten or even banned from working in the quarries. One of the priests told Uncle Phil the conflict resulted in a lot of people being chased out. Uncle Phil concluded something like that must have happened to Grampa; he got caught up in a labor problem and was chased away, and he somehow got on a ship to America.

Grampa didn't talk about it much, and he came alone, so there was no one else to tell the story. When he heard about Uncle Phil's snooping and his resulting theory, he was not happy. According to my dad, Grampa's only response was, "That's not exactly what happened." Then he changed the subject.

How he made his escape, if it was an escape, was also not clear. We did know from some old pictures he was tall and slender – over six feet of sinewy muscle. And handsome, with a full head of thick, wavy hair. Like most northern Italians, his coloring was a bit lighter than the Sicilians and Italians from the south, where most of the immigrants came from, and his features were less Mediterranean, more middle European, and he had a pencil-thin mustache similar to the one Rudolph Valentino had in the movies in the '20s. Altogether, Grampa was a head turner; young ladies of the time would have noticed him.

Surprisingly he was literate, not common back then among poor immigrants. His aunt and uncle taught him how to read and how to sign his name. He was limited to Italian, of course, but at least he was comfortable with the concept of reading.

Even more unlikely, he had a little bit of money. Living with his aunt and uncle, he claimed, he was able to save most of his earnings, meager as they were, while working at the marble quarry. So, he had enough to pay for his passage and food. Finally, he had a likeable manner that drew people in. This remained true into his old age. He would have made a good confidence man, if he had the least bit of guile in him, which, people who knew him would agree, he didn't.

It was assumed these attributes combined to get him to Genoa, on board the ship, and past whatever immigration official greeted him in New York.

CHAPTER 7

JOURNAL – THE SOFTEST PILLOW

5am, Monday, 12-15-2014

According to Grampa, when he saw fit to talk about it, there was only one mishap in his journey to America. The customs or immigration agent in New York who processed his entry spelled his last name incorrectly on his papers, and Grampa became Pietro Antonio Rossi. He lost the "ni" at the end of Rossini.

In the grand scheme of things this may seem like a minor issue, but to Grampa at the time, it was a major crisis. The way it happened with the immigration process and the quick transfer to land transportation, it was all a blur; he didn't catch the error until he got to Fredonia.

When he finally examined his papers and saw the name "Rossi," he said he went right to the authorities in western New York. They brushed him off. He said they acted like it wasn't their problem; it happened hundreds of miles away in New York City. Probably they saw it as a big paperwork magillah, the resolution of which had no potential benefit for them; just one of those dagos getting worked up over nothing. Grampa said he persisted until he sensed that they all, including the foreman at the farm, started getting impatient with him. Caution made him back off. He would deal with it later, at a time when he was in a more secure situation. He certainly didn't want to get sent back to Italy.

What he was unable to communicate to the authorities in his almost nonexistent English was that the name "Rossini" was one of the great names of Italian art and culture. The great operatic composer Gioacchino Rossini, who had composed "The Barber of Seville" and "William Tell" and many other famous operas, was Grampa's relative, albeit a distant relative. He said the distinction of being part, even a remote part, of the family of a great composer was everything. It put him as close as he might ever get to being somebody. That was why we watched The Lone Ranger TV show. The theme music, the overture from "William Tell," was his family music, his only meaningful tie with his origins.

As it turned out, correcting the name change never happened.

Hence, my name is Rossi, Peter Anthony, after Grampa.

Having the same name, and being the oldest in my family, and living next door, resulted in Grampa and me becoming very close. When he got laid off for the last time, never to return to the Ford Rouge foundry, he was sixty-one and I was three. About then, my mother started working part-time at the A & P store, and Dad, not infrequently, was working two jobs. So, Grampa and Lucille, living next-door, became the go-to baby sitters. Especially Grampa.

I was like a special "retirement project" for him. He spent a lot of time with me, talking to me, explaining things, as if we were almost equals, not adult and child. At one point Uncle Phil started calling us "Big Pete and Little Pete." Keep in mind this started when I was only three or four. It went on until I was approaching adulthood.

Some might think, when reading about this, that my parents were somehow negligent, and Grampa stepped in to fill the vacuum. Not the case at all. My parents were attentive and supportive and always there when I needed them. Certainly, Dad worked two jobs a lot, which made him scarce sometimes, but so did a lot of dads in those days. It was just when I was small and very impressionable, Grampa was there every day, and took the ball, namely me, and ran with it. Maybe it was the oldest grandchild thing; for whatever reason he was devoted to me right from the beginning.

When I was real small, we only went for walks, sometimes just around the block, sometimes up to the confectionery store, where he bought me ice cream, sometimes to the park where he pushed me on the swings or watched while I came down the slides.

When he thought I was old enough, he took me to Tigers' games down at Briggs Stadium. Al Kaline was the big star then. We also went to the Shrine Circus at the Fairgrounds a couple times, when it was in town. The second time I had too much cotton candy and threw up in Grampa's car on the way home. We never went back to the circus.

We also went to cool places around Detroit, like Belle Isle, the big park in the Detroit River. I remember one summer day we were on the south side of the island, looking at the gray-green water in the river flowing left to right down from Lake St. Clair to Lake Erie and the big rusty looking freighters slowly gliding along. Standing on Belle Isle, we could see the Ambassador Bridge to Canada off to our right, just a few miles west of us. I asked him to take me over the bridge just to see everything from up high. So, he did. We drove around Windsor and had lunch at a fish & chips restaurant. Windsor's fish & chips were the best. From a little boy's perspective there wasn't much other difference between Windsor and Detroit; they were both blue-collar factory towns. But beneath the surface they were very different. Windsor was a small, tidy city of almost exclusively European immigrants with a relatively homogeneous culture, while Detroit was a thriving American metropolis about to become a boiling cauldron of racial conflict.

Few white people saw it coming. Maybe Grampa did. One time, when The Harlem Globetrotters were in town, he took me to a game. It was at the old Olympia Arena where the Red Wings played. Somehow he'd gotten two pretty good seats; we were only about ten rows back. Halfway through the game he asked if I noticed, "All the good guys are black and all the bad guys are white." The good guys were the Globetrotters, of course, and the bad guys, as Grampa called them, were a bunch of pretty mediocre basketball players called the Washington Generals. All white. It was a nuance, a reverse racial stereotyping, maybe only a coincidence. But there may have been a subtle message there. And Grampa wasn't objecting, he was just pointing it out. Truth was at my young age I hadn't noticed, and I didn't get his point. In later years I came to suspect that Grampa saw something that most white people at the time weren't onto. Black people were angry. As preposterous as it may seem, most white people didn't understand that. Why would black people be angry? What do they have to be angry about? Years later we all started to catch on. I think Grampa was way ahead of his peers.

He'd evolved a great deal since he came to America more than 40 years before. He learned to speak English with only a slight accent, sounding somewhere between Italian and Detroit blue collar. He said the 'Rossini' to 'Rossi' incident at the immigration center had convinced him he had to learn the language. His first wife, Katrina, was his tutor. Before she died, she also taught him to read and write his new language. She was a great teacher. By the time his children were in school he could help them with their homework, and he became a regular at the library and in bookstores. Every day he devoured the Detroit News from front to back. That was at a time when newspapers were thick, not just with advertising but also with news and editorial. He couldn't get enough of what was going on in Detroit and Michigan and the country as a whole.

A by-product of this literacy and his life in general was that he came to love America and things American. He applied for American Citizenship, quickly passed all the requirements, and was sworn-in in 1920. He became a close follower of American politics. FDR was like a god to him. Ten years after FDR died, Grampa still talked about him, and how he'd saved the country from the terrible Depression and the even more terrible Nazis.

Grampa also became a Tigers' fan. He thought baseball was the great American pastime, so it became his also. He never actually played baseball, except games of catch with me, but he was a real fan. And a real American. He wore overalls and smoked a pipe and drank beer instead of wine, and just tried to do what he thought were American things. I remember him making an offhand comment once about the Italian immigrants at the Knights of Columbus hall who were always saying how much they missed home. He said, "If it was such a great place, why don't they go back?"

The point is Grampa was an easy person for a little boy to idolize. He paid attention to me, and talked to me, and took me places, and was just so good to me. He was insightful. He saw things that got by the average person and pointed them out to me. I spent a lot of time with him through those formative years. Much of what he said served to guide my thinking for a long time.

I think part of his influence on me was that I was not a rebel. They say the oldest child tends to be the most responsible and respectful of authority. That was me. I became what he wanted me to be. Even his patriotism rubbed off on me.

But it was more than that. Grampa was a straight arrow. He believed in fairness and kindness and in doing his part. He always looked for ways to convey those values to me. A favorite example was the Longfellow poem, *The Village Blacksmith*. It was in one of the books Katrina gave him. (Apparently, she wasn't teaching him English from "Dick and Jane" books.) In it Longfellow wrote about the blacksmith:

Each morning sees some task begin
Each evening sees it close
Something attempted, something done,
Has earned a night's repose.

Grampa memorized those lines. He recited them every chance he got. He said, "Petey, those are good words to live by. It means you gotta do your job everyday." He said the blacksmith was a fair, hardworking man who held up his end, which gave him a clear conscience, and "a clear conscience is the softest pillow." That was another of his expressions –"a clear conscience is the softest pillow." I loved it. I used it as I grew up, and in Vietnam, and when I was a cop. When I was in business, I put it on the conference room wall. It made tough decisions easier. I always tried hard to be fair and work hard and do my part. I always went for the clear conscience. As a result I had a soft pillow and slept well for a long time. Life is hell, if you can't sleep, if the pillow gets hard. I've learned a few things about that, too.

Grampa never gave up on imprinting these values on me. *The Village Blacksmith* and the softest pillow and the Lone Ranger speech. He even brought the speech up the day I came back from Vietnam and visited him in the hospital. He was so happy to see me he cried. So did I. Two days later we had the big conversation, when he told me "exactly what happened", which explained a lot and further directs what I'm doing now. He died a month after that, so it was almost like a death bed scene.

CHAPTER 8

DYLAN & PETE

Wednesday, December 17, 2014. Dylan was an early riser. Most mornings he was dressed and downstairs in the kitchen drinking coffee by 5:30. After a workout and shower at the gym, he'd be in the office by 7:00. This morning was different. His eyes were open, but he felt drowsy. He usually rode the express from sound asleep to wide awake with no stops in between. The little bedside clock, a gift from Henry, projected the time on the ceiling. Dylan, lying on his back, could see blurred red numbers up there. Did they read 6:15? *Could it be that late?* He rubbed his eyes to clear the sleep out.

Yeah, it was 6:15

What day is it? Yesterday was Tuesday? Yeah, Tuesday. He couldn't remember coming to bed last night. It was the second time that happened since last Friday, White Castle day. Two lost evenings out of the last five. Two others he'd had quite a bit to drink, but at least he could remember going to bed. He categorized those two nights as "tipsy." "Tipsy" was far less condemning than "lost." Sunday night, the only sober night out of the five, Henry was home. He didn't like Henry to see him drunk. A few months ago Henry said, "Drinking diminishes you." Dylan's response was to drink only when Henry wasn't there – sort of cheating. He wasn't sure which was worse, being diminished or cheating.

The binge-like string of nights was directly related to Pete. He dreaded the day when he'd have to tell Pete he couldn't help him. Would it end their friendship? Thinking about it made him feel lonely.

He turned his head to check the red numbers on the ceiling: 6:20. He was going to be late for work, or at least later than usual. No matter, he'd still be one of the first ones in. He wanted to stay in bed. He closed his eyes thinking about Pete. Such a good guy. He didn't deserve what happened.

Dylan remembered their first meeting.

It was a job interview 20 years ago, the summer of 1994, at the old office in Southfield. Dylan was responding to a help wanted ad by a company called PARsafe, a commercial and residential security company. They were starting up a personal security arm. He got a phone call to come in for an interview.

Two years out of the Navy, he was working at Henry's new restaurant as the company gofer, even though he was an equal partner. Just trying to keep the place going. Roof leaks, stopped-up sinks, trucks in the alley with boxes to unload, cracked floor tiles, toilets that wouldn't flush, dishwashers and waiters who didn't show up. When he wasn't fixing and schlepping, he kept the books: checking supplier invoices, paying the bills as close to on time as cash flow allowed, doing payroll, all the money stuff.

And the pay sucked; after he'd written the regular checks for everyone else, he got what was left, which averaged to about a third of his SEAL pay, a third of not enough. The restaurant gig, starting as a labor of love, had become a depressing burden. Doing what he was doing, he could be easily replaced. It was time to move on, get a real job. They could hire a new gofer. Dylan could still do the books at night.

Dylan carried his resume in a white, 9"x12" envelope. They already had it, but just in case. The problem was it showed little job diversity. He'd put down the last year in the restaurant as Business Manager. A bit of a stretch. The year before, when he first got out, he worked as a waiter in the restaurant where Henry was a sous chef. The rest of it was twelve years in the Navy, nine of it as a SEAL. Before that he was in high school. Granted the SEAL experience was diverse in itself, but some of the most interesting things he'd done were classified – activities he couldn't talk about.

Making E-8 (master chief petty officer) in less than ten years was a rarity and a big plus, but he wasn't sure how that would sell out in the real world. What were the chances a civilian interviewer would appreciate it?

Then his reason for quitting the SEALs, would the guy want to press him on that? He dreaded how it would come out. Bye, bye, job. In spite of the potential unpleasantness, he committed to going through with the interview. Worst case, he'd get some useful practice.

He arrived ten minutes early for his appointment. Entering the building, he did his usual mental inventory of his surroundings. Dylan was accustomed to "seeing" everything in his immediate environment, noting people or objects that might pose a threat. Henry laughed at him for "looking for monsters under the bed," because in his current life there were virtually no threats or at least few that he was trained to deal with. But he couldn't help it. The SEALs had ingrained it in him.

The building was small, about one half the size of a neighborhood strip mall. The outer office was modest: three padded wooden visitor's chairs around a coffee table, an unread copy of the day's Wall Street Journal on the table, two framed Ansel Adams-like photos on the wall, a wood veneer receptionist's desk. No ash trays. A seeming lack of pretension. They'd apparently saved money on the interior decorator. Dylan remembered it as a comfort for his interview nerves.

The receptionist was 40-ish and attractive, maybe not a movie star, but nice-looking. Casual dress. Dylan gave his name and said he had an appointment with Mr. Rossi at 9am. She nodded, and instead of telling him to take a seat and picking up the phone, she called over to the open door on her left, "Mr. Armstrong is here."

Within fifteen seconds a man stepped through the open door and smiled. He extended his hand to Dylan and said, "Morning, Pete Rossi."

Dylan replied, "Morning, sir, Dylan Armstrong, pleased to meet you."

Dylan did a perfunctory scan. Rossi was average height; not heavy, not skinny, maybe 175 lbs.; plain face, nothing big or small or out of place; no visible scars or tattoos; dark brown hair with some gray moving in, not long, not short, not wavy, combed straight back: pale blue dress shirt; no tie; khaki pants; brown oxfords, more durable than expensive; same with the watch, maybe a Seiko or Citizens. Dylan concluded the most remarkable thing about Pete Rossi was his complete lack of distinguishing characteristics. He'd make a great spy. You wouldn't notice him in a crowd.

Rossi pointed at the door, "Come on in." He turned to the receptionist, "Liz, emergencies only, ok?" It sounded more like a suggestion than a directive. The receptionist smiled and nodded.

Dylan went into the office first, and Rossi closed the door behind them. Dylan did his usual scope of the room. Brown carpet, thin commercial nap. Pinewood bookshelves. Two metal file cabinets, another wooden veneer desk. A black polyester office chair behind the desk, similar to the economy model Dylan had at the restaurant. Two guest chairs in front of the desk with the same look of moderate austerity. On the front wall a framed blown-up photo of an older man with a thick moustache. It was hung so Rossi could see it from behind his desk when he looked up. No ostentation, just a place to take care of business. Nothing in the room said, "Look at me, I'm successful and important, and you should be impressed." More comfort to Dylan.

Rossi stepped behind the desk, sat down, and motioned Dylan to sit in one of the guest chairs. Dylan took his seat, sat military style, erect in the chair, legs not crossed. Rossi opened the folder on the desk blotter, and with his forearms sitting on each side, looked down at its contents. Dylan assumed it was his resume. Rossi was quiet. Dylan wondered whether to say something. Decided it was Rossi's turf. Just wait.

Rossi raised his head and did a quick inspection. Dylan was a clean cut young man: 6'2", about 200 lbs, sinewy frame, close-trimmed brown hair, military bearing, blue eyes, conservative suit and tie. Sitting almost at attention, Dylan confidently returned his gaze.

Rossi smiled and got right to the interview. "Are you from around here?"

"Livonia. Grew up there." Livonia was a middle class suburb of Detroit.

"Family still there?"

"Yeah. My mom's a librarian. Dad's in construction."

"Must have been Bob Dylan fans."

"Actually it was Dylan Thomas, a Welsh poet. Pretty sure it was Mom's idea. She's the literary one. You probably know this, but that's where Bob Dylan got the name, too. He was originally a Zimmerman from Minnesota. Anyway I think Mom came up with it before she'd ever heard of Bob Dylan. I was born before he made it big."

Rossi shifted gears and said, "Let me tell you what we're talking about here. This new Personal Security Division has no employees. Right now we're looking for a director who would be responsible for hiring his own staff. This person will go out with me on prospective client calls to line up business. As each piece of new business becomes a reality, we'll add staff to handle it."

Rossi paused to let Dylan take it in.

He continued, "We have reason to be optimistic based on some thumbnail market research and a few unsolicited inquiries from existing clients. Mexico and South America seem to be the areas where personal security is most in demand. The Big Three and some of their tier one suppliers are planning to send more of their people down there, and some of those places can get kind of hairy. So, if we can be ready in time, we have a chance to benefit from the opportunity."

He finished, "Sound like your thing?"

The Big Three were GM, Ford and Chrysler, and the tier one suppliers were huge companies that made the parts the Big Three assembled into cars and trucks. Everyone in Michigan knew that. But the rest of it startled Dylan. He squinted and said, "You mean as director of the division?"

"Yeah, sure." Rossi saw Dylan's confusion. "I assume you had some leadership chops as chief and master chief. You must have been in charge of people and units."

"Well, yeah, but I wasn't…I wasn't expecting…" His pulse had picked up its beat. He could feel it and hear it. *Was the thumping audible to Rossi?* He had no idea the job was this prime. He had to regain control of himself. "Yes, yes uh yes, it very much sounds like my thing."

"Good, then. Let's get back to you. Why the Navy and the SEALs?"

"My dad was a Marine. Thought I'd try to outdo him." As the words escaped his mouth he wanted them back. Too flippant. Could lead into an area he'd rather avoid. Not a good answer.

Crossing his legs, he took another shot at it, "I was right out of high school; didn't think I was ready for college; and the Navy had this thing about seeing the world. So, I guess I wanted to try something that would help me grow up. I did the SEALs because, well, what happened, after I'd been in the navy for a while, one of my Chiefs suggested I check it out, and when I did, it just became an irresistible challenge. Have to admit when I actually got through the training, I was as surprised as anyone."

"Quite an achievement."

Dylan felt a tinge of dissonance in the response. They had met only minutes before, so he wasn't sure. Is something wrong? Does he already know?

Months later, in a more relaxed conversation, Rossi told him his version of the interview. He said he'd picked Dylan's resume out of about sixty that came in from the want-ad. He screened all the resumes himself – no recruiting service. Most he discarded in less than two minutes. About a dozen were interesting enough for more consideration. Dylan's jumped out at him. Spoke Spanish fluently. Some Arabic. Nine years as a SEAL. Chief petty officer and then master chief for over five years. Only 32 years old. He was a Navy chief at the age of twenty-five. In Pete's military days that was almost unheard of. Yeah, he liked him a lot. But something wasn't right. He couldn't put his finger on it.

As the interview proceeded, Rossi asked about Dylan's SEAL training and experience – what he actually did during the nine years. Dylan answered in generalities, explaining apologetically that much of what he did was classified. Rossi assumed it was futile to try to probe, so he didn't push it. He also knew the national security claim was sometimes an angle used by con-men as a smokescreen to hide things. Rossi was not an untrusting person; he tended to see the best in people, but he cautioned himself to try to maintain a healthy wariness.

Rossi had tried to confirm Dylan's work history by calling the Department of Defense. The person at the other end of the line who had access to the files, a Navy 1st class petty officer, wasn't very helpful. When Pete said the name Dylan Armstrong, there seemed to be an attitude change on the other end of the line. Did he imagine it? The PO confirmed some of the basics: Dylan's rank, time in service, honorable discharge, etc. but little else. It was troubling. Making E-8 in less than ten years was in Dylan's favor. It was a notable, extraordinary achievement. They confirmed that, but little else. For Dylan to have advanced so quickly through the ranks there had to be successes, letters of commendation, medals. When Rossi asked about such recognition, the answer was, "I'm sorry, sir, but I can't go into that." What the hell did the guy do? Win the cold war, single handedly? Rossi didn't get a good feeling. Maybe it was about national security, but if it was, what the heck is he doing here in my office applying for a job? Something was missing. Something not right.

If he was so good, why did he leave after 12 years in? Rossi hoped to clear it up in the interview. How could an E-8 just walk away?

So he asked, "Seems like you were having a pretty successful career. Why'd you leave?"

Dylan had been well trained to deal with hostile interrogations. Water boarding, physical pain, sleep deprivation, all techniques he'd been exposed to in his SEAL orientation. There were also less physically demanding procedures, where you were studied by eyes and cameras for subtle giveaways of secrets you were trying to keep covered. You could not show you were affected by the questions or the subjects. You could not give signals to the interrogator that he had just entered a sensitive area. You couldn't let him know he was getting warm. Or that you were getting warm.

Under Rossi's gaze Dylan had the feeling that some of that training was failing him. Maybe it was because he wanted this job so much. It was getting damp inside his suit coat. He looked down, then up at Rossi, and then over Rossi's shoulder at the file cabinet with the computer monitor on top.

His planned answer was something about how the challenge wasn't there anymore, it was time to move on, and he wanted to take his training to the private sector. He started to say it, then hesitated. He still wasn't looking at Rossi's face. Over Rossi's other shoulder was the picture of the woman and the girl. No doubt Rossi's wife and daughter.

Dylan started rambling about the service being no place to start a family, or to raise kids. He hoped he was saying what Rossi wanted to hear, or what he would at least accept as a reasonable explanation.

But as the words came out of his mouth, he felt ludicrous saying them. It was like the day he told his father.

Suddenly the interview was not going right. He was tangling himself in a lie. The situation was becoming untenable. He really wanted this job. He'd already started thinking about telling Henry he was leaving the restaurant.

But telling the truth would be the end of the interview. The end of something he had started to get his hopes up way too high for. He was flipping around between embarrassment and dismay and anger. He felt his face flush and give him away.

Rossi sat silently and observed it all. Something had happened. Suddenly Dylan Armstrong was different. He'd just become very nervous or upset or maybe ill.

Dylan knew he had to say something. He looked down at his lap, "It's hard to explain. I just had to get out. It was getting too difficult."

"I don't understand. What happened?"

He couldn't avoid saying it, even though it would be the end of his chances at the job. He really wanted to get away from the restaurant, and this job seemed so right. It was as close to the perfect opportunity as he was ever going to get. It wasn't fair. The embarrassment faded into just dismay and anger.

He looked Rossi in the eye and blurted it out, "I'm gay! I was a *gay* SEAL. The Exec found out. They didn't want me anymore. They made me quit."

He stood up abruptly, moved to the door, and said, "Thanks for the interview. Sorry to have wasted your time."

Rossi was stunned. *What'd he say!?* The concept of a gay SEAL was just so extraordinary. Rossi had never considered it. He knew little of the gay scene. In spite of his ignorance, he assumed the stereotypes were like all stereotypes, mostly untrue. But a gay SEAL. What a stretch. The macho world would just hate it. He smiled. Then he broke out of his brief lapse. Dylan was gone.

Rossi ran out of his office to the front door and into the parking lot. A vehicle was pulling out into traffic. He waved his arms, but the vehicle accelerated and left him standing by the office. It was a GMC Sierra pickup. Another macho stereotype shattered.

CHAPTER 9

DYLAN — THE GRIMACE

W*ednesday, December 17, 2014, cont.* Dylan opened his eyes. He smiled to himself. Thinking about that first interview with Pete made him feel good. He was still in bed. Not ready to get up. The red numbers on the ceiling were now at 6:40. He set his head back on the pillow. It had been a rocky night, partly because of the dream. He hadn't had the dream in a while, at least a couple months. It tended to show up when he'd gotten a little drunk, or was stressed about something. Truth be told those two conditions were working in tandem a lot lately.

It was a simple dream. Not exactly a nightmare, not horrifying, no chain saws or dentist drills, but still upsetting in a visceral way. He would wake up in a sweat with his pulse racing, then lay awake struggling to get back to sleep. To calm his body he would try to think comforting thoughts. When he eventually drifted into sleep, the dream would recur and recur and recur, as if on a film loop.

The dream was a simple visual, an image of his father's face with a stunned, disbelieving, angry, disgusted expression. No words. Just a pained grimace.

Dylan couldn't forget the first time he saw that look. It was the day they had the big talk.

He'd shown up at the front door of his parents' house on a Saturday afternoon in August, 1992, a day after his release from active duty. At that point his parents knew nothing of what had happened. He and Henry flew in to Metro the night before and stayed at a motel in Farmington Hills. Henry had already landed a job as a sous chef at The Golden Mushroom, an upscale restaurant in nearby Southfield. They agreed Henry would start apartment hunting, while Dylan broke the news to his folks.

Dad was home alone, Mom in Grand Rapids visiting her sister. George Custer Armstrong (his real name) flung open the screen door and hugged his son with joy and genuine affection. *Would he still feel the same in an hour or two?* Standing next to each other on the front porch of the brick bungalow in Livonia, George was two inches shorter than his son and, thanks to middle-age and a preference for beer, at least 25 pounds heavier.

After the happy greeting, father and son went inside and down to the partially finished basement. Dad had converted about one third of it into an early version of a man cave. He'd put down an 8'x12' blue and gray Detroit Lions rug in the corner farthest from the stairs. It was the only floor covering in the basement, so you walked across bare cement to get to the carpeted area. His neatly organized workbench and tool pegboard sat in the opposite corner to the right of the stairs. Two unpainted iron stanchions ran from the floor to the I-beam across the center of the unfinished ceiling. A leather sofa and a Lazy Boy recliner, both reclaimed from the living room upstairs, formed an L and defined the edges of the finished area. A large TV sat in the corner. TV tables for snacks and beverages bookended the sofa. Dylan assumed the small refrigerator against the wall was stocked with beer and soda. A small table, with outdoor magazines displayed on top, sat next to the fridge.

There was no desk. No need. This wasn't an office. Dad wasn't into whatever you did on desks in offices. Mom handled the bills and paperwork. He was a man's man, an outdoorsman, an ex-marine who worked as a construction laborer building houses – pouring foundations, rough carpentry, roofing, and such like. He abhorred the thought of ever having a "desk job." Absolutely no need for a desk.

The walls in that corner of the basement were decorated with photos, one of Dylan in his dress CPO uniform and others of fishing scenes. Dad was a serious angler. Going fishing was their primary father/son activity before Dylan went into the Navy. They even went to Alaska once to catch halibut. Other than fishing, to Dylan's boyhood disappointment, they didn't do much together.

A very subtle distance existed between them. George was a big sports fan, especially the Lions and Red Wings. Dylan wasn't. He tried, but he never generated much interest in team sports. His sport was swimming, a mostly individual activity, at which he excelled. All-State in fact. In his senior year he won the individual medley event in the State Finals, one of his few achievements to win Dad's praise.

When they went fishing, there wasn't much talk, especially later when Dylan was in his teens. Dylan wondered why. *Doesn't he like me? Can he read my thoughts? Does he know? What was there to know?*

Even Dylan didn't completely get it. *Should I tell him? Probably not.* It didn't take a genius to understand that the crusty ex-marine, the construction worker, would have great difficulty accepting the inconceivable issue that Dylan suspected about himself. He just had to keep it inside. Forever.

Books also played a role in the distance between father and son. Dylan was a reader of books. Dad's reading didn't go much beyond the Detroit News sports section and Field & Stream. Dylan on the other hand devoured books of all genres – even so-called literary books. He got it from his mother, the librarian, who was very different from her husband, real life evidence that opposites attract.

She started to read to Dylan almost as he was coming out of the womb. He could read his children's books himself by the time he was four. In school he was years ahead of his classmates, and the gap continued to widen as he grew older. When he encountered conflicts he didn't understand, about religion or sex or the like, he used books to resolve the confusion or sometimes just to escape. By high school he was reading serious literature – college level and beyond. Not just fiction. Dylan read biographies, history, current affairs, even some science-related best sellers, books his dad wouldn't even think of reading.

He came to believe that reading was a major factor in his decision to join the Navy. It had set him apart from his classmates, filling him with knowledge and understanding they didn't yet have. It made school one big bore. The teachers were boring, the homework was boring, and the other students were boring. Intellectually and academically, he belonged in a more advanced environment. The boredom was so stifling, he paid almost no attention, daydreaming through it all, thinking about water and boats and far away travel and sometimes about the boy in the next row. He managed to pass all his classes with above average grades, but he never reached the academic heights he might have achieved if he was at all interested. For Dylan school lacked intellectual stimulation. Bottom line: he didn't want to sit in any more classrooms.

When he joined the Navy out of high school, he detected a change for the better in his dad's attitude. And when he applied for the SEALs, and was accepted, the proud father was all-in. George Custer was now Dylan's biggest fan. He conceded that gaining his father's respect and approval was a factor in doing both the Navy and the SEALs. In retrospect Dylan wasn't sure if he comprehended at the time how much of a shell game he was pulling on his dad, hiding the real Dylan by going the all-macho route.

It worked. But it was a lie.

On that day in the basement he came to truly understand the extent of the deception. And it would stay with him for the rest of his life.

Dad got a couple beers from the fridge. Not the Budweiser but the imported Molson's he stocked for special occasions. He was all happy eyes and grins, seeing his son, the Navy SEAL, for the first time in months. Right away he wanted to know if Dylan would have enough time this trip to go fishing.

Dylan remembered starting with the old standby, "Dad, I have something to tell you."

His dad's eyes lit up and his grin widened into a happy open-mouthed smile, "What's her name!?"

"No Dad, it's not...uh..." Dylan had rehearsed this speech enough in the last few weeks to have it memorized, and already he was headed off script.

"Dad, I had to make a big decision. Things just weren't going right."

"What is it, son?" Dad's mien changed, concerned, sensing Dylan's discomfort.

"I quit the SEALs, Dad. I'm out. I'm a civilian." Blurting it out was not in the script either.

His father's large head seemed to tilt slightly, as if straining to hear, not believing what he thought his son had just said. He was confused. His greatest source of pride, of self esteem even, greater than his own time as a U.S. Marine, his son, the war hero Navy SEAL, was what…quitting? What was he saying?

He leaned forward in his chair with alarm all over his face, "What do you mean? Why? You're a master chief petty officer. You're a SEAL. You only have eight years to go, and you'll have a life-time pension!"

His father was all blue-collar, not a rich man. At 54 everything was about getting to the point in life when he could hang up the tools, collect his retirement checks, and go fishing. His son obviously didn't understand how hard it was to get there. He'd have a pension in hand when he was only 38-years old. He could coast to the finish line! Why give up his head start?

Dylan tried again, "Dad, I didn't want it to turn out this way. You see, I didn't have a choice. This was the only way." A pause. "There's something…" his voice trailed off.

"What? There's what?"

One more time. "This is really hard. I don't know how… I guess there's only..." Another long pause with Dad hanging there, waiting. "Dad, I'm gay. They found out. It was a pretty bad scene. All I … I managed to get out with an honorable discharge. It was the best I could do."

That was when Dylan saw "the grimace" for the first time. The muscles in his dad's forehead and around his eyes and mouth seemed to contract toward the middle of his face, as if he'd bitten into the world's bitterest lemon or been sprayed by a skunk. He held that expression long enough for Dylan to recognize the grimace as a look of *revulsion*. His father was more than unhappy; he was on the verge of nausea.

The tone of the conversation changed, different from any they'd had since he joined the Navy. At first his dad couldn't put a sentence together. Finally, he said "Why? When did you get this big idea? Why are you doing this?"

"I didn't *do* anything, Dad. I didn't make a decision to be gay. I just am. It just happened … a long time ago. Way before I went in."

The ex-marine was losing the battle to control himself, "But you were normal!"

"I'm still normal, Dad. Just gay."

"We'll have to talk to your mother. See what can be done." As he said this the look of revulsion briefly returned.

Dylan was now calm. He was trained to be calm in the face of adversity. The look from his father was as adverse as any threat he'd ever faced as a SEAL.

"Dad, nothing can be done. It's not a curable disease. It's not a disease at all. It's the way I am. I got used to it a long time ago. Unfortunately, the Navy didn't. I'm happy. I have a partner who is a great guy. I'm as in love as a person could be. I guess … I should've told you a long time ago. Maybe it would have made a difference."

After that, nothing between them was ever the same. The ex-marine, raised in the homophobic culture of the 40s and 50s, and still living it as a blue collar man's man, could not accept that his son, the Navy SEAL, was a queer, a faggot, a three-dollar bill, a fudge packer, or any of the pejorative terms for homosexual he'd been using since he was 13-years old. They never went fishing again, even years later when Dylan splurged on a nice boat.

And Dylan was left with a recurring and disturbing dream of the look of revulsion on his father's face.

CHAPTER 10

JOURNAL – SAIGON

5am, Wednesday, 12-17-2014

I arrived in Saigon in October '73, when the war was pretty much over. (We lost by the way.) I was an M.P. and had just made 1st lieutenant. In that year most all of our combat troops were withdrawn. We still had some Special Forces in the field along with support personnel for the ARVN, South Vietnam's army, but our main combat troops were gone home.

I became part of a skeleton crew to keep things in order in Saigon, the capital city, while the rest of our people got packed up and out. It took another 18 months before we did the final evacuations in April of '75. As it was, we still left a lot of stuff behind.

I stayed to the end, or actually three days before the end, April 27. Most Americans, who were alive on April 30, 1975, the last day, saw the Embassy rooftop helicopter scene on TV. The brass called it Operation Frequent Wind. Some think it should have been called "Operation Tails Between Our Legs." Someone suggested the "frequent wind" was caused by the propellers of helicopters taking off from the Embassy roof. Desperate South Vietnamese citizens were climbing over each other struggling to get on one of those copters. They believed if they didn't get out before the last Americans were gone, they would be slaughtered by the Viet Cong. As it turned out, many of them were right.

My path to Saigon was atypical. After graduating from Wayne State with a degree in Business, I entered the Detroit Police Academy. I completed the training within three months, graduated, took military leave and joined the Army. Since I had a college degree, and enlisted rather than being drafted, I was eligible for officer training. Because of the Police Academy, I went from OTS to MP School.

That worked for me, because as an MP I could get real law enforcement experience, doing much the same as I would as a civilian. It also meant there was little chance the Viet Cong would shoot at me. I had little affinity for getting shot at. As it turned out, by the time I got there, the Cong were not shooting at any Americans, at least not very often.

In Saigon, we were down to only three MP units. As the junior officer, they were mine. I supervised all of their activity, which was mostly patrolling the city. Our job was to try to keep the few remaining GIs in Vietnam from hurting each other when they came into the city for relaxation. Though the combat troops were mostly gone, we still had GIs over there with regularly recurring needs, the kinds of needs that could be easily met in any big city in the world.

Saigon is a big city, but we were able to focus our resources on the limited commercial areas that catered to GIs: small sections of the city with large numbers of B & Bs (bars & brothels). You'd also find, sprinkled into these areas, a few places catering mostly to local residents. They were known to the GIs' as "gook joints." It was a time and place where being politically correct didn't count for much.

As we did our rounds, we pretty much ignored "gook joints." They were not our business. However, one night in October of '74 a pivotal incident occurred in one of them, Pho Phan's. Pho Phan's was a noodle house. (I think "pho" means "noodle soup", and Phan is a fairly common Vietnamese surname.)

Saigon had no shortage of noodle houses. That I should intersect with that one on that night had long term significance for me. It was a life-changing coincidence, and a contributing event to where we're going here.

The Pho Phan eatery was small and on a narrow street near several establishments that catered to GIs. I recall a portico over the front entrance and swinging double doors, like a saloon in the Old West. Saigon was close to the Equator, so it was almost always hot; swinging doors were common.

As was my custom I was out on patrol for a couple hours during the busy time just to keep my hand in. The busy time started a couple hours after dark and ran until the middle of the night. We went out in a Jeep, only two of us, a corporal and me. The corporal drove. The night sky was clear. As usual, it was warm and humid. We rolled slowly along the narrow streets hoping not to find trouble, and indeed, not expecting to. With the war over we seldom did. Except for this night.

About midnight we rolled by Pho Phan's at maybe 10 miles an hour. Our attention was on the GI B & Bs a few doors down. So we were startled to hear loud voices along with what were clearly crashing sounds, like maybe breaking furniture, all coming out of Pho Phan's. The loudest of the voices was American. Many of the words started with the letter "F" and several others used variations on that theme. Some of them were quite slurred, but increasingly angry, with the louder crashing noises providing a percussive background.

I jumped out of the Jeep before it came to a full stop, hoping all the while that one of my crews was already in there dealing with the disturbance.

No such luck; I was first in.

The place was very small. Typical low ceiling, better light than most, but then it was a "gook joint." No need for dim lighting. About six tables on the left and a short bar on the right. Five people in the room, one American soldier, an officer, sitting on the floor between two tables, holding his head, looking dazed. One of the tables on its side, dishes broken and scattered on the floor. Two Vietnamese, a man and a woman, cowering back in the corner behind the tables. One Vietnamese man on the floor near the bar holding his hands up as if to protect his head, and one very big American soldier standing over him with a chair leg in his right hand, weaving, having trouble keeping his balance, and yelling. He was at least 6'4", 250 lbs.

The grip end of the chair leg was round and about two inches in diameter. The other end was square and much thicker. A formidable club.

His slurred message was something about how "it was your fucking fault, all of you; all you mother fucking gooks who can't take care of your own fucking country." Something like that.

Complicating matters, there was an oak leaf on his shoulder. He was a major. An Air Force major. As a rule majors, especially Air Force majors, didn't get drunk in Saigon and attack the locals. On rare occasion maybe Army or Marine, but not Air Force. People joined the Air Force to avoid physical confrontation, or so I assumed. Further complicating matters, I was a 1st lieutenant. Unfortunately, I didn't have time to consider these details, because someone had to do something fast to keep that little guy on the floor from getting his noggin bashed in by the giant standing over him.

I yelled, "Stop! Police!" Admittedly, not very original. I was still in the doorway about 10 feet from the drunken monster major. He hesitated and tried to turn toward me without falling down.

Didn't work.

He went down on his side. When really big things fall, like a tall tree, though it's happening very fast, there's the illusion of slow motion. Then the big thing hits the ground, and the noise tells you it was going pretty fast. Thus for the major.

Once on the floor he made movements that confirmed both that he was trying to get up and that he was very drunk. Right then it became clear that his intent, if he could get to his feet, was to use the chair leg on me. He managed to get to his hands and knees. His knees were about 18 inches apart, helping him keep his balance.

Keep in mind, in spite of being an MP, I'm no Jack Reacher. (Actually nobody is.) While the big guy struggled to get up, I quickly circled behind him and kicked him as hard as I could in the crotch. It was about as much as I could put into a kick without falling down myself. In the NFL it would have been a 50-yard field goal.

He did a classic face plant and moaned a terrible sound and showed no further intention of trying to stand up. I got one handcuff on him. The other hand was between his legs holding his crotch. I couldn't get it out to cuff it. He was very strong. (What the hell was he doing in the Air Force?) By this time my driver was in the room. With our combined strength we got his other arm out and the other handcuff on it. Then he threw up. His face was right on the floor next to the mess he was making. We had to make sure he didn't choke on his vomit.

After getting him clear of the mess, and feeling confident that with his hands cuffed he could not get to his feet without assistance, we went around to the others in the room to see if they were ok. The two people in the corner were unharmed, at least physically. The little guy on the floor by the bar was mussed up only a little. No cuts, nothing broken. Apparently, he'd been pushed rather than knocked down. Turns out he was the owner of the place. The other American officer had a busted lip and a knot on the back of his head from hitting the floor.

While the major lay there semi passed-out, we concentrated on the other officer. Though slightly dazed, he appeared to be sober. He was an Air Force captain. He explained he was a close friend of the big major, whose name was Kovach. They'd come from Tan Son Nhut, the huge air base near Saigon. The major got a "Dear John" letter from his wife early that afternoon. He was devastated and wanted to come into Saigon to get drunk. His friend, the captain, suggested they just go to the Officer's Club on the base. The major insisted on Saigon, where he could blow off a little steam. The captain kept trying to keep him on the base. The major insisted on Saigon and started crying. The captain gave in and, as a good friend, went with him.

Once in Saigon the major consumed an enormous amount of alcohol at three different GI hangouts near Pho Phan's. The captain, on the other hand, nursed his drinks, trying to stay sober. They ended up here at Pho Phan's to get some food. The major had a plate of noodles and drank some of the local wine. At that point he just went off. The captain tried to restrain him and somehow got elbowed in the mouth and knocked down. The captain said the major wasn't normally like that at all. The letter and the booze did it to him.

We turned our attention back to the shop owner. He wanted us to get the major off his floor and out of his place. No, he would not be pressing charges. He was very grateful for our arrival and assistance. The captain paid him $50 for the broken furniture. He took it and thanked him. Now he just wanted all of us out of there. The three of us got the major to his feet. I uncuffed him so we could put his arms around our shoulders. The captain and I half carried him, half dragged him outside and over to the Jeep. I didn't want to take him back to our headquarters holding cell. The captain said his car was only a block away. We loaded the major into our Jeep and drove to their car.

The major was now out cold. Somehow we got him out of our Jeep and into their sedan. They drove off slowly and we headed back to our hotel, The International, which also served as our MP headquarters. It was 1:15am in Saigon. I went immediately to my room and fell into bed.

That night I didn't sleep well. Normally when a soldier gets drunk and turns violent, we bring him in and put him in a holding cell overnight. We didn't do that with the major. We just let him go back to his base. No reports, no charges, no paperwork, nothing in his service jacket.

Certainly as Officer-In-Charge I did have some procedural leeway, but early on in my Vietnam tour, my inclination had always been to go by the book. Everybody gets the same treatment. It was only fair. Kind of a "Grampa" thing. Reminder: I'm the oldest child in my family, and research shows we oldest children are most likely to act responsibly and be respectful of authority. We also tend to be pretty good about following the rules.

In Vietnam, my rigidity was challenged. As time went on, I became more accepting of the concept of extenuating circumstances. Purists refer to this as "situational ethics." Usually they say it with a sneer. With the major there were three of those situationally ethical circumstances in his favor.

Number 1: he was out cold and wouldn't be causing any more trouble that night in my jurisdiction or any one else's.

Number 2: his friend, the captain, was sober and willing to get him back to his base.

Number 3: the "Dear John" letter. Admittedly there was no mention of Dear John letters in the UCMJ (Uniform Code of Military Justice), but from my point of view, Vietnam was bad enough without having to suffer loss on the home front.

I kept telling myself it had nothing to do with him being a major. On the other hand I was certainly aware of his rank. So maybe it was another extenuating circumstance, the biggest of which was Vietnam. You had to be there. In Vietnam the sense of corruption and dishonesty in high places, both there and back in the States, was immersive and corrosive, bringing everyone down. I had become willing to bend the rules. Under the circumstances (there's that word again) it seemed proper and, I confess, easier.

In any case, I had a restless night. The next morning I was on the horn to Tan Son Nhut. I found the captain at his desk in an admin office. Don't remember exactly what his job was. He assured me they made it back to the air base safely, and thanked me for letting him take the major back with him. The major was pretty much out cold all the way back, but the captain was able to rouse him and get him into his quarters without creating any attention.

He hadn't spoken to the major yet this morning, but he imagined the big guy had a colossal headache, not to mention a limp from how his balls must ache. I told him I was just checking to make sure they got back ok. He thanked me profusely and assured me they owed me one but had no idea how they could pay it back. I asked out of pure curiosity what the major did. The captain said he was one of the two or three top guys in logistics; getting people and equipment in and out of Vietnam. The captain thanked me again. We hung up, and I expected that was the end of it.

Three days later, shortly after arriving at my cubicle, my phone rang. I answered, "Good morning, Lieutenant Rossi."

The voice on the other end was a deep bass, "Good morning, this is Major Kovach at Tan Son Nhut."

At least my groin kick hadn't altered his voice. Still, important orifices in my body puckered slightly. Was he still limping? Had I made a life long enemy?

As for the latter, apparently not. He said, "I just called to apologize. And I want to thank you for stopping me from doing something really stupid."

I don't know if he heard the relief in my tone when I said. "Don't worry about it. All in a night's work."

He asked, "How long you been over here?"

"One year last week."

"Take any time off yet? Go anywhere?"

"Took three weeks in August and went to Hawaii. Might be getting rotated out in a few months. I suppose we'll all be getting rotated out pretty soon."

"You get any time and want to go somewhere, call me. I can get you to most places you might want to go. I owe you a big one."

"Like I said, don't worry about it. I wasn't looking for favors. But thanks for the offer. Never know where and when you might need a friend."

"No, you never know. Anyways, you got one. And thanks again. If I ever get back to the city, I'll look you up. Buy you a drink, if you're not on duty."

"Sounds good."

The phone clicked at the other end. The deep voice was gone with no reference to sore balls. I was glad the whole matter was over.

CHAPTER 11

JOURNAL – CAPTAIN PHAN

5am, Thursday, 12-18-2014

As it turned out, the whole matter wasn't over. It's amazing how life turns out to be a sequence of events like dots on a chart. Who would have thought that seemingly unrelated incidents in Saigon in 1975 could be traced to an assassination in Virginia in 2015, forty years later?

When I came into the office the next day, I had a phone message from a friend and colleague, Captain Phan Boa of the Q.C. (Q.C. stood for Quan Canh, the South Vietnamese equivalent of the U.S. Military Police.) He asked me to call him at my convenience.

Captain Phan was a cop, a good cop. Remember, South Vietnam was a third-world country. So it should come as no surprise that corruption was prevalent, especially with people in positions of authority – politicians, bureaucrats, military and police. In Saigon it had always been thus.

It was a quagmire of arrogant, uncooperative, bribe-addicted bureaucrats and politicians. Phan, on the other hand, was the exception, a beacon of integrity and dedication.

When I arrived in Saigon, my predecessor introduced me to Phan and told me there would be times when I would need his help, and when those times came, I should trust him. It was the best advice I got during my stay in Vietnam. On occasion we American M.P.s would need to go into parts of the city that were otherwise off limits or considered out of our jurisdiction. Instead of playing the turf war game, Phan would help us get in and out without creating a fuss. And in the event his people arrested one of our GIs, Phan would deliver the miscreant directly to us without delay. No ransom or extortion. No quid pro quos. He also knew how to cut red tape when we needed a permit from a bureaucrat to do something related to our mission. Or, if he became aware of an impending crisis, he made sure we were warned, so we could be ready with the appropriate response. All in all he was a friend indeed.

As a practical person I nursed this relationship. We checked in with each other at least weekly. We shared info and rumors. We had lunch together almost monthly. On receiving his message, I promptly returned his call.

After an exchange of greetings, he said, "I rang you to express my deepest gratitude for your actions the other night in Pho Phan's. My brother is the proprietor who you protected from harm by the very large GI. Thank you, Lieutenant Rossi, thank you very much." He spoke in an almost academic speech pattern with a slight British accent. In one of our lunches, he said that he'd spent 10 years as a youth in France, England and Canada and went to college in Australia. He'd also visited the U.S. briefly during his time in Canada. His father, now deceased, was in the export/ import business, and the family spent a great deal of time traveling and living abroad.

I responded, "You're very welcome, of course, Captain, but it was nothing. Just doing my job, you know how that goes."

"My brother said you acted quite courageously against the drunken ferocity of a man of great hulk. He also said you were very courteous and considerate. I assured him it was your nature. Nevertheless, he would like to invite you to a traditional Vietnamese dinner prepared in your honor."

I was hesitant, "Please don't misunderstand, Captain, but I'm not sure how that would look. You know the Army pays me to do these things."

Phan persisted, "I told him you would be reluctant to accept such an invitation, since it might imply that he was somehow in your debt when you were, as you say, 'just doing your job.' However, my brother is somewhat old fashioned about such matters. He feels obligated to honor you and return your courtesy to him. Accordingly, he laid responsibility on me, his younger brother, to make sure you attend. If you don't, he will be very disappointed in me. And he is the family patriarch. It will have a very negative affect on my status in the family. You simply must attend. I assure you none of your superiors will ever get a whiff of it."

"I have the feeling, Captain, you're putting me on. But, what the hell, if your brother insists, I'll be there."

My other concern was the concept of a "traditional Vietnamese dinner." It would be what the GIs referred to as "gook food," like eyes and brains and other parts most Americans would have trouble swallowing without gagging. Yucky.

The dinner took place about two weeks later at the restaurant. Due to its small capacity, it was closed for the occasion. Several noodle variations were served, each with its own distinctive flavor, and each delicious. The other "delicacies" I accepted without asking questions and found them to be edible, even tasty. Overall, the meal was very good. Not yucky at all.

It turned out to be a family event. All of Captain Phan's family attended. Though his parents were both deceased, in life they had produced six children, 4 boys and 2 girls. The oldest was the Pho Phan proprietor, whose first name was Hien, the youngest, Captain Phan. I remember musing to myself that I was in the middle of the "Phan clan." Adding to the pleasantry and my comfort level, most of the adults spoke very understandable English.

The full family story, on the other hand, was somewhat grim. The two middle brothers were soldiers, both killed in the war. One had been married. His widow attended the dinner as did the two sisters. The husband of one of the sisters was a soldier who also died in the war (that's three), and the other sister's husband was in attendance, but only because he was too disabled to still be fighting. He was minus one leg and one eye. Sometimes we forget that the South Vietnamese lost 280,000 soldiers, more than five and a half times as many as we did, plus an astounding figure of over one million civilians. Sitting at their table, I was struck by the enormity of the tragedy wrought on their country and their family.

Captain Phan brought his wife and their only child, a baby boy. His wife was young and very pretty. The baby was happy and friendly and seemingly very bright. The oldest brother, Hien, who ran the restaurant, had been spared military duty due to his age. His wife also attended. All in all a beautiful family decimated by a war for which they held no responsibility and an incomplete understanding.

I was honored to have been invited to their table. They all welcomed me and seemed grateful for my actions to protect their patriarch. The thought of Grampa and my Lone Ranger instructions flashed through my mind. But for only a moment. What I'd done was routine, not heroic. I just did what had to be done. I had not fulfilled a Grampa imposed destiny.

To my relief there was no political elephant in the room. The Phan family did not appear to blame the U.S. for what was happening to their country. In contrast to the anti-war turmoil back in the States, this family was genuinely cordial to the American presence.

Ironically, the only American at the table, me, was less convinced of our innocence. We didn't start it, but we did make it worse. Or so I felt. Of course I wouldn't openly criticize my leaders to my hosts or almost anyone for that matter, but in my closely held thoughts, I was losing faith. I was backsliding, as they would say in the pulpit. I was coming to believe our demi-gods in the White House and the Capitol Building and the Pentagon were maybe not as omniscient or omnipotent as we thought, nor as they thought.

Keep in mind I was no left-wing, pinko peacenik. I was an authority-respecting, rule following, speak when spoken to, moderately conservative, flag-saluting, oldest child. And I had no political agenda. I didn't assume one side or the other had the right answers.

However, the evidence was piling up that our military leaders were sometimes incompetent, sometimes dishonest, and sometimes corrupt; furthermore, they were abetted by similarly disposed – not to mention, blindly ambitious – political leaders in Washington. From both parties. Between them they had used this small, densely populated strip of geography as a beta war to stem what they perceived as the "domino effect" of the rising tide of Godless Communism.

Admittedly, when I got to Vietnam I was already aware that all was not as advertised. At first I adopted the British counsel to "keep calm and carry on." As time went on and more damning information came out, I started to feel a little dirty. My pillow was becoming overly firm.

The dinner with the "Phan clan," was a watershed event for my tarnished outlook. Their attitude helped. They were not inclined to shift blame for their tragedy to the invading Americans. They understood that we did not come to prey on them. They thought we'd made mistakes, but not with malice aforethought. They were grateful we had tried to help. Too bad we weren't infallible.

I was encouraged. For more than a year I'd been absorbing guilt, a sense that the averted glances of the people on the street were accusatory. The Phans turned that around. They wordlessly accepted their nation's share of the failure. They were simply trying to survive their horror, not litigate it. Or so it seemed. I left their home feeling inspired in a way, wanting to restore a positive attitude, to do the best I could each day, much like the Village Blacksmith and the Phans. Certainly Grampa would approve.

The remaining uneventful routine in Saigon was broken only by my monthly lunches with Captain Phan. We normally got together on the third Tuesday of the month. Our March, 1975 lunch was at the Army Officers' Club. By then it was clear the Viet Cong would soon have Saigon surrounded, and we would all have to be the hell out of there before they crossed the city limits.

Obviously the captain could not stay. He'd be near the top of the Cong's list of people to deal with. He would be quickly executed or sent to a work camp where he could be held for the rest of his life. If he tried to hide in Saigon or anyplace else in Vietnam, he would be found. I was curious about his plans. At the end of our lunch I asked him where he was going.

His eyes turned away, "We are not quite sure. We might be able to get to Thailand."

Might be able to get to Thailand? Was I asking something I shouldn't? Maybe he had a plan he couldn't share. But his vagueness alarmed me. I cared about him.

I pressed on, "How would you do that?"

He shifted in his chair, eyes still avoiding mine. "Overland is probably too treacherous. I am trying to find a boat. I have a little money."

Not a reassuring answer. Everyone in Saigon was trying to find a boat. Now I was getting uncomfortable.

"Sorry for being a pushy American, and if you are getting out, and it's top secret, just tell me to stay out of it, and I will. But if you're really 'looking for a boat', I'm concerned."

His head was down, tilted to his right, staring at the floor next to the table. Without meeting my eyes, he rotated his head to stare at the floor on the other side of the table. As his face passed my gaze, I saw a tear running down one cheek.

He didn't have a way out.

Back at my office, I called Tan Son Nhut and got through to Major Kovach's office. The enlisted clerk answered, "Logistics."

"This is Lieutenant Rossi, Army Military Police. Is Major Kovach in?"

"May I tell him what this is about, sir?"

"No."

There was a pause during which the clerk apparently decided not to get into it with me. "One minute. I'll try to find him."

It took less than 15 seconds. "Kovach here."

"Major Kovach, this is Lieutenant Rossi. I hope you haven't forgotten me."

He sounded pleased to hear my voice. "You know I couldn't forget you, Lieutenant. You're still here. How ya doin'?"

"Fine, thank you. I'm going to get right to it, Major. I need to get a family out of Saigon, Vietnamese people. I understand you can make that happen."

"Uh … I'm … what exactly … what family?"

"Major, I hope this doesn't sound disrespectful, but remember when you said you owed me a big favor? Well, this is that kind of situation. I need to get a man, a woman and a child out of Saigon before the stuff hits the fan."

"Lieutenant, there are lists of approved evacuees. Are they on … who are they?"

Sounded like I was going to have to push a little, but with caution. One more try at begging. "Major, the man is someone who has been of great assistance to this office and American Forces in general. If he doesn't get out before the Cong take over, he will almost certainly be executed. The woman is his wife. The child is their baby…about 18 months old."

His voice took on an officious, bureaucratic tone, "Lieutenant, I'm really not sure if I can do anything at this time. Maybe if they increase the number of flights … but everything so far is pretty full."

Time to squeeze a bit. "Major, please let me lay out the complete circumstances in this case. To begin with … I don't know exactly how to say this … uh, excuse my candor, but we both know you are in a position to make adjustments to those manifests. And we both know those lists are filled with corrupt politicians and bureaucrats who've mostly been pains in the ass since this mess started. My man, on the other hand, is an allied soldier, a Vietnamese M.P., who has consistently helped us keep our guys from hurting each other."

I paused to bring my voice and blood pressure under control before weighing in with a round of heavier artillery. "He also is the brother of the man whose restaurant you damaged. The brother of the man you were preparing to do great bodily harm to before I stopped you. The brother of the man who refused to press any charges against you."

Another pause to keep my voice from getting blatantly disrespectful and to give gravitas to the coup de gras. "There's also the payback issue to me. Again, excuse me for being so blunt, but not only did I save you in your drunken condition from committing a major crime, I also elected not to file a report on any of it – a report that could have had a negative impact on your career. As you are probably aware, my action, or lack of it, was a violation of procedure, which technically could have resulted in some form of reprimand or even discipline to me. I did it because I felt there were special circumstances at play. No disrespect, sir, but in return I'm asking you for a similar procedural 'adjustment,' one that certainly is justified by a truckload of 'special circumstances.' It will assuredly result in saving a good man's life. As support staff, you and I don't get many chances to do that kind of thing. As for the threat to an innocent wife and child..."

"OK, OK, let me get back to you. What's the timing on this? When will they be able to go?"

My relief at his quick cave-in was palpable, a slight tingle from my ears to my thighs.

I had to clear my throat, "Major, I'm sure they can be ready in a day or two. But we shouldn't wait more than a few days." I tried to convey a sense of urgency. Delays, even short ones, are dangerous.

He said, "I'll get back to you this afternoon."

Three days later Captain Phan, his wife and baby were on a flight to Okinawa. The captain took my address in the States, though I never expected to see or hear from him again. But you never know.

CHAPTER 12

JOURNAL – THERE WAS A GIRL

5am, Friday, 12-19-2014

Harper Hospital in mid-town Detroit was founded during The Civil War. 1863. It has a rich history of medical innovation including being the first hospital in the world where open-heart surgery was performed. That was 1952. The heart machine used in that operation was designed in part by, what else, an automotive engineer.

Fast forward to July, 1975. Harper Hospital was in a new building and had come a long way since 1863. But it still looked and sounded and smelled like a hospital. Pale sea-green walls, cream colored ceilings, heavy steel doors, marble-looking vinyl flooring, Formica countertops, a collection of easy to disinfect hard surfaces with noisy acoustics. They all gave it away.

The man in room 522 was a heart patient. 83-years old. His cardiologist said his condition was such that, even at Harper, surgery was not an option. He might live for six months…and he might not. He was fully aware of the prognosis.

He was worried. Not that he was going to die. But that his secret would die with him. He did something over 60 years ago in his distant youth, and even though he believed it was the right thing to do, he'd kept it a secret for fear of condemnation. It was time to tell someone.

When I entered his room, Pietro Antonio Rossi (nee Rossini) did not see or hear me. The old man's eyes were closed and his breathing was labored, like someone with late-stage heart disease.

I came to the hospital directly from Detroit Metropolitan Airport. The previous afternoon I picked up my active duty separation papers at Fort Leonard Wood in Missouri, took a bus to St. Louis, and found a cheap motel near the airport. The next morning I was on the first flight to Detroit. My parents met me at the gate and brought me to the hospital.

While Dad parked the car, Mom and I went up to the room. She stayed at the door as I approached the bed. A hospital sheet and thin blanket covered Grampa to his chest. His face had the taupe color of someone who hadn't seen the sun recently. An IV drip line was attached to his left hand and arm. I hesitated when I saw his eyes were closed, but the irregular breathing suggested he was awake. His hearing was failing, too, so I bent over and spoke directly into his ear, "Grampa, it's me, Pete."

Grampa's eyes popped open, and he was momentarily speechless. Tears formed and his voice quavered, "Oh, Petey. You made it."

From the day I joined the Army, Grampa harbored dreadful concerns I wouldn't come back alive or in one piece. Even when I got back stateside, he still worried. No one told him I was coming home soon, so when Grampa saw me healthy and alive, he was both surprised and full of joy.

The reunion was emotional. We were both in tears as we took each other in. I avoided mentioning his condition. I didn't know how much he knew.

Instead we talked of my immediate plans with the Detroit Police Department and reminiscences of our adventures as "Big Pete and Little Pete."

When they brought his lunch, Mom and I left. We went home, had our own lunch, after which I unpacked my luggage. Later in the afternoon I returned to the hospital alone, so Grampa and I could continue our reunion. I went home around 8:30 that night when the Visiting Hours were officially over.

I wasn't scheduled to start with the DPD until the end of the month, so while Grampa was in the hospital, I visited him every day. Back in the dark ages of the 1970s, hospitals had restricted visiting hours. Visitors were considered a nuisance. You had two or three hours in the afternoon and the same in the evening. They gave out visitors' passes in the lobby to control the friends and loved ones ostensibly from tiring the patients but mostly from getting in the way of doctors and nurses.

I got around all that by wearing my uniform with the MP arm band and a few medals on my chest. As I thought they would, the "hall monitors," to borrow a term from high school, assumed the medals were for doing something heroic, when, in fact, they were just for showing up. Hospital personnel also seemed to respect uniforms. It may have had something to do with the prevalence of a strict hierarchy in the medical world. Strict hierarchies and uniforms go together. In any case nobody said a word to me. Each day I walked through the front doors, past the lobby desk and up to the room.

Grampa was in a semi-private room. The doctors were ready to send him home once they "stabilized his vital signs." His blood pressure kept going up and down.

We had long discussions and long silences. He would doze off during the silences. While he was sleeping I went down to the cafeteria for coffee or a sandwich.

Our conversations avoided typical hospital visitation small talk except for maybe a daily weather report. No "how are you feeling" or "are the nurses taking good care of you?" We had a lot of good territory to cover. Grampa laughed as I told him about the Phan's and Major Kovach in Saigon. He was curious what happened to the Phan's. I didn't know, but was sure they were better off than if they'd stayed in Saigon. Grampa suggested it might be a "Lone Ranger" story. I thought it probably didn't quite come up to that standard. Then he followed with a less intense version of his "Lone Ranger speech."

Into the second day of my visits I sensed an ever so slight change in the tone of his conversation. A couple times he went silent and looked at the wall with that stare people get when their mind leaves the room but their body stays. At first I thought he was having an episode of some kind.

I asked, "Are you alright Grampa?"

He shook his head and looked down at the covers and said, "Yeah, yeah, just thinking."

"About what?"

"Oh, not much. Just the old days." Still not looking at me. It was as if he knew he didn't have much time left. I wished I was a mind reader. I suspected whatever he was thinking would make a good story. Maybe I could get him to tell me.

On the third day, right after I filled him in on the weather, Grampa replied, "I'm probably going home tomorrow. They think they've got the blood pressure settled down." He didn't sound glad or sad. Again his eyes were averted from my face.

I said, "That's great! Back to Lucille's cooking." My enthusiasm was forced. I hated the thought of Grampa going home without being fixed. I wanted them to keep him for a while, and somehow come up with a cure or at least a postponement of the inevitable.

We had several minutes of silence, with his eyes going from the wall to the covers and back. I got up and cranked the bed so he was sitting up a little bit more. As I sat back down in the chair, his eyes turned to me, and he focused with an intensity I hadn't seen since I was a boy.

"Petey," he said. "You gotta remember the Lone Ranger thing. The time will come. Sometimes a bad situation needs to be corrected. You can't just let it go. You can set things right. Maybe keep it from happening again. There was a guy said 'The only thing necessary for evil to triumph is for good men to do nothing.' You shouldn't let bad guys get away with it. You should do something."

He was agitated in a way I wasn't used to seeing. But his eyes didn't wander. They stayed locked on mine.

I didn't respond, couldn't respond. Grampa was on the verge of saying something big. The scene created a visceral reaction in me, as if the room had suddenly gotten much cooler. I told myself to calm down; my brain needed to function. Something of consequence is going on here. Time to be a cop. Take advantage of my training and experience. When the suspect is feeling guilty, and thinks you know he's guilty, you're supposed to push him into a full evidence-riddled confession.

But it was Grampa. What a terrible thing to think. On the other hand, maybe it was what he wanted. He wanted somebody to know something. He wanted it to be me. Or was I over-reading the intensity and grimness on his face?

I thought about his condition. Not a time for tension or emotion. But it must be important. Don't let this opportunity disintegrate. Be calm, even casual. I edged my chair closer to the bed. In my gentlest manner I asked, "What is this about?"

The old man's eyes wandered away. His right hand pushed the covers down to his waist, then it went up to his head and swept back his thinning white hair. "I don't know where to start. It's kind of a long story."

I waited. I fought the tendency to fill the air with comforting words. Just let it happen.

"Well, there was a girl."

How many life-changing stories start with "Well, there was a girl?"

A girl? When? Where? I tried not to show a physical reaction, like shifting in my chair. Has he ever told this story before? Does Lucille know?

Don't interrupt. Let him do it his way, at his pace.

"Her name was Bella, short for Isabella." He chuckled, "Bella means 'good' or 'pretty girl.'" More thinking. "That she was…a pretty girl."

He looked away from the blanket toward me, "I first saw her when I was about 18. She was almost 16. Her family was big, lots of kids. Age-wise she was in the middle somewhere. They were poor farmers, tenant farmers. Small piece of land."

He paused and shifted his eyes to the wall. I said nothing. My heart rate picked up a few beats. He's going to tell me "exactly what happened."

"We met at a big celebration party in the center of town. It was a national holiday or something, like Fourth of July over here. I don't remember exactly what it was. She was with her parents and brothers and sisters. I saw her and stared at her. She was real pretty. She caught me looking, you know, almost like a voyeur." He looked up with a mischievous half smile. "But she held my gaze. I wasn't too bad either, you know. And I was real tall. Girls liked that."

I smiled and nodded.

He continued, "I didn't forget her. I found out who she was, and in time we managed to be at the same places at the same time. She was always with her family, of course. But our little meetings were as close as you could get to dates in those days.

"Pretty soon everybody knew we liked each other. I even visited her at her family's little house. All those kids in that little house. Must have been eight or nine kids.

"After a while people assumed we were sort of engaged. Her family liked me." He smiled, "Maybe I was a good catch. I was a quarry worker."

Another pause. He looked past me to the other bed in the room. It was empty. The guy went home this morning. Grampa's eyes dropped to his lap, then up to meet mine. An embarrassed look weakened his face.

He started again, "What happened was they were real poor. When the kids got a certain age, they tried to find work. Bella was very pretty. So, she found a place right away. She was 16 when she went to work in one of the rich family villas, the Pavoni family.

"See, most of the land was owned by just a few rich families. Same with the quarries. The Pavoni's owned the land Bella's family lived and worked on. The Pavoni's were very rich. Lots of servants.

"Bella was pretty and very shy. Just what the rich people wanted. Signore Pavoni actually told Bella's father he had an opening for her."

The words were coming now with less effort, "She went in as a maid. She washed clothes, and made beds and cleaned the rooms. She lived there. Came home one day a week. Every week I would go to her house on her day home. Just to see her. It was what I looked forward to all week long. I was only 19, but I was in love, for sure. We were going to get married right after she turned 17.

"One week I went to her house on the day she was supposed to come home, and they told me she wasn't there, and she wasn't going to be there. No explanation. Just that I should leave.

"The next day I found one of her brothers who said she had come home earlier in the week and she was crying, and later her father took her to the church and came back without her.

"It took me a while to piece it all together, but I eventually got the whole story. Another brother told me when she got home she was terrified and ashamed. She insisted on being taken to the convent. She could not marry me. She had been defiled. Signore Pavoni had raped her. She tried to resist, but he overpowered her. When he left her, she ran away.

"Another quarry worker told me it was not the first time for Pavoni. He apparently was accustomed to having his way with any servants who pleased his eye. He always got away with it. He made sure his victims were particularly vulnerable to his wealth and status. In Bella's case, if they made a fuss, the family would be evicted from their little farm. They would have no way to feed or shelter themselves. And the authorities, even the priests, turned a blind eye. He was just too powerful and rich.

'I went to the convent to plead with her, tell her it didn't make any difference, I still wanted to marry her. But the nuns in charge wouldn't let me see her. It was like she'd disappeared."

A pause. He picked at his IV line. "I was sick. Lovesick, I guess. I couldn't eat. I couldn't work. I just wasn't able to concentrate. At work I almost lost a big block of marble and a whole team of oxen over the side of the trail. They sent me home from the quarry.

"I had a little room in our house, and for a couple weeks I hardly left it. Just lay in bed.

"Finally one day I got up and went outside for a walk. I just walked not really knowing where I was going. At some point I found myself near the convent. So I went to the gate. But they still wouldn't let me in. I started thinking I would never see her again. It hurt my stomach, I was so sad. None of it seemed fair.

"I left the convent and walked some more. I ended up at Pavoni's estate. I sat on a hillside and just looked at the villa. I'm not sure what I was thinking. Why was I there?

"For several days I went back and did the same thing. Just sat there and watched.

"After a few days I noticed a pattern. He came out each day in the late afternoon and went riding on one of his horses. He had a stable of horses. He considered himself a horseman. There was a riding trail through a lot of trees. He always took it. He would go for more than an hour, some days almost two."

Grampa paused again, his eyes searching my face for empathy. "I stopped going to the convent. I gave up. They would never let me in. Uncle Giacomo wanted me to go back to the quarry and ask to get my job back. I told him I would. Next week.

"I went to Pavoni's again. This time I hid on the riding trail. He came riding along. He was so close I could see the wrinkles around his eyes. He was bald and his lips were kind of thick. During the Depression and the war, when I saw pictures of Mussolini, they reminded me of him." He gave another grin, "So, I didn't like Mussolini right from the beginning."

The serious look returned. "When they sent me home from the quarry, I took my whip home with me. It was under my bed. The last day I went out to Pavoni's place, I took the whip. I'm not sure what I thought I was gonna do with it. Maybe give him a few lashes. But it would have been stupid. No way I'd get away with it.

"Anyhow I took it. In a way it gave me confidence. Confidence to do what? I didn't know. I hid near his riding path, and when he came along, I got this sudden impulse. I lashed out at him with the whip, and it wrapped around him, and I pulled, and he came off the horse. I ran over to him not really knowing what to do next, and he just lay there on the ground. I checked him, and he was dead. His eyes were open. No pulse or nothing. I don't know if he hit his head or broke his neck or what. But for sure he was dead."

Grampa searched my eyes for assurance that I wasn't horrified. I tried to cover my shock.

He continued, "I just sat down next to him sort of stunned. Then all of a sudden I had this feeling as if I'd done something good. As if I'd just slain Goliath. It was like a sense of triumph over evil. It was a very wonderful feeling. I'd made the world a better place. Bella was redeemed. Her shame was obliterated. The score was even.

"I wanted to go back to the convent and tell Bella I'd fixed everything. I looked for a piece of proof that I'd done it. He was wearing a ring. I pulled it off his finger. So I could show it to her.

"After a few minutes reality started creeping in. They would figure out I did it. His family was rich and powerful. They would use that power to get retribution. I would be punished, maybe hanged. What should I do?

"I thought maybe I could make it look like a robbery. But there was no other jewelry. I searched inside his riding coat. Found nothing. The horse was still standing there. I looked inside the saddle bag. There was a small purse. Inside the purse was money. A lot of money. At least it seemed a lot to me. More than I'd ever seen before. I took it.

"Then I got up and walked away. Just walked away. I took the whip and the ring and the money. I didn't know what to do with the horse. So I left it.

"At first I just walked. After a while I started to run. Didn't know where I was going. It was getting dark. I still hadn't seen anyone. I came to a road and went back to walking. I wasn't even sure what direction I was going. Turned out it was north toward Genoa. I kept right on walking in the dark. In the morning as it got light, I was afraid someone would see me, so I hid in a stand of trees and slept for a few hours. I stayed there till it started getting dark again. Then I ventured out on the road and ran and walked all that night too.

"At one fairly wide stream I threw away the whip. Maybe they were looking for a tall guy with a whip. I didn't know. The stream was deep enough that you couldn't see the whip down at the bottom.

"Eventually I got all the way to Genoa. It took almost 4 days. Along the way all I had to eat was fruit from trees. And I drank water out of streams as I came to them. On the last day nearing Genoa, I bought some bread and cheese and milk in a little market.

"All the time I was walking and hiding, I also did a lot of thinking. I was trying to figure out what lay ahead. Where should I go? How long before I could go back and see my Aunt and Uncle? How would I get to see Bella again?

"There were no good answers. I started to accept the worst. Everything was over. Not that I had done the wrong thing. No. It had to be done. He was evil. I did the world a favor, but the world was not going to forgive me for it, much less reward me.

"When I got to Genoa, I decided to go into the city. I was careful. I didn't know if they would be looking for me there. I went in after dark looking over my shoulder a lot. But nobody seemed to pay any attention to me. I started to think maybe I was far enough away from Carrara. Maybe I would be safe for a while. So I stayed in Genoa.

"Genoa was not like anything I'd ever seen before. It was a real city, a major seaport. Columbus was born there. First thing I went down to the docks and I threw Pavoni's ring in the water. I didn't want to get caught with it. I was still afraid of somebody spotting me and turning me in to the authorities.

"After a few days I got some work on the docks, probably because I was a big guy and pretty strong. After a couple months I used Pavoni's money to get papers and passage on a ship to America.

"They never caught me. I got away with it. But I never saw Bella again or my aunt and uncle. I was always afraid to go back.

"My consolation was that I stopped him. He would never do it again. I would never see Bella again, but he would never see *anything* again. He deserved worse, but it was the worst I could do. If there's a hell, maybe he went there."

He stopped talking. It'd been quite a speech. He looked down at the covers. Either he was tired from his long monologue or afraid to look at me for fear of seeing disapproval on my face.

I stood up and took a step over to the bed. Put my hand on top of Grampa's and tried to convey reassurance. "Quite a story, Gramps."

I asked, "Did you ever let your aunt and uncle know you were okay and where you were?"

He said, "I was afraid to write to them at first. Maybe the authorities would find out, and they'd know where I was and come and get me. Finally I had a friend write a letter for me. I could write, but I thought maybe it would get through better, if it wasn't in my handwriting. Maybe I was being overly careful.

"We even went up to Buffalo and over to Canada to mail it. For the postmark and stuff. The letter didn't tell them where I was, just I was okay. I wrote about every few months for a couple years. But I never heard from them, 'cause they didn't know my address or anything. I found out they both died in the influenza plague right after the war, the First World War."

I asked, "How come Uncle Phil couldn't find out anything when he was there?"

A hesitation, "He wasn't looking for the right people."

"I don't understand."

"I changed my name."

"What do you mean?"

"I changed my name so they wouldn't find me."

"You changed your name…to what?"

"Pietro Antonio Rossini."

"That wasn't your real name?"

"No, I made it up in Genoa, when I was trying to get hired to work on the docks."

Grampa confessed all of this without emotion. Like it was no longer a big deal. The story was out. Might as well tell all of it. I looked for the chair. I had to sit down.

"Grampa, let me get this straight. Your real name is not Pietro Antonio Rossi or Rossini?"

"No, I made all that stuff up." He was gaining confidence again in telling his story. Now that he'd told someone, it all made sense to him. Me, on the other hand, I was reeling.

"So what about the thing with the Customs guy when you got here and Rossi vs. Rossini?"

"That actually happened. It wasn't important, but I pretended like it was, to make my story better. Actually I didn't really care."

"So what is…or was your real name?"

"Ferrari, Gioacchino Ferrari."

After a brief pause to let it sink in, he continued, "See, Gioacchino was Rossini's first name. That's where I got the idea. I just traded his first name for his last. Pietro Antonio was my little brother's name. He died before he was a year old, before my parents died. I guess I wasn't terribly creative. Just borrowed some names I knew."

"You were a Ferrari? Like the car?"

"Yeah, but don't get excited. We're not related. It was a common name. It's the Italian word for metalworker. It's like Smith over here."

"Ferrari is the same as Smith? I'm really a Smith?"

"Yeah, but...so what. It's just a name. You're whatever you make yourself. If you want to be Rossi or Rossini, go ahead.

"You can even be the Lone Ranger."

CHAPTER 13

DYLAN & HENRY

Saturday, December 20, 2014. The red numbers on the ceiling said 6:45. Another late morning. He didn't move to get up. Dylan was starting to wonder if he was going to make it to the New Year and the meeting with Pete.

The hours between 6pm and 11pm were the problem. Each night he came straight home from the office. Got home no later than 6:15. On the drive home he was full of commitment to take it easy that night, short of going cold turkey. After all, he had to have at least one drink when he got into the empty house with no one to talk to and nothing to do but think about all the things he didn't want to think about. Henry was seldom home before midnight, and Dylan was aware of all the lore about drinking alone. But, what the hell. Everybody had a cocktail just to unwind from the commute. Didn't they? He had to have one.

Since he wasn't up to cooking lately, dinner came down to leftovers or takeout. He ate at the kitchen table with a book, and, of course, his drink. His latest read was about a new theory on the mysteries of the Bermuda Triangle. Not exactly a page turner. The first drink went so fast a second drink became a must. Then it somehow got out of control. He'd progress to a third, fourth, fifth. He rationalized that the alcohol helped him to *not* think. Or at least not think about the pressing issues that were piling up, the most pressing being the lunch conversation with Pete. Poor Pete, his grieving mind simmering for almost 15 years; finally he comes up with a bombshell solution: commit the crime of the century. And Dylan the only obstacle standing between Pete and that disaster. Anybody would need a drink under the circumstances.

Dinner last night was later than customary – 8:15. Afterward Dylan brought the gin bottle up to the bedroom along with a glass full of ice cubes and his book. This morning the big black Hendricks bottle and an empty glass were sitting on the bedside table next to the little projection clock. One of the things about a Hendricks Gin bottle is a person can't tell by looking at it how much gin is left in it. You can't see through the black glass. He may have emptied the bottle; he couldn't remember. And now just looking at it, he couldn't tell. He could pick it up to try to feel if it was empty. But that wouldn't always work either with a Hendricks bottle, because the bottle glass is so thick, the weight, even if empty, might still fool him. Make him think plenty of gin was still in there. He wouldn't know until the next time he poured a drink if last night he'd finished the whole damn bottle, which was what his headache and the time reflected on the ceiling told him had likely happened.

He didn't feel well. Along with the headache, he had what might delicately be described as an uneasy digestive tract. When he shifted his weight to get out of bed, he felt lightheaded. The totality of symptoms clinched it; the bottle must be empty.

Recent experience told him he could dispatch these symptoms with two or three, maybe four, large gulps of gin – the proverbial "hair of the dog." However the other side of that coin – the bad news – was that it confirmed, in something of a paradox, his very rational self-diagnosis of approaching alcoholism, which was one of the things he didn't want to think about. The ex-Navy SEAL, the perfect physical specimen (as perfect as you could expect for fifty-two), the four- to five-day a week gym rat, the healthy diet enthusiast, he was countering it all by becoming a lush.

What had happened to him?

He pulled the heavy comforter off his body and slid his feet to the floor. Sitting on the edge of the king-size Victorian bed, he surveyed the large master bedroom. The French motif with dusty rose walls and light-colored ornate furniture reminded him it was clearly Henry's room. Henry had furnished it exquisitely over the years via antique shopping trips to DuMouchelles downtown and other Midwest bastions of "old tasteful things." Dylan withdrew from those weekend excursions years ago.

To his eye, the large bed and even larger room were intended for more than one person. Henry was sleeping down on the main floor now, in the guest room, because he found it increasingly difficult to negotiate the stairs. So they hadn't slept in the same room in over a year. They hadn't made love in longer. Both ominous dots on the chart labeled "Dylan and Henry."

He looked across the room to the window on the back of the house – the sunrise side. The drapes were open. Still, the view was almost black, not unlike his mood. It was past mid-December, tomorrow would be the so-called shortest day of the year. Traces of light from the rising sun wouldn't appear for an hour. Even later if the gray snow clouds remained.

Besides his drinking and the new problem with Pete, there were other matters about which he wanted to *not* think. Some had been festering for a while. Henry's health for starters, which led directly to what was happening with their relationship. Nor did he want to think about their precarious finances – the restaurant was losing money – or his feeling of burnout with his own job. They all seemed related. Except for Pete. That one stood out there all by itself.

The depression from the hangover confirmed that his life was evolving, even spiraling, in the wrong direction. Where did it all start? Possibly with his father and "the grimace." No, don't blame him. He was a victim just like the rest of us. A couple years after the big talk, his parents had separated. The opposites no longer attracted. Dylan suspected he was the primary factor in their break up.

In the over twenty years since the talk, most of his family communication was restricted to his mother, until last year, when she died. Except for the dream. Dad continued to speak through the dream. Now the old man was in a nursing home suffering from end-stage dementia. Dylan visited monthly, mostly out of guilt. He told himself he had nothing to feel guilty about, but it was still there. Sometimes he thought he saw a flicker of recognition on his dad's face, but most often not. At least "the grimace" wasn't there.

Dylan brought his wandering mind back to the present. He needed to focus. First, take a good, hot shower.

At 7:10, showered and dressed, Dylan sat alone at the big table in the kitchen sipping black coffee. He could hear Henry snoring all the way from his room down the hall. When they met almost twenty-five years ago, Henry didn't snore. So much had changed. Dylan reluctantly admitted that his beloved Henry was no longer the man he'd fallen for. Henry's good looks, sartorial splendor, insightful wit, fine cultural tastes, even his health, had all diminished, if not disappeared completely.

It was late spring, 1990. He first saw Henry in a used book store in downtown Sarasota right after Desert Storm. Dylan's SEAL unit was stationed at MacDill Air Force Base in Tampa, where the U. S. Strategic Command was headquartered. ("Strategic" being a euphemism for "Anti-terrorist.") Sarasota was a little over an hour's drive from McGill. He loved the little Florida city for its restaurants, shops, cultural events, and, importantly, its relative safety. Not physical safety. As a Navy SEAL he was in no danger of being mugged. But as a gay man in the service, especially as a gay SEAL, he had to cover up his personal life. It was a time when gays in the service were still a threatened species. He had to find hiding places. Sarasota was a good one.

Henry was not a big man, about five feet seven and at the time about 175 pounds, not fat but stocky. His medium complexion revealed little hint of the impact of Florida's skin-damaging sun. The round cherubic face simultaneously gave off mixed hints of mischief, innocence and kindness. His trimmed sandy moustache matched his hair well enough to suggest that one or both had been given special attention with a chemical substance. Dylan guessed his age at about forty.

Henry's wardrobe was coordinated to draw attention. The man was costumed, if you will, in a lightweight silk, muted-coral sport coat, with a cream-colored pocket square that not only matched his dress slacks and open-necked silk shirt but also his Panama hat. The hatband was coral, matching the sport coat. Accessories included a gold braided necklace, an onyx pinky ring and a coral cloth watchband, again matching the sport coat and hatband. The shoes were tan alligator loafers. Fingernails manicured. Peacock would be too strong, but the ensemble was an award-winning achievement in look-at-me attire, almost as if he employed a wardrobe consultant and dresser.

Dylan had tried not to stare, but the sight was magnetic. He believed the dramatically dapper man to be gay, and he estimated the odds to be high enough to risk an encounter.

They were both rummaging in a bin filled with books by late 19th and early 20th century authors. Dylan saw Hemingway, Fitzgerald, Conrad and even Joyce on the covers. He ventured, "Have you seen any James?"

With a raised eyebrow the man looked up and responded, "Henry James?"

Dylan didn't know of any other James, "That's the one."

The man looked back down at the table, "Not since English Lit 202."

The response reminded Dylan that few besides himself cared for the dense literary material of the late 19th century, and, as the son of a librarian, he was more than an avid reader; he was a bookworm. He muffled a chuckle at the sarcasm, trying not to break through the muted tones of the bookstore. In his estimation the cleverness of the remark sent the man's gay quotient, which was already near a six on a scale of ten, up to at least an eight.

He tested the man with a little flattery, "Interesting that an author born in the USA would be taught in an English Literature class. But, you're correct. He did almost all of his writing while living in London."

The man bit, "Sometimes I amaze myself with the far flung reaches of my arcanity."

Arcanity? Dylan thought, *Is that a word? If I know what it means, I guess it is.*

The man looked up, and when their eyes met this time, they instantly acknowledged each other's special status. The conversation progressed to a coffee shop a few doors down Main Street. His name was Henry Dawson. He was a sous chef at one of Sarasota's boutique restaurants.

It was the first day of a long, committed relationship. They were not quite Mutt and Jeff, but close. Dylan, at 6'2," with a muscular build, was what the gay world called a "bear," big and masculine, bordering on macho. Henry was compact, slightly effeminate, closer to the gay stereotype, what the character, Kramer, on TV's Seinfeld might call a "fancy boy" with the quick disclaimer, "not that there's anything wrong with that."

In the years since, they'd been through a great deal together, protecting each other from the sticks and stones of a sometimes hostile society and nurturing each other's special abilities and characteristics.

Now, 24 years later, they were "drifting apart." Dylan thought it an inapt expression for couples. Snow drifted. Boats drifted. People changed. Some people. Not Dylan. At least, he thought, not much. But certainly Henry. He was no longer the funny, dapper little man with the carefully matched outfits and accessories.

For one thing Henry had gained more than 130 lbs. He never let Dylan see him on a scale, but the report from his last physical was in the file in the den, and Dylan had sneaked a look. It said Henry, all five-foot seven-inches of him, now topped out at 310 lbs.

Obesity, like poverty, is not a stand-alone condition, particularly at the age of 63. No, it has cousins. For one, old fat people almost always suffer from hypertension. Henry's blood pressure readings were off the chart. Blood sugar issues are another close relative. Henry was diagnosed with type 2 diabetes four years ago. Diabetes is a precursor to vision loss. In the last few years Henry's eyesight had faded more than it should have simply for his age. Diabetes also often led to neuropathy, a deadening of surface nerves usually in the hands and feet. In addition to causing pain, neuropathy often resulted in problems with balance. Henry's balance was becoming less dependable. His poor vision and balance caused him to walk carefully, taking very short steps with his feet apart, almost a shuffle, resulting in an aversion to stairs and upstairs bedrooms. And, of course, he was impotent. Thank goodness, he could still make it to the bathroom in time.

In a feeble attempt to camouflage his obesity, Henry had adopted an inelegant wardrobe of work clothes consisting mainly of loosely fitted, untucked, paisley-patterned, pajama-like garments. When Dylan commented, Henry brushed it off by saying it was what all the chefs were wearing these days. Dylan resisted responding, "You mean all the fat chefs."

Not surprisingly, Henry's quick wit and light sense of humor had abdicated to cranky sarcasm, taking with them what had been a gentle kindness. On many different levels Henry wasn't very much fun to be around anymore. And that among other things was causing Dylan to find solace inside a gin bottle. As he thought these thoughts, he looked across the kitchen to the old liquor cabinet which had once been, before electricity, a real ice box. Another of Henry's finds. Dylan knew it held several fresh bottles of gin among other fermented delights. He chided himself for feeling the need to *not* think.

CHAPTER 14

DYLAN – THE ISSUES LIST

Saturday, December 20, 2014, cont. In deference to the delicate signals coming from his stomach, Dylan prepared a gentle breakfast of dry toast and one poached egg. No use challenging the forces of nature.

While picking at the meal, his mind returned to the issues. Giving up on the food, he walked down the hall to the den, his thinking room or more aptly these days, his drinking room. He located the pad of lined paper and the pencil on the desk. He sat at the desk and made four columns on the top sheet of paper. At the top of the columns he wrote in headings: Problem, Solution, Chances, and My Influence. He wanted to list each problem, determine the solution, estimate the likelihood of the solution being realized and further estimate the potential of being able to affect that outcome himself.

In the "Problem" column he wrote: (1) Father/Dream, (2) Henry's Health, (3) Our Future, (4) Money/Restaurant, (5) Job, (6) Drinking, and (7) Special Project. "Special Project" was code for Pete's crazy plan.

Before filling in any of the other three columns, a wave of hangover-induced procrastination came over him. The best thing to do, he thought, was take a long walk. Maybe down toward Belle Isle. Sometimes walking helped overcome mental inertia.

The air outside was cold, about 30 degrees, but partly due to his military training, cold or hot temperatures had little effect on him. He tore off the sheet of paper, folded it, and put it in his pants pocket. It was 8:10. Henry was still snoring. He put on a wool crewneck sweater, a fleece-lined hoodie, gloves and walking shoes and headed out, walking toward Jefferson Avenue.

As Dylan came through the kitchen door following his walk, the antique clock dinged 9:15. Henry was sitting at the kitchen table eating breakfast, still in his bathrobe. His plate overflowed with pancakes, bacon and maple syrup. He precariously overloaded his fork and swiftly drew it to his mouth. Dylan remembered that fat people tended to put too much food in their mouths at one time. The word "stuffing" came to mind.

As Henry chewed and swallowed one mouthful down to a manageable remainder, he cheerfully announced, "I think I have good news."

"Wonderful. I could use good news." Dylan felt relief that Henry seemed to be in a pleasant mood. He pulled off the hoodie sweatshirt and sat down to remove his walking boots. They were wet from the light snow.

Henry said, "We're having a very good December. Four more parties booked for the week between the holidays. That will be about 50 for the month. It'll be a very good fourth quarter."

"Up from last year?"

"Well, I'm not sure about that. But it should make the year better than we thought."

"So the year will still be a loser, maybe even more than last year, but just not as bad as we originally thought." As soon as the words came out, Dylan wanted them back.

"Get up on the wrong side, did you?" Henry's good mood was gone. He went back to scoffing pancakes and bacon.

The restaurant business had been something of a roller coaster ride for Henry and Dylan. When they first met, Henry dreamed of owning his own bistro. After coming to Michigan and putting in a year at The Golden Mushroom, he got it, albeit with Dylan as partner. In keeping with his underdeveloped sense of modesty, he called it "Henry's." The restaurant was located in the close suburb of Ferndale; one of the first new restaurants in that somewhat diverse, blue-collar community which to everyone's surprise would soon develop a gay presence while simultaneously becoming a go-to place for trendy restaurants. After a couple years of mild struggle, "Henry's" caught on, and began to turn a nice profit.

Henry was the creative force in the kitchen, emphasizing an avant garde menu. The mundane business side was left to Dylan (not unlike their personal finances). Even after moving on to the personal security business with Pete, Dylan kept an eye on the books. And they were ultimately successful. Unfortunately, after over 10 years of good, profitable business, Henry's ego drove him to want to expand. Without the obviously wasteful exercise of serious market research, he picked the wealthy community of Grosse Pointe for a "Henry's" restaurant, which he believed it needed badly. Most importantly it was geographically desirable, only 15 minutes from their home in Indian Village.

Dylan went along with a certain degree of trepidation. His concern was that the start-up costs would be excessive. And he was right. In lieu of selling the boat, they had to borrow.

Surprisingly, several banks were willing to loan.

So, Henry and Dylan took them up on it. In the summer of 2007 "GP Henry's" had a spare-no-expense grand opening. The restaurant crowd from the Pointes showed up in sufficient numbers to reassure Henry that his market prescience matched his culinary skill.

Within months the "Great Recession" was decimating the stock market, and housing valuations were tanking, along with the bottom lines of many banks. Though Grosse Pointe's old money was hardly affected, its new money was in trouble. Accordingly, very few people – at least not enough – came back after the wonderful grand opening. At Dylan's insistence, they closed the doors the next spring and set about paying off their debt to the bank, Dylan convinced he had to be more forceful the next time in controlling Henry's underdeveloped sense of risk. The good news was that he managed to right their financial situation without selling the boat or second mortgaging their home.

Six years later, 2014, they were clear with the bank, but the other restaurant, the original, was now losing money. It's a truism in the business, that trendy restaurants are ultimately victims of a fickle audience. So it was with "Henry's." Except Henry didn't accept it. He rejected Dylan's suggestion they close down and move on, maybe even retire. Henry was sure that with a few adjustments, they could make a comeback. In the meantime, Dylan was paying for the losses out of their personal nest egg, their retirement fund, another concept Henry didn't seem to comprehend. In their arguments, Dylan got the feeling he was turning into his father.

—o—

After Dylan's grumpy faux pas at breakfast, the remainder of their day together was awkwardly quiet. Clearly, Henry was no longer a happy man, and discussions about the restaurant put him even more on the defensive. Dylan wished he could escape to his boat, but it was December and it was Michigan. Finally, around 3:30 that afternoon Henry went in to the restaurant, not to return until after closing that night. Now with Henry gone for the rest of the day, Dylan sat at the kitchen table and went back to his sheet of paper with the four columns and seven rows. When he filled in all the columns and rows it read:

Problem	Solution	Chances	My Influence
Father/Dream	?	?	?
H's Health	Lose 100 lbs	Low	None
Our Future	?	?	?
Money/Rstrnt	Close it	Low	Little
Job	Quit	Low	Depends
Drinking	Quit	?	100%
Special Project	Quiet reason	50%	50%

He reread it, focusing on Chances and Influence. His dismal analysis added to his depression. The only issue he had solid control over was "Drinking." It reinforced why he wanted to drink. He looked across the room at the old ice box/liquor cabinet. He stood up, walked across the kitchen, opened the cabinet and took out a new bottle of gin.

CHAPTER 15
JOURNAL – PARSAFE

5am, Monday, 12-22-2014

It's important to reiterate that getting here, this ominous place we're in, has resulted from a convergence of seemingly unconnected events, not unlike the proverbial "perfect storm." My business was one of the events.

Grampa died in late August of 1975, which was even more sudden than we expected, but certainly best for him. I elected not to tell his story to anyone, as momentous as it was, though I was tempted to tell my dad. I'm not exactly sure why I didn't. I wondered why Grampa told me. Did he want me to be the messenger to the family? I concluded not. He was passing on a legacy of sorts, to the one person least likely to judge, and who might someday benefit from the knowledge.

Considering our relationship, his death wasn't terribly cataclysmic for me. I suppose I'd had time to get used to the reality of it before it happened, or maybe it was because of that conversation at the hospital. He saw it as a deathbed confession, and what usually happens after deathbed confessions is the confessor dies. Which he did.

As I write it out it seems a bit cold to say, life went on. The 20 years from Grampa's death through 1995 were what might be called the normal years. I did the police thing, got married, started a new business, solidified and grew the business, had a child, and became 20 years older. All were interesting events, but none earthshaking. And all were part of the seemingly disconnected biographical algorithm that produced the extraordinary outcome we're heading toward.

My police career didn't last long, only 5 ½ years, the last three with the Robbery Section. Robbery is where I picked up the foundation for the rest of my working career. No, I didn't become a thief.

I was put in the Robbery Section because one of the captains was impressed with the academics of my resume. In those days most cops did not have college degrees. Apparently he spent time, or had someone do it for him, going over personnel files. He was looking for a person who could handle an unusual desk assignment. The prize went to me. He wanted me to collect and organize in-depth data on reported robberies in hopes of spotting previously unseen patterns.

In 1978, when cops didn't have computers, it was all compiled with pencil and paper. First I phoned all the robbery victims and conducted detailed interviews, asking a lot more questions than were part of the original perfunctory investigation.

The new, additional data was considerable. I recorded it in notebooks, categorized it, summed the totals on an accountant's adding machine, and typed up monthly reports. Without a computer, of course, it was all done manually. (One of my fellow cops referred to it as a "hand job.")

The reports didn't produce a "eureka" moment, though they revealed trends that led to some altered investigative techniques; and much to the captain's credit, they helped in catching some bad guys. During my last year, certain categories of robbery actually declined a bit.

But prize assignment or not, I was restless. No Lone Ranger opportunities appeared on that horizon. Showering one morning, it dawned on me that the best thing to do about robberies, rather than solve them after the fact, was to prevent them in the first place.

So after a lot of soul searching, and kitchen-table talks with Donna, I made the momentous decision to quit the Force and start my own little security business. This was a big decision, mostly because we were just married and were trying to prepare ourselves financially to support a big family, which we both wanted. Well, mostly Donna wanted, but what made Donna happy made me happy.

I met Donna just before Christmas of '78 at a cop party. Her girlfriend worked in one of the precinct stations. I don't remember exactly what she did; just that she was Civil Service, not on the Force. She invited Donna along to the party with the hope that each of them would meet up with a handsome, and eligible, young police officer. I started a conversation with Donna, and she decided to settle for eligible by itself. We were married in May of '80.

As for quitting a secure government job and starting a fledgling business, it helped that Donna was bringing in a good paycheck. She graduated from Walsh College with a very handy degree in accounting, after which she was quickly hired by a fast-growing marketing company. She did double duty by helping me with the books.

Our new venture was a consulting firm where, using the knowledge I'd picked up from my robbery reports, I counseled business owners on how to better protect their property from theft and vandalism. I also sold some of the required equipment.

The name of our company was "PARsafe," which I got from combining my initials P.A.R. with the generic security word "safe." I momentarily considered using the word "Ferrari" in the name, but quickly rejected it in fear of having to explain it. Granted, it's a little egotistical to name a company after yourself, but when I did it back in 1981, it was such a small business, didn't seem like anyone would notice. Actually it was Donna's suggestion, when I told her I was trying to think of a name.

My last paycheck as a police officer was dated December 31, 1980. Due to economic conditions, it was a bad time to start a new business, but we struggled through. We grew slowly, and in no year did we ever lose money. By 1995 we were doing quite well.

At the beginning my role in the new business was as the expert consultant, the trusted advisor who understood the problems and knew the solutions. And for a while it was true. Our product line consisted of simple items like deadbolt locks, break-resistant floodlights, grated windows and the like, low tech to the extreme. In a way I was a glorified locksmith.

In time the selling of equipment, versus the consulting, took over the revenue mix. As the consultant my role faded somewhat compared to good sales people I'd hired who could move inventory. Soon security cameras came to be a must-have product. I had no trouble keeping up with that, and they contributed to the bottom line nicely. However, as in the rest of the world, the dominance of mechanical devices began to diminish. Electronic devices controlled by computer chips were the new alpha solutions.

Eventually I sensed that the "glorified locksmith" was threatened with extinction, delivering a small hit to my ego. Struggling for survival,

I took a "Village Blacksmith" approach: I showed up early in the morning, every morning, did a lot of grunt work (which somebody had to do), and when dragooned for client meetings, pretty much kept my mouth shut. It worked. The business thrived.

With the business doing well, the challenge for me as the boss was to keep up with tomorrow. Grampa once told me there were "more than two inevitable things in life, not just death and taxes. There was also change, and just like death and taxes," he added, "most people won't like change either."

I vowed to try to accept and learn the new business model, and was marginally successful. But it was a constant game of catch up, because the technology wouldn't stand still. Someone called it "technology creep." To my credit, as the business grew, I surrounded myself with very good people who were generally younger and seemed to understand the new world innately.

In the mid-90s the meteor known as the Internet crashed into my little dinosaur world. The times they were a-changing; the Internet was quickly becoming the new medium for business communication and, consequently, a big threat to business security.

An example pertinent to our story: in the Motor City, automotive design engineers at the Big Three were designing new cars on their computers. They'd been doing so for years. It was called CAD, the acronym for Computer Aided Design. Now, using the Internet, they could collaborate online with other automotive design engineers across town and across the country, even the world, in "real time." (A bit later I found out that "real time" meant "right now.") This was a major time-saving and cost-cutting breakthrough. One problem: the data to be transmitted was highly classified, and the Internet was a relatively insecure medium. To keep their secrets from the inquiring minds of the competition, they needed a protective barrier called a "firewall," deftly borrowing the term from the barrier between the engine compartment on a car and the passenger compartment. It was a new kind of security, cyber security.

They needed these Internet firewalls to keep the new breed of enemy out of their stuff. The new breed of enemy, however, could be very computer savvy. The most sophisticated of these thieves carried the seemingly diseased moniker, "hacker." Hackers had been around for a while, but with minimal impact because of minimal Internet use. In the new Internet world, with so much confidential data being transmitted, they presented a security threat that dwarfed the traditional concern of someone breaking in to the business through a door or window.

In any case the firewall issue came up in late 1995 at a weekly meeting of the PARsafe sales staff. We'd been in business for 15 years and then employed over 50 full-time people including eight salespeople. A salesperson named Leanne said one of her customers asked if we knew a company that did Internet firewalls. We didn't. I barely understood what she was talking about. Another of the salespeople said something about it being a project for "Silicon Valley."

CHAPTER 16

JOURNAL – JOEY

5am, Tuesday, 12-23-2014

At this point we need to rewind even further to 1984.

It was February of that year. I was sitting in my office reviewing invoices for those rent-paying security cameras, when the phone rang. I answered and a vaguely familiar voice asked if I was Mr. Rossi. Trying to recall who owned the voice, I said, "Yes sir, it is."

The voice replied, "Is this the Mr. Rossi who once served as United States Army Lieutenant Rossi of the Military Police in Saigon in 1974 and '75?"

His delivery immediately gave it away as Captain Phan. My voice took on a tinge of excitement as I replied, "Yes, Captain Phan, it is the same. How are you? And where are you?"

He was in San Jose, California, where he and his family had been for almost eight years. They were sent there directly from Okinawa as part of a major resettlement of Vietnamese refugees in that part of California.

As he spoke, it became clear that after a slow start, Captain Phan had assimilated well. He worked as an advisor to the San Jose Police Department. Whenever they had an issue with a member of the Vietnamese community, Captain Phan was their go-to guy. The board of education also recruited him to help out with adult classes in English as a Second Language, another paying gig. Later I learned he also served as the de facto mayor of the Vietnamese community in San Jose. This role led to several opportunities for additional compensation, all legal and above board. Clearly the Vietnamese diaspora served him well.

He asked me to come out and visit, an invitation I couldn't accept at the time because of the demands of my little start-up business. We stayed in communication, though, and four years later in 1988 Donna, Keenie (our four-year old daughter) and I did go out there, and were treated like royalty by his little family and much of the Vietnamese community.

His little boy was 14 years old. The boy's Vietnamese name was Phan Thanh Gia, Gia being what we would call his given name or first name. Here in the U.S. he was "Joey," a slight phonetic manipulation of "Gia." His father, Captain Phan – who everyone still called "Captain"– had translated "Gia" to "Joey" in honor of the American G.I. Joes who gave their lives or limbs in Vietnam.

Once again it amazed me that they accepted the devastating U.S. presence in their homeland as an event worth honoring, while many of our own people condemned us as homicidal invaders.

In spending time with the family, it became clear that Joey was a special kid. His mother said he was an exceptional student. He was already taking advanced courses in computer science. What I didn't understand then was that San Jose was ground zero for the high-tech revolution, just coming out of its infancy. This was Silicon Valley, a sobriquet for Santa

Clara County and environs that hadn't yet become a household name to the rest of the world.

Joey, of course, was a child of the Valley. Since the age of two he'd been breathing the same air as Jobs, Wozniak, Noyce and a multitude of computer geeks who were in the process of taking over the world of commerce. What would become clear in the future was that when it came to the inner secrets of motherboards and the software that controlled them, Joey was a savant with few equals.

As a family, Donna, Keenie and I went out there three more times before 1995. Each time we were drowned in affection and special treatment. Then, late in 1995, I went out alone on business to set up meetings with a couple companies claiming to have expertise in Internet security. My goal was to try to partner with a company that knew something about the so-called firewalls.

Of course I had dinner with the Phan's and explained why I was there. Joey was home for the dinner. He'd completed his BA at San Jose State two years earlier at the age of 20, but did not continue in grad school. Later I learned of his concern they weren't teaching the important stuff, and even if they were, he knew more about it than the teachers. He said he was freelancing as a computer programmer on "special projects," then changed the subject.

Joey was Vietnamese by birth, but American by everything else. At 5'9" he was taller than his dad and most of their refugee community. And when he spoke, everything came out American. Self-assured, effusive and outgoing in manner. Very American. By comparison the stereotypical Asian tended to be more reserved. Joey's personality erased the visual image his skin color and facial features projected.

When he sat down at the table, he was open and welcoming, asking me about Donna and Keenie and the business. I mentioned the evolution we were going through at PARsafe. When I got to my mission for the trip, something in his demeanor changed. He became quiet. It was as if he ran out of small talk. I might not have noticed except, other than me, he was the only one who'd been talking. I thought maybe he wasn't feeling well.

After the meal, as I was leaving, he walked me out to my rental car. Glancing over his shoulder back at the house, he said, "Can we meet someplace and, like, talk?"

I was startled.

He said, "Just act normal. Like, don't look at the house." I tried to follow his instructions, but I was confused and didn't feel at all normal.

Trying to recover I said, "Of course. Is everything Ok?"

"Everything's awesome," he said. "Just have an idea to help you, but not here."

I got a phone number and a time to call him. Still trying to look normal, I got into the Toyota sedan and drove off.

That night I didn't sleep well, thinking about what he might be telling me that his parents shouldn't hear. My straight-arrow nature was nervous. I didn't like cloak and dagger, and conspiring to keep secrets from parents and friends was way out of my comfort zone. Keeping secrets beyond Christmas gifts and surprise parties was about my limit. I suppose I wasn't even very good at doing surprise parties.

I called him the next morning before my first meeting. "What's up, Joey?"

His response didn't help soothe my angst. "Can we meet somewhere? Maybe we shouldn't talk on the phone."

Shouldn't talk on the phone!?

With an effort to sound calm, I said, "Sure. What are you doing for lunch?" I amazed myself. Did I actually say that?

"No plans. Meet me at the park, The Guadalupe River Park. It's a real big park where we can talk." He gave me detailed directions to an area with picnic tables. "I'll bring a couple sandwiches and bottles of water. Is water ok?"

"Yeah, water's fine." *Meeting in a park? What the hell?*

I found the picnic tables. Joey was sitting at one between the street and the river. The table was well off the walking paths and somewhat isolated by shrubs and a couple trees. It was late October, a few leaves on the ground, first signs of color change, the sky a bit cloudy for my image of California, temperature a little cool. Everything about the setting added to my discomfort. What could he want to tell me that would require this ... I didn't even know what to call it.

"Hi Joey." *Could he sense the caution in my voice...the concern?*

"Afternoon, Mr. Rossi. How did your meeting go?"

He was sitting near the end of the table facing the nearest walking path. As I walked up, he stood and went to the other side of the table, turning his back to anyone who might be watching.

"I'm not sure. Maybe not so good. Didn't seem like what I was hoping for. We'll see."

"Don't think you're going to find what you need in the other meeting either." It was a let's not beat around the bush response.

"Why? Is that what this is all about? What's going on?"

"Here." He pushed a wrapped sandwich and a bottle of water across the picnic table. "Hope ham and cheese is ok. There's mustard in a packet in there, if you want."

"Ham and cheese is fine."

"Mr. Rossi, I'm going to be very candid. Those companies you're meeting with, they, like, probably can't help you. In fact I don't think there're any companies around who can do what you need. At least not yet. Maybe in a couple years or so. But not yet."

He unwrapped his sandwich but left it on the paper. "The problem you're trying to deal with is kinda new. But it's gonna become, like, a totally big problem. So in time people will be seriously looking to solve it. They're, like, not there yet, I don't think." He picked up one half of the sandwich and took a large bite.

"We needed all this secrecy for you to tell me that?"

With his mouth moving the food around, "No, I'm getting to that part." Was he that hungry, or was he chewing on the sandwich as a stall… building the suspense?

"Ok, why don't you get to it." *Did I sound rude?*

Big swallow, "Mr. Rossi, what I'm about to say is totally not for publication. You can't talk about it with anyone. Especially my father. Deal?"

I didn't want to agree, but my curiosity was busting out all over. I caved.

"Deal."

"Mr. Rossi, do you know what a hacker is?"

"Yeah, kind of. I've heard the term, but no, I guess I'm not sure exactly what it means."

"It's a person who can break into a computer network and look at whatever's there. They do it via the Internet. They can steal the data or manipulate it or, like, pretty much do whatever they want. They're the people who firewalls would keep out."

I should've known that. "Yes, now I remember. So what about hackers?"

He took another bite of his sandwich, stalling.

"This is, like, the secret part." A pause, then, "I'm a hacker."

He let that statement sit there in the open air of the park. My sandwich was still in front of me, undisturbed. I cringed out, "Mightn't that be illegal?"

"Yeah, pretty much."

Wow! Now what do I say?

"And your father doesn't know?"

"He would be totally unhappy knowing I was, like, a potential criminal."

"So why are you doing it?"

A pause for reflection. "Because I can, and it's fun. I haven't done anything to harm anyone or any company. We just go in and look around. For the challenge. For the fun of it, you know. See what we can see. Haven't stolen anything…so far."

"We?"

"Yeah, me and a couple buddies. We're not, like, criminals, but what we're doing would totally not be well received in polite computer company, if you know what I mean."

Both sandwiches were sitting in front of us, barely touched. "Why are you telling me this?"

"I think I can help you with your problem. Please excuse the lack of modesty, but as hackers go, I'm pretty good. We, like, cover ourselves by saying we're programmers, but basically that's what a hacker is – a very good software programmer. Totally good."

He took a sip of his water. "I know how hackers do it. So, who would be better at figuring out how to stop them? Who could build a better firewall?"

I said nothing. Was my mouth hanging open? He waited for me to respond. A bird was chirping in one of the trees. I looked around. No one else was in that part of the park. No baby carriages or senior citizens or strollers of any kind. Almost eerie. Can a hacker arrange for a city park to be cleared out?

"You can build a better firewall? And you would do it for me or with me? Why me?" My questions were a stall. I needed a moment to figure out a nice way of telling him to get real. In truth I had no idea if he was making sense or not.

"Mr. Rossi, two reasons. Number one, in my family you are, like, revered. If it wasn't for you, my father would be dead. No telling what might've happened to me and my mother. We owe you everything, totally. I've been taught that since my infancy. Short of committing murder, I'd do anything to help you. Maybe even I would commit murder."

"Number two, I need legitimacy. My friends and I are on the verge of, like, criminal activity. Working to help you build network firewalls would allow us to do what we're best at and put us on the right side of the law. The solution to your dilemma, like, answers both issues. I can help you when nobody else can, and I can help myself at the same time. We could even tell my dad what I was doing."

My mind started to work. Did what he say make sense? He could see I was considering what he said. Trying to work it out. He picked up his sandwich and let the silence simmer his proposal. As a twenty-two year old, his sense of timing was exquisite.

"Ok, Joey. Tell me how we pull this off."

CHAPTER 17

JOURNAL – DONNA & KEENIE

5am, Wednesday, 12-24-2014

Before we get to Donna and Keenie, let me wrap up Joey's part of the story.

In a nutshell, we tried Joey's proposal, and it worked. Within 18 months, we were spectacularly successful, on our way to an entrenched position as the foremost source for Internet firewall technology in the auto industry. As for Joey, he stayed with us for two and a half years, then moved on. He left us in great shape with a formidable staff of brilliant little hackers bent on creating cutting edge cyber security systems for our clients. Our little company would never be the same.

Nor would I.

The resulting success, which ultimately went well beyond my expectations, is one of the converging factors taking us to where we're going in this story. Wrapping it together one could say: Grampa inspired it, Vietnam and Joey made it possible, and Donna and Keenie made it necessary. Most interesting is the feeling that all of this fits together too well, almost as if it were predestined.

So let's get to Donna and Keenie, the core of what we're about here.

When we married, Donna and I agreed to a big family, thinking we'd be happy with four or five kids. When I quickly said, "Sure, why not," she responded, "Thank you" in a way that made me feel like it was a good thing I agreed.

We ended up with only one child, Keenie. There was no clear medical explanation for our semi-barren results. We tried all the tricks, up to and including a fertility clinic. We took pills and shots and such-like, but nothing happened. No more kids. Just Keenie.

As I said, the push for a big family was mostly Donna's doing. I went along, but it was for her sake. I'm not exactly sure why she was so obsessed, something in her own only-child upbringing, I guess. Whatever it was, having lots of kids was a paramount goal in her life.

So, when our big family didn't happen, she changed. Over seven or eight years her hopes and expectations slowly evolved to doubts, and then into hurtful reality. It was as if she went through those stages the grief counselors talk about, except in Donna's case, when she finally got to acceptance, she was a different person.

A good analogy is the story about the frog and boiling water. If you throw a frog into a pot of boiling water, it'll jump out. But if you put it into a pot of cold water and slowly raise the temperature, the frog won't notice the gradual change and will eventually cook to death. The change in Donna was gradual and subtle. From day to day you wouldn't notice it, only looking back over a longer period of time, you might see that part of her died.

She lost interest in most social activities, like her book club, and the neighborhood hen parties, and lunches with friends, even business dinners with me. Our sex life diminished, as if she agreed with Vatican doctrine that it was really only meant for procreating. She became a loner, taking long solitary walks, and escaping to an empty room to read a book, and going alone to afternoon movies. She only did these things, of course, in Keenie's absence, like when she was in school or involved in lessons or supervised recreational activity.

No, Donna did not neglect Keenie. When Keenie was with Donna, she was the center of Donna's everything. "Smothering" is too strong a description of her parenting style, "doting" maybe not strong enough; whatever term you use, she gave continuous support and attention to her only child. Again, it might have had something to do with Donna's own childhood; perhaps she felt lonely or neglected as a little girl. I don't know. I think about it often, but I've never figured it out. Donna didn't talk about it.

In spite of the potential to be spoiled, Keenie somehow turned out to be the perfect child, as if there was no effect from her mother's split personality. She was intelligent, considerate, funny, athletic, outgoing, pretty, everything. She was the room lighter-upper. She made great friends; she made good decisions. She didn't mind her mother's need to be the mother of all mothers. For me, in lieu of the withdrawn Donna, Keenie was a safe harbor to come home to at the end of a business day. We were friends.

The name Keenie, by the way, came from my suggestion. When Donna was pregnant, we both made lists of boys and girls names, and then rated each entry on the other's list. I think I've mentioned that I like to do things in an organized way. Donna, the accountant, was the same. Looking back, it's almost comical how anal we were. To my surprise,

Donna really liked the girl name at the top of my list – Isabella Katrina, Grampa's two first loves – except she wanted to reverse them, Katrina Isabella. Okay by me. I didn't tell her where I got those names, pretended like they just popped into my head. So when a girl came out, that was it. I was thrilled. As she learned to talk, Katrina became Keenie. That's how she said her own name. Katrina was a little too much for her at 18 months. Donna called her Keenie. I called her KeenieBelle, only among friends, and before I found out she didn't love it so much.

She and I became especially close after I joined the golf club. Keenie was about ten that first year at the club, and I enrolled her in the junior golf program. With a proud Daddy looking on, she showed real potential. Our pro, Mr. Martin, said, "Don't get in the habit of betting with her. In the long run it's gonna cost you."

It helped that she was willing to practice. To her, it wasn't just about competition and scoring. She got pleasure out of the feel of a good swing and a solid hit. Each one was a personal achievement.

Three or four evenings a week in the summer we could be found together on the practice range or putting green. Not surprisingly, the practice worked for her. She improved greatly. For me, not so much. I never got better than a middle handicap. It didn't bother me, because I was out there mostly for the therapy. It helped me to really focus on something that wasn't important. Took my mind off of what I didn't know about computers and firewalls. I was also there for the joy of being with her. Her presence was a great comfort in my life.

Donna tried a bit half-heartedly to take up the game. I'd meet the two of them at the club after work, and they'd both be on the practice tee. When I got there, Donna would bag her clubs and go find a place to sit and read. Sometimes after a short practice, Keenie and I would go out and play a few holes. Donna seldom went out on the course with us. When we came off the course, the three of us would have a light supper and go home. No partying with the other members. Donna always wanted to get home.

CHAPTER 18

JOURNAL – THE FAMILY MEETING

2pm, Wednesday, 12-24-2014

My affectionate little nickname, KeenieBelle, was shelved during the summer before she entered high school. She put the end to it herself.

It happened in the summer of 1998 at one of our family meetings. (We had family meetings maybe for the same reason we made so many lists.) Keenie had just turned fourteen.

She said, "Dad, we're gonna have to lose the 'Belle.' I'm going to be in a more mature place. No more cutesy names. How about from now on we just go with Keenie. That's cutesy enough; don't you think?" A precocious fourteen-year-old.

My response was something like, "Oh." Of course, I agreed, like the worshipful father I was. I dropped the "Belle" from that day on.

That was the same family meeting where Donna brought up the idea of a private school for Keenie.

Keenie was startled. She asked, "Why, Mom?" There was opposition in her tone. It was unusual for Keenie to oppose her mother, especially when her mother was simply attempting to guide and shelter her.

Donna, not sensing the depth of her concern, smiled and said, "Well, mostly for a better education."

Keenie said, "You mean better than Northville?"

That's where we lived. It's an upscale suburban community. We moved there before Keenie entered kindergarten. It was a little expensive for us then, but, ironically, Donna said the schools made it worth the extra money.

Still not getting the intensity of Keenie's resistance, Donna pressed on. "Private schools have much smaller classes. The teachers will be able to give you more personalized attention."

"Mom, my grades are just fine. Do you think I need special tutoring?" She was digging in her heels.

The family meeting was turning into a debate, and so far, I'd stayed out of it. Though it had never happened before, because we'd always come to unanimous agreement on our family issues, the prospect loomed that we might end up having to take a vote. The worst part of it was the possibility I was going to have to be the tie-breaker. Not good.

On my scorecard Keenie was winning this debate. Maybe I wasn't being objective. Of course, I'd never been purely objective about anything having to do with her. In fact I was trying to think of a good reason to back Donna. As parents we're supposed to stick together. I could say to Keenie that if she was worried about the money, it wasn't a problem anymore; the business was doing very well. But I knew it wasn't money. It was being separated from her friends and community at a time in life when social needs are so central to everything. My heart was on her side. I didn't want this to go to a vote. Could either of them sense my discomfort?

Donna, becoming aware now that Keenie's tone had taken on a defiant edge, made a lame attempt to end the discussion, "Honey, we simply want to protect you." Since this was the first I'd heard on the subject, I wondered who the "we" was. Nevertheless, I held my tongue and kept my fingers crossed.

Then something happened, something I don't think had ever happened before. In speaking to her mother, Keenie raised her voice and added sarcasm to her protest, "Protect me? From what? Am I a 'bubble girl?'"

Suddenly the air in the room reeked of insolence, a foul odor when emitted from words spoken by an otherwise loving child.

Donna paused, looked at me, and seeing no rescue, made a defensive thrust, "It's just that private schools are usually safer."

"Mom, safer than Northville? What's the danger? Did I miss something? Has there been a secret crime wave?" More points for Keenie. Northville had no crime. At least none I was aware of.

Keenie then threw in her knock-out punch, "Mom, what about all the extra-curricular activities that those little private schools don't have. The good colleges look for that on your application. Most of those little schools don't have girls' golf teams and stuff."

All this from a fourteen-year old.

I was in trouble. I wasn't going to save this situation, or more importantly, I wasn't going to save myself. I'd have to vote. And as much as I hated to irritate my wife, Keenie was right. I had to do the right thing, or Grampa would turn over in his grave, and the pillow would be hard.

The outcome of this dispute, both short and medium term, can be summarized thusly: (1) in the fall Keenie went to Northville High School, the school of her choice; (2) in order to help her mother accept the defeat, her grades, which were already quite acceptable, went to new heights with straight A's; (3) she made the golf team as a freshman and became team medalist as a sophomore; (4) she grew even more valuable to me as a family anchor in place of Donna's increasing indifference; (5) following my suggestion, Keenie joined the debate team where she also excelled; and (6) for an extended period of time, sexual activity in the master bedroom of our house was completely absent.

The long term outcome, however, was far more momentous. It started quite innocently. Two years later, in the first week of her junior year, Keenie was given a writing assignment by her English Composition teacher. It was a simple exercise: pick an interesting word and support why you chose it in two- to three-hundred words. Keenie picked "equilibrium," and her teacher, Mrs. Rumsfeld, was so pleased with her little essay, she had her read it in front of the class.

CHAPTER 19

JOURNAL – THE LONE RANGER CARD

5am, Friday, December 26, 2014

The male voice said, "Is this Mr. Peter Rossi?"

The call came in on the 13th of September, 2000, a Wednesday, at 3:15pm, my mid-week "play hooky" time. I was clearing my desk to leave early, hoping to get to the club in time to hit practice balls before playing a few holes with Keenie.

The voice carried an ominous tenor. I wondered if they'd put a customer through whose Internet firewall had been compromised. Certainly they wouldn't give him to me, Mr. Dinosaur. Maybe he'd demanded to speak to whoever was in charge. Those calls were supposed to go to the IT director, not me. Definitely, not me.

Yet something about this one sounded different. There was a hesitance, a discomfort.

"Yes, sir, what can I do for you?" Still thinking customer.

"Mr. Rossi, this is Detective McBain from Northville. You are the father of Katrina Rossi, right?"

"Yes." My body stiffened as I said the word.

"There's been an incident here at the high school. You should get over here right away. It involves your daughter."

Standing behind my desk, my knees buckled, and I caught myself by putting my hand on the blotter. "What happened? What'd she do?"

He said the unthinkable, "There's been a shooting. We called your wife; she's on the way. Please hurry."

The police estimated the whole incident took less than fifteen seconds. At about 2:30pm, a man stepped into his wife's Creative Writing classroom, aimed a 38-caliber, snub-nosed revolver at her and fired till it was empty.

The gun held six bullets, one of which hit the teacher in the shoulder, knocking her down and sending her to the hospital, though not causing life threatening damage. Another hit a male student sitting in the first row in the right arm, breaking the bone, but leaving him, after a short recovery, capable of leading a full, unencumbered and presumably happy life. Three more lodged in the far wall of the classroom, surprisingly not hitting any of the large windows on that outside wall. The other bullet hit Keenie, who was standing in front of the class reading her essay. It hit her in the neck, piercing a carotid artery. The coroner estimated she bled out in about thirty to forty seconds. The first EMT arrived about seven minutes later.

She was gone.

⊸o⊷

I went with her. Or at least the existing version of me went somewhere. That Peter Rossi, the simple, gentle, straightforward man, open and unassuming, that person went away that day and never returned. The replacement version, somewhat more nuanced and complex, installed in the old body, is here now. I'm more skeptical, suspicious, sarcastic, calculating, more easily angered, and certainly sleep-deprived. The new Peter Rossi, namely me, is obligated – maybe compelled is a better word – to find an answer, a suitable redress for the events of that day, to correct a terrible error, to restore some semblance of fairness and balance to the world, perhaps even to play the Lone Ranger card.

PART II

CHAPTER 20

JOURNAL – ARE YOU SURE?

5am, Saturday, 12-27-2014.

I am told the funeral was a big event for Northville – a relatively quiet village about 30 miles from downtown Detroit. In addition to curiosity seekers, there were relatives and teammates and classmates and teachers and neighbors and PARsafe employees and customers, and old friends like the Phans from California, and cable news trucks, and big-time print journalists, and a mix of state and local politicians, including the lieutenant governor.

Due to the heavy medication, it was all a blur to me. I remember little of it, which is good. I don't want to remember it. For poor Donna it was even worse. To say she was inconsolable misses the depth of her grief. She was a mess. Can't imagine what she would have been like without the medication. They'd sedated her so heavily, she'd fall asleep in the middle of a conversation; she needed help just to walk. It's embarrassing to admit I was of no comfort to her, none at all. Understandably, she was no help to me either.

In the second week I cut back on the drugs a bit, and in the third week, when I went back to the office, I was down to a manageable dose. At the office, it was apparent, even more so than before, that I was of little use. Before the shooting my contribution had been marginal. Now I just wasn't interested. I was empty. My being had been hollowed out like a pumpkin. There was no nutrient left.

I thought I'd be able to use the job to distract from the grief, but it didn't work. The only reason I kept going in, and I hate to say this, was because being home with Donna was worse. After the funeral, in one of her more functional moments, she moved out of our master bedroom into an upstairs bedroom from which she rarely emerged. On the few occasions when she came out while I was in the house, she didn't speak, simply giving me an occasional glare. No doubt, in her fog of narcotics, she'd somehow managed to remember the family meeting two years earlier, when I cast the deciding vote, sending Keenie to the public school and, eventually, to her death. In the ensuing years, as I lay awake, which I did almost every night, I recalled the accusation in her eyes and painfully conceded she was correct. I had played a role in the tragedy. I couldn't claim the role of completely innocent victim.

During my third week back at work, in mid-October, sitting in my office, staring at the big photo on the wall of Grampa, I started to think it was time to get out of the business; sell it and move on.

Move on to what? No idea. But I had to change my life. I could not function as before. I had nothing to contribute. My feeling of incompetence was exceeded only by my sense of guilt.

I recalled getting calls in the past year from high tech companies about a merger. At the time I put them off, without completely turning them down, because I was only 49, and retirement seemed premature. I was savvy enough to know they didn't really mean merger. They wanted to acquire us. That meant I'd soon be retired, especially once they caught on to how little I knew about the cyber firewalls, the part of the business they were after.

Sitting there in a deep funk, doing nothing, I reconsidered. The grief counselors tell you not to make big life-changing decisions while you're still reeling from a terrible loss. But now, except as a place to escape from Donna, I had no interest in the office or what was going on there. Nor was it likely I ever would. I needed to go somewhere to figure out what had happened, and to find a way to offset my guilt, a crushing guilt, not simply for failing to be an adequate paternal shield for my precious Keenie, but for virtually pushing her in front of the oncoming train. I had to do something to offset my culpability.

The big picture on my office wall was no longer comforting. Now Grampa seemed to be arching an eyebrow, looking at me, questioning if I'd gotten the message.

(Dylan called on Christmas Eve. We set a date to get together: Saturday, January 3. That's one week from today. To make sure I finish everything, I'll be doing double writing sessions most days from now till then. They'll start this afternoon.)

JOURNAL: 2pm, Saturday, 12-27-2014

Joey's immediate response was simple.

"Are you sure?"

That's all. No tedious lecture about making big decisions too soon. Just "Are you sure?" A comprehensive, cautionary, merciful response in three short words.

For three weeks I'd been showing up at the office. The old me would not have done that, just *show up*. The old me *went to work* each day with a purpose, like the Village Blacksmith. To others, there may be no difference, showing up versus going to work, but to me there was a critical distinction. I knew just showing up wasn't right.

I still came in early each morning, but only because I'd been awake for hours. The new me closed the door, sat at my desk, tried to think clearly and be productive, looked out the window at cars in the parking lot, not really seeing them, and did nothing. Finally, I picked up the phone and called Joey.

He was in the Far East on a consulting trip. It was the middle of the night there, so I left a message, asking him to call me at his convenience about a business matter.

He called back the following Monday late in the afternoon, just off the plane. I filled him in on my thoughts, and asked for advice on how to get started. I went to Joey, because I assumed the key to a successful sale was the firewall business, and for that he was still my go-to expert.

When he asked if I was sure, I replied, "I'm not sure of anything anymore, Joey, but things have changed, and it's going to happen sooner or later, so we might as well get started." It was the clearest, most definite statement and longest string of words I'd put together in weeks.

Silence on his end for several seconds, followed by fifteen minutes of insightful background info on how to go about it, including appropriate cautions. I took notes and thanked him.

The next day, I went into the office and set out to write a plan based on my notes and what I'd retained in my head from Joey's brief telephone seminar. I'm big on writing things down, especially plans, even when grief-stricken and a little drug addled. I read the first draft, crumpled the paper up in my fists, and threw it in the wastebasket. I went through the same process three more times before admitting I was in over my head.

I reached for the phone again.

Joey flew in the next week and went to work as our broker/consultant with a traditional ten per cent cut. He said he'd do it for expenses, but I insisted on paying him the standard fee.

After we did the social pleasantries, he got right to the core question. "What do you think the business is worth?"

I had no idea, but took an optimistic stab, "Maybe five million. Our success with the firewall business should be worth a lot."

His surprised look dashed my hopes for a moment. He asked, "You've heard of the high tech bubble?"

I nodded. It was the year 2000. On CNBC, which I watched with regularity, all they talked about was the "high-tech bubble." Or so it seemed.

Joey said, "Mr. Rossi, I've set up meetings with three high-tech companies. All three of these outfits want what you have, a foothold – more than a foothold, an entrenched position – in the potentially huge automotive internet security market. *That's* the reason they're coming here. It's not to buy a *business*. It's to buy a *market*.

"The strengths of the people who run these companies is math and computers. But business, the financial stuff, not so much.

"The key to dealing with them is remembering about "the high tech bubble;" they're all sitting on piles of cash. They're not used to it. They don't know how to deal with it. It's, like, burning holes in their corporate pockets. They're on what's called a cash-rich spending spree. When Greenspan said the market was showing signs of 'irrational exuberance', he was talking about people like these guys.

They know you've turned the corner, and, they believe, like, the sky is the limit. Your position is, like, gold to them. You're where they want to be. They see the firewall stuff as a cash cow, like minting money. Throw in your algorithms and a few of your key people and their checkbooks are open. They don't give a byte for your tangible assets or your book value or even the rest of the business. Once the deal is done, they'll either sell all that other stuff or close it down."

I didn't want that to happen, but decided to let it go for the moment.

Joey said the Silicon Valley guys would make a first offer of at least $15 million. Their first offer would be just that, a *first* offer. Soon after, when they found out who their competition was, the offers would go up. "Remember," he said, "they've got money to burn, or at least they think they do. They're like the business equivalent of 'new money' trying to move into Grosse Pointe. They want to live there, no matter what it costs."

It all ended within two weeks with an astounding offer of $62 million, 15% in stock, which I had to hold for at least 18 months. Joey wanted nothing to do with the stock. He said, "The bubble is gonna burst on all these guys in a couple years and their stock will be worth, like, shit." He corrected himself, "Excuse my French, their stock will be worth a fraction of what it is now. 'The Sword of Damocles' is swinging real close to these guys, all of them, the whole high tech scene. It's, like, they just don't seem to get it." His cash take was over five and a quarter million dollars.

As he predicted, they wanted nothing to do with the basic security business, so I sold it, minus the personal security section, to key employees for the lowest amount our tax lawyer said was allowable. I sold the personal security section to Dylan alone, again for the minimum allowed. Unfortunately, the key employees couldn't keep their segment going. They only lasted up to the big business downturn in 2007 and 2008. Dylan's piece, however, made it through. He cut costs to the bone and struggled through. He's still in business.

By the end of the year, I was clear of the whole shebang, and had more money than I would ever know how to spend.

CHAPTER 21

DYLAN – LOSING ON ALL FRONTS

Saturday, December 27, 2014. This holiday season, more so than any he could remember, Dylan needed cheering up. He no longer doubted he had a drinking problem. Since the day, two weeks ago, when he made his issues list and quickly proceeded to get drunk, his willpower had lost several more battles with the gin bottle.

He'd unintentionally made it harder on himself by taping his issues list to the mirror in the master bathroom. He saw it each morning and some evenings, provided he was still sober enough to make out the scribbling. He'd pretty well memorized it: (1) Father/Dream, (2) Henry's Health, (3) Our Future, (4) Money/Restaurant, (5) Job, (6) Drinking, and (7) Special Project plus the two columns of percentages.

He understood he was losing on all fronts, but the worst was the booze, because it was the only one he had sole control of.

Today was Saturday. Henry had stayed home from the restaurant, which was unusual. The weekend between Christmas and New Years was a busy time in the restaurant business, but Henry spent most of the day in bed, because he wasn't feeling well. It seemed like almost every day Henry was at some level of not feeling well.

Clearly, his health was diminishing. He was only 64, same age as Pete, but he seemed much older. Dylan remembered reading there were two classes of old people: young/old and old/old. The difference was health. An elderly person, who is relatively healthy, is still young/old. Once their health fails, they're old/old, and old/old people almost never get better; they just get sicker and sicker until they die. He diagnosed Henry as old/old.

He dreaded the prospect of a period of lingering, bedridden illness for Henry, with a corresponding lingering sentence of care-taking for himself. He was ashamed for having such selfish feelings, but he couldn't stop from wanting it to be over.

Another selfish thought crossed his mind: maybe a swashbuckling adventure with Pete would take his mind off all this shit.

He had to get rid of that thought.

Three days ago on Christmas Eve, he called Pete to extend holiday greetings and to momentarily distract him from the sadness of being alone again on that most difficult of nights to be alone. 13 days had passed since their White Castle lunch. During that time, he hadn't heard from Pete, giving him a thread of hope that Pete had somehow seen the light and scrapped his crazy plan. Pete quickly disabused him of such thoughts when he said, "I should be ready to go in a week or so. When can you come over to take a look?"

Dylan's heart sank a little; his issues list reappeared in his mind. They set a date: Saturday, the 3rd of January. Dylan felt like a little kid making a dentist appointment. He lied and said, "I'm really looking forward to it." It was going to be difficult, maybe even a bit cruel, bringing Pete back to reality. He was sure Pete wouldn't be dissuaded by simply being told it was a bad idea. Dylan would have to demonstrate why it wouldn't work, and how it could fail on so many levels. He needed a careful, considerate approach.

He started forming a strategy. First he would thoroughly read Pete's write-up, then he would listen attentively to Pete's added comments, if he had any. Dylan knew he might have to feign genuine interest and open-mindedness, but let Pete say his piece. Dylan would nod at all the right places. Ask a few inoffensive questions. Be positive. Do *not* be sarcastic. Do *not* reveal any preconceived objections. Once Pete takes him through everything, go back and tactfully ask about how this part would work in a real situation, and suggest how that part may have too many uncontrolled variables, too many moving parts. Break it down gently until it dawns on Pete that it's too risky, has little chance of success. By all means do *not* preach. Let it come to him independently, in a way that he thinks he's discovering it on his own. Don't appear to be trying to lead him.

Dylan couldn't believe he was plotting like this against the man to whom he owed so much. The man who had believed in him and stood up for him, when so few others would.

The January 3rd meeting was now one week away. Dylan vowed once again to stay sober for those seven days. He needed sober, non-hangover time to think clearly, to prepare a very diplomatic argument to convince Pete to abandon his radical plan. Dylan needed his wits about him. This time he'd stay sober.

Somehow.

CHAPTER 22

JOURNAL – LESTER'S TRIAL

5am, Sunday, 12-28-2014

One day in late October of 2000, only six weeks after the shooting, while the negotiations for the sale of the business were still ongoing, I came home and Donna wasn't there.

She left a note saying she was gone to Clearwater, Florida, where she'd rented an apartment for six months. She somehow managed on her own to contact a rental agent who pre-paid the rent and also arranged and paid for her plane ticket. The cleaning lady, Merle, helped her write the note. Merle also helped her pack. It made me wonder, once Donna got off the plane in Tampa, how the hell she would get from the airport to the apartment by herself. She was much worse off than I was.

The next day I called her cell phone and left a message to make sure she had enough money. She didn't call back. I soon found out she could still write checks, withdraw cash from the ATM, and use the charge card. I thought, quite uncharitably, that she was not so overwhelmed by grief and medication as to not be able to figure out the money part, my new cynical side raising its ugly head. Later, I admonished my pettiness, because except for minimal groceries and gas, she spent very little. The new me had to be more closely monitored to assure a proper level of civility and consideration for others. It didn't come as naturally as it used to.

Then in early April, just before the six months was up, and near the beginning of Lester's trial, I got a note from her saying she still couldn't bear living in what she called, "that house," meaning our Northville home, the house with all the Keenie memories; she was going to spend the spring and summer in northern Michigan. The same rental agent found a small cottage near Petoskey. It was a modest place; even though Donna was aware we now had a bottomless pit of money. I simply responded with an "OK," knowing I was part of the reason for her not coming back to Northville. That hurt a lot. It didn't help that I agreed with her take on me.

She didn't come down-state for even one day of Lester's trial.

It started in April, seven months after the shooting; surprisingly soon considering his mental condition. Usually with the sanity of the defendant in question, there are long trial delays while the court determines if the defendant is capable of assisting counsel in his own defense. Not so in Lester's case. The criminal justice system decided to move ahead despite testimony by a psychiatrist that he was suffering from acute symptoms of PTSD.

My recollection is that back then (2001) the courts weren't yet tuned in to PTSD and its symptoms. Of course, Lester's court-appointed attorney did not put him on the stand; he was too fragile. The prosecutors would have pit-bulled him into chewable pieces.

Every day of the trial I sat in the same seat, in the first row right behind the prosecutors. Apparently that seat was reserved for me, because the first day the bailiff directed me to it, and each day thereafter it was empty when I got there. The court room did not have that traditional men's club mahogany look you see in the movies. More of a cafeteria style with light oak veneer and metallic trim, but it was still a court room, divided up so as to keep all the key players properly separate from each other, with the judge sitting in a dominant, somewhat elevated position.

Michelle Rumsfeld, Keenie's teacher, was on the stand for the better part of the second afternoon. She had fully recovered, at least physically, from her bullet wound in the shoulder. She came off as the stereotypical high school English teacher, one who could have been sent over by central casting – neither tall nor short; maybe a little overweight but not what you'd call heavy; orthodonticly straight, snow-white teeth that dominated her otherwise ordinary face; thick glasses with tortoise-shell frames; gray-blue eyes; slightly graying brown hair, shorter than a bob, longer than a pixie; articulate; sincere; just what you'd want for your child's English teacher. And in spite of being a prosecution witness and Lester's ex-wife and his intended target, when talking about him, she showed little animosity. It was more rueful affection.

She related that two years before the shooting, the day after his 35th birthday, he was in a near-fatal traffic accident, and from that day forward he was not the same. She said he was working as an appliance repairman when it happened. He'd been doing that kind of work for several years. He was good at it, mechanically inclined, knew how to fix things and good with people. When the accident occurred, he was *not* wearing a seatbelt. Michelle thought this to be out of character, because she knew him as a sensible and safety conscious person.

Michelle said it appeared he was on his lunch break between service calls, possibly in a hurry; maybe running late for his next call. She said Lester remembered nothing from that day, so to some extent she was speculating about exactly what happened. Driving north on Haggerty Road, about to cross Eight Mile Road, (he may have been headed to the McDonald's just north of Eight Mile) a Dodge Ram 3500 pickup, one of the biggest and heaviest pickups on the road at that time, left-turned in front of him. (The driver of the pickup claimed the light was turning red. Other witnesses said it had just turned yellow.) Lester couldn't or didn't stop. When his service van hit the pickup, it was believed to be going about 35 mph. Witnesses described the collision as a bomb-like thump with Lester's smaller van compressing into the larger pickup and stopping dead. Although his little van stopped, Lester didn't. Without the fastened seatbelt his body kept going at 35mph. His forehead collided with the windshield, fracturing his skull and severely damaging his neck.

He also broke three ribs on the steering column and his left wrist when it somehow got tangled in the steering wheel. It took three firemen and two EMTs 45 minutes to extract him from his van after which he was helicoptered to University of Michigan Hospital.

He was unconscious for two weeks.

The bone structure of his skull healed in due time as did the muscles in his neck and the broken ribs and left wrist and the cuts on his face and neck and arms. But inside his skull, his brain cortex didn't respond to treatment. The frontal lobe, the part right behind the forehead, suffered the most damage. The doctors called it a "closed head injury." Something inside there was broken, and they couldn't fix it. After three months of hospital and nursing home rehab, they released him and sent him home to try to function in society.

As luck would have it, the frontal lobe is the part that holds the knowledge of how to fix broken appliances. Now through his damaged brain receptors, the schematic of a refrigerator looked more like an inescapable maze. He lost his job.

That wasn't all. According to Michelle, he suffered from severe headaches; bad enough to take his breath away. The pain pills didn't help, because the doctors cut off the good stuff, the pills that really muffled the pain, to guard against addiction.

She said he also had dizzy spells where sometimes he actually fell down. And there was intermittent memory loss – one time he went on an errand in their neighborhood and got lost. Nightmares were frequent. He would wake up sweating and crying.

The scariest problem, according to Michelle, was his fits of anger. He would unexplainably fly into a rage. He claimed "people were *blanking* with him." That's the way she put it in her testimony, electing to bleep herself. Neither of the attorneys or the judge asked for a clarification. Lester had major people problems. She said he believed just about everyone he came in contact with was "blanking with him," including his bosses, fellow employees, doctors, store clerks, the list went on. She added that she herself was probably at the top of that list. Two different times during his rages he had hit her; the second time she moved out. She even got a restraining order against him. In spite of the court order, she said, he would still follow her when she left her apartment. At times she could see his car. It was scary. But she never thought he would try to shoot her.

She said he tried other lower paying, menial jobs like dishwashing, cleaning offices and cutting lawns but couldn't hold onto them, because he couldn't get along with his fellow workers or supervisors. Everything stoked his anger. There was more than one fist fight.

He didn't have any money. The insurance company was still holding out on a settlement and his disability claim hadn't been approved. (In October of 2000, a month after the shooting, while he was awaiting trial in the Wayne County jail, his Social Security Disability claim was approved, legally confirming his unsuitability for gainful employment.) He had to move into his mother's house. Lived in the basement. More fuel for his internal fire. That's what Michelle called it, "his internal fire."

Various medications for his condition had been prescribed, which, before the shooting, he'd taken only on occasion; and one doctor had recommended hospitalization in a psychiatric facility, which he steadfastly refused.

He was unemployed, not quite homeless, though feeling very much alone, severely brain damaged, causing him to be mentally unstable bordering on delusional, and periodically angry. Very, very angry.

And he was allowed to purchase a handgun at a gun show.

The prosecution team, in carrying out their duty to protect society, argued to the jury that he was able to distinguish between the concepts of right and wrong; furthermore, his ability to carry out the purchase of the gun proved both that he knew what he was doing and that he was capable of premeditation; and so on. All the while the specter of the beautiful, innocent teen-ager he'd killed haunted the court room.

His defense attorney, appointed by the court, attempted to portray Lester as a brain-damaged victim of a terrible automobile accident, whose resulting actions were beyond his control. After a few hours of deliberation, the jury went with the prosecution and found him guilty of a range of crimes including first-degree murder.

The judge, possibly less convinced, did not give Lester the maximum sentence, but nevertheless put him away for a long time in a maximum-security state prison.

To an objective observer, Lester might have been perceived as another victim of the crime, though certainly less sympathetic than Keenie. To me, separating him from society to prevent him from doing more harm seemed appropriate, but ideally, it should have been in a more humane place than the big house. Considering his mental and physical condition and the nature of the facility, it was reasonable to assume he'd never see the outside again.

I remember trying several times in the courtroom to get close enough to look him in the eye. On one occasion I succeeded. Of course, by the time of the trial, and probably because of his incarceration, he was taking his medication with prescribed regularity. What I saw was fear and loneliness and confusion. I felt as much pity toward him as anger. It appeared as though he didn't completely understand what he'd done, or why he did it. His finger did pull the trigger, but in my judgment, the broad culpability, the moral responsibility for it all, belonged elsewhere.

Lester Rumsfeld was not a Signore Pavoni or a Goliath. The Lone Ranger would not consider him a suitable candidate for special attention.

CHAPTER 23

DYLAN — A PLACE TO READ

S*unday, December 28, 2014.* Dylan didn't drink on Saturday night. Not even a glass of wine. Come Sunday, he kept himself busy by taking trips out of the house to run errands or just get away. Whenever he felt himself starting to backslide, he'd grab his car keys and get out. After four trips, one where he circled Belle Isle six times, when he got back to the house, it was still only one o'clock.

He went to the den and turned on the Lions' game, thinking it might suffice as a four-hour distraction. He gave up at half time. They were losing and playing badly. Made him want to have a drink. Periodically Henry would shuffle past the door. His sluggish steps gave the house a nursing home feel, reminding Dylan of what the future held. Dylan went for his car keys again. This time he drove all the way out to Twelve Oaks, the big mall in Novi, almost an hour from the house. He strolled the mall for over two hours, just wandering and doing a little window shopping. Finally he made a purchase, a conscience-salving gold bracelet for Henry that was marked down to a post-holiday sale price.

When Dylan left for the mall, Henry was dozing in a living room chair. The sound of the kitchen door closing startled him awake. He looked at his watch. In an hour he'd need his insulin shot. He'd get the paraphernalia now and put it on the kitchen table in plain sight so as not to forget. Forgetting shit was another problem these days.

He put on his glasses. He'd need them later to administer the injection. Getting out of the chair, he had to use every muscle in his body, or so it seemed. He carefully made his way into the bedroom for the insulin and a syringe. Looking into the dresser drawer, he remembered he'd used the last syringe in the packet this morning before breakfast. He checked the bathroom for a spare pack. None. Ditto, the kitchen.

He'd have to wait for Dylan to get back from wherever he was, because the only other place they'd be was upstairs in the master bathroom. He hadn't been up there in a while, but thought he might have left a few up there when he moved downstairs.

He couldn't wait too long to get the syringe. His body needed the insulin in evenly spaced doses. If Dylan wasn't back within a half hour, he'd have to call him. He turned on the kitchen TV and sat down at the table to wait.

At 3:20, he started to feel an episode coming on. He found his cell phone and tried to call Dylan. The phone was dead. He'd forgotten to charge it. He couldn't delay any longer. He'd almost lapsed into a diabetic coma once before, and it was scary. He'd have to get the syringe himself. He reluctantly shuffled for the stairway. He hadn't attempted the stairs in over six months. It wasn't that he couldn't climb the stairs. Sure, it was a tough slog, but mostly it was the balance thing. At his weight, falling could be a disaster, and he was still rational enough to acknowledge it.

He opted to not risk a fall and instead scale the stairs on his hands and knees. He tipped his upper body forward until his hands landed on the fourth step, his knees coming to rest on the second step. He moved his hands up to the fifth step, then his right knee up to the third. It was not easy. He could feel the strain in his thigh. Then his left knee. His hands again. Then his knees. After six steps, he thought he understood why Homo sapiens had decided to walk upright. The perspiration on his chest and neck was running freely. He had to stop to catch his breath. He looked up to the top of the stairs. His hands had only four steps to go, the knees six. As his hands got to the top, his thighs ached. He crawled forward until his left knee ascended the last step.

He was tired, breathing hard. Instead of making the effort to stand, he crawled the few paces to the master bedroom door, got inside the bedroom and crawled past the walk-in closet door to the bathroom. The doors were all open, simplifying his effort. Inside the bathroom, he crawled over to the sink cabinet, opened the middle drawer and used it for balance, while he pulled himself up to the counter. He had to take care not to put too much weight on the drawer. Dylan would be upset if he broke it. Standing now, he found no syringes on the counter; he tried the medicine cabinet on the side wall. He opened the cabinet, and there they were. Close to exhaustion, he leaned over the sink with his elbows on the counter to catch his breath. Luckily, the insulin bottle was in his pocket. He'd put it there while searching for the syringes downstairs. He straightened up and tottered over to the toilet, put the seat cover down, plumped his squat 310 pounds down on top of the cover and proceeded to administer his insulin shot.

For several minutes, he sat there resting. He noticed a slip of paper taped to the mirror over the sink. With great effort, he pushed himself to his feet to get over to the sink and get a closer look at what was written.

Just after 6:00 Dylan returned from his trip to the mall. When he entered the kitchen, Henry was sitting at the table, drinking a cup of tea, staring into space. He looked up with a sad question mark on his face, but said nothing.

Dylan said, "What?"

"You've been gone for a long time. Where'd you go?"

"Checking out the bargains at the mall. Got this on sale." Dylan handed him the little unwrapped gift box.

Henry looked at the box, opened it slowly. When he saw the bracelet, he looked up at Dylan standing over him, "Who's it for?"

Dylan said, "Well…you. Who else would I buy a bracelet for?"

Henry's eyes turned watery. He couldn't speak. After a long pause, he recovered and said, "Thank you." It was almost a whisper. He got up from the table, shuffled down the hall into his bedroom and closed the door.

Dylan asked himself, "What the hell was that about?"

It was 5:15 on Sunday evening. He looked at the liquor cabinet. He needed four more hours, and he could go to bed sober. He fixed himself a light dinner, Mrs. Grass's chicken noodle soup and a tuna fish sandwich. While he ate, he read a book about Quantum Physics, supposedly explaining it to the average person. It took a lot of deep concentration to try to wrap his mind around the alien concepts. When he looked up, it was almost 7:30. He gave up on Quantum Physics, went into the den and turned on "60 Minutes" to catch the last half. Due to the NFL games, the broadcast was delayed. The program had just gotten underway. Surprisingly, not one of the topics made him feel like he had to have a drink.

At 8:30, he rose from his recliner and scanned the bookshelves for a page-turner that would similarly not awaken any gin cravings. He spotted Elmore Leonard's "Swag" and grabbed it off the shelf, as if it was the last copy available in the bookstore. Halfway up the stairs he was already smiling about the funny characters and dialogue he was about to re-encounter.

After an hour and a half of reading, he went to sleep and got seven hours of peace, uninterrupted by alcohol induced frustration dreams or an overtaxed liver.

At quarter after six Monday morning, Dylan was in the gym in Grosse Pointe starting an extra long workout. He worked six of the machines, before heading for his favorite part, a swim in the pool. He did laps for almost forty minutes. Returning to the house at 8:30, he showered, shaved, dressed in walking clothes, had a poached egg with muffin breakfast, and set out for a long walk to Belle Isle, where it was bitter cold, even for him.

On his return, he joined Henry at the table for coffee and a quick scan of the Free Press. It was 9:30. Henry was up fairly early, because he didn't go to the restaurant yesterday, Sunday being a usually slow day.

"I'm going to stop by the Eastern Market for a few things on my way in today. I'll probably get in a little early, so I'll be starting a full review of the place."

Something about the tone made Dylan look up from the paper. "A full review?"

"Yes, it's time. You're right. You've been right all along." Henry emitted an alertness Dylan hadn't detected in some time.

"What do you mean?"

"The restaurant, of course. It's time to look at our options." Then he added, "As you've suggested." He was looking directly at Dylan to see his reaction.

"Uh…oh…uh…did something happen?"

"Nothing happened. I just woke up, I guess. Maybe it was the bracelet. Something else, I'm going on a diet starting today. I could wait until the New Year on Thursday, but then it would be a 'resolution.' You know what happens to them."

For a moment, Dylan had a flashback of the old Henry. What was going on? All he could say was, "Yeah."

The place where Dylan had always managed to stay sober – the office – was closed due to the holidays and would stay closed until after their meeting. All that time he'd be at home where he did most of his drinking. He needed to be out, but he could only take so many long walks and do so many reps, treadmill steps and pool laps at the gym. It was more exercise than even he could handle. What to do? As much as he enjoyed reading, sitting around the house was too risky. He'd be too close to the liquor cabinet. He couldn't trust himself. He had to think of something.

Dylan's mother, bless her soul, would have been disappointed it took him so long. Dylan was wracking his mind over finding a place to read, where he would not have easy access to booze. On Sunday night, when it dawned on him that public libraries don't serve alcohol and do provide comfortable places for reading, he laughed out loud. He'd use the library, his mother's place of business, for a brand new purpose – to stay sober. He thought Mom would approve.

He pulled into the parking structure two blocks from the Main Branch of the Detroit Public Library at 11:00 a.m. on Monday, December 29. He sat in the car for ten minutes wondering what was going on with Henry, hoping it was real and would last. It made his list less depressing. Maybe he could change some of the percentages. That day he read a collection of Mark Twain's short stories, which added to his positive mood.

CHAPTER 24

JOURNAL – THE SHRINK

5am, Monday, 12-29-2014.

Donna's escape strategy didn't work.

In August of 2000, in her secluded little rented cottage near Petoskey, only 11 months after Keenie's death, she swallowed all her sleeping pills, pulled a plastic bag over her head, and tied it tight around her neck. The pills put her into a deep sleep, enough so that even the diminishing presence of oxygen inside the plastic bag would not wake her. The cleaning lady found her two days later.

The last iota of doubt was now removed: I was alone.

I got that call in my hotel room in Rome on the next-to-last day of a three-week trip to Italy. The purpose of my trip, other than to distract me from my grief and guilt over Keenie, was to try to confirm Grampa's story. I'd never doubted him when we were Big Pete and Little Pete, but the coincidence with my own situation was so bizarre, I wanted to try to settle in my own mind that he wasn't having some kind of hallucination or false memory. Also I had a lot of time and money on my hands.

In a nutshell, his story held up. There really was a Signore Pavoni, and the records said he really did die in a horse-riding incident, and it happened in 1912. Furthermore, he was a landowner of some consequence in that part of Tuscany.

There were also several Ferrari families living in the area at the time. One Ferrari couple named Giacomo and Chiara died in 1920, just as Grampa said. The only Rossini's from anywhere near Carrara, a family of eight, immigrated to America in 1929, which I noted was a bad year to leave home.

The day after the phone call about Donna, I came back on my scheduled flight – no need to rush – and dealt with the arrangements for her burial. For this funeral I took no drugs.

As I said, the primary symptom for me, following Keenie's death, was an inability to sleep. My pillow had hardened. Except for the heavily sedated first week, I rarely got three hours in any one night. To this day that condition has abated very little.

The side effects of long-term insomnia are not fully appreciated by people who haven't been through it. I can testify that not being able to sleep over a long period of time is a version of hell. It's easy for me to see why sleep deprivation is used as an interrogation method, bordering on torture. I am continually tired, paradoxically not tired enough to sleep, but reduced to very low energy. At times I can't concentrate on even normal activities, like reading or watching TV. The effort it takes to do simple tasks, like writing this journal, can be exhausting. The condition is omnipresent, day after day, night after night. It not only diminishes my body, it alters my thinking. On bad days, I am disorganized, at times irrational. On really bad days, I feel symptoms of depression. I tried sleeping pills, only mild versions, of course, for fear of addiction, but they're not up to the task.

In desperation, right after Donna took her life, I saw a shrink, hoping he might help me get some sleep. His name was Ronald Curlew. My Internist recommended him. I went to Dr. Curlew weekly, cancelling only a few appointments due to travel, etc.

During our sessions, I cried sometimes, telling him about Keenie. Conversely, when he asked about my youth and parental influences, I related a happy, secure childhood, which was true. Dad and Mom were great. I was a well-adjusted kid. Nothing to blame on my parents.

The only possible issue with me was the exceptional relationship with my grandfather, which for some reason I never mentioned to him. I'm not sure why. But I do remember being aware of not talking about it. Maybe it was the Lone Ranger thing.

Several times, I brought up the ineffectiveness of the sleeping pills. We talked about a stronger dose, so he bumped it a little, but not enough, the specter of addiction again being the controlling factor.

Our weekly ritual went on for about 18 months, showing little progress. After each session, when I left his office, I felt about the same as I did when I entered back in the first week. It occurred to me that maybe I wasn't a good candidate for whatever it was Dr. Curlew did. It's been said, that, like hypnotism, some people are not good candidates for analysis.

Apparently he was getting frustrated too, sensing that little had changed since we began. Finally, near the end of a session, the good doctor let his impatience show. He said I had to stop holding back. I said I didn't know what else to say, mentally crossing my fingers about Grampa.

He told me I needed to open up more and start taking control of my life in a positive way. I needed to pull myself together and just get over it.

I felt like I was talking to Dr. Phil.

That was our last session. I came out of it with the suspicion Dr. Curlew was right. It was up to me. I had to do something. But what? And why didn't I want to tell him about Grampa?

That night I slept less than two hours.

After the trip to Italy, and I admit, as a result of my findings there, Grampa's Lone Ranger speech crept back into my thoughts with increasing frequency. The loss of Keenie was as if a circuit had been tripped, an essential circuit of my life, and seemingly an essential circuit of a just world. I wanted to be able to press a button that would somehow reset it.

Maybe others in my situation also feel such a need, albeit helplessly. But in my case, with the windfall sale of the business, I had the wherewithal and the time to attempt extraordinary deeds. And, of course, I had Grampa's example and his ever-present Lone Ranger directive. So I began a halting, disorganized pursuit of the reset button.

I wasn't sure where it would take me. At the beginning I assumed it was *not* going to result in physical harm to another person. Possibly some radical or daring act would be required, probably a serious financial commitment, but certainly nothing that would result in someone's death.

As a result, most of my waking hours, of which there were an overabundance, were spent trying to uncover an event or circumstance – a *non-animate* Signore Pavoni – that could be altered or corrected; possibly a few statutes or gun laws that could be fixed in a way that would prevent or reduce the occurrence of similar shootings. Such changes could compensate to some degree for the loss of Keenie and the damage done to Donna and serve as memorials to them.

Toward that end, I became a gun control activist. Not a marching, chanting, sign carrying activist. More a behind the scenes researcher and financial donor. From the start I believed the source of the tragedy to be *the sale of a pistol at a gun show to a person officially known to be mentally deranged and court-certified as a domestic abuser, with no attempt or requirement to obtain a background check, all under the legal guise that it was a private sale.*

Certainly, such transactions could be minimized in the future. First, the private sale loophole should be closed. Period. No exceptions. And second, the existing, but inadequate, system for maintaining a registry of persons who should not be allowed to purchase a firearm should be made workable. There are other gun control issues, of course, but those two were my focus.

CHAPTER 25

JOURNAL – KNOW YOUR ENEMY

5am, Tuesday, 12-30-2014

To make a long story short, by 2005 my gun control activist approach bore little fruit. My side in the conflict made no progress on political or legislative solutions for my targeted issues. We lost every legislative battle, even the small ones. The gun lobby said all that was necessary was proper enforcement of existing law, and then did everything they could to insure such enforcement didn't happen. If anything, we were going backward. Too many federal and state senators and representatives were under the political and financial spell of the gun lobby.

All my research efforts – the reading and web surfing and traveling and meetings and letter writing – were in vain. As were my financial donations. More than five years after Keenie was killed, nothing good had happened nor was going to happen soon, possibly not even during my lifetime. It was beyond my reach. The gun lobby's resources dwarfed my fortune. The hope that my Signore Pavoni, my Goliath, would *not* be a real live human being was dimming.

I needed a plan B.

Lying awake night after night, I tried to dissect the problem. In those five years, what had I learned? Why did we, the gun control advocates, lose every battle? Or seem to? Our team kept getting our butts kicked. We were never even competitive. Why? We were on the side of the angels. We should win at least a few. What were we always doing wrong? Or conversely, what were they always doing right? Analyzing this dilemma became my new substitute for counting sheep.

Meanwhile, an ominous image, the Lone Ranger rearing his white horse, was gaining purchase in my nightly ruminations.

This persistence to do something might be seen as the proverbial road less taken. Other people suffer horrible tragedies in their lives, including the most tragic of all, the death of a child, and they don't come to this place. Despite immense suffering, they eventually get back to their lives, doing what they did before. Not that they forget the loss or get over it. No, they don't forget. It's always with them. No amount of alcohol or drugs or praying can keep it blocked out. When they sober up, or leave church, it's right there again. Nevertheless, they grind it out, year after year, for the rest of their lives, in quiet, impotent desperation. They won't live long enough to be rid of it, try as they might. They have no options, no recourse. There is nothing they can do. The pain remains until they die. Maybe that's why Donna did what she did. Maybe she saw her act as a less painful short cut.

Neither course is available to me. My situation is different. There are factors which do not allow me to simply exist in a continuous state of grief or just give up and end it all. I not only have the desperate need, I also have the resources, the time, and thanks to Grampa, the destiny. I have to do something. I have to make it right. I'm obligated. I *must* seek a meaningful, suitable redress, to restore balance, to achieve Keenie's revered equilibrium.

Once I've done that, perhaps the pain will go away; perhaps I will feel like I've done my duty for Keenie, and even Donna. Perhaps I'll feel as Grampa did, that I've conquered evil and made the world a better place. That's not an unreasonable goal, especially for someone in my circumstances. I really don't see that I can do anything less. Perhaps when I've done it, I'll get a good night's sleep.

Investigators and journalists and historians who read this may wonder what else was going on in my life while I stumbled about looking for a solution to my dilemma. I suppose the truthful answer is: not a great deal, particularly in view of the vast amount of time available.

I do a lot of walking, when I'm not sitting and reading. I'm kind of a slow reader, mostly because of the lack of sleep. It translates into drowsiness, short of sleep, making it hard to concentrate, especially if the material is denser than *USA Today*.

I've traveled; some business, some pleasure. The business part relates, of course, to the money. A big bunch of money requires attention. As an investor, I took the conservative route and went for financial diversity. My money's divided into many different piles. Some of them have done alright, others not so much, and taxes take some of it, but I still have more than I'll ever need.

As for pleasure there've been a couple of women in my life – not at the same time, of course. Neither of them knows anything about what I'm up to. No need to tell them. It would be foolish to do so for obvious reasons.

The first, Carrie Rhinehold, was a widow. Her late husband was one of my PARsafe clients and a good friend. Carrie was his second wife, kind of a trophy wife, a good looker. She took an interest in me after Donna died. Carrie and I traveled a bit, mostly to Europe. Turned out we had little else in common. After a couple years we went our separate ways.

Then there was a Mexican woman, Patricia Paar. Also not bad looking. I met her at a place in Mexico called Lake Chapala. She's actually half Irish. Her father (the Irish half) did well investing in energy and left her a little money. As with Carrie, Patricia and I travelled quite a bit. She showed me all over Latin America. And she helped me learn Spanish. I've become reasonably fluent. It was good with her for a while, but she got the feeling my mind was elsewhere too much of the time, which, certainly, it was. So, last year (2013) she said, "Adios." I miss her.

Lake Chapala is Mexico's largest body of fresh water. About an hour southeast of Guadalajara. I discovered it in 2004. A lot of us norteamericanos, including quite a few Canadians, winter there. Some stay year around. Most years I'm there from November to April. I do make occasional trips out to take care of business and personal matters, but most of the winter I'm in Mexico.

I mentioned reading. In spite of the challenges I've become a serious reader, like Dylan, which brings us back to our purpose here. In the moments between everything else, I read. When you can't sleep, it helps a little. One book I came across, The Art of War, gave me a clue about how to proceed.

In that oft-quoted treatise, written over 1500 years ago by an insightful Chinese military leader, a major path to victory is to know your enemy, which, in strategic importance, comes right after knowing yourself. Since knowing yourself is so much more difficult, I concentrated on the enemy, namely the NRA, The National Rifle Association.

In truth, the NRA was not the only enemy, but it was near the top of the pyramid of enemies. Not being able to beat them, I joined them.

I became a closet NRA member. No bumper stickers or window decals on my pick-up, especially since I didn't own a pick-up, but if I did, it wouldn't have revealed any signs or opinions one way or the other. I stayed undercover, because my motives were pure espionage. I wanted to know what they were doing, what made them so successful, why they were winning. If I could better answer those issues, maybe I could develop a viable response, a new plan.

CHAPTER 26

THE FUNDRAISER

Wednesday, May 10, 2006. "Ladies and gentlemen, this is an unusual gathering." The speaker paused and looked around the room making eye contact with as many in the audience as his careful timing allowed; not too fast, not too slow. In response, the chatter in the room ebbed to a gentle murmur.

Rossi sat in a middle row near the outside aisle on the speaker's right. The position allowed him to scan the room to establish a rough head count. He gauged 20 rows of chairs, 16 chairs per row, about two-thirds full. Between 200 and 250 people.

The speaker was J. D. Ramirez, a former justice of the New Mexico Supreme Court and, according to the program, an authority on the Second Amendment of the U.S. Constitution. He continued, "I am very much humbled by your attendance and grateful to each of you for being here." His tone was genuine. He seemed to care.

"As patriotic Americans, we share an interest in a critically important issue...an issue essential to the safety of our families, and the protection of our way of life, and the security of our nation." Platitudes, for sure, but delivered by a gifted storyteller. His baritone voice was buttery, modulated to convey earnest concern, and held to a limited decibel level, to encourage close attention. The murmur in the room faded to silence.

The man, appearing to speak from the heart, used no script or notes. Sincerity oozed from his pores while he gave the impression of talking directly to individuals in the audience, rather than to the audience as a whole.

As he continued, Rossi, the skeptic, noted the elements of the speaker's compelling style. Beyond his pacing and soothing voice, he looked good. Only a discerning eye would detect the care taken to achieve such a look. He was well preserved for the fifty-four years Rossi's Internet search had revealed. A touch of color, maybe from a bottle, muted the whitening hair to a more distinguished gray. His face was in that trustworthy category of "almost handsome," no feature outshining the others, the unblemished skin gently tanned. Rossi estimated his height at about five feet, ten inches. His well-toned, size forty-medium torso was enhanced by expert grooming. Not flashy grooming, but judicious elegance in every detail.

The cut of the suit gave his body an overall trimness, the coat draped to show no evidence of the handgun Rossi suspected was holstered underneath. The cost of the entire outfit from shoes to coif exceeded the quarterly wage of the average American.

The speaker was practiced in the choreography of persuasion. He took advantage of the value of direct eye contact with individuals in the audience. His body control was that of an accomplished thespian, performing rather than "speechifying." Rossi speculated he'd polished his stage moves through years of practice in front of audiences and mirrors. His feet did not move except to emphasize a point by stepping from the lectern toward the audience, or it seemed, toward a single person in the audience. His shoulders and torso and hips gave off no nervous shifts or tics and moved only to support dramatic hand or arm gestures. His head tilted occasionally to give the audience an opportunity to chuckle at an absurdity he raised.

Ramirez was a master, a true mesmerizer without the swinging watch. Rossi couldn't remember anyone this good on his side, the gun control side.

The presentation took place in a small boutique style hotel about a mile from the convention site for the Annual Meeting of the National Rifle Association. The event was not listed in the NRA meeting agenda. Furthermore, according to the program placed on each of the chairs, it was not part of or in any way affiliated with the NRA meeting, which Rossi thought was a bit of a stretch. The sponsoring organization was listed as the American Gun Council. The AGC was a behind the scenes group primarily tasked with fundraising for the gun lobby. Rossi assumed everyone in the room was registered for the much bigger annual NRA meeting down the road. To assure an exclusive, select attendance, this event was by invitation only. The invitees were all, in a word, rich. They had the means, and possibly the inclination, to make substantial monetary donations to the cause, the gun lobby cause. Rossi was surprised to have gotten an invitation. How did they identify him this quickly as being in that category? So far, he'd taken a very low profile as an NRA member.

The host hotel for this presentation was somewhat pricier than the main convention hotel, and conveniently, most of today's affluent audience had chosen this tonier lodging for their own stay. The medium-sized ballroom was nothing short of opulent, with what Rossi perceived to be genuine crystal chandeliers. The large wall paintings depicted 19th century aristocratic scenes, foxhunts and the like. Rossi assumed they were originals. The folding chairs, with comfortable, wide seats, were a cut above those you'd store in your basement with the family card table. Two long, well-draped bars, one on each side of the room, employed a total of six bartenders, pouring generous drinks that were, of course, on the house. Whose house seemed of little concern.

Behind the well-stocked bars, the walls were covered with paisley-textured wallpaper in a champagne hue, closely matching the event's drink of choice. Single malt scotches, aged bourbons and other expensive spirits were also available. Almost no one drank beer. The multitude of beer drinkers had been culled and remained at the main convention hotel. Rossi asked for Vernors, and when the bartender gave him a confused look, he switched it to ice water.

In the back right corner of the room, during the warm-up to the speech, a tuxedoed band played standards and mood-lifting "golden oldie" country classics. When the speaker took the stage, most of the audience was already well tenderized by the refreshments and the music.

The speaker presented the usual political talking points of the gun lobby, acknowledging that on most of these issues he was probably "preaching to the choir." He warned that each of them should clearly be afraid, afraid for their personal safety and the safety of their family, acknowledging that they all probably understood that part.

He went on to explain that, most critically, they needed to be afraid of their own inattention and carelessness, not inattention and carelessness in using and maintaining and securing their personal firearms; no, that wasn't the threat. The real threat was in making even small legislative concessions to the opposition. To do so was to begin a slide down a "slippery slope." Being less than vigilant in responding to that most pernicious threat of all, the slippery slope, the small concessions, would be their downfall.

This angle struck closest to Rossi's question of why his allies, the gun control advocates, could not seem to win even the small battles, the common sense issues.

In the talk, the opposition was not openly defined. It wasn't necessary. Rossi, along with everyone in the audience knew who the opposition was. It was the liberal do-gooders (all of whom were assumed to be Democrats) who would minimize or restrict the rights of law-abiding American citizens to conveniently purchase and use firearms. Any small concession to these miscreants would potentially open the floodgates to their real objective, the repeal of the Second Amendment.

The ease of acquisition, the satisfaction and security of possession, and the recreational pleasure each audience member received from using and collecting guns could be taken away, because their basic right of gun possession, as guaranteed in the Second Amendment of the Constitution, could ultimately be revoked. Such an injustice was a certainty, if they let down their guard for even a moment, if they weren't acutely wary of the slippery slope of small concessions.

To Rossi's surprise, the speaker did not draw on his purported Constitutional expertise regarding the Second Amendment. He made no academic references to the Constitution's stated need for a "well regulated militia" and its importance to "the security of a free state."

As a matter of general principle, most pro-gun messages invoked God, something to the effect that it "was not just a Constitutional right but also a God-given right." Today's speaker was not remiss in doing so. To Rossi's disappointment God's position in favor of gun rights was not explained. Perhaps there was no need to clarify. It made sense to the core audience, so why get into it.

Donations at this event would go to the aptly named Sniper Fund, a fund reserved for donors of over $10,000. The money would be used to defeat particularly insidious liberal candidates who posed the greatest danger to every American's Second Amendment rights, especially the opposition (read Democratic) candidate for president, whoever that turned out to be. Rossi wondered if anyone else in the room picked up on the negative implication that the money would not be used to support good candidates, only to defeat bad ones. Hence, the name "Sniper."

Prior to Keenie's death, Rossi had never been a particularly political person. He showed up at the polls, usually voted Republican due to his personal conservative outlook, but wasn't active in or emotionally committed to political issues. On several occasions, he'd even voted for a Democrat.

Now he had one political issue that mattered to him, and he saw it as not particularly conservative or liberal. He wondered how conservatives got to be gun rights people and liberals ended up on the other side. He thought maybe you could ask that about other issues as well.

When Ramirez finished his surprisingly short talk – Rossi timed it at 12 minutes – he walked to the front of the short riser and stepped down to talk directly and intimately with the audience members. He was accompanied by a guy named Martindale, who'd introduced him before the speech. Rather than split up, so as to talk to more people, Martindale stayed right next to Ramirez as he worked the room.

Rossi managed to get in a few words with Ramirez and felt that in his direct personal conversation, he was less impressive, a bit detached, perhaps a trace impatient. Throughout the post-speech socializing, Martindale stayed close and watched him intently.

Nevertheless, Rossi acknowledged, Ramirez' little speech had been effective. He'd taken boilerplate arguments – big brother regulations, government arrogance, violation of the American way, contempt of the wisdom of the forefathers, sanctity of The Constitution, threat to the personal safety of the citizenry, denial of the joy of gun ownership – and woven them into an emotional blanket of persuasion. When he threw in fear and patriotism and God, the audience members couldn't get their checkbooks out fast enough. The next week, Rossi did some online research and found that, at that event alone, the gun lobby raised over $2,700,000. Rossi's side, the gun control advocates, couldn't raise that much money in three months.

He conceded Ramirez was good, the best Rossi had seen or heard. Conceivably, he was key to answering Rossi's why, "Why do we, the gun control advocates, always lose, even the little battles?" Maybe Ramirez fell into the class of a Signore Pavoni, a person who could be held responsible for what had happened to Keenie, a candidate for the Lone Ranger to deal with.

There were other candidates, of course, but so far none who stood out in such a singular way. The top NRA officials didn't fit Rossi's criteria. As combative as they appeared, they were no more than placeholders. One goes away and a similar one is right there in line to take his place. Nor were they the real power behind the NRA; the real power were the manufacturers and the sellers, who were too numerous to deal with via Grampa's template. Rossi couldn't assassinate a whole raft of people. That would make him a serial killer or mass murderer. Illogical as it seemed, if he was going to do this, he wanted a meaningful one-time assassination that would make a difference. It had to be a single person of both genuine and symbolic consequence.

Rossi had been trying to find an individual who could be held most responsible for what happened to Keenie. He'd identified a few candidates so far, but none who stood out in as singular a way as this guy. Over five and a half years had passed since the shooting. He considered adding the name, J.D. Ramirez, to his list, while wondering if he was a true Signore Pavoni.

CHAPTER 27

THE GOOD WRIST

M*onday, June 19, 2006.* Using an alias was an essential part of his grandfather's template. Rossi was not yet fully committed to the Lone Ranger solution, but he saw a new identity or multiple new identities as a possible future need. At some point he might want cover just as a precaution. You never knew. It didn't hurt to be prepared.

During the summer of 2006 Rossi spent a week on a solo road trip through parts of the Midwest. In each of five nearby states he picked out a mid-size city where he visited old cemeteries, roaming randomly through the gravesites. He would stop at some of the smaller, more modest headstones and write down the engraved names and dates. He was not in any way acquainted or knew anything about any of the deceased whose names he was collecting, except their year of birth, gender, and the year of their death.

By week's end he'd gathered forty-five names, all males born between 1946 and 1954, within four years of his own birth, all of whom had died in their early to mid-teens.

He then called the Social Security Administration to determine which names had a Social Security Number, and which of those numbers were still active, meaning the SSA hadn't been notified after the deaths to close the accounts. Back in his Army MP days, Rossi learned it was not uncommon for grieving parents to neglect to notify the SSA when their child died. Nowadays most funeral directors include the notification in their list of services. But back in the day, some of them didn't.

In a case where the SSA was not notified, the deceased's number and account stayed on the books, remaining open, even though there was no activity for decades, because the agency didn't know the person was dead. This little bureaucratic glitch only applied to people who'd died before a date in the nineteen eighties. Rossi wasn't sure of the date, and the SSA avoided publicizing it. In such cases an enterprising imposter could assume that person's Social Security identity. Rossi intended to do just that, and his conscience was not troubled by the theft, since the dead boys and their loved ones would in no way suffer any real loss.

Rossi knew the SSA wouldn't give him the actual SSNs without good solid ID, but he didn't need the numbers yet. He'd get them later when he had good credentials to work with. All he needed at this point was to know the deceased had registered with the SSA and that the SSN was still valid. So he called and told the clerk he was checking an employee's number, gave one of the names he'd gathered, along with a nine-digit number he made up, and waited for the clerk to tell him the number was wrong, which he already knew. If the clerk told him the person did not have a number or was deceased, meaning they'd been notified, he just scratched that name off his list.

After each one, he hung up and redialed, getting a fresh clerk, of which there are seemingly hundreds. He made a second list of those who did still have active numbers, and stopped after five. Five should be enough. To get five good names, he had to go through thirty-three from his original list of forty-five, which took a day and a half, mostly because of the time spent on hold.

The whole process of getting a good ID package was long and detailed, but he had plenty of time. Once he had the five names, he'd have original-looking birth certificates made. He could get copies, but copies weren't sufficient. He needed originals, or fakes that looked like originals. Then he'd get five disguises. They'd have to be distinct, not five versions of the same disguise. He would rent a cheap apartment in the name of each of his five deceased men. He did this because they would each need an address, a place to mail the driver's license, bank statements, etc. The apartments would be in five different mid-west cities. He chose Cleveland, Indianapolis, St, Louis, Des Moines and Milwaukee. He would then get a driver's license for each one. With the licenses in hand, he'd go to the five local SSA offices in the respective cities, each in appropriate disguise, and get a copy of the Social Security card for each of his resurrected men. The card, of course, would have the SSN on it. He would then have passport photos taken in each disguise. With the SSN and the driver's license number and the home address and the passport photo he would be able to get a legitimate passport. The final step was to open a small bank account and credit card account for each name. He had to make sure he didn't get the elements mixed up; he couldn't put the guy with the Wisconsin license in a Cincinnati apartment. So, he carefully set up five separate color-coded files. He also spent a lot of time driving to the various cities to carry out all of the necessary steps. He drove in order to minimize his tracks. Flying left a lot of evidence behind.

Having accomplished his first step, getting the five names from the SSA, he phoned an old friend in Huntington Woods, a close-in suburb of Detroit, and scheduled an appointment.

Jim Bailey had a replica of the PARsafe logo on the wall in his carriage house art studio above his garage. He designed the logo for Rossi over thirty years ago, working as a freelancer when Rossi's little security business was getting started.

In the commercial art business Bailey was known as an illustrator, a sub-category under the broad heading of artist. Illustrators were the ones who could draw. They had the ability to accurately replicate visual images with their pencils, pens and brushes. They were artists in the original sense of the word. The good illustrators, of which there were few, could paint a picture that looked like a photograph, an exact replica of the subject, preferably an inanimate subject. Lesser talents sometimes deprecatingly referred to these illustrators as "good wrists." Bailey ranked high in that group of good wrists.

In the time before computer software encroached on the field of commercial art, Bailey's talent was in great demand, particularly for use in print advertising and promotional materials. He was one of the top-paid commercial artists in Detroit, which, because of the auto industry, was one of the largest commercial art markets in the country. Then one day, computers, equipped with new graphics software, and operated by less talented souls, made Bailey's special talent semi-obsolete. The new computer artists could produce similar results in a few hours, compared to the days it took Bailey and his fellow illustrators.

Nonetheless, Bailey hung on, and thanks to his persistence and willingness to adapt to the new technology, he managed to make a living. But the salad days were over. The term "scraped by" best described his financial status since the mid-eighties. He'd supplemented his income by painting still-life pieces and landscapes in oil and acrylic, which he sold at summer art fairs.

Now he was sick. Very sick. Pete drove out to Bailey's house to deliver a special assignment. When he came into the little home studio, seeing Bailey for the first time since Keenie's funeral, even though he'd been warned, he was startled. The man had lost at least 75 pounds. His face emitted a gray pallor, and every time he spoke, he generated a little coughing spell. When possible during their conversation, in lieu of talking, he spared his damaged lungs by nodding or gesturing.

The lung cancer diagnosis had come a year ago. The irony was that he didn't smoke. Never had. Unfortunately, a fellow artist, who shared a studio with Bailey, was a veritable chimney, providing further evidence to the claim of second-hand smoke contagion.

Rossi got the full story from Bailey's daughter, Debbie, when he called the week before.

She said, "The doctors haven't given up yet, but his attitude isn't good. He's real down. The insurance is done, and he's just about out of money. Don't know how they're planning to keep him alive, but they're not going to get paid for it, at least not by him or his insurance company. He's skeptical of what their commitment will be, once they know he can't pay. And he hates the thought of being a deadbeat."

Rossi said, "Give me the names and phone numbers of the medical providers. Tell him those bills are taken care of. He doesn't need to worry. And tell him it isn't charity, because I have a special project for him, and he'll earn every penny."

She hesitated, "What kind of project? You know he doesn't have much stamina. He's not well."

Rossi said, "It's personal, between him and me. And don't worry. If he hasn't lost his talents, he can handle it. He'll be able to take his time. It's not going to be a typical job, you know, with a rush deadline."

Debbie assured him that Bailey had not lost his eye or his "wrist."

Rossi brought copies of the birth certificates of the five dead men who had SSNs. He needed original birth certificates, or at least high quality fakes that would pass as originals. They would be used to obtain driver's licenses and passports. Bailey was to produce these undetectable fakes, and he had to promise secrecy ("You can't even tell Debbie."). Rossi explained they were to be used for a special top secret humanitarian project he was working on. He was honing his new skill as a liar. He assured Bailey they would not be used to cheat anyone out of money or valuables. As for workmanship, his faux originals would only be examined by the naked eye, no microscopes or electronic devices. They only needed to look real enough to get by the perfunctory inspection of the government clerk who would process the license or passport request for each one.

The bottom line is that Jim Bailey produced perfectly sepia-toned birth certificates with stamped embossments and sharp creases to look like they'd been folded and filed away for over half a century, and on fragile paper that appeared to be dried out and fraying from age. Rossi put them in an envelope and filed them for future use.

CHAPTER 28

THE WARDROBE CONSULTANT

Wednesday, September 20, 2006. "Let's do that brown one and all three of the gray ones and that sandy-colored one."

Rossi pointed at five of the eight wigs sitting on the counter, each with a color-matched mustache.

It was late September, 2006, just over six years since Keenie died. He was in a wardrobe/costume shop in Hollywood, where they outfitted actors for the film industry. The wigs he selected were made up in three different hair styles, giving him a variety of looks. The moustache styles varied also. He pointed at the full beard that went with the gray wigs, "That, too." He might only use one or two of the mustaches. He'd decide later.

The shop also had a wide selection of accessories including eyeglass frames with clear lenses, tinted contact lenses, fake faded-looking tattoo decals, fake pierced ear jewelry, and gum line inserts that temporarily altered the shape of an actor's jaw or cheek bones, like Marlon Brando did in "The Godfather." Brando used tissue. Rossi took a few of each. He also took a tube of the putty-like substance the clerk said could be used to broaden the bridge of his nose.

The clerk, or as she called herself, the wardrobe consultant, was quite helpful in pointing out all the accessories and options. Most of her customers were wardrobe stylists from the film production companies, pros who seldom wanted her input. So it was a bit of an ego trip for her to be able to "consult" with a real person who was actually going to wear the stuff. She took a genuine interest in his needs.

When he got home, he worked in front of a large dressing table mirror, the one Donna had used in their master bedroom. He tried on the various disguise pieces. He mixed and matched them until he came up with five distinctive looks. When he was satisfied with each look, he went out and tested it with people who he thought should recognize him – neighborhood grocery store cashiers, a waitress at a diner he frequented, a neighbor walking by in the grocery store parking lot. He even spoke to some of them – "I'll have to pay cash. I left my credit card home.;" "Make that a de-caf.;" "Think we're going to have an early winter?" – None of them did double takes or paid any unusual attention to him. All the disguises worked.

He had the passport pictures taken in five different combinations. Years later in his assassination journal, in spite of his stated commitment to "the whole truth," he would only make a passing reference to this preparation.

CHAPTER 29

JOURNAL – THE HIGH COURT

2pm, Monday, 12-29-2014.

In June of 2007, President Wheeler released the name of his nominee for the recently vacated seat on the Supreme Court. The nominee, Jesse D. Ramirez, was unknown to most of the country.

Not unknown to me. In my undercover investigator role, I attended a gun lobby fundraising event a year before. Ramirez was the speaker, and after his presentation, I spoke to him briefly.

He'd been very effective. Of course, I didn't like him for that reason, but the rest of the audience was in awe. He put on quite a show and raised a whole truckload of money for their cause. I remember thinking at the time he might make a good candidate for my Signore Pavoni. I made a note to find out more about him and later put it aside as an overreaction to the emotion of the moment, so there'd been no follow-up. One of the problems with my Plan B was its inconsistency, a lot of starting and stopping.

His nomination for the High Court refreshed my interest, got me going a little bit. The name was a surprise to the political world. Nobody in Washington knew much about him. He wasn't on any of the media lists, short or long. That morning news departments were all scrambling for info on him. Preliminary reports had Ramirez as a close associate and behind-the-scenes legal advisor to the president, particularly during the campaign for his second-term. At one time, he'd served on the New Mexico Supreme Court and once he argued a Second Amendment case in a federal appeals court. He did some work related to constitutional law for a conservative think tank before joining the White House. He was also involved in fund raising for one of the conservative PACs. He was on his third marriage and had no kids. The Democrats didn't like his resume, but the Republicans loved it, except the part about not being able to stay married. In his favor, the Republicans controlled the Senate, where the confirmation hearings would take place. He would be the fifth conservative justice, assuring their control of key Court decisions.

I knew a bit more, and held an admitted bias against his fund-raising prowess for the enemy, the gun rights lobby. My immediate reaction was to lament how damaging this was going to be to our side. Any reasonable chance of winning cases at the high court was now out the window.

People reading this may remember he zoomed through the Senate "advise and consent" process, one reason being President Wheeler had just returned to D.C. from his son's funeral. Everyone felt sorry for him, even the Democrats. The whole country, including the liberal media, wanted to avoid the appearance of partisanship, especially since the nominee seemed more a personal choice than political. Democratic senators discreetly remained quiet, also not wanting to give President Wheeler, a Republican with a little more than a year left on his second term, a hard time about anything, even his choice for the Supreme Court. Anyone who thought about speaking up against Ramirez risked being shouted down. One group, a committee of gun control advocates, put out a statement protesting his nomination, which was summarily ignored. The American Bar Association committee which traditionally vets Supreme Court candidates gave him a "qualified" rating, a downgrade from their top rating of "well qualified," but certainly better than "not qualified." The gun lobby weighed in by quietly putting several million dollars behind the confirmation, most of it in the form of promised – and threatened – future campaign donations.

As a result Ramirez didn't get a political vetting in keeping with the times. Probably didn't make much difference. Most of the bad stuff about him, of which there was plenty, was known by only a few people, none of whom were likely to spill the beans. And Ramirez had managed to keep the dirtiest dirt to himself; even his wife didn't know.

As it happened, it took me more than five years after his High Court appointment to get a good look into his secret closet. The reason it took so long, not to put too fine a point on it, I'd been equivocating again. What happened was my enthusiasm for the whole Lone Ranger idea had diminished. All I had on Ramirez was his fundraising prowess on behalf of the gun rights people, and his power as a Supreme Court justice to rule against sane gun control policy. As effective and powerful as he was, and as much as his efforts overwhelmed us, it was hardly enough to justify the kind of serious retribution Grampa envisioned. Plus the guy was a Supreme Court justice for crying out loud. No way I could pull that off. There'd be all kinds of security and media around and friends and family in the way. It was just too crazy to think about. And, of course, I was tired.

So instead of a real Lone Ranger target, Ramirez became more of a hobby for me, a fantasy target to help perk up the boring or sleepless times. It was stimulating, almost fun, to think about what I might do, *if only*.

It added to the game to try to learn more about him, follow his activities, watch the news for mentions of him. Surprisingly, there was very little, even on the Internet. Maybe I overestimated his importance.

I did find some articles he'd written for legal journals, mostly Second Amendment issues, plus one on the concept of "originalism," the idea that the Constitution should be interpreted according to what the framers intended when they wrote it. Apparently, it's a very conservative position. Most of his writing was unreadable to me. The legal jargon was dense.

The overall lack of fodder against him further diminished my interest. I couldn't assassinate a guy for his political opinions. I just didn't have enough to justify doing anything. Coincidentally, the previous winter I met the Mexican lady, Patricia, and we'd already started talking about a trip to Peru, which was another distraction.

On occasion, however, something would happen to bring me back. I'd be jolted into a renewed interest. For example I had occasional nightmares about Keenie and Donna. I'd see Keenie holding up a school paper in front of her face, trying to stop a bullet. Or Donna looking at me through a plastic bag. Unsettling to say the least, and interrupting what were relatively sleepless nights to begin with. These little touches of my personal PTSD would get me thinking again.

Throughout the years, periodic shootings, some of which were rightfully called massacres, lit up our TV screens and dominated the front pages of our newspapers. Of course the worst were the school shootings. Every time one of those horrors came on, I'd get a pad and paper out and start drawing up a new action outline.

The final straw was Sandy Hook in late 2012.

When that one came down, there could be no more backsliding. It was clear the political protestations – the thoughts and prayers from Congress and the president – wouldn't result in any meaningful action. I'd have to do something.

But what?

CHAPTER 30

JOURNAL – NEW MEXICO

5am, Tuesday, 12-30-2014

By 2012 Justice Ramirez was the only target on my list. The problem was I didn't have enough on him to take anything like Lone Ranger action. My mind was not so dulled by lack of sleep that I couldn't understand that. Through his fundraising acumen he was central to the success of the enemy, the gun rights lobby, and as a Supreme Court justice he was the ultimate roadblock to our causes. But it wasn't enough. I had to find someone who would truly offset Keenie's death. Someone whose loss could balance the ledger. He was the closest I'd come, but the case against him didn't pass the test.

For lack of anything better to do, I decided to try to learn more about him. Maybe find some juicy morsels to better support his candidacy as my Signore Pavoni. His fundraising proficiency for the gun lobby made him a real bad guy to me, but what if he was otherwise a saint with adoring grandchildren? What if he also raised large amounts of money for St. Jude's Hospital or something?

He was from New Mexico. Seemed like it would be a good place to start. I went there in March of 2013.

Raul Ramirez, J.D.'s brother, was first on my list of sources. I didn't expect to get anything meaty from him; it was just a place to start. Maybe I'd pick up a few leads.

I got to Raul's place about mid-afternoon on a Saturday, not having called ahead. When he opened his front door, I introduced myself as Gerald Renfro, a free lance writer from Chicago. To go with the fake name, I wore a disguise including a big walrus moustache. I was going more for unkempt academic than pin-stripe corporate. I told him I was writing a book about the behind the scenes' lives of the current U.S. Supreme Court justices which included his brother, Jesse. Raul agreed to talk with a "why not" shrug of his shoulders and showed me in.

His house was up in the northwest corner of New Mexico, just east of Farmington and the big Navajo Nation Reservation. We sat at the kitchen table. The large kitchen, in what once may have been a farmhouse, had a rough-hewn rural sort of charm with a little Aztec flavor thrown in. Both the table and kitchen chairs were hardwood. The chairs had maroon, home-made cushions, matching the home-made cloth valances over the windows.

Raul was 51, ten years younger than his brother, the justice. The ten-year youth advantage didn't show. He reminded me of the Indiana Jones line, "It's not the age, honey, it's the mileage." His odometer was showing a big number.

Raul was taller than his brother and heavier. His speckled gray whiskers were either a misguided attempt at the "stubble" beard or a week-long shaving oversight. The thinning hair on his head hadn't quite reached comb-over status. His skin was leathery, possibly from long-term exposure to the New Mexico sun. His deep brown eyes were surrounded by early signs of puffiness, which skipped down to a double chin, then to a paunchy stomach. A can of Coors, one clue to the excess flesh, sat in front of him. Further evidence was the five empties on the kitchen counter. He was off to a good start on what had the potential for a weekend spree. When he offered to have me join him, I opted for diet cola.

The un-tucked, pale blue tee shirt barely reached his beltline, which was substantially lower in front than in back. After his stomach, the extra flesh stopped. From there on down he was almost scraggy; his faded, denim pants were baggy. Nothing about him replicated his brother's elegant grooming or trim condition.

Raul wanted to talk. May have been the beer. Guess I showed up at the right time. Leaning forward in his chair, his forearms and hands resting on the table, as if protecting the not yet empty can of beer from thirsty predators, he said he worked for the local power company as an electrician, maybe promoting himself from lineman for my benefit. Said his wife was a social worker employed by the New Mexico Department of Indian Affairs. She worked with the Indians on the nearby reservation. She was part Navajo herself. That afternoon she was over in Shiprock, the biggest town on the Rez, for a tribal event of some sort. She and Raul had just celebrated their 25th wedding anniversary. No kids.

I asked a couple background questions on his childhood and upbringing, hoping it would lead to talk about his brother. He told me their father, Hector, was a cattle rancher and part time dabbler in oil exploration. He'd been big-time successful in both. Their mother, Imelda, was from Spain. They met overseas after WWII, when Hector was in the

Navy. Hector and Imelda had three kids, including one girl, who married a banker. All three kids grew up on the cattle ranch south of Albuquerque. Both Hector and Imelda were now deceased.

Nothing about the justice yet. Trying to segue gently I asked, "How often do you talk to J.D?"

Sitting up straight and folding his arms across his chest, he said, "He's a goddamned U.S. Supreme Court justice," as if that answered my question. He took a big chug on the beer can, tipping his head back until it was close to empty, then resumed his forward-leaning, protective posture.

Not sure if he was joking or angry I said, "Yeah, I know. It's why I'm here." Raul's demeanor was almost threatening. I told myself to be careful. Keep it general and maybe vague, "What's he like?"

Raul sat up straight again, refolded his arms across his chest and said, "I'd say he scores very high on the asshole quotient."

My, my. He was upset about something, not trying to cover it up, daring me to ask more. The beer had taken over. He got up from the table, turned to the refrigerator, opened it and grabbed another can. By my count that would be seven. "Sure you don't want a beer?"

"No thanks, not just yet. Gotta get my notes right."

As he popped the can, he asked, "You know anything about Mexican culture?"

"A little, I guess." I didn't tell him I'd been wintering in Mexico for years.

"Ever hear of a Criollo?"

I'd heard the word, but couldn't remember what it meant. "I guess not. Nothing comes to mind. What is it?"

Raul said, "Like most cultures, Mexicans are divided into socio-economic classes. The three main groups in Mexico are Criollos, Mestizos and Indians." All of a sudden the pissed off, beer drinking, electrician/lineman was a learned college professor, not drunk at all.

"Criollos are Mexicans who come from 'pure' Spanish breeding." When he said "pure," he did an air quote.

"No one in their family lineage has Indian blood. Not a drop. Some of 'em thinks their shit don't stink." (Back to the lineman.) He interrupted himself for a long swig of beer.

"Criollos are a minority in Mexico, but they make up much of the upper class. Doesn't take many people to make up the upper class in Mexico. They've got money and tend to control the economy and the government. They're usually better educated; they have lighter skin, and as a rule, their features look more European. Most Mexicans, on the other hand, come from mixed heritage – Spanish and Indian. They're called Mestizos. Some Criollo's use that word like they're referring to cockroaches.

"J.D. is a Criollo, as am I. The difference between him and me is: it's real important to him. He thinks he's genetically superior. He doesn't think of himself as a Mexican, 'cause too many Mexicans are Mestizos. Indian blood. He thinks Indians, coming from a primitive culture, are inferior beings, sub-humans. Basically, Jesse is a U.S Supreme Court justice of Mexican heritage who doesn't like Mexicans."

A long swig of beer.

"Truth is, it's all irrelevant. Both me and J.D. are Americans. We never lived in Mexico. We were born here, as was our father. But we've got that "ez" at the end of our name, so everybody thinks of us as Mexicans, which is fine with me. It's my heritage. But it just kills J.D."

"And on top of that he thinks any Criollo who marries a Mestizo or an Indian is some kind of racial traitor, diluting his pure bloodline, like mixing fine, expensive bourbon with Old Crow. He thinks I'm a disgrace to my family and my ethnic heritage."

He definitely wanted to talk.

"When Rainey and I got married, he refused to come to the wedding, which really pissed me off at the time. But I got over it."

I thought, *or not*.

"After awhile I decided it was just as well he wasn't there. He was such a big pain in the ass."

"Was?"

"Well, I haven't seen much of him in years, so I can't say about lately. But back in the day, he certainly was."

"How so?" I tried to look only mildly interested.

Pause to gulp on the beer can, "Don't know where to start. Probably shouldn't be tellin' you any of this, but he used to get my goat sometimes."

He was calming down. I didn't want him to clam up on me, so I tried to prime the pump a little, "What was he like as a boy on the ranch?"

"I guess he was about as nasty as a boy on a ranch could be. Almost mental, like he was a product of inbreedin' or something, which would be real irony." That made him chuckle.

His words were getting louder and more emphatic. And the chuckle bordered on an outright laugh. The beer was kicking in for sure.

Have to keep him talking. I said, "For example?"

He thought for a moment. "One thing was the guns. Lotta' people like guns. But J.D. took it to a different level. He totally got off on 'em. He thought he was Billy the Kid or somethin'. Used to practice a quick draw. Got so people were afraid of him."

"Just handguns?"

"Mostly. Revolvers. Thirty-eights, like in the cowboy movies. He loved to do target practice. He'd shoot at soda cans full of water. Pretend he was in a gunfight. Fast draw the shit outta' those cans. The water'd spray up in the air when he hit one. Shoulda' seen his face. Like someone winning the Publishers' Clearing House. He loved the noise, the loud cracks when he pulled the trigger. The louder the better. I wondered what went on in his head. One time he filled one of the cans with gasoline. When it went up with a real deep whomp and then a whoosh as the flames jumped in every direction, his eyes got so big, like he was gonna cream his jeans. He got so jacked, it was scary.

"Used to shoot at small animals. Use 'em for target practice. He'd wound 'em, let 'em limp away, then start shootin' at 'em again till he killed 'em. One time I caught him shooting at an armadillo from about ten feet. He didn't need to do that. They don't hurt nobody. Real nice, huh? Thinks he's better'n an Indian. Asshole. Finally Dad rationed his ammunition. That really pissed him off. Yeah, when it came to guns, he was a little crazy."

I skipped past the "crazy" comment. "He never used a rifle?"

"Oh, he'd use anything. But you get closer with a pistol. It was kind of a Wild West gunfighter thing with him. He seemed to like that feelin'."

"His interest in guns why you say he was nasty?"

"Oh, no. Lots of people like to shoot once in a while. It's the way he did it. Another thing, he didn't seem to like people. He was unpleasant, unless he wanted something. Then he could be real nice, a goddamned chameleon. Change colors on a dime. He was always nice to Dad. Needed him for ammo and gas money and college tuition, like that. Rest of the time he was just a real asshole. Wasn't even the worst of it."

"What was worse?" I was trying to become his best friend; the beer was helping.

He paused, as if wondering if he was going too far. Then he took the bit and raced ahead, "Well, there was a problem on the reservation. It was Indian girls. Little Indian girls, I think. But I was pretty young myself then, and it was hushed up, so coulda' been a lotta things, I guess."

"Little Indian girls, you mean minors?"

"Yeah, I think so."

"When did this happen? How old was he?"

"When he got caught was his first summer back from college, I think. He woulda' been about 19 or 20. Probably shouldn't be tellin' you this."

"What're you saying?"

"Nothin' I guess. Just some suspicions of mine. Nothin' you can put in your book."

No, I thought, don't worry. There isn't going to be a book. But does this mean he's a real Signore Pavoni?

Raul took another long swig of beer, tipping the can up and glugging noisily until it was empty. He got up from the table for another trip to the fridge, number eight, again asking me if I was ready for one. Clearly a generous host.

Trying to keep the incredulity out of my tone, I asked, "What happened? Did he get caught? What was the outcome?"

"Apparently, a couple of the girls reported him to the tribal police, but Dad squelched it, somehow. He musta' paid somebody off. I don't know."

What if he was just playing with me? I'd have to confirm it all. How would I do that?

"Raul, you think there's anyone else might know something about any of this?"

A pause to think. Took a swig of the beer in his hand. "I don't know. Be hard. Long time ago. Some of the ranch hands knew stuff. But that was over forty years ago. May not be any of 'em left. At least none who want to talk about it. But you never know. He was a mean little bastard back then. Wasn't very well liked. I can give you some names. You never know.

"Maybe Vicky, my sister. Or maybe not. She's got some health problems. Might not want to get involved. I'll give you her number. If she doesn't want to talk to you, don't pester her, or you'll have me on your ass. She's been through a lot. No need to upset her any more."

We talked for another hour or so, during which he had at least two more beers.

He said, "J.D's been married three times. Might be one of the wives would know something worth writing about. Wouldn't be surprised.

"I remember there was a period not too long after he got out of college when he worked for a guy who was into what they called direct marketing – direct mail, telemarketing, stuff like that. J.D. did some legal work for him. I'm not sure what. He also got into sales training with him – teaching people how to sell stuff. J.D. got pretty good at that. He was a real whiz up on a stage in front of an audience. Never understood that. Didn't seem like something he'd be good at. One on one he wasn't much of a personality, unless he was sucking up for something."

"What was the guy's name, the guy he worked with?"

"Hodgeson…Hobson or something."

"Know where he is now?"

"I think he's in real estate in Albuquerque."

"J.C. was on the New Mexico Supreme Court. How did that happen?"

"I don't know. He did well in law school. Top grades. Probably sucked up to the professors. One thing, J.D. was a whiz bang fundraiser for the gun people, you know, the NRA and so forth. That turned into a Republican thing of some kind. Might be how he got appointed. He resigned when his term was up. He never stood for election. He could'na got elected to anything, I don't think. He wasn't much good with people, 'cept for the fundraising, and when he needed somethin'."

He gave me the names of a couple hands who worked the family ranch when he and J.D. were young, men who might still be alive and findable.

Then his wife, Rainey, came home. She told him no more beer, and he, apparently, wasn't inclined to cross her. This new restriction also ended his interest in talking to me.

I left with my brain overflowing. Juicy, juicy material. I sat in the rental car trying to take it all in. Raul didn't like his brother. His brother was addicted to handguns. His brother was kind of two-faced. His brother was a racist when it came to Indians. All lamentable faults but not capital offenses. The one rumor-like allegation – his brother raped little girls – was the potential tipping point. But it would have to be verified. When I started the engine, I turned to look at the house. Raul was at the kitchen window, watching me. Was he feeling regret about blabbing to me?

JOURNAL: 3pm, Tuesday, 12-30-2014

My motel was north of Albuquerque on U.S 550 just east of the Rio Grande. The drive from Farmington was long, but scenic in a southwestern kind of way. Along the way I stopped for dinner and didn't get to the motel till well after dark, which was okay, because I never went to sleep till late anyway.

Most of that night and the next morning I spent searching the Internet. Didn't find much. The exception being the law firm where Ramirez once worked. It went on the bottom of my to-do list. Late in the morning I went down to the old family ranch where I struck out on surviving ranch hands from the time when J.D. was allegedly such a bad boy.

J.D.'s sister lived in Rio Rancho, an upscale suburban community on the northwest side of Albuquerque. Some of Rio Rancho was more upscale than the rest. The most upscale part was where J.D.'s sister's house was. She was the middle child, four years younger than J.D., and a widow. Her husband died of a massive heart attack two years earlier.

The Spanish style, beige, two-story house sat back and up high on a large piece of choice property. The long circle drive was surrounded by southwest landscaping including a mix of turf, decorative stone and well-trimmed low shrubs. The banker husband must have worked at a big bank.

Rather than just show up on her doorstep, I phoned ahead. She was expecting my call; Raul had forewarned her. She agreed to see me that afternoon but without great energy or enthusiasm in her voice.

A young woman answered the door, attractive, business-like outfit, in her 30s, said her name was Kim. She led me to a patio in the back. It was a nice day in March, allowing us to sit outside.

An older woman and a man were waiting there. The man, maybe in his fifties, wore a priest's collar on a short-sleeved black shirt. He reached out and said, "Mike Lopez."

I took his hand and said, "Gerald Renfro."

The woman introduced herself as Victoria. I remembered Raul called her Vicky. She didn't look well, no color to speak of. Her face and body language showed the same weariness I'd heard on the phone. She was 57 years old; and like her brother, Raul, she looked older than her years.

They sat me in a chair facing Victoria and the priest with Kim almost between us on my right. We were all in matching wooden chairs with comfortable built-in, cloth-covered padding. For a few seconds, which seemed much longer to me, no one spoke. The scene had an ominous, somber air to it. It reminded me of the meeting with the police lieutenant in Northville, thirteen and a half years earlier.

I wondered why the other two were there. Was Kim a lawyer? I hoped not. If she was, I probably wasn't going to learn much.

Victoria read my thoughts and broke the silence, "Kim is my daughter. I've had some health issues, so I asked her and Father Lopez to sit in."

What was she afraid of? Why a support team?

Kim spoke next, "Mom is still recovering. She's been through a lot lately." I didn't know what she meant by "a lot."

When she heard from Raul, she called Kim and the priest, and they agreed to help, assuming I showed up. It still wasn't clear to me why she needed them. Did Raul tell her I might be dangerous?

I decided to start as I had with Raul, with a general, ice-breaker type question, "When was the last time you talked to Justice Ramirez?"

Another brief silence, then Kim jumped in, "Mr. Renfro, what are you going to do with this information?"

"Well, as I explained to Raul, I'm writing a book about the private lives of all the members..."

Victoria interrupted, "Who are you?"

The little old sick lady got right to it, didn't she?

When I planned this trip, I knew I'd have to conceal my identity. Years ago I had false ID made up that looked authentic. It was in my wallet, along with some recently printed business cards. I was still in full disguise: wig, bushy mustache, horn-rimmed glasses, and a fake semper fi tattoo on my arm. Nevertheless, the directness of Victoria's question rattled me.

"Uh...I'm Gerald Renfro." I fumbled for a card, wrote my cell phone number on the back, and handed it to Kim, who was nearest. The cell phone was a throw away I'd bought just for this trip.

Victoria was staring at me, as if trying to solve a puzzle. "What books have you written?"

Her question told me they'd been doing some research. Probably Googling Gerald Renfro. This was going badly. Still, I didn't want to give up without trying. Before I left home I knew at some point I'd have to rely on the new me, who, I suppose, wasn't that new anymore. Over the years I'd become more comfortable with lying. If Grampa could maintain a big lie for all that time, I could tell some little ones.

I dove in, "Nothing that's been published. But if I can confirm some of what Raul told me, and find a good editor, that might change."

"If you've never been published, how do you pay the bills?" She wouldn't let it go. For a sick, worn out person, she held on like a Terrier with a ring toy.

I might have to get way out there with the mendacity. Fortunately I'd rehearsed this scene. I anticipated that at some point Gerald Renfro might need to be somebody who, with plausibility, could not be found on Google. To justify the anonymity, I picked a couple of professions that didn't get a lot of publicity.

"I've made a living as an accountant for a few smaller companies and sometimes as a locksmith. My writing is a long time avocation. Mostly for myself; to keep my mind working. Getting published has never been a priority. Now that I'm retired, I thought it might be fun to one day find my book in a bookstore. Something to be remembered for. It's not about money." A little tingle passed through my shoulders as I went on with such effortless guile.

Victoria continued to press, but with a slight change of tone, not as accusing, "Are you really going to do all the justices, or are you just after J.D.?"

I struck a "not sure" pose.

"Good question. I was planning to do them all, but after talking to Raul, the other eight are looking kind of dull. I may have to change my plans." I can't say I enjoyed lying, but it was as if there was a reservoir of deception welled up inside me and pushing to get out. I'd crossed over into a make-believe world, except, unlike Alice, I was the maker.

The priest maintained his silence, seeming to concentrate on my answers.

I added, "If you don't want to talk to me, I won't pressure you. Raul was rather firm on that. I'm here because I need confirmation of what Raul said, another source. I know I'll have to have more than one. Otherwise, no publisher will touch it."

I knew nothing about libel law. It just sounded good to me. I wanted some reassurance that Raul wasn't a complete kook. Once I had that comfort level, I could proceed with my Lone Ranger plans.

She followed up, "Raul's very smart, very intuitive. And he's a good man. We're very close." Was that code?

She paused, as if to catch her breath; talking was work for her. "You probably think he's just a laborer for the Utility up there. Well, he's a lot more than that. He helps people, especially the Indians. Truth is he doesn't really need that lineman job. He's got plenty of money. He was well taken care of in the will. He called me last night. Said he told you some things. Said he had a little too much to drink. Sometimes he does that. He's not happy with his older brother."

Another pause. "He had questions about you." In spite of her drained condition, she was trying to be thorough. "He thought maybe you weren't exactly what you said you were. He didn't know what, though. He didn't think you were law enforcement either, maybe a private investigator. Maybe working for a lawyer or for the Democrats. I don't have any reason to want to…be involved in anything like that."

It was a mouthful for her. She was tiring, slowing down. The priest remained quiet, just watched intently.

I deflected her question, "Raul did have a lot to say. I don't know what else to tell you; I've got no proof of who I am or what I'm doing. The book is only a bunch of notes so far. But if I don't get some kind of confirmation of what Raul told me, it can't go in the book. The lawyers will throw themselves on the presses before they'll allow it to be printed."

I'd never lied so much in my life. Why were we even having this conversation? Was she going to confirm Raul's allegations or not? If not, what difference does it make who I was? On the other hand, she certainly wasn't going to admit that her Supreme Court brother raped young girls. Was she?

She interrupted the flow, asking if anyone would like coffee. Kim did, and Victoria arose from the chair with some effort. The priest broke his silence, "Let me help you." They left Kim and me on the patio.

We didn't speak until Kim said in a soft, almost whisper, "Her prognosis has changed."

I said nothing, but the expression on my face gave off a question mark.

She explained that her mother was undergoing cancer treatment. She'd just come out from under the grief of her husband's death, when she got the cancer news. A double mastectomy and two rounds of chemo had taken their own toll. Some kind of radiation was still to come. That's what she meant when she said her mother had "been through al lot lately."

Kim said, "When she was first diagnosed, it was 50/50. Now they're less confident. Apparently, it's spreading."

Still not speaking, I gave a look of sympathy.

"Is that why he's here?"

"Not exactly, mostly he's here to check you out. Mom thinks since he's a priest, he should be a good judge of character...know when people are telling the truth...whether they can be trusted. They're probably in there talking about you now."

Apparently Kim had already decided in my favor.

"I think she knows some things about Uncle Jesse. She told Father Mike, and he convinced her she should go public, but it's very embarrassing. Uncle Jesse is her brother," still just above a whisper.

"She doesn't know what to do. It's a family thing. She's not exactly close with Uncle Jesse, but she thinks it's time to try to mend fences. She also thinks he may have changed. In her condition…in case it doesn't go well…I hate to say that...she just wants her family to be closer. She doesn't want to do anything to drive them further apart. When she goes, she wants everyone to be friends. Kind of a pipe dream, maybe, but… she just cant' go out and tell the world her brother, the Supreme Court justice, is a...has had problems. On the other hand she'd like to get it off her conscience like Father Mike says." Kim put her hands up in front of her eyes and swept them back over her hair in a gesture of frustration.

I started to feel guilty. If they only knew what I was planning. I wanted to change the subject. I asked, "What do you do?"

"Therapy, psychotherapy. I work with abused women and children, mostly."

OMG! Does she know what's been said about her uncle?

"I might as well tell you," she looked at the door wall through which her mother and the priest had exited the patio. "Mom is very ashamed of her brother, and she wishes he wasn't in such a public position, you know, a Supreme Court justice. And she's afraid…afraid of what he might do. Of course, he's only one of nine…still he's in a terribly powerful position. Some say it's more powerful than the president. But again, he's family. It keeps her awake, sometimes. Me, too."

"What might he do?"

"There's no telling. I'm not supposed to make long distance diagnoses, but he…one thing he does, he manipulates people, he can be frightfully persuasive, and he has no regard for the truth. It's all too scary."

"Raul told Mom he'd been drinking a bit when you were there, and he might've been a little too talkative. He was having second thoughts about some of the things he told you."

Like what? She wouldn't say the words. Nobody was willing to spell it out, to say the terrible words, not even the professional psychotherapist.

Victoria and the priest returned; he carried the coffee tray. She went to her chair and sat down as he distributed the filled cups. Everyone took it black.

After a sip, I decided to get right to it. "Victoria, I think we ought to get this over with. If you want me to leave now, I will. No hard feelings. You just need to take care of yourself and get better."

I didn't want to give up on what Raul said about young Indian girls, but what the hell, it seemed like I already knew the answer. Everybody was dancing around it. No need to put this lady through any more trouble. She had enough without me nosing around.

"Mr. Renfro," she hesitated and looked at the priest, "What would you like to know?"

"Tell me about his friends. Who was he close to?" Semi innocuous information.

She said, "I'm not sure I know much about his friends. I'm not close to that part of his life. He's been gone from New Mexico for a long time. There was one guy he met through a shooting club. Name of Martindale. Though I don't think they were really friends, like most of us might have. They were both into political stuff. I don't think he really had friends like most people do; you know, people to get together with and have a drink or go to a party. Mostly, he knew people who were involved in Republican activities and guns and stuff."

I remembered the name, Martindale, from the fundraising event where I first came across Ramirez. Disparate details were coming together, slowly coalescing. At this point I didn't care what she told me. I pretended to write a few notes and tried to figure out a way to end the interview.

Then she started up again, "Jesse loved to shoot, especially hand guns. It was kind of a cowboy thing. He seemed to get a kick out of acting like a cowboy. Through the shooting club, or Martindale, I'm not sure which, he got involved with the NRA. And from that he got into Republican politics. I don't think he really had any deep philosophical political positions on anything, he just liked the guns. Then somehow he got into fundraising for political candidates. J.C. was real good at fundraising. Never understood it. Didn't seem like it'd be his thing."

I wasn't going to ask the tough questions. The woman was sick. Just get out of there. I looked at my watch, suggesting I was on some kind of schedule, thanked them as sincerely as I could muster, and left.

I headed back to my motel planning to call the others on my list. After a quick shower I was going out for an early dinner, when my cell phone rang. I answered, "Renfrow."

A woman's voice said, "One of them is Marlene Descheene, and she's in Las Cruces." The voice spelled out the name "Descheene," then silence, followed by a click and a dial tone. The caller spoke quickly, hoping to disguise her voice. Sounded like Kim to me. Dinner could wait.

JOURNAL: 5am, Wednesday, 12-31-2014

I turned back to my room, opened my laptop and got on the Internet. It took me an hour and a half to find a Marlene Descheene in Las Cruces. Dinner followed and included two glasses of wine – a little celebration. The next morning at 4:45 I was headed south on I-25. Las Cruces was down near El Paso, Texas and the Mexican border. It took almost four hours.

I stopped at Dunkin' Donuts and had a light second breakfast before going to the woman's address. Got there about 9:30. The house was a significant downgrade from Victoria's Rio Rancho digs.

I knocked four times, each progressively louder, before she answered. Apparently the knocking woke her up. I asked if she was Marlene Descheene. She eyed me up and down with suspicion. When silence no longer sufficed, she confirmed her identity by asking, "Who wants to know?"

Her gray hair was disheveled and she was wearing a knee- length, pale green bathrobe. She was short; about 30 pounds overweight, and desperately needed a makeover. Marlene had put 56 years into life, paid a substantial toll and gotten no change. She was no longer an innocent little waif, certainly not someone a prosecuting attorney would want as a star witness. With me as prosecutor, judge and jury, that wouldn't be a problem.

Standing at her front door, she kept looking over my shoulder. Turned out she was living with her boyfriend, Manuel something or other, who, she said, was out of town. Her behavior suggested he was illegal, not uncommon for Las Cruces. She scanned the street again, as if looking for a team of ICE agents. It took me a few minutes to convince her I was there about her, not Manual. Finally, she asked me in, and as with Raul, we sat at her kitchen table.

I gave her a different cover story than I'd used with Raul and his sister. I said, "I'm a private investigator, looking for information on a series of sexual assaults back in the early '70s on young girls on the Navajo Reservation. Your name came up as possibly one of the victims."

"How'd it come up?"

"One of the other girls. I'm not authorized to give their names."

"Why do you want to know?" A bit hostile, but also a bit interested.

"I work for an attorney who's trying to help out the victims, maybe get some kind of settlement."

That got her attention. "Was the guy's name Jesse Ramirez?"

I paused, as if reluctant to reveal privileged information, then giving in, "Yes, it was."

"What are you gonna do? What kinda settlement they talkin' about?"

"Don't know, but it could be big. He's very wealthy."

That was the icebreaker. She said, "It's true." Now, like Raul, she wanted to talk. "I was thirteen, hitchhiking. I didn't want to tell my parents, but he messed me up some; I had bruises, my blouse was torn. My mother could tell somethin' happened. She asked me questions. When I told her, she told my father, and he got real upset with me, like it was partly my fault. Then they took me to the tribal police to file a complaint. Then a few weeks later, they suddenly got over it. Like night and day. They bought me a new pair of tennis shoes, the best shoes I'd ever had. That was it, a pair of tennis shoes. Right after that my parents bought a new car, first one they'd ever had. Somethin' happened there."

As she talked, I got the impression the whole experience had set the tone for the rest of her life. She not only got raped, she also got screwed.

The evidence was starting to form a pile. Not quite piling up, but close. I wanted to believe her; the sonofabitch had raped young girls. Raul thought so, and in his somewhat inebriated state, blurted it out. The girl, Marlene Descheene, identified him by name without any prompting. And the voice on the phone – almost surely his niece, Kim – believed it also. If it was true, he was the same as Signore Pavoni. And Bella and Keenie were the same. And Grampa and I were the same. Two parallel sets of dots lining up on the chart. What more do I need?

Since I was already in New Mexico, and had spent the better part of a day in cars, airports and airplanes getting there, I decided not to cut my trip short and to continue sleuthing. You never know; something absolutely 100 percent convincing might turn up.

On the fourth morning I visited J.D.'s estranged wife, Cynthia. She left him two years earlier and moved to Taos, the art community up in the mountains north of Santa Fe. Though not an artist, she had enough money to be welcome to hang out with them.

She wasn't a particularly attractive woman, kind of short and thick, with a jaw maybe a bit too big for her face. She could have used a makeover, or maybe it wouldn't have helped.

I started with my usual, a wide-open question, "What is Justice Ramirez like?"

She thought about it, avoiding my eyes, "Oh, alright, I guess."

My interviewing success in the last three days made me bold enough to push harder, "Why are you in Taos instead of with him in Washington?"

"We didn't have a good marriage. I guess that's why most people separate." She apparently believed a straight question deserved a straight answer.

I gave her another push, "When did it go bad? What happened?"

She caved real fast, deciding to just lay it out, maybe get it over with and get rid of me quickly. "It went downhill right after we were married. I hung on as long as I could, almost eleven years."

"What was the problem? Did he do something wrong?" Maybe a little too forward, but what the hell.

She said, "He wasn't very loving or much fun to be with. He was inconsiderate. Everything was about him. After awhile, I felt like he was just using me, like he'd only married me for the money." Turns out she'd inherited a pile of it.

"Nothing in common?"

"Sometimes we'd ride together."

"Ride?" The word startled me.

"Yes. We both like horses. One of the few things we had in common. Not much else."

He rode horses? Like Signore Pavoni? Well, well. My stomach made a small flip.

I said, "What did he do other than horseback riding?"

"He had his guns. He set up a range out back at the country house. Spent some time out there. And he travelled. Kept going off on long trips to the Far East, to Thailand. Never asked me to go with him. One time I made up my mind I was going whether he liked it or not. I don't like to talk about money, but I was paying for his trips back then, at least part of the costs. We ended up going to Hong Kong and Macao. It was boring as heck. He didn't want to do anything. We spent all that money to get there and did nothing. Never even went to the casinos. I got tired of it. I never went with him after that."

Still trying not to think about Signore Pavoni and horses, I asked about abuse. Bringing it up was awkward, almost rude; nonetheless, I plowed into it. She said no, he'd never hit her. Very matter of fact. After pausing, she qualified it, "He could be very abusive in things he said, though. Lots of sarcastic, hurtful words." Another pause. "As bad as that was, it was worse when he just stopped talking to me altogether. Ignored me. It was like he no longer cared enough to insult me. So I left.

"I hated Washington anyway. Nobody there was truly nice to you. People in Taos are friendlier. So is the climate."

"Why haven't you divorced him?"

"No need yet, but probably someday, when he does something to make it necessary. Money's not an issue. I sold the house in Chevy Chase. I'm not supporting him any more, except I haven't sold the country house yet. He uses it quite a bit, I think. I guess he's doing alright financially. I'm not sure how. All the travel is pretty expensive for his salary. I'm pretty sure he goes first class all the way."

"Who are his friends? Who does he socialize with?"

She was quick and clear, "He doesn't have any, least he didn't then. He and President Wheeler got along during the second campaign; Jesse was a major fund raiser. Just amazing how charming he could be up in front of a crowd or asking people for money in a meeting. Anyway he got in with the president pretty good. He didn't see the president all that often socially, but he had a lot of meetings with him.

"There was a guy named Martindale he met with every once in a while and another one named Straight, but they weren't exactly friends. They just talked political stuff, fund raising and such. Didn't seem to me they liked each other that much. Most of the time they'd go into the den and close the door. They had that interest in common, politics, but nothing else, as far as I could tell. J.D. never said anything that made me think he actually liked them."

I left thinking about horseback riding. Was it just a coincidence? Do a lot of people do that? Another pair of dots on the parallel lines on the chart.

The two ex-wives wouldn't see me or even talk to me on the phone once I told them what I was about. I wondered what they knew, and what they were hiding, and why. Maybe nothing. Just didn't want to stir up bad memories.

Near the end of the day I called the justice's old legal firm. Talked to a guy named Everitt. His answers were guarded. I asked him about the state supreme court and why J.D. didn't run when his term was up. He said I should ask J.D. I asked him about guns; if J.D.'s interest in them was a little over the top. He said, "What's over the top?" I asked if he'd ever heard anything about a problem on the reservation. He said no. After that he said he had another appointment, said he had to go and hung up.

Next I called the old partner, Hobson. As Raul guessed, Hobson was now in real estate. Said he was too busy to meet with me. I asked about the nature of their partnership. He said he had some customers with him and he'd call me back. He never did.

I was out of New Mexico on the fifth day, and after getting home, my fake persona, Gerald Renfro, disappeared, never to be seen again. Well, almost never. Those five days were good for me. I was inspired.

CHAPTER 31

JOURNAL – THE LAST NAIL

5am, Thursday, 1-1-2015

New Mexico was 21 months ago. In the interim I've been quite busy, busier than I've been for years. The focus of my busyness has been the justice, of course. And my research reveals astounding information about him. Specifically, I investigated his tendency for unexplained travel to the Far East. The answer to that one is, as Grampa used to say, a doozy. Grampa might also have called it the last nail in the justice's coffin.

Here's what I found and how I found it.

Per the justice's wife, his favorite destination is Bangkok, Thailand, and he goes there at least quarterly. Lying awake (as usual), I wondered why. What kind of secret activity takes him there? An off-shore business? Politics? Or a girlfriend? What is he hiding, all those airplane hours away? And, if his purpose is clandestine, how does he pull it off without anyone taking notice? Maybe I should go with him next time. Without his permission, of course.

First I went to Washington to get a closer look. In fact, since New Mexico, I've been in the D.C. area multiple times, often enough to have lost count. I've purposely not kept a written record. I use my own car and pay for everything in cash. No airlines, no rental cars and only cheap motels, a different one each trip. And I keep a safe distance from my target, so there will be no cell phone photos on Instagram or Snapchat of me standing near him.

He lives in a small rented condo in Georgetown. Cynthia, his wife, left him sometime in 2009. She owned the house they lived in and sold it, further confirmation that she left with no intention of ever returning. As she indicated to me, she still owns a country house in Fauquier County, Virginia which he uses occasionally, almost like a Russian dacha. He goes out there about every other weekend, when he isn't traveling to Bangkok, of course. The rest of the time he resides in the Georgetown condo.

I've been in the condo twice. Both uninvited. Both B & E's, courtesy of my old locksmith tools, which for some reason I never disposed of. My touch was a bit rusty, but the door locks on the condo were less than stellar. Both visits were after dark while he was out at the country house.

The country house is about sixty miles from D.C. I've been in it five times. Again not as an invited guest. Getting into the country house was more of a challenge. The locks on all the outside doors were beyond my limited skills. Even the windows were fairly burglar-proof. But my experience in the residential security business served me well. (I'll explain in a minute.)

I've thoroughly surveyed both places inside and out. Except for the basement at the country house which was sealed up like a submarine. One time, I was actually in the country house with him. I was there when he arrived, and I elected to stay, allowing me to closely watch his movements inside the house; track his habits. That was a bit risky, so I only did it the one time. And I got out of there post haste when he went into the john. Point is: I've become familiar with the layouts and surroundings of both places, which has led to the decision that the country house is the place to do it. It's nicely isolated, and he never has visitors out there. Actually he rarely has visitors anywhere.

While in the Georgetown condo, I logged onto his home computer. The password is on a list in his desk. (Real secure.) I reviewed his calendar on that computer and was able to confirm that he keeps it up and follows it. The calendar is how I know he plans to go to the country house on Feb. 13, how he will get there, and what time he expects to arrive and leave. If his plans change at the last minute, and he doesn't show up on schedule or gets there early, we'll simply abort, go home and reschedule.

The computer is also how I found out about his Far East travel. Someone made reservations on his computer to go to Bangkok. The reservations were made in the name of Joseph Howell. Who could that be? Joseph was scheduled to fly out of Atlanta's Hartsfield Airport (not Dulles) on Saturday morning in September, 2013. The routing called for a plane change in Los Angeles, then non-stop from there to Bangkok. All first class.

In an envelope in his bedroom sock drawer (how original) there was a passport, credit card and other ID for Mr. Howell. The passport picture looked (surprise) a little like Justice Ramirez with longer, darker hair; horned rim glasses and a moustache. So he does travel incognito. Fake ID, disguise, and leaving from an airport where he is unlikely to encounter someone who might recognize him, especially in disguise. Pretty sure it's illegal to fly with false ID. Particularly if you're a Supreme Court justice. As it turned out, there were two people on that plane with false IDs and disguises. Mine were far more convincing than his, but his were sufficient for his purposes, I guess.

The question was, *why Bangkok, Thailand?*

The answer should've been obvious, at least to anyone inclined to believe the worst. It wasn't to meet a girlfriend. Not exactly, but sorta. Actually, a plethora of girlfriends. All very young. So young as to be considered minors by law and social norms. So young that having any kind of sex with them is called statutory rape, at least in the USA. Not to mention the likelihood that you're providing support to a human trafficking operation. Travel pros know that among Thailand's many attractions, the availability of child prostitutes is foremost: young girls and boys – very young, if you prefer. You can find actively commercial underage sex elsewhere – it is sex, after all – but why not go to the world headquarters? Pedophilia and underage sexual predation is to Bangkok as snow is to Buffalo. (I later found out that a sexual interest in post-pubescent boys or girls is not technically considered pedophilia. Pedophilia refers to children before puberty. Most 12- or 13-year olds are pubescent or post-pubescent. Hence, my usage of the term "underage sexual predation.") Clearly, J.D. had not experienced some miracle cure; he still liked young girls, preferably 12- or 13-years old. Sating his special need was too risky on home turf, so he went to the other side of the planet where no one would recognize him.

And he always went first class, adding up fare and lodging numbers he shouldn't have been able to afford. Where'd he get the money?

Bottom line: all the dots on the chart were in place. J.D. Ramirez was a clone of Signore Pavoni. He was my Goliath. The Lone Ranger card was in play.

CHAPTER 32

JOURNAL – THE PLAN

5am, Friday, 1-2-2015

Now to the details of how we're going to do it. This plan is guided by three overarching considerations.

First, we'll take every precaution, as I have right along, to assure we're not apprehended. The primary concern*: don't get caught*. I've already paid for this crime. No need to be punished again. I'm convinced it's the right thing to do. The guy is evil. Even without the Keenie motive, I'm doing the world a favor, like Grampa did. So, I don't want to rot in jail for it, or certainly not expose Dylan to retribution of any kind.

The second consideration is to inflict no collateral damage. We will carry out this mission so as to assure *no innocent bystanders will be harmed* in the process. That's one of the advantages of the farmhouse. No one else will be around.

The third major consideration is to be humane. This aspect is important to me. Maybe another Grampa thing. The Lone Ranger would likely feel the same way. Our method must assure the justice *does not suffer unnecessary trauma*. We're not barbarians. The objective is to correct an imbalance in society, nothing more. (Except the hoped for by-product of me being able to sleep again.) We are not seeking to inflict pain or anguish. As deplorable as he is as a person, we will take no pleasure in hurting him. Nor would we want to cause extra grief to innocent loved ones, though apparently, he has no loved ones, innocent or otherwise.

Beginning with our priority to maximize immunity to detection, we will do the following:

- Avoid exposure to surveillance cameras throughout the trip. This means travel by car. No airports or train stations or bus depots. And during the trip, no toll roads. I've mapped out a route to avoid the toll roads in Ohio and Pennsylvania. It'll add about 75 minutes to our trip. Not a problem; we'll have plenty of time. For further assurance that we're not inadvertently photographed or filmed, I have electronically scanned the last 30 miles of the route and found no operational road-directed surveillance cameras.
- *Not* stop in gas stations, restaurants, or official rest areas. Our vehicle, a black Tahoe, will carry the necessary food, drink, gas and equipment to meet all our needs for the entire round trip. We will only get out of the vehicle in remote areas to stretch our legs and pour gasoline from our onboard gas cans into the tank, and, of course, to enter the farmhouse. As for bodily functions, we will have equipment inside the vehicle to handle that.
- *Not* stay in a motel. We will leave my apartment in Southfield at 4:30 a.m. on Friday, returning about the same time Saturday morning.

Each of us will be able to sleep in the vehicle, while the other is driving. (Might not be an issue for me.)

- Leave no forensic evidence. They won't find DNA traces, fingerprints, footprints, or tire prints at the scene. While there, our sleeves and pant legs will be secured with elastic bands, preventing hair and skin flakes from escaping. The hair on our heads will be cut closely and covered with watch caps. From arrival to departure we'll wear latex gloves. Of course, we won't use the toilets or sinks or any appliances. If a microscopic trace of fabric from our clothing rubs off on any surface, it will not be traceable to us, because all our articles of clothing, including Dylan's, were purchased months ago with cash at Target. No chance a clerk will remember that purchase or the purchaser. The clothes will be donned upon arrival at the scene, removed immediately after leaving, and when we get home, burned in a high temperature burn box. The ashes will be indistinguishable from moon dust. The assassination will be carried out in a manner that will give the justice no opportunity to bite or scratch us. Nor will he shed any blood, at least not to an extent that we could be contaminated by it.
- Avoid exposure to eye witnesses. The farmhouse has been selected primarily because of its remote location, a rural area made up of a mixture of crop and horse farms. The house is set well back, at least a hundred yards, off a two-lane, paved road, and it's surrounded by evergreen trees. It can't be seen from the road or from any neighbor's house. The nearest neighbor's driveway is over two hundred yards away. All the nearby houses are also set considerably back from the road. The entrance to the Ramirez driveway is on a tree-lined curve in the road, obscuring it from any neighbor's home or driveway; and the road, though never rush-hour busy,

has enough traffic so a casual observer would not take notice of an unfamiliar passing vehicle.

Bottom line, we will be able to arrive, carry out our mission, and leave without attracting bystander attention or neighborly curiosity.

- Enter the house without disturbance. Security at the farmhouse is considerably tighter than at the condo, but not impregnable. There are no motion sensors. There is no security system, per se, since the remoteness of the area precludes prompt police response, but the doors and windows are modern, heavy duty and resistant to break-in. Either he or Cynthia, his estranged wife, had them upgraded. (As mentioned, the same with the basement door, which is off the kitchen. Wonder what he keeps down there. No dead bodies, I hope. Maybe just his extra guns.) I didn't even try to pick any of those locks. I found another way – the automatic garage door. I can open it with an electronic code grabber, a common device for home burglars back in the day. I learned about it years ago, when I started PARsafe. It's what I've been using to get into the country house. They also didn't upgrade the lock on the door from the garage into the utility room in the house. It's pickable. So the electric garage door and the inner door to the utility room will be our path of entry.
- Take advantage of the long weekend. We'll arrive at the scene on Friday right about sunset – 5:45 pm – when there's still enough natural light to allow us to see without turning on our headlights. About thirty minutes later, near 6:15 pm, when it's close to total darkness, the justice will be dropped off by a driver from the Court. On a normal Friday night they would arrive earlier, but due to the government holiday on the following Monday and the resulting three-day weekend, Friday traffic out of D.C. will be even heavier than usual.

The extended weekend is also good, because it'll likely delay anyone finding the body until Tuesday morning, costing investigators an extra 24 hours before they get started. Those 24 hours are built in as an extra precaution. According to statistics, every hour lost after the crime occurs reduces investigator's chances of solving the crime. If we don't screw up, no physical evidence will be found at the crime scene. But if we do, when they find it, it'll have deteriorated for another 24 hours. Likewise with witnesses. There should be none. But if someone does see something, the accuracy of their memory will have diminished accordingly. Ditto surveillance cameras. Should we somehow get caught on video; most footage from Friday will be erased by Tuesday. This is probably being overly cautious. But it gives a little extra advantage, so why not take it.

- Hide the car. After being dropped off, the justice will enter the house through the front door. I'm confident of this, because in the past 21 months, I've observed him do it three out of three times. Our vehicle will be parked in the open space in the two-car garage. The other space is occupied by his car which he leaves in there. The garage wall facing the porch has no windows, so from the front porch, he can't see into the garage. We have to go in through the garage, anyway. Might as well get double duty out of it.
- Related to the second primary consideration, no collateral damage, we have one important factor in our favor: the federal government does not supply personal security to Supreme Court justices, except while in the Court building itself, and during official activities offsite. In other words, in their private life, they're on their own. (This policy may change after February 13.) Hence we won't have to take out any body guards. The driver who drops him off will leave and not return until Tuesday morning.

Furthermore, the choice of venue, the country house, assures remoteness, away from passersby and others who might somehow get in the way.

As for the third consideration, minimizing his suffering and conscious trauma, we will employ no guns, including stun guns, explosives, knives, axes or blunt instruments. The act will be carried out so as to assure Justice Ramirez has minimal awareness of what's happening. At worst he'll experience only momentary confusion or concern of a possible threat.

Some might argue that a bullet to the back of his head, causing instantaneous unconsciousness and death, would be the most merciful, the victim not ever knowing what hit him. But the logistics of that scenario are not foolproof. He could make a sudden unexpected move just as we are ready to fire. We might only wound him, or miss him entirely, necessitating further shots and causing him pain or acute emotional trauma. Handguns are intrinsically inaccurate. It's why Keenie got shot. The possible outcomes of gun play are several, all potentially risky. If we don't get him with the first shot, we might end up getting shot ourselves.

Even if successful, killing him instantly, a bullet to the back of his head from a :38 caliber pistol – it would have to be a :38; that's what Lester used – would result in a large gaping wound in his face, producing large amounts of gushing blood, not to mention skin and bone and brain tissue. Dylan or I or both of us could get splashed with human detritus. Not a pretty picture.

We'd also have to deal with GSR – Gun Shot Residue. Too much bother.

Furthermore, the exit wound would be ghastly, and the pictures in some of the media, like the supermarket tabloids, would convey us as brutal monsters. I don't want that, I'm not sure I can explain why. It's just me.

And another side of me doesn't want it to be a gun because that's the way he would have done it. I don't want to do anything his way.

In any case, to achieve a most humane outcome, here's what I've come up with: we'll administer a two-part lethal injection, the first part sedating him, the second stopping his heart, similar to capital punishment executions and euthanasia. His awareness of a threat to his person will be slight and brief, and except for a pin prick in his leg, there'll be no pain whatsoever. The necessary drugs are used every day by Vet's to euthanize animals. I've researched the appropriate dosage: 12 grams of the second drug, the lethal one, for the average adult human. I have 20 grams to be safe. It can't be traced to me, because I stole it from a vet's office. Nobody knows I have it.

Admittedly, the injections will be a bit dicey to administer, since he very likely will be carrying a handgun, likely a .38 revolver, a weapon with which he is proficient. Fortunately, he carries it in a shoulder holster under his left armpit, limiting a quick draw to only his right hand. That's what we have to control for a few seconds, his right hand. He can still draw the gun with his left hand, but it would be very awkward and slow, and take more time than he will have. We need only restrain his right hand for the few seconds it'll take for the sedative to make him too drowsy to be able to use the gun effectively. The sedative is very fast-acting.

This scenario requires that Dylan and I will have to choreograph and rehearse the necessary moves, which we'll do thoroughly. It'll all happen right after he enters the house. As he has done each time I've observed him, he'll first turn on the foyer light, then close the outer door. To hang up his overcoat, he'll step across the foyer and slide open the closet door on the wall opposite the outer door. He'll reach for the closet door with his right hand, putting his back to us.

We'll be hiding on opposite sides of the archway leading from the foyer to the room on the right of the front door. Dylan will step around the archway, take two steps, and grab the justice's right hand, while I step forward, bend down and put the sedative needle into a muscle in his thigh.

The thigh muscle is thicker than the shoulder, neck and back muscles. That's why I'll inject there. Since this has to happen quickly, I need a thick muscle, which will minimize the chance of the end of the needle going completely through and out the other side. It's better if the sedative flows directly into the muscle. Muscle tissue has less sensitive nerve endings (very little pain) and an abundance of veins and arteries and capillaries, assuring a quicker transfer of the first traces of the sedative to his brain.

For the second part, the lethal drug, we'll do a vein in his arm, assuring fast delivery to the heart. He'll be fully unconscious by then, giving us plenty of time to find a vein and do an effective injection. After that injection his heart will stop beating within ninety seconds, maybe less.

We'll then carry the body to the den, about fifteen steps, and put it behind the desk, where it won't be visible to anyone trying to look inside the house through the window. The den has a window that looks out on the porch, but the venetian blinds make it difficult to see in.

One little confession: another reason we won't use a gun is because there's a darker side of me that craves sticking it to the gun lobby. (Excuse the pun.) He'll be concealing a handgun on his person, but it won't do him any good. He'll be outshot, so to speak, by a couple of syringes. So much for the extra personal security of carrying a handgun.

There it is, all of it, I think. Dylan will be here tomorrow.

CHAPTER 33

THE FIRST READING

Saturday, January 3, 2015. Dylan's eighth straight day on the wagon. He arrived at ten in the morning, fresh and alert, no hang-over for a whole week. Still he was nervous. He could tell Pete was nervous, too. They were like two teenagers on a first date.

Pete led him into the spare bedroom where the computer sat on a desk, turned on, waiting for Dylan to start scrolling. Dylan sat down on the desk chair in front of the computer and shifted his weight to get comfortable. He began to read. Pete went into the kitchen to make a cup of tea.

Normally a fast reader, this time Dylan's eyes lingered on sections, intently studying certain pages, rereading and taking notes.

It wasn't what he expected; indeed much of it startled him. He'd known Pete for over two decades, never hearing about his grandfather's old country exodus, or the Lone Ranger speech, or how Pete came to know Joey's father in Vietnam, or the insufferably long stretch of insomnia.

Dylan did know, too well, the horrible tragedy of Keenie and Donna, and how it had torn Pete apart. Dylan had been there through all of that.

He revered Pete as the epitome of a good man, the best of the best. He remembered that long ago job interview, when he'd rudely burst out of the room in a fit of shattered hope, how Pete phoned him that afternoon and asked him to come back. Pete offered him the job right away, a breakthrough opportunity for Dylan, with never a mention of his quitting the Navy or his sexuality or his abrupt departure from the office.

Working with Pete, Dylan learned to respect his judgment and goodness as much as any other person in his life. The chance to buy the personal security part of the business for almost nothing was the icing on the cake. Pete was truly a good friend.

But he'd said nothing of all these supposed indicators of destiny he lived through, nor given any indication of his insomnia. Dylan had no idea of the driving forces or the depth of Pete's suffering.

Pete stood in the kitchen near the microwave. It'd take Dylan about two hours to read the whole epistle, a long time for Pete to just sit and wait. When the microwave beeped, he put a tea bag in the cup to steep. He carried it over to the breakfast nook, sat down at the table, and looked out the window. The apartment was on the fifth floor. He'd moved out of the house in Northville about five years ago and into a mid-rise apartment building in Southfield.

His desire to hang onto Keenie's memory by staying in the Northville house was overcome by its impracticality. It was a big house. He was alone. He spent the winters in Mexico. He travelled the world. The house was an albatross. So he sold it, but with a commitment to make sure the next place had enough room to prominently display all the big walled pictures of Grampa and Keenie. The Southfield apartment sufficed.

It was January in Michigan, cloudy, gray again, like the day at the White Castle, but without the snow. The weather made him think about Lake Chapala in Mexico. No snow there, for sure. Lots of sun and blue sky. He hadn't been there since early December, and he wouldn't be going back until after wrapping up the business with the justice.

He was both tired and nervous. Most nights in the last week he'd slept a little better, relieved that the end was in sight. However, last night he relapsed, a worry crossing his mind about Dylan's reaction. What if Dylan said, "No?" Could he possibly pull this off himself? The thought made him restless. He was back to very little sleep.

He stood up with his cup of tea and walked over to dump the remainder in the sink. He looked at his watch. Dylan had only been in there ten minutes. This was going to be a long vigil. He decided to go for a walk. No, that wouldn't work. It was nineteen degrees out there. He pulled the car keys off the hook by the door, and told Dylan he was going out and, "If you get done before I get back, call me on my cell."

Dylan read carefully and took occasional notes. He intended his notes as talking points to convince Pete to scrap the proposed outrageous venture. He could see how the totality of seemingly related events, especially the Bella/Keenie connection, would appear to someone in Pete's state of mind to have a persuasive flow, a magnetic draw toward a common resolution. But assassinating a Supreme Court justice? That was a stretch. Dylan saw it as a desperate leap in logic, and made notes on it, wondering if he could make Pete see the same.

Pete pulled out of the parking garage and drove north to I-696. He crossed over the freeway, electing to stay on surface streets. He wasn't going anywhere in particular. Just driving, taking up time, trying not to dwell on the possibility that Dylan would turn him down. He needed to get onto a busy street with heavy traffic and stop lights, anything to distract him from pessimistic thoughts. He went over to Telegraph. A person could depend on Telegraph to be congested, even on Saturday morning. He took it north for over ten miles, all the way to Pontiac.

As Dylan neared the end, the section on how the killing would actually go down, (Pete still resisted calling it a killing) he took more notes than he had for all the preceding sections together. This part, supposedly, was his area of expertise: special ops. He read carefully, looking for signs that Pete hadn't done adequate reconnaissance. He remembered telling him years ago, the intel had to be reliable, or the operation would fail. Dylan kept looking for an opening that would let him plant a seed of doubt. He wondered if Pete would appreciate the concept of "the fog of war." Shit happens. A covert operation like this was like a military battle. A British general once compared confusion in battle to pain in childbirth, saying it was the natural order of things.

As he read through the section, it became clear Pete had done his usual thorough homework, covering contingencies that hadn't even occurred to Dylan. There were no obvious holes. His seed of doubt might not take root in this garden.

Then he got to the lethal injection part. He sat up straight. His eyebrows jumped up his forehead. The fuck-up meter went wild. There it is, he thought. Way too many moving parts. Talk about potential for confusion in battle. How could something not go wrong? It gave him his first real opening. He had to be calm when he talked about it with Pete. Handle it carefully.

When Pete made the u-turn just before M-59 to head back, he'd been gone for twenty-five minutes. On the way back south he stopped at his favorite deli in the strip mall at Maple Road and got two corned beef sandwiches. When Dylan finished, they could talk over lunch.

Pete continued south past his turn off all the way down to Eight Mile Road, driving as slowly as traffic allowed, all the while an ominous feeling gnawing at him. When Dylan arrived, he wasn't right. Something was going on with him. At Eight Mile Pete u-turned again, back north toward the apartment. When he opened the door to the apartment, he'd been gone for over an hour and a half.

Dylan got to the final sentence and saw his name again, reprising the troubling thought of how much his friend was counting on him. Dammit! How could he let him down?

During the reading, Dylan's mind would briefly wander to the issues in his own life, and the early signs of a possible turnaround. He didn't want to jeopardize the recovery that seemed to have started. Henry was almost a week into his diet and had already contacted a broker about selling the restaurant. Dylan, himself, hadn't had a drink in that time and had suffered little withdrawal. It wasn't as hard as he thought. He was feeling better on several levels, especially his concern about his relationship with Henry. This venture would put everything at risk. He couldn't do it, even for a million dollars. Nor could he leave Pete hanging out there on his own. He had to find a way to bring Pete back to reality, to bring him down gently. He'd start with the crazy lethal injection thing.

Just remember to not call it crazy.

Dylan got up from the computer, feeling stiffness in his lower back, bending forward at the waist, then as far back as he could, stalling. Pete had returned about twenty minutes earlier, announcing that lunch was available whenever he was ready.

He entered the kitchen and neither spoke. No eye contact. Pete pointed to a chair with a plate in front of it. The sandwiches were still wrapped, sitting on a serving dish in the center of the table. Another dish held chips and pickles.

Pete broke the silence, "What'll you have to drink? I have Oberon and Bud Light and Diet Coke."

"Uh…I think just a water. It's still early for me," not mentioning his new abstinence protocol.

Pete got ice water for him and a Diet Coke for himself. As he sat down, he looked directly at Dylan and said, "Well?"

Dylan shifted in his chair. "I didn't know a lot of that stuff, Pete. I kept getting surprises." He bit into his sandwich.

Pete said, "Now you know."

Dylan said nothing.

Pete said, "So what do you think?"

"Pete, I just feel bad. I didn't know all you were going through. The insomnia must be hell." Stalling, not sure where to start. How should he do this? He needed more time to think.

Pete waited.

Dylan asked about Major Kovach, "You ever hear anything about what happened to him?"

Pete said, "No." The impatience beginning to show.

"What about the Indian girl in New Mexico?"

"Nope. Nothing. I let that one go."

Dylan took another bite of his sandwich. Pete's remained on the plate, untouched. He could hear Dylan chewing, no other sound, not even the usual January wind on the window. If awkward discomfort could make a sound, it would have been cacophonous in that kitchen. He thought he saw tiny beads of perspiration on Dylan's forehead.

Pete's stomach turned over. It was going to be "No." He was going to have to do it by himself.

Or not at all.

Dylan stared at his plate, like a small child being scolded. Internal conflict showed in his body language.

Breaking the silence, Pete said, "Talk to me, Dylan. In or out?"

Dylan remembered the old Pete, who would never have said such a thing, would never have put another person in such an uncomfortable place. Dylan couldn't make eye contact. He wanted more time to figure out a tactful way to talk Pete out of it, a way that wouldn't hurt him. Nothing came to him. Finally he went to the needles, "I'm really concerned with the lethal injection part. A lot could go wrong there."

Pete thought about what he said. Maybe he's not out. Just wants to discuss options.

"Yeah, you're right. It'd be tricky. I thought we could rehearse it, keep going through it till we got it down. Don't want to use a gun."

Dylan nodded, head still down, eyes on his plate.

Pete said, "Maybe a taser to freeze him, while we inject the sedative. Ever use one? I'm not sure how they work."

Dylan sensed the conversation was going in the wrong direction. He'd given the wrong impression. He wasn't interested in a better way to do it. He wished he could think of a way to say what he wanted to say. He was tongue-tied. Finally, he squeezed out a stall, "Pete, I have to think about this. You've had more time than me. I need to figure everything out."

He started to get up from the table, "Give me three days, and I'll have it clearer in my mind." He didn't know why he picked three days instead of one or two or four.

He picked up his pad of paper, "I'll go over all this stuff and get back to you at the beginning of the week." He started to walk toward the coat closet.

Pete startled him, "Hold it, Dylan. You can't take the notes out of here. Somebody might see them. I have to burn them. Sorry." He reached for the pad under Dylan's arm.

"Oh…I didn't think." Dylan surrendered the pad without resistance. He was embarrassed, confused. He just wanted to get out. "I'm sorry…it's…I need a little time." His mind was racing. He was too warm. He needed a drink. When he got home, the gin bottle would be there. He could almost hear the ice cubes crackle. Just one drink. Just one would help.

CHAPTER 34

DYLAN – ACT LIKE A SEAL

S*aturday, January 3, 2015.* When Dylan came through the kitchen door, Henry was sitting at the table with papers spread out in front of him. He smiled as he looked up.

"Where you been?"

"With Pete, going over some things." He glanced at the liquor cabinet.

"Oh." Henry nodded his head, "Going over some things."

Dylan scrambled to come up with a follow-up, "He has a new venture he's looking at. Wanted my thoughts. Didn't have much to add."

"New venture?"

"It's a government thing. I didn't really understand it."

Henry gave him a lingering, uncertain look of disbelief with an unspoken question inside it, "*Why are you lying to me?*"

Dylan felt like a complete piece of shit. More than ever, he wanted a drink. If he walked over to the liquor cabinet at that moment, it would be equivalent to a full confession. He looked away from Henry, walking out of the kitchen toward the stairway. Over his shoulder he said, "I need a shower."

Henry watched him down the hallway and muttered to himself, "Yeah, I guess you do."

Dylan did take a shower: a long, soaking shower alternating very hot and very cold water, as if to shock his body and mind enough to regain control of each. It was something the SEAL trainers might have put him through, when they were forging him into a superior fighting machine.

When he turned off the water and exited the shower, he felt better. It still works, he thought. He dressed in warm clothing and went downstairs. Henry was no longer at the table. He could get to the liquor cabinet unobserved. He stood at the doorway to the kitchen, torn. It was there, right across the room: a comforting numbness, a release of tension, a brighter disposition – all the wonders of demon gin. But a false and incapacitating condition. The battle in his brain was waning, less intense than last week. The gin was losing. A small but decisive defeat.

What he needed was to finish the psychological disinfecting process the shower had started. He turned and walked down the hall, looking for Henry. He was sitting in the living room, a cane next to his chair. Since his self-revelation last week, Henry had taken to keeping a cane close by, acknowledging his infirmity, so as better to conquer it.

Dylan sat in the chair facing him.

"I have to clarify something. I was not completely forthcoming with you earlier."

Henry nodded, "No shit."

Dylan went on, "Pete has come up with an idea…a project, an outlandish project…and he wants me to help him. He's offered me a lot of money, but it's just too…I really can't say any more, even to you. The problem is, if I don't help him, he may try to do it by himself, and I have to try to stop him. I can't tell you any more. I hope you can understand. Look, since last week, we – you and I – seem to be really back on track, and that's what's most important."

Henry remained silent, but curiosity was eating at him. He didn't give a shit about keeping secrets. This one had to be juicy. Finally he said, "Something less than 'completely forthcoming' isn't it?"

"C'mon, Henry. You can't put Pete between us. He's been too good to us, both of us. And he doesn't deserve betrayal."

Henry smiled, "Ok, you can't blame me for trying. Just one thing. How much money?"

"A million."

"Holy shootski, who do you have to kill?"

"Hi, Pete, it's Dylan." He was talking to Pete's voice mail. It was Sunday, the day after their meeting. Pete was down at the soup kitchen. Dylan expected as much, but didn't want to wait lest his momentum wane. He had to get it over with. He had to start the process of walking Pete out of this inextricable maze he'd designed himself into.

"Pete, I want to be completely candid. I have real concerns about the whole thing." It was easy talking to a machine. "I'm ready to talk about it. Call me when you get this. We'll set something up. I'm going to San Antonio tomorrow morning, and I'll be back on Wednesday. Maybe we can do something on Thursday."

Pete didn't get home until after nine o'clock that night. The tone of Dylan's message was discouraging. So he put off the return call till morning. When he reached Dylan's cell on Monday, Dylan answered. He was about to board the plane. They set up a time on Thursday morning at Pete's place. Pete was already trying to figure out a new plan. Something he could do by himself.

They didn't meet on Thursday. Henry died.

On Tuesday afternoon the cleaner found Henry's body in his bed. Time of death was estimated by the medical examiner as Tuesday morning between midnight and eight o'clock. Cause of death unknown, but probably either a massive heart attack, stroke or both. Foul play was not a factor. He'd died the way everybody says they want to die, peacefully, in his sleep.

Dylan came home from San Antonio a day early and began the process of dealing with death. At the funeral home viewing, Pete noticed that Dylan did not appear to be grief-stricken, at least not inconsolably so. Dylan had come to the same realization. The presumed cause of death had convinced him Henry's poor health was beyond recovery. He might have lessened the pace of his downward spiral, but he wasn't going to make a difference with the more serious symptoms. If he'd lived, the remainder of his life would have been difficult, gradually more so each month. His eyesight was worsening, as was his ability to walk. If the cardiovascular event had been less severe, while not killing him immediately, it would have further debilitated him, perhaps to the point of being a helpless invalid. Henry wouldn't have liked that. Not at all. And Dylan drew a certain amount of consolation from the peaceful nature of Henry's passing.

Dylan's issues list was still posted on the bathroom mirror – Father/Dream, Henry's Health, Our Future, Money/Restaurant, Job, Drinking, and Special Project. On Saturday night after the funeral he pulled the paper and tape off the mirror, and threw them in the waste basket. He was going back to being a SEAL; at least he was going to act like one. No more fear of the variables of life. Let the "chips fall" and "shit hit the fan" and all those clichés.

He was going to do the right thing.

CHAPTER 35

THE SECOND READING

Sunday, January 11, 2015. Dylan arrived at Pete's apartment at ten in the morning, the day after the funeral. It was normally Pete's day at the soup kitchen, but Dylan told him they had to talk, and it wouldn't wait.

When he got inside, Dylan said, "Before we talk, I need to read your write-up again. It'll only take about an hour, I'll be skimming. Just want to get a few things clear in my mind. You can go out and get us lunch, like you did last time. I'll be quick."

Pete was puzzled but did as Dylan suggested. When he returned, he set the nook table as before. Sitting down with the sandwiches (this time pastrami) in front of them, Pete wondered what strategy Dylan would use to try to talk him out of it, and what the hell was the hurry? It could have waited until tomorrow, a non soup kitchen day.

Dylan came into the kitchen and said, "I want to make a deal. The lethal injection makes me nervous. It would take some fairly complex coordination. Let's find another way. And you won't have to pay me any money."

Pete's eyes were locked on Dylan's face, wondering if he'd heard him right. What happened? The loss of Henry?' Dylan's demeanor carried an intensity Pete hadn't seen in years. Dylan doing it for nothing was not an option. Money was of no consequence to Pete. He had more than he'd ever spend. Dylan, on the other hand, would need money. More than he had. The fallout from this could be major. He might have to disappear for a while, a long while.

Pete put his elbows on the table and his hands over his face, rubbing his forehead with his finger tips, stalling as he put together a response. Pulling his hands down, he said, "I want to counter."

Dylan shifted uncomfortably. He hadn't expected that. His confidence level diminished. "Look, Pete; I'm not gonna refuse, you know that. I owe you too much. It's just…"

Pete interrupted, "I've been doing a lot of thinking. And some research. The stun gun thing really stinks. You have to actually touch the guy with the gun. So it's almost as risky a dance as the needle. And it's really painful to the guy. The Taser is just as gruesome, plus it leaves behind residue that can be traced. We might be able to get around that part, but it's a risk we should avoid. And with the pain issue…neither is a good option for my taste."

Dylan had a response, "What about a small caliber handgun? You know, a .22 or something. He won't feel a thing…beyond the first nanosecond. You can do it without the mess. The bullet doesn't come out the other side of his skull, just stays inside and rattles around. No mess, no ugly photos."

"I don't have a .22. I'd have to go out and buy one. Unless I steal it or get it on the dark net, which I don't know how to do; it could be traced back to me. Even then, it adds risk. At this late date, it'd be a rush. Makes me uncomfortable."

Dylan said, "You can't trace the shell, because it get's all messed up inside the guy's skull."

Pete thought about it, "Listen to us. I've never had a conversation like this before."

"Well, now you've lived."

No more comments, as they chewed their sandwiches.

Finally, Dylan said, "What was your counter?"

Pete put his sandwich down, sipped his Diet Coke, set it down, looked at his hands and said, "Do it my way, and we'll make it three mil."

CHAPTER 36

JOURNAL – WE'RE READY

8:00am, Thursday 2-12-2015

Fourteen and a half years is a long time to be on a mission. That's how long it's been since the shooting, longer than the war in Afghanistan. In that span, a great deal has happened.

Lester, the shooter, died in prison eleven years ago. He succumbed to injuries received in a fight with another inmate; his damaged brain unable to withstand more trauma.

His ex-wife, Michelle, gave up teaching; it was probably hard for her to work in a classroom, after what happened. She opened a little bookstore and gift shop and eventually remarried.

In 2011, the high tech company that bought our firewall business was acquired by an even bigger high tech company. As Joey predicted, cyber security has become a major business consideration throughout the world.

Joey, by the way, is skyrocketing toward billionaire status. I try to visit him at least once a year. His dad, the Captain, is in his 70s and still holding sway in the Vietnamese community in Northern California.

Tomorrow is the day. We leave early in the morning. Dylan will be here tonight around eight, and he'll sleep in the guest room.

I've gone over everything five times, some of it more. We rehearsed our little needle dance a dozen times on a full body mannequin.

I made one trip back to D.C., just to verify things, and turned up nothing new, except I tried to check out the country house basement and couldn't get past the door locks. They're big time, heavy duty secure. Makes me wonder. Can't get distracted, though. All the same, I do wonder what's down there.

Nothing else to record. When it's over, I'll make a full report. For the record.

CHAPTER 37

JUSTICE RAMIREZ

F*riday, February 13, 2015*. One thing for sure: no more frigging New Mexico. The whole state was toxic. No longer "The Land of Enchantment," at least not for the justice. He swore that when he got off the Court (and who knew when the hell that would be), he wouldn't go back to New Mexico. No matter. Who'd want to anyway? Just a big rocky desert with mountains and a river running through it.

He'd have to find someplace new; and not D.C. either; *no damned way*. He should never have come here in the first place. Too much frigging aggravation.

He wished he had a place to just vanish. If he left, as in "disappeared," he wouldn't have to worry. Get lost in a big city. A guy could hide in plain sight in New York or L.A. No, he wouldn't like L.A. Too many beaners.

Maybe overseas. Madrid would be good. Pure Spaniards. No Mexicans or Indians, frigging animals. He could brush up on his Spanish.

Bangkok would be fun, but he'd never learn that weird language. Bunch of gook talk. He'd just visit there as needed.

If he could only go somewhere; sleep late; not read anything denser than USA Today or American Rifle; have a late lunch in a sidewalk café; maybe a little target practice once in a while; a little riding on the weekend; an occasional afternoon delight with a young primitive; a martini at cocktail hour, maybe two; no MSNBC or CNN, and no nosy law clerks; no having to deal with anyone who might get inquisitive about…whatever. At his age a man should be able to relax. People are too damned judgmental.

Ramirez looked out the right-side, rear window of the black government sedan as it snailed across the Theodore Roosevelt Memorial Bridge over the Potomac River and into Virginia. Down below, Theodore Roosevelt Island stretched to the north. The February day was cold, but no snow. The water around the island was not frozen, but the gray current had an icy look.

The driver, Sweeney, made no attempt to speed their progress, just stayed in his lane and crawled along. Ramirez wanted to tell him to push it a little, take a few chances. When the next lane opens up, cut into it. Wouldn't do any good. He'd tried before. Sweeney was such a wimp; he wished he could get a driver with some balls.

It was 4:15 on Friday afternoon, a time when freeway traffic was normally slow. Due to the long weekend, this trip was going to be slower than slow. Traffic was literally bumper to bumper. Monday was a government holiday – President's Day. Federal employees and the hordes of parasites that drew their nourishment from the government, along with the bankers and teachers, all headed out to enjoy the next three days somewhere else, as was Ramirez, anywhere but D.C. He figured with Sweeney driving, it was going to take nearly two hours to make his escape to the farmhouse.

It wasn't really a farmhouse, because it wasn't really a farm, only ten acres of mostly-wooded land way out in Fauquier County. Cynthia bought it for the privacy. She called it the country house. The neighbors or people passing by on the road couldn't see the house. She liked the idea that no one in this unfriendly part of the country could be watching her.

The place had a riding trail through the woods and on to the neighboring property, which he and Cynthia used when they rode together, but that was over three years ago. There was a horse barn back of the house, but no horses. Cynthia took hers, when she moved back to New Mexico. She'd decided once and for all that any place near the nation's capital was not for her. Since she left, he had to stable his horse, Alhambra, at a nearby horse farm. Tomorrow afternoon, if it wasn't too cold, he'd go over and ride the trails in the nearby state park.

Now, what to do for the next two hours, while Sweeney did his sloth-like routine in traffic. Two bad this car didn't have a little bar in it. It's cocktail hour. A Supreme Court justice shouldn't have to ride in the back of a car for two hours at cocktail time without a cocktail. These things never seemed to get properly thought out. Probably a Mexican in charge of the transportation amenities.

He reached over and opened his briefcase. The Smith & Wesson .357 Magnum sat on top of some Court papers he'd thrown in there for show. The gun was fastened into a shoulder holster. He preferred a shoulder holster, because that's what the real ballsy heroes used in the old movies. The .357 was Dirty Harry's gun, which made it good enough for Ramirez. People said it was heavy and awkward, but it made him feel good, like a real man. He took off his overcoat and suit coat, pulled the holster strap over his head and fastened it. It felt good under his armpit. It belonged there. He put the suit coat back on but left the overcoat on the seat.

He folded his arms across his chest and over the seatbelt. Seatbelts were a real pain in the ass. A liberal conspiracy to take a man's freedom away. He let his chin settle on his chest just above his crossed arms. This was his thinking position. Sweeney would look in the rearview mirror and assume he was asleep. Often as not nowadays he was.

All he cared about was getting away from the Court. The drudgery was endless. Why didn't he foresee what a drag it would be? Who gives a damn about "stare decisis" and the "commerce clause" and whatnot? Boooooring! The only thing that counts is the Second Amendment. The rest of it is all so much horse puckey.

Life would be less onerous if he didn't have to pretend so much. He had to be nice to all of them, even the law clerks. They were all such jerks. They should be more respectful of his special legal expertise. Sometimes he sensed the condescension. Bunch of uppity assholes.

Even if they treated him better, he supposed he'd still be walking a tightrope on what might come out someday. For sure something's going to come out. The world had changed. And not for the better. It seldom changed for the better.

He'd been on edge ever since the phone calls last year from Everett and Hobson. Some writer was asking dangerous questions again. Who was he? And where'd he disappear to? Wonder if he talked to Raul?

Why the hell did he let himself get put on the U. S. Supreme Court in the first place? He should have learned his lesson after the stretch in Santa Fe. He'd come to think he was invulnerable. In truth it's Martindale's fault. The Supreme Court nomination was his idea. That would've been the time to head it off. He could've just said, "No thanks," and slid into comfortable obscurity. Of course, if he wasn't on the Court, the gun people wouldn't be taking care of him the way they are. Still, he knew it was a bad idea right after he was confirmed. He'd kept a low profile ever since. No publicity. No photo ops. No grand standing questions during the oral arguments. Just hunker down. People on the street didn't even know who he was. Just a face in the crowd.

What's amazing is nobody bothered to look very hard when Wheeler put him up. The Senate confirmation process was a breeze. The president's son had just come back in a casket from the Middle East. The whole country was in mourning. Wheeler's approval rating was sky high. He still had 18 months to go before his second term was up. Nobody wanted to get crossways with Wheeler. Everybody was trying to be nice…afraid to stand up.

Plus there was the ethnic thing. People assumed with a name like Ramirez he was a Mexican. Democrats didn't want to hassle a Mexican for fear of upsetting all the Hispanics. They needed the Hispanics at election time. Christ, if they only knew. Still, it was his own fault. If he'd been thinking straight, no way would he have allowed himself to be nominated. He rarely admitted fault, even to himself.

Straight and Martindale would get there between 6:30 and 7:00 tonight. This was the first time they'd made the delivery to the farmhouse. In the past they came to the condo, and he took it out to the farmhouse on one of his weekends. He didn't want to do that any more. The condo just wasn't secure enough to keep that much money around. Couldn't bank it. And he didn't like hauling it out to the farmhouse himself. Too risky. He'd insisted. They were a little irked, but so what. It was only once every three months. They could alternate. They didn't both have to come out. Maybe they didn't trust each other.

Tonight they would act like they were glad to see him, but he knew they were just using him. He told himself he didn't care as long as they paid him, but truth be told, he cared. It was starting to wear on him. They'd shortened their visits, wouldn't stay to talk politics; just long enough to deliver the briefcase and be able to say they were there; soon as they could, they'd be headed back to be with their real friends.

He looked out the window at the passing cars in the next lane. Fat chance Sweeney would think about merging into the faster lane. He wondered if someone with a name like Sweeney could be a Mexican.

He wished he could relax. Sure as hell, somebody is going to put it all together. He couldn't get that call from Everitt out of his mind. A guy was asking questions about something that happened up on the reservation. That was over *forty* years ago. How the hell could that come up again? Why would anyone care about that now? They were just Indians for Christ's sake. What the hell else were they good for? He'd made sure they didn't get pregnant.

Pops had taken care of it, and it all went away; clear evidence that power and money go well together and can work wonders. Only restriction on him was he had to stay away from the Rez.

He slipped into pondering the mysteries of the libido. This matter with very young girls had always been with him. It wasn't the powerful driver it used to be, but it still sort of lurked there, made him restless, sometimes. Skin color seemed to be part of it. Why? When he was young, he never asked these questions. He just did it, because he wanted to. Now, at this age, he wondered.

He was grateful for one aspect of it. Certainly the inclination for young girls was better than if it were young boys. Guys who went that way were clearly sick. He was sure of that. But why didn't he find as much appeal in grown women as with the young ones? Deep question.

Back in the day, he couldn't stop thinking about those Navajo girls. He went up there to the Res' looking for them six or eight times that one summer. You could find them walking along the road alone, hitch-hiking. They were asking for it. Three times he got lucky. One didn't even resist. The other two were the problem. His dad was really ticked. But after all this time, damn, the statute of limitations was up many years ago. Hardly anybody knew about what happened, and most who did must be dead. How the hell did it come up again? Why would anyone care about that now?

Had to be Raul. Raul was still upset. He needed to get over things. It's that squaw he's got.

When he called Cynthia, to see if she knew anything, she said some guy talked to her, too. Asked a lot of questions. She said she didn't tell him anything, but he wouldn't put it past her to get in a few shots.

She said Raul may still be getting back at him for what he did, not going to the wedding. It was 25 years ago, for Christ's sake! What the hell did he expect? Thank God they haven't had any kids.

Now there was the gun money. Fortunately, nobody who knew about it could talk. They'd get hurt as much as he would. Certainly it's not illegal for them to pay him to appear at some of their VIP events. At least it shouldn't be. But if it got out, the shit would hit the fan. They'd say he was influence peddling. Those assholes at the Court would be so damned sanctimonious. Just thinking about it riled him up. Every one of them would be demanding his resignation, which he would love to be able to provide, if only it wouldn't give Harwell a chance to make another liberal appointment. Since succeeding Wheeler, Harwell had already put one bleeding heart on the Court.

Ramirez hadn't paid taxes on any of the money. That's how they got Capone. Maybe he should move it. Get it into some kind of offshore setup.

Shit. It's a house of cards.

When will this damn limo ride end. We're still more than an hour and a half away. Just calm down, take a little nap while the sun sets in Sweeney's eyes. Serves the goddamned wuss right.

Ramirez woke up when Sweeney pulled into the driveway. It was well after six. The moon was hidden by the clouds. Darker than usual for this early in the evening. Good thing he had a porch light with a sensor. The car stopped in front of the porch steps. He did not put the overcoat on. He draped it over his arm, grabbed the briefcase, and opened the right rear door of the car without waiting for Sweeney. He'd learned some time ago that Sweeney wasn't getting out of the car in this cold or in any other weather for that matter. He'd felt like a fool the first time, sitting there waiting for him to open the door.

"Goodnight, Justice. Have a nice weekend. See you on Tuesday morning."

Ramirez closed the door without replying.

CHAPTER 38

MARTINDALE & STRAIGHT

F*riday, February 13, 2015.* "Whit, I got a problem. Gonna have to bail on you. Can't go tonight."

"What? Stick me with him all by myself? That's bullshit."

"Look, Whit. I just can't. If I'm not on that plane with Evie this afternoon, she'll turn me inside out."

"Hell, I've got plans, too. I could be over at Greenbriar with Gloria. Goddammit, Ken. You've known about this for three weeks. I've told you before; he's getting to be too much. I can't deal with him by myself anymore."

"For Christ's sake, Whit, he's your man. You found him. You've been dealing with him for years. And it's practically on your way. You'll only lose an hour or so."

"Fuck, Ken, I could've been there sitting with a drink by the pool yesterday. Pulling out at the last minute like this completely sucks.

You know I don't like being alone with him anymore. And it's your fucking money, not mine."

"Whit, I'm sorry. But Evie's been on my ass for days. I thought she'd give up by now, but it's only gotten worse. If I'm not on that plane with her, she'll cut my balls off. She's got her mind set on dinner in South Beach tonight, and she means it. She'd be seriously pissed. I have to be on that plane."

Martindale continued to protest, "For Christ's sake, she's gonna have a whole week of fancy dinners on that cruise ship."

"Whit, it's not that kind of cruise. We'll be roughing it, helping crew the ship. It's a big goddamned sailboat. No TV, no cell phone, no caviar. Six days and no civilization. Evie's idea, not mine. I suppose they'll feed us well, but no seven-course gourmet sit-downs."

Not exactly Whit's idea of a vacation. Roughing it. Shit. Why would you spend money for that? That's like paying to mow your own lawn.

"I guess you picked your poison. But next time, Ken, he's all yours. I'm telling you right now, so you can plan on it. Next time, I'll be on my second martini at the club, and you'll be dealing with him all by yourself."

"Jesus, Whit, I'm sorry, but…"

"Go fuck yourself. Hope your plane doesn't crash."

Whitford Audley Martindale would have to make the delivery by himself. It made him nervous. Ramirez made him nervous. He always had. For some reason his discomfort with the guy had grown since he went on the Court. Ramirez was always out there, but now he was just too much. Like he had no feelings. He didn't care about anybody. It was all about him. Martindale admitted Ramirez had always been that way. Just seemed to bother him more now.

This whole process made it worse. The money had been going on for six years. It was Straight's idea. Martindale didn't think they needed to pay him. He was ours and always would be. Straight said nothing was forever, especially with a fruitcake like Ramirez. Straight said we could guarantee his Court vote on anything with a little bit of money. The guy had none of his own left, or very little. His wife bankrolled him. If she gets tired of him … well, Straight was right on that one. Ugly old money bags Cynthia is history.

Still Martindale didn't like it. He got the bag this morning. He wasn't expecting it. Up till now Straight always brought it to Ramirez's place, and Martindale met him there. Now he understood why it came to him. It arrived at his office, delivered by a stranger, someone he'd never seen before. According to Straight, each payment was withdrawn in relatively small chunks from two different bank accounts – one of his own and one belonging to the gun guys. Not Martindale's gun guys. Somebody else's. They changed the banks every year or so. Martindale didn't even count it. He wanted to pretend he didn't know anything. Straight's supposed to have checked to make sure it was right. Martindale simply took it out of the bag and put it into his briefcase. The risk here was ridiculous. This was seriously against the law. The shit just kept getting deeper. They'd turned him into a bag man. Not worth it.

He wondered what Ramirez did with the money. Probably in some offshore numbered account. Time to get clear of him. Too much was happening. Martindale wished he could take it all back. If he hadn't made it happen, Ramirez would be out of his hair by now. He was so pissed, he shut off his phone. No more bad news calls today.

Had to admit, Ramirez was one of the best fundraising pitchmen he'd ever seen. Now he wished he'd never met him. The guy wasn't right. Never had been. He was missing something. Fucking mental case. All the shit was really starting to bother Martindale. This would be his last delivery. He promised himself.

CHAPTER 39

NOBODY EVER COMES HERE

F*riday, February 13, 2015*. The headlights of the government limo, a black Lincoln, came around the last trees at the top of the long, curved driveway and sprayed across the front porch of the house at 6:25pm. Sunset on the horizon was forty minutes earlier. Invisible clouds blocked the moon and the stars, leaving the sky as dark as the car.

Pete and Dylan waited inside the house in the room next to the foyer behind the archway walls, one on each side. Light from the car flashed through the vertical slit between the curtains and the window molding. They heard the approaching purr of the motor diminish as it came to a stop, followed by a car door slam, then steps on the porch.

Pete thought of Grampa, crouching near the riding path in Italy, waiting for Signore Pavoni, oxen whip in hand. Grampa didn't know he was about to take a life. This was different. Pete had been planning for years to do just that. He thought of Keenie. Would she approve? Of course not. A bad thought. Now was not the time.

The sound of a key turning the bolt and the tight-fitting door resisting, then a little swoosh as it let go. He was in. He stepped to the closet door. Pete looked at Dylan. Dylan nodded.

Simultaneously they stepped from behind the arch walls. Ramirez had his back to them. Two quick steps. Dylan' got to him first. He put his left arm around Ramirez's left arm and chest, and with his other hand grabbed the right wrist. The overcoat and briefcase fell to the floor. Pete went down on his haunches and poked the needle through Ramirez's suit pants into the back of his thigh. Ramirez struggled to get his right arm free, but Dylan's strength prevailed. After a few seconds, which seemed much longer to Pete, Ramirez resistance began to slip away along with his balance. Dylan held him up, and then gently laid him on the floor as he lost consciousness.

They took off his suit coat and Dylan set it on top of the overcoat. Pete pushed up Ramirez's shirt sleeve and searched for a prominent vein for the other injection. It took a couple pokes to get it right, but for a guy with no medical training, Pete thought he did alright. Piece of cake. In three minutes it was over. They carried Ramirez into the den, Dylan's hands under the armpits, Pete's holding the ankles. Everything as planned.

They maneuvered the body behind the desk and gently laid it on the floor, as if not to bruise it. Dylan knew it no longer mattered; the justice was beyond feeling pain or even bruising. He only did it that way to accommodate Pete's sensitivities.

Pete straightened up and looked around the room. The face on the little digital clock on the desk read 6:31. A black cord ran from the clock to a wall plug next to the desk. Pete unplugged it. It stopped ticking. The 6:31 stared back at him.

He looked around the room and saw several pictures on the wall of Ramirez posed with people he didn't recognize, except President Wheeler, and one with Martindale, the apparatchik with the gun lobbying firm. Pete had met him, but couldn't remember his first name.

As he stared at the picture, something interrupted his thoughts. He heard a sound, an intrusive sound, mechanical purring, like a car. Then he saw a moving flash of light, similar to the car lights when Ramirez arrived. The sound stopped, and the light went out. Silence. He could feel his heart beat accelerate, his skin flushing. He was breathing hard, as if he was running. He wanted to run, but his legs wouldn't respond. Where could he run to?

Then a louder noise. A thunk. Outside, but nearby. Now his pulse made his whole body vibrate, percussing like hip hop music in a gangbanger's car.

The thunk was the slam of a car door. Somebody was out there.

No! Nobody ever comes here. He'd watched this place. The guy had no friends. This can't be happening. Not now! Why now?

He went from paralysis to vertigo, as if the earth had stopped revolving on its axis, but his body had continued to spin. He had to hold onto the back of the desk chair. He was squeezing it so hard his hand was trembling. Could the whole room be flying? Of course not, nothing was moving. He was hallucinating.

He looked at Dylan. Dylan's head was tilted, like the RCA Victor dog, listening, trying to pick up faint sounds. Dylan met his gaze. Pete thought he saw an "I told you so" expression.

Dylan saw pure panic in Pete's eyes. Helplessness. Pete's mouth was open, nothing came out.

The doorbell rang. Pete thought he heard Dylan say, as if to himself, "I think it's for me."

Dylan stepped to the door of the den, looked over his shoulder at Pete, and said, "Stay here, don't move and don't make a sound." Pete was sure he could follow those instructions. Dylan disappeared toward the front door.

Pete listened. It was all he was capable of. He heard the closet door open and something drop on the floor. Then the closet door closed. The doorbell rang again. The front door opened and he heard Dylan say something about pest control. Then someone was inside the house with Dylan. Mumbled words. Seconds passed, then a strange sound, like a grunt, then a shuffling sound, then quiet.

Dylan called out, "Gimme a hand."

Pete realized Dylan was yelling to him. He shook his head, trying to clear it, pulled away from the desk chair and half stumbled out to the foyer.

It was Martindale.

Dylan was holding him up by his armpits. His overcoat was open and off his right shoulder, like he'd started to take it off. It appeared as though he'd fallen backward into Dylan's arms. His face was turned awkwardly to his right, eyes open.

Dylan said, "Grab his ankles. Let's get him to the den."

Robotically, Pete bent over and picked up Martindale's legs by his ankles. They carried him across the room, into the den, and laid him down next to Ramirez. Pete reached down to check his pulse.

Dylan said, "No need."

Dylan left the den and quickly returned with a small briefcase and said, "He set this on the floor when I offered to take his coat. I put Ramirez's stuff on the floor in the closet."

Pete gave him an uncomprehending look, setting one hand back on the chair for support. He was confused, not sure if his senses were conveying reality to his brain, wondering why the hell Dylan cared about a briefcase at a time like this.

Dylan put the case on the desk, tried to open it, until he saw the combination lock. He looked back up at Pete, who appeared to be attached to the chair in a cathartic state. Dylan returned his eyes to the briefcase and studied the lock. He lifted the case off the desk, shook it, wondering.

Giving up, he set it on the floor next to Martindale's body and said, "C'mon, let's get out of here."

Pete, still dazed, hesitated, stepped over to the wall, reached up to the 5 x7 picture of Ramirez and Martindale and lifted it off its hook.

Dylan said, "What're you doing?"

Pete made a mumbling sound, shook his head, set the picture face down on the desk, next to the unplugged clock, stepped toward the door, and, in an almost imperceptible voice, said, "OK."

PART III

CHAPTER 40

YOU CAN CALL 911

T*uesday, February 17, 2015.* Sweeney, the limo driver, turned in to the long drive at 7:15am. The sun was near the horizon, starting to reveal what promised to be a cloud-free blue sky. The air was brisk, but not bitter cold; a winter morning delivering an early glimmer of spring. All in all, Sweeney saw it as potentially a good day, a day for optimism.

He absorbed the mood. Traffic going in after the long weekend would still be congested, but not as bad as it was coming out Friday night. With luck they'd be back to the Court by nine o'clock. He'd be done with the old toad before coffee break.

As he drove up to the house, he noted something was off. Why was a BMW sitting in the middle of the driveway right in front of the porch? Did old Mr. Speedway get a sporty new car? He just bought that new big-ass Mercedes. Where's he get the money?

The house was still. Usually, when Sweeney pulled up, the justice was coming out the door. He waited a few minutes, considered honking the horn, and decided not to risk screwing up a happy morning by irritating the old SOB. He went up on the porch and rang the bell. No answer. The extra secure door had no sidelites, so he couldn't peer in. He tried to look through the windows on the porch into one of the rooms in the front of the house. The draperies and blinds were all closed. He walked around to the side of the house and looked into the garage. He could see the Mercedes. Didn't make sense.

He called the justice's cell. No answer. Now he was getting ticked. The morning's promise was taking an ominous turn. What the hell's going on? Why the fuck didn't they tell him the schedule had changed?

He called the Court and got through to one of the U.S. Marshals, who knew nothing.

He called his dispatcher, Jolie. She'd be in early. If a schedule change was made, she would know.

She said, "Let me look." Pause. "Nope, the screen says you're supposed to make the pickup at 7:15."

Now what, he asked himself.

Jolie said, "Maybe you should call 911. Maybe something's wrong."

He didn't want to call 911. No telling how long before they'd show up. And what would he tell them?

He said, "Jolie, if something's wrong, why is there a BMW parked in the driveway?"

"Is that his car?"

"I don't think so. His car's in the garage."

"His car's in the garage, and there's a BMW parked in the driveway?"

"Yeah."

"And you think the presence of the BMW, which is not his car, is a clear sign nothing is wrong?"

The way she said it, put him on the defensive, "Well, that's not exactly what I meant."

"What exactly did you mean?"

"Look, Jolie, I don't want to argue with you; I just want to get old 'sweetness and light' down to the Court building, so I can go home."

"Aloysius, my man," (that was his first name, resulting in just about everyone calling him Sweeney) "seems to me like you got three choices. You can do nothing and just keep on arguing with me, or you can leave and go home, or you can call 911. Since I'm not going to argue with you anymore, that leaves two choices. If you leave and go home, you probably get reprimanded, maybe even suspended or fired. If he's inside there, being held hostage at gunpoint by the guy who owns the BMW, you may even be charged as some kind of accessory to the crime. So, if I were you, I'd call 911."

The Fauquier County sheriff's deputy walked around the house and checked all the windows and doors, trying to find an entry point that wouldn't require major property damage. He didn't find any soft spots. The place was unusually secure.

Then he called in the tag number on the plates on the BMW.

The locksmith had to weave through four law enforcement vehicles – two sheriff's department, two state police – parked at various angles in the long driveway, plus Sweeney's limo and the

BMW. Two FBI agents, coming from Alexandria, and a U.S. Marshal from the Supreme Court building in D.C., weren't there yet.

It took him almost ten minutes to get the front door opened, using power tools. He was on his haunches on the porch in front of the door and fell backward from the stench.

The sheriff and a state trooper went in, holding handkerchiefs over their faces, walking single file, touching nothing. Within five minutes an FBI Evidence Response Team, two FBI investigative specialists, an FBI special agent, two more U.S. Marshals, a Virginia State Police homicide investigator and a Virginia State Police forensics team were on their way to the scene. The driveway was going to get crowded.

Two uniformed state troopers started putting up yellow crime scene tape along the front of the property. Eventually it would wrap almost two of the ten acres. The Fauquier County sheriff and two deputies, about to be made seriously insignificant, but reluctant to leave the scene, stood and watched as the others scurried about. Ultimately, the deputies directed traffic and parking out on the road. The sheriff went to his car, pretended to make a few phone calls and otherwise tried to look busy.

At 9:15, the first TV news truck was stopped by a deputy fifty yards short of the driveway and told to park on the shoulder. By noon media trucks and cars lined the road for a couple hundred yards in each direction.

This was going to be a big one.

CHAPTER 41

MAGGIE FOSTER

T*uesday, February 17, 2015.* Maggie was sitting at the poker table in the Tampa casino when she got the call. The omnipresent cell phone, positioned in front of her on the black vinyl rail of the table, buzzed irritably.

The poker room was big – fifty tables – one of the largest in the country. Each table sat nine players, sometimes ten for the big tournaments, plus a dealer, all in comfortable leather chairs. Large full-color framed photographs of smiling winners adorned the bright rose-colored walls, trying to create an air of fun and excitement.

She looked up to a less inspiring sight, the see-through, gridded drop-ceiling, interspersed with solid black panels, each of which held a protruding dark-tinted glass node large enough to hold a high resolution video camera. The invisible cameras were positioned to assure clear sight lines to each table so as to capture the moves of all the dealers and players. Also to remind them they were being watched. Maggie marveled at the overall crime-detection potential and the oppressive implications, which made her wonder if George Orwell had ever been in a casino.

She was on a poker vacation, having flown down from D.C. on the previous Saturday, Valentine's Day. She'd come to the Tampa casino for a big Texas Hold'em tournament, a major event in the poker world. Big-money players were in town from all over the country. Some were professional or top amateur poker players, and others, well, they had big money.

The featured event, the high stakes tournament, didn't start until Friday, and she had no intention of playing in it. She was here for the preliminary games. The week prior to the big tournament was filled with satellite tournaments and medium- to high-stakes cash games, warm-up activities for the impatient and their predators. The cash games were an opportunity for the very good players to relieve the anxious, poker wannabes of money they didn't need. The lead-in week served as a kind of insurance policy for the good players, helping them cover their expenses for the week, and also to pick up a little take home, in case they didn't win money in the big tournament on the weekend.

Though not a professional, Maggie's poker skills were considerable. She could hold her own with most players, pros included. She'd been playing poker for almost 40 years, starting as a kid with her Dad and his friends. In college the poker table helped her pay for books and earn pocket money. Then in the late 90s, she discovered the mother lode, No-limit Texas Hold'em, Hold'em for short. Thereafter, she supplemented her government income by playing in medium-stakes Hold'em games.

This week Maggie expected to win, because she usually did. It was one of the reasons she was here, to win money.

Another reason was to hone her skills at reading people. Maggie was an FBI special agent with a reputation for getting her man, or woman, as the case may be. Her academic resume emphasized the study of human behavior. She had a Bachelors Degree in Criminal Behavior and a Masters Degree in Cognitive Psychology. Her doctoral thesis, which she never completed, featured law enforcement interrogation techniques. She'd been through FBI analyst training, but rejected that rating in favor of special agent status.

Throughout college she'd been at the top of her class and, after three years with the Illinois State Police, she accepted the Bureau's overtures. Her strength was her ability to sense what the bad guys were thinking, and when they were lying. Hold'em was good practice for that. She saw the game as a form of exercise, a periodic workout to stay in shape, and this week, the Tampa casino was the gym.

In Hold'em being good with cards and numbers and figuring odds in your head was a basic requirement. You had to know the percentages. Maggie could do that. Statistics was her second major as an undergrad. But being good at math was only the entry fee; it got you in the door. It helped you win when you had the best cards. Getting to the next level – winning when you didn't have the cards – involved strategic thinking, even game theory. It required patience, discipline and ruthlessness. You had to be willing to deceive and manipulate your opponents. Good Hold'em players mastered the art of deceit. Like criminals, they had to lie. It was an essential ingredient to their success. So Maggie used the game to hone her professional skills – picking out when they were lying.

The other reason she came down was to have fun – playing poker was fun – and because she needed air, air for the soul. Too many people in D.C. were afflicted with acute ambition. The lack of moral oxygen was suffocating. Viciousness abounded. Dedicated public servants were paralyzed with fear, afraid to express opinions, afraid to disagree, afraid to make decisions, afraid to take actions on their own, afraid to put anything in writing. The ultimate fear was of getting sucked into a career-ending political whirlpool that could take away their most prized possession, their government pension. JFK said that Washington was a town of "Northern hospitality and Southern efficiency." Maggie thought he was being too kind.

She often wished she'd stayed in New York City, where she was posted for almost fifteen years. New York people were sincere and helpful, or so she remembered. She smiled to think she would say that about the Big Apple, where incivility was one of the arts. But compared to D.C., NYC was a rose garden. Maggie came to Tampa to relax and play and block out the D.C. rancor and duplicity. Here at the poker table she could focus on an activity where the sharks weren't cloaked as public servants.

The cherry on top of the sundae would be Ted's arrival from Chicago on Friday. They were going to celebrate Valentine's Day a week late. Ted Howe was her man. He was kind, intelligent, funny, serene and good in bed. They'd had a long distance romance going for five years now. Ted was an aeronautical engineer based in Chicago. Out of college he went to work for Boeing. Later on he did seven years with the Department of Defense and now worked as a consultant. Not surprisingly, his two biggest clients were Boeing and DOD. His duties put him in the D.C. area about thirty per cent of the time, which worked out well for Maggie. She never felt like she had too much of him. At 57, he was still easy on the eyes and fun to be with. To her, their setup was close to perfect. He was her sanity base for when the zombies started coming out of the cemetery. So instead of playing in the big tournament on the weekend, she'd play with Ted in the Florida sun. At least that was the plan.

When Maggie arrived at the Tampa airport on Saturday, it was mid-afternoon, sunny, 74 degrees. She was comfortable in medium-weight grey slacks, a white short-sleeve blouse and grey casual flats. The winter jacket, sweater and gloves she'd worn to Dulles were all stuffed in her large shoulder bag along with her purse.

The purse contained her government issued 9-mm Sig Sauer, FBI badge, wallet, keys, lipstick, compact, Kleenex, etc., etc. Walking to the baggage area, it occurred to her that if, at that moment, she had to stop a terrorist from escaping, she'd first have to find her purse inside the shoulder bag, then find her gun in the holster inside the purse, then pull it clear of the holster and all the paraphernalia in the purse, then go into a shooting crouch, all before she could take action. By that time the guy could be in Orlando. In moments of retrospection she chided herself for not taking the gun responsibility more seriously. The NRA would not be happy with her.

She picked up the mid-size Korean rent-a-car and drove directly to the casino hotel. On Saturday afternoon it took only twenty minutes. She'd made her reservation almost three months ago and got one of the last available rooms. It was a big week at the casino.

After checking in, she showered, changed into her poker uniform – jeans, sneakers and sweat shirt – before going down for an early supper in the hotel deli. She left half of the corned beef sandwich uneaten. It wasn't up to her standards. New York had spoiled her.

She found the poker room, looked it over and sat down to play for a few hours. She won $900. Sunday she played a little longer, winning only $300. At nine o'clock she went back to her room and called her daughter, Gabby. Gabby was in law school at Columbia. Her father, Maggie's ex and a commodities trader at the Chicago Board of Trade, was picking up the tab. He could afford it. He was a very smart guy. Just not as smart as Maggie. Right after Gabby was born he made the mistake of cheating on her. When she questioned him, he lied. Even then she knew, almost as if she was born with it.

In Maggie's heart Gabby was the only person in the world ahead of Ted. Gabby's existence made Maggie's mistake with the ex worthwhile. When apart, they had long phone chats every Sunday night, filling each other in on the week's events. They cut this one a little short, because Gabby was working on a major project. Maggie went down to the Poker Room, played for a couple hours and broke even. Cards were terrible.

She took Monday off and tried to read at the pool, but it was too chilly to sit outside. February weather in the Sunshine State could be checkered. She opted for a little window shopping, a massage, manicure and pedicure, and a Cuban sandwich in Ybor City.

Back in her room on Monday night, she checked the cable news. A guy named Martindale was still missing. Martindale was a lobbyist for a conservative political firm in D.C. Maggie'd never heard of him. Late Friday night, almost 72 hours ago, his wife reported that he hadn't shown up to join her at a resort in West Virginia. She said she had no idea where he was, and it wasn't like him not to call. His disappearance was the lead on all the cable news channels. Fox News was apoplectic. Maggie turned off the TV and read herself to sleep.

Now, on Tuesday afternoon, with three days still to go before the big tournament, she was looking forward to a full day in the poker room. The action and the winnings potential would increase each day leading up to the tournament. Today, her plan was to put in at least 12 hours at the poker table with a few short breaks.

She was at a $5-10 table, a middle level where the stakes and the skill levels were neither too high nor too low. Today, tomorrow and Thursday she would likely pay for the trip and also put a nice deposit into her retirement fund, both while engaged in her second favorite activity. Her favorite activity would have to wait until Ted came down on Friday.

When her phone buzzed, she was in a hand. Though the ringer was off, the vibration from the buzzer was still intrusive. She had just looked at her pocket cards – jack/ten suited – one of her favorite holdings. They presented a wide range of potential winning opportunities.

On the phone's second buzz, she glanced at the screen. The caller had a 202 area code followed by seven zeroes. Shit, headquarters. Had to be something important. Nobody there would be calling to ask about the weather. She'd have to take the call. The phone buzzed again, number three. To Maggie it sounded like a dentist's drill.

Maybe she could get through the hand before it went to voice mail. No. Bad idea. She couldn't risk letting it go to voice mail. That would really piss off the big guys back in D.C. She was expected to have the phone on and close to her person at all times.

The phone buzzed for the fourth time. How many rings before it goes to voice mail? She thought eight, but wasn't sure. The dealer looked at her, as if to ask, "When are you going to turn that off?"

She looked at the phone again. Why would they be calling her on vacation? Her internal crisis sensor told her it was not a routine call. She visualized a crime scene at the caller's end with blood spread around like a Jackson Pollock painting, bodies and body parts scattered to all points.

If it was serious, they were going to tell her to abort her vacation and head back to the office. She didn't want to leave. The fun was just starting. Then the name Martindale flashed through her mind. Holy Shit!

The phone buzzed again. Five. She couldn't just turn the goddamned thing off. Please don't go to voice mail. Not a good idea to wait for another ring. She picked up the phone and blurted, "What is it?"

A poor choice of words. Fortunately, the person on the other end was Fran Berkley, the good-natured administrative assistant to T. J. Collins. Fran was not one of the tight asses. "Hi, Maggie, T. J. wants to talk to you." T.J. Collins was an executive assistant director, meaning he was tied for second in line to the director of the FBI. Fran added, "Sorry, if I interrupted something. Is everything OK?"

"Not so much. What's up?"

"I'll let him tell you. Just hold while I switch you in."

T. J. sounded a bit out of breath, "Maggie?"

"Yes sir," concern now in her tone as she walked slowly away from the table, muffling her voice, head down, mouth touching the phone. The dealer mucked her coveted suited jack/ten. She continued to drift toward the empty tables, looking for an isolated spot where she could talk.

"I hate to do this, Maggie, but we've got a situation here. Can you get to the airport by 3:45? Fran's getting you a seat to Dulles on a Delta flight."

She looked at her watch. It was 2:29. "What's going on? Do I get any...uh, what kind of situation? Can you tell me anything?"

Collins was Maggie's boss's boss and something of a mentor.

"I'm sorry, Maggie. All hell's breaking loose around here. I'm a little...they found two bodies in Virginia this morning – Whit Martindale and Supreme Court Justice Ramirez. The president is going off the charts. Martindale's a big republican politico, and you know who Ramirez is, neither is exactly a friend of the administration."

He added, "The president wants a joint task force with the best people from everywhere. I told the director I wanted you to head this up from our side. There'll be a meeting tomorrow morning at the White House and probably a press conference. You need to get out to the scene tonight. It's not far from Dulles. Can you make that flight?"

"Holy mother f... I'm...what...yes, yes, I'll get there," looking at her watch again. "It's 2:30. I'll get there. Can you have an agent come here to the casino hotel and get my rent-a-car and turn it in?"

"Sure, Fran can call the office down there."

Maggie said, "He can get the keys at the concierge desk. Make sure they hold that plane for me, just in case. Use your shit." The urgency made her forget who she was giving orders to.

From the poker table to the departure gate she felt like she was in an abbreviated version of the reality TV show, *The Great Race.* She furiously gathered her stack of chips, cashed them in and ran to the hotel elevator. Fortunately she was in jeans and sneakers. The ride to the fifth floor and her room seemed interminable. Did T. J. say a meeting at the White House? Oh, my God.

She ran from the elevator down the cream-colored hall seven doors to her room, opened the door, grabbed her suitcase and shoulder bag from the closet next to the door, threw them on the bed, ran around the room throwing belongings into the appropriate containers, checked to make sure she had her gun, badge, phone, wallet and keys, and shuffled as fast as she could into the hallway and back to the elevator with the rolling suitcase bumping along behind her and the shoulder bag bouncing off her hip.

Once on the elevator she looked at herself in the full-length elevator mirror. Hair okay. The thick, reddish-blond, medium short locks worn in a semi-bob almost always held up in frantic situations. Make-up okay. She hardly wore any to begin with. The jeans and sneakers and sweatshirt were neat and practical, but hardly traditional FBI attire. They'd have to do. Her winter coat and gloves were in the shoulder bag.

Did he say the White House?

She shuffled off the elevator and ran/walked to the concierge, dropped off the keys with a $20 bill and a quick explanation to give the keys to the first FBI agent who showed up. Also asked the concierge to notify the reception desk she was checking out. They already had her credit card info. More run/walking to the lobby door and the first taxi in line. She got into the cab at 2:49. The cab ride was a bit harrowing, since rush hour in Tampa in February is pretty much the better part of every weekday. Got out of the cab at 3:24, probably enough time to do the check-in lines. The problem could be the damned handgun procedure. She hoped T. J. had done his magic to hold the plane. If he'd dropped the ball, she might not make it.

Good news was the check-in people were on full alert for an FBI VIP, specifically Senior Special Agent M.A. Foster. Bad news was they assumed Senior Special Agent M. A. Foster would be a man, very likely a man in a conservative business suit with a briefcase. What they saw stretched their credibility – a woman, not exactly young, but admittedly attractive, somewhat hurried, and dressed like a female Columbo. The whole package threw them. It cost valuable time for the ticket agent and his supervisor to accept that Maggie was the VIP this plane was being held for.

Then, of course, there was the paperwork on the handgun. Armed federal law enforcement people, when traveling on duty, were expected to carry their weapons on board with them. The pilots' union, on the other hand, demanded they be properly cleared. To a security conscious air travel community, both conditions made complete sense. To a flight crew and a planeload full of passengers full of hurry, it was serious aggravation.

At 3:46 Maggie was running down the jet way to a reconfigured Boeing 737. Two flight attendants and a co-pilot were standing just inside the door of the plane, not smiling. When Maggie reached the door, the co-pilot said, "Welcome aboard." Still no smile. Then added, "May we leave now?"

Maggie walked past him as if she hadn't heard him. She had a middle seat in coach near the front of the plane. As she sidled up the aisle to her seat, she saw disgruntled looks on the faces of several passengers. She wanted to tell them this wasn't her idea. Instead she tried to feign preoccupation.

As she settled into her seat, her thoughts bounced between two dead VIPs in Virginia, the blown poker playing opportunity, a meeting in the a.m. at the White House, and a slightly delayed airline flight. Under her breath she said, "Fuck it."

CHAPTER 42

THE WALK THROUGH

Tuesday, February 17, 2015. Josh Henley, a young agent from the Alexandria office, picked Maggie up at the airport and filled her in on what he knew, which was very little. The Fauquier County sheriff had held a brief news conference at 1:30pm, revealing the identity of the victims and estimated time of death, but little else. Prior to that, according to Josh, they notified the two new widows.

She asked, "What did he say time of death was?"

"They're not sure yet. Been at least three days since they were killed. So, sometime Saturday, maybe Friday. Driver from the Court dropped the justice off on Friday evening about 6:20. The other guy disappeared about then. So sometime after that."

In the car on the way out to the scene, she called T.J. He was in a meeting with the director. Fran said she'd have him call as soon as he came out.

Maggie said, "You're there kind of late. Any news?"

Fran said, "It's all hands on deck right now. Latest is the president's doing a TV thing tonight at nine."

"Everybody all jacked?"

"If the president's jacked, everybody is. Lots of people walking around real fast. Fast walking is the surest sign that people are jacked."

"He doing it from the Oval Office or Press Room?"

"I think Oval Office. Doubt if he wants to face the press."

"What's he going to say?"

"Maggie, this is Fran you're talking to. I don't get consulted on the president's messages to the nation. All I know is people are walking real fast past my desk."

"Well, be careful you don't get run over. Ask T.J. to call me, when he has a moment."

"Will do. Soon as he has one of those."

When Maggie got to the farm house at 6:55pm, the night air was cold, near freezing. She donned her winter jacket and a pair of plastic gloves from the car. She told Henley to stay in the car until she had a chance to do a walk through alone. He stayed with the car at the bottom of the driveway. To get to that parking spot, they had to weave their way through about ten TV and radio trucks, which Josh said was down from more than twenty-five earlier in the day.

As she got out of the car, a young state trooper approached and handed her a thick envelope marked "Confidential." Her name was written on the outside. It contained copies of all the crime scene photos.

The note inside the envelope said simply, "Call me" and was signed "Olen." Olen Richards was the Evidence Response Team

Leader assigned to the case. An Evidence Response Team is the FBI version of a CSI forensic unit. She'd worked with Olen once before and remembered him as being thorough and involved. He liked doing what he did.

Before calling him or looking at the photos, she walked the scene, invoking the investigator's vanity that with her unique powers of observation she might notice a telling piece of evidence, something everyone else missed. Of course, to achieve the necessary objectivity for such perspicacity, her mind had to be clear, unadulterated by anyone else's opinions or observations, even the photographer's.

Starting outside, she took out her flashlight and walked the full perimeter of the house. Because of the trees and the setback and the dim light, she could see no other houses, not a glimmer of light in any direction. She checked all the windows of the country house, walked over to the out building, looked inside, back to the house and up the porch steps.

Stepping through the front door she picked up a faint odor that she assumed was the smell of rotting dead bodies. The day's activities had apparently aired the place out quite a bit, but not completely. The door on the other side of the foyer was closed. It was a louvered bi-fold door. She pulled it aside, noted it was a closet, and peered in. Empty hangers, but a folded suit coat on top of a somewhat disheveled overcoat lying on the floor next to a briefcase. She started her walkthrough, going from room to room looking for something out of place or extraordinary, trying to conjure up what had happened.

In the kitchen the door to the basement was open. She went down the stairs into an unfinished, low ceilinged, large single room. The walls were poured cement. No carpeting, no attempts at décor. Two small windows at the top of the back wall and two more on one side wall, all four covered with taped-on newspaper instead of curtains or blinds.

The only pieces of furniture were a card table and a folding chair by the wall opposite the stairs. Dust marks indicated a computer or similar object had recently been on the table. Black cords led from a router to a surge protector outlet. Another long cord from the outlet to a ceiling plug. No printer. Crime scene people must have taken the computer.

The opposite wall held a large gun safe, built into the wall about a foot off the floor. Possibly installed recently, or at least well after the walls were poured. It was closed and locked. Why?

After a quick last glance around, she went upstairs, walking through the kitchen to a family room and ending her tour in the den.

The bodies had been removed, leaving only the forensic chalk marks. Nothing of note, except maybe the little unplugged clock, stopped at 6:31, the photo of the two victims face down on the desk next to the clock, and a space on the wall with an empty picture hook that may have earlier held the photo. Significant?

Still standing, she opened the envelope from Olen, took out the photos and gave them a quick peruse. The bodies appeared to be in the early stages of decay. Martindale's head was turned at a peculiar angle, maybe a broken neck. No obvious blood on either body.

The photographer paid special attention to the little unplugged clock, the face-down photo and the empty hook on the wall. There were at least two photos of everything she'd seen in her little walk through including the coats and briefcase on the closet floor. So much for her unique powers of observation. After the second time through the photos, she went out to the car and called Olen.

"Hi, Mags," he answered.

She didn't like "Mags" from him. Maggie was okay, but "Mags" was presumptive, assuming a closeness they didn't have. Ted could call her Mags. He could call her anything he wanted, but not Olen. Before responding, she realized, in view of the task at hand, she was being petty. She let it go.

"Hi, Olen. Whatcha got?"

"Are you sitting down? This is going to take awhile. Your ankles might eventually feel distressed."

"I'm sitting. Hit me."

"Note taking device?"

"Got it." She propped the iPad on her knees.

"Start with Ramirez. Time of death between 6p and midnight, Friday. He died from an injection of a toxic substance similar to pento-barbital, which is a drug used for lethal injections, like in executions, and in euthanasia, both animal and human. It's assumed to be a less traumatic way to go. I'm estimating he received about 15 grams, which is more than enough for a person of his body weight."

He paused to take a breath. Maggie remembered Olen was a heavy smoker and overweight.

He continued, "Can't be absolutely positive about that amount. After this long, some of it might have deteriorated, but it's a reasonable approximation. They also injected sodium thiopental, most likely as a sedative prior to the intravenous injection."

"They? More than one killer?"

"Had to be. The whole two-stage injection thing would be damned near impossible for one guy. Ramirez was armed. One person would have to tie up his gun hand while the other injected the sedative. A lone assailant could have gotten himself shot up real good."

"So, just two? Not three, or four or more?"

"Would've been overkill, excuse the expression. Only needed two. Other guys would just be standing around. Probably just two."

"What about the other guy – Martindale?"

"Same time of death. His spinal column was severed up high at the C3, C4 level. Clean through, almost like a knife. Whoever did it was tall and strong, probably right-handed and was familiar with the technique."

"I get strong, but why tall?"

"Looks like he had to do it from behind, over Martindale's shoulder. Martindale is six one. The killer had to be at least that, probably more."

"Pretty sure it was a man?"

"Almost for sure. Unless she was a certified Amazon."

"Why right-handed?"

"The head was turned to the right. If he did it from behind, which is most assuredly the case, he had to put his right hand on Martindale's chin and pull. Stands to reason, he'd use his strongest hand for that."

"The other one have to be a man?"

"No ma'am. Could've been either."

"What else?"

"You see any reports yet?"

"Just the photos."

"Forensically, there's nothing else. It was a very professional job. Don't even know how they gained entry, unless Ramirez let them in."

"No hair follicles or stuff under their fingernails or anything?"

"Not a whit."

"So you got nothing?"

"Just one item, a real lulu." He paused to catch his breath again. Maggie suspected he was enjoying her anticipation.

"OK, Olen, you got me on the edge of my seat here. Let's hear it."

"There was a small briefcase. Apparently belonged to Martindale. Combination lock. His initials."

Another pause, "Would you like to know what was inside?"

"C'mon, Olen."

"One hundred large. Large as in thousands. Thirty-four packets of mostly twenties, some fifties. We counted it twice."

"They just left it?"

"Yes ma'am. Found it with the bodies, lying next to Martindale."

"So, in your vast experience and wisdom related to criminal investigations, you'd probably rule out robbery as a motive."

"Seems like a reasonable assumption...in view of my vast experience, etc."

"Why wouldn't they just take it 'cuz it was there? I mean, it's money."

"Calls for the knowledge and judgment of a top dog investigative analyst like yourself, not just a humble forensic scientist like me. Nevertheless, I've pondered the question. I'll give you the benefit of those musings, if you like."

"Hit me."

"Number one: they didn't know what was in the briefcase, because they couldn't open it. Not knowing it contained one hundred thousand simoleans, they had no reason to take it, especially since, if found on their person, it could tie them to the scene." Deep breath. "Two: they left it behind by mistake, in their rush to get the hell out of there, before another potential sacrificial witness showed up. And three: they didn't need the money." Another breath pause, "You probably don't want to waste a lot of time mulling that last one.

"So, milady, those options help you in nailing something down?"

She didn't like "milady" any more than "Mags" but reminded herself this was the wrong time to get chippy. "We'll see. What happened to the computer in the basement?"

"We dusted it and then Fontaine sent it to "Cyber" for their perusal. Cyber's got the cell phones, as well."

"Sam Fontaine?" Sam was an FBI senior special agent.

"Yeah, he officiated as the lead from the Federal side, till you got there."

"Anybody else I should know about?"

"The state police guy, a detective name of Battinelli. Didn't say much. Don't think he likes us."

"Anything else?"

"Not at this time. Except, good luck. You might need it on this one."

"Yeah, we'll see. Oh, Olen, one more thing. What's with the safe in the basement? What was in it?"

"Don't know. Goddamned thing is like Fort Knox. Couldn't get it open without blowing up the neighborhood. There'll be a guy from the safe company out there in the morning. Coming from Milwaukee."

Breath pause, "Couldn't get him here today, because of the weather up there. Claims he couldn't tell us what to do over the phone. He's some kind of "safe whisperer" or something. Specializes in opening these safes when the owner dies or forgets the combination."

"What time tomorrow morning?"

"He's due in on the flight out of Chicago following his connector flight from Milwaukee. Be mid-morning, unless they have more weather issues."

"OK, Olen. Tomorrow, then. Wait. You said a professional job. You mean, like a contract killing?"

"It was very neat and quick, well planned, no loose ends. No traceable evidence left behind. Doesn't seem like something amateurs could do. And Martindale's neck was about as clean a break as you'd see. Somebody with experience."

"No chance this was a random thing?"

"Hardly."

"You do many contract killings in your time?"

"Not that I can remember. At least none of this nature."

"Ever hear of one where they used lethal injection?"

"Contract killing? No, I guess not. Might be a first."

"OK thanks, Olen. Talk to you."

As she took the phone from her ear, she heard a faint, "You're welcome."

She started a to-do list below her notes from the phone call. She paused and stared at the windshield, slipping into a deep thinking mode, trying to understand what had happened here. Moments later something distracted her. Josh was talking to one of the people from a TV truck. She opened the car door and called to him.

When he got into the driver's seat, she said, "Friend of yours?"

"No, just a cameraman."

"What were you talking about?"

"Asked me how long I'd been here?"

"Oh. What'd you tell him?"

"Since this morning."

"That's all. He didn't ask anything else?"

"No, that's when you called me over."

"How long you been with the Bureau?"

"Next week it'll be fifteen months. A year and a quarter," his tone indicating pride in his agent status.

"Listen carefully. You want to make it to sixteen months, you don't talk to the media. Any of them. Cameramen or drivers or janitors, whatever the hell they tell you they are.

"And, until this case is wrapped, if some hot chick talks you up in a bar, be suspicious. Don't just assume it's because of your cute dimples. If she, or anyone with her, brings up this case, lie. Tell them you're CIA, and the Russians are coming. Don't tell anybody anything about this case. Not even your mother."

She paused, conscious of the sternness in her voice, then continued in a less parental tone, "We're about to go to war. The media, for the most part, are one of the enemies. They have nuclear capability. The way to stay safe, and inside the bomb shelter, is by not talking to anyone about this case. At least no one who doesn't have an FBI badge, and who doesn't out rank you. Clear?"

"Very clear."

"Any questions?"'

"No ma'am. No questions, very clear."

"Good. Let's get back to the city. I need to get to the office."

"Maybe one question."

"Shoot."

"Am I going to work on this case?"

"Not decided yet, but you might as well give me your cell number." As he recited it, she put it in her phone. Then she gave him hers.

He hesitated and put a serious look on before saying, "One more question."

"I'm listening."

"Do you really think I have cute dimples?"

She tried not to smile.

CHAPTER 43

NOT ENOUGH JUICE

Tuesday, February 17, 2015. On the drive in they listened to the president's talk. He was appropriately stunned and appalled. He was more than stunned and appalled, he was angry. He said these murders were a violation of the example we make to the world as a civilized nation and a threat to our national security. He reassured the country that the killers would be found and brought to justice. Maggie wondered how he knew that.

The speech took slightly over nine minutes. It passed the grade for astonishment and anger, but for Maggie's taste, it was a little short on genuine grief. She'd voted for his Republican opponent, making it easy to find him disingenuous. He signed off with the obligatory "God blesses," and the talking heads began dissecting the nine minute oration for special political meaning, particularly how it might affect the latest polls and the next election.

She turned off the radio to answer her phone. It was Fran. T.J. Collins was going to be tied up in meetings for at least an hour and would talk to her when she got in, assuming she'd be in before midnight. Maggie had a fleeting resentful thought that it was presumptuous of him to assume she was coming into the office at this late hour. Then she got real. Of course she was coming in.

She went back to thinking about the scene. What actually had happened there? How'd they get in? Why lethal injection? What was the briefcase full of money about?

At 9:45 pm, Maggie stepped off the elevator onto the top floor of FBI Headquarters. She noted that people were indeed walking fast.

She went directly to Fran's desk, "Where is he?"

Fran was focusing on her computer. "In the director's conference room. They're expecting you."

"Is Fontaine in there?"

"Don't know. Haven't seen him for a while."

She walked toward the director's conference room, tapped on the door, opened it and entered. She was still in her poker sweatshirt, jeans and sneakers. Sitting at the big table were six of the top officials of the Bureau – one woman, five men – all in traditional business outfits, all with jackets off. The men, except for the director, had loosened ties and rolled up sleeves.

It was her first time in this exalted enclave. She did a quick, single-glance inspection of the room. She saw a 12-foot oak conference table surrounded by about twelve to fourteen chairs, vinyl-covered, hardly plush. No bar, at least none visible. A small table in the corner with a coffee maker, cups, cream and sugar. The walls were the only exception to a very ordinary meeting room. They were covered with an excess of plaques and eight by ten photos, both black and white and full color. It was a room decorated by a man of either little pretention or on a highly restricted budget. She knew it wasn't the latter.

The director, Nathaniel Parker, sat at the middle of the table with Naomi Sarrano, the head of FBI Public Affairs and his go-to spokesperson, sitting next to him. Parker always kept her close by. He had good D.C. instincts.

The others, sitting on the other side of the table, were T.J. Collins; Arnie Povich, head of the Crime Division, who reported to Collins and was Maggie's immediate boss; Executive Assistant Director Karl Maas, head of the Terrorism Division; and someone she didn't recognize, sitting next to Maas.

She scanned the faces of the assembled group for clues to their mood. T.J.s' face showed concern. The others revealed stress or anger, and she thought she picked up a whiff of animosity from at least one of them.

Povich said, "Dressed for success?"

In spite of being Maggie's direct report boss, Povich wasn't a fan. T.J. Collins had recruited her from New York and put her in Povich's section without consulting him. She'd heard the rumor that when Povich retired, which was only a couple years out, she was T.J.'s choice to replace him. Povich had heard the same rumor and appeared not to embrace it.

Director Parker, a southern gentleman by birth and resume, stood up, a gesture of his heritage, and said, "Welcome, Special Agent Foster, please have a seat." He pointed to the empty chair next to T.J. Collins.

He added, "We know you've had a hectic day. It's been unsettling for all of us." Maggie wanted to interpret the remark as a subtle rebuke to Povich. If nothing else, the Director was a patron of civility.

He continued, "We're in the throes of getting organized. Maybe you can tell us where you are on everything. T.J tells me you've been out to the scene."

She said, "Yes, I went there from the airport. Did a walk-through, reviewed the photos and talked to Olen Richards. He's head of the ERP. I've seen no written reports yet. Nor have I talked to the sheriff or anybody with the state police or Fontaine. I understand he was our lead on the scene today. Thought he might be here in this meeting."

Povich responded, "Sam had to leave. Personal issue."

She thought that was odd. What personal issue could tear an agent away from a crisis like this? Something not being said. She had an advantage over Povich in these situations. He was a lousy liar. When he was telling less than the truth, she could tell. That shadow of mendacity was on his face now.

The director pulled it back to the main issue, "Any conclusions … thoughts?"

The question made her a little uncomfortable. It was starting to feel like an audition. She wanted to say *I sure as hell haven't solved the case yet,* but instead went with, "Lots of questions."

Povich wouldn't let it go. "No insights, no nothing?"

She noticed Naomi roll her eyes. Perhaps an ally.

Maggie said, "A bit early yet to have answers. So far, mostly questions."

T.J. said, "We all have them. What's at the top of your list?"

Maggie said, "The thing that jumps out is why lethal injection? And why for Ramirez and not Martindale? Both key questions. We answer those two, we'll be well ahead of where we are now."

T.J. asked, "Any others?"

Maggie recited a top of mind list, "What was Martindale doing there? What's the money in his briefcase about? How'd they get in, or did Ramirez know them well enough to let them in? And if so, who does he know who'd want to kill him? And what's in the safe downstairs? Like that."

Director Parker leaned forward onto the conference table. "Yes, ma'am, all good questions. We have them too. Any theories?"

She wondered if she should reveal the thoughts that ran through her head on the ride in. Decided she had to say something. "Two sort of conflicting things have struck me. First, it was well planned, almost professional. We're not dealing with stupid. They left no evidence at the scene. So, we can't count on the typical criminal IQ to help us catch them. We may have to get lucky.

"Second, it's very early to jump to conclusions, but there may be an easy explanation for the two different causes of death."

The director said, "Oh?" Everyone shifted ever so slightly in their chairs. She had their attention.

She took a deep breath. "Perhaps they just ran out of juice. They didn't have enough drugs to do two people."

While everyone thought about that, she continued, "If that's what happened, you can further surmise that they weren't expecting him. He walked in on them, or drove up the driveway on them, before they could get out of there. They had to kill him. He wasn't an intended victim. The old 'wrong place at the wrong time.' Collateral damage."

Silence in the room while they digested the common sense of that. Maas, feeling he had to say something, was first, "Lot of conjecture there. Prosecutor would have a hard time building a case around all that speculation." Maggie wondered if his grin was forced, or if he was having gas pains.

She responded with a straight face, "I'm sorry if I gave the wrong impression. I wasn't trying to build a case for trial. We're certainly a long way from going to trial." She hoped it didn't sound like she was talking down to him, even though her next comments were basic law enforcement dogma. "Mr. Maas, I'm simply trying to better understand the crime, so I can build a properly directed investigation. Getting a handle on motivation could keep us from going off on wild goose chases. If the two killings carry separate motivations, as would be the case if he surprised them, the difference in our strategy would be significant." Right out of Criminal Investigations 101.

He stared at her and said nothing.

She continued, "The possibility that Martindale was not an intended victim stems from the whole idea of a murderer using lethal injection in the first place. Of all the options available, lethal injection, especially a two-stage lethal injection, would not be anywhere near the top of the list for simplicity and efficiency. A pro would simply use a small caliber handgun to the back of the head.

"It's worse if you know the subject is armed. That means you're going to need two people to do the first needle. And as well planned as this thing appears to have been, it's reasonable to assume they were aware he'd be carrying.

"We have to assume the lethal injection was done for a reason, a reason that for the moment is mystifying. You just don't come up with something like that randomly. The lethal injection was carefully planned, as was the whole operation. So, why not do Martindale the same way?"

She paused to let that sink in. "Probably because he wasn't part of the plan. They had to improvise with him. And Olen said whoever did it, whoever ripped Martindale's spinal cord simply by turning his head, knew what he was doing. He's done it before. So, if they're good at killing people the easy way, we're back to our first question, 'why all the trouble of a lethal injection?'"

A not well-concealed smirk crossed Naomi's face. Did that all go down too quickly for her? Or was she enjoying Maggie breaking it down to basics? Or what?

Parker said, "That's an interesting theory. We'd like to think on it." Maggie thought it sounded like an imperial "we." If not, how did he know the others would like to think on it? And what difference would it make in the conduct of the investigation? Is he going to think on it, and then tell her to forget it? Was he going to tell her how to conduct the investigation? What the hell was going on?

He said, "Agent Foster, there's another issue needs settling. We have a bit of a situation here. The question has been raised whether this is a possible national security or terrorism case. Would you care to add anything on that issue?"

Whoa! The lights all went on in Maggie's head. It was a typical D.C. "alpha male" meeting. Maas was trying to take the case away from T.J. Collins.

Maas had a reputation for taking personal ambition to new levels, but this gambit might be a new indoor world record. Behind his back, some called him the "uber climber," adding the subtle ethnic slur to compound their disdain. "Uber" was a German word. Maggie remembered reading somewhere that Maas's heritage was Dutch, not German, but to most that was too fine a hair to split, the German descriptor stuck to him.

Before joining the Bureau, he'd been a young, aggressive, prosecuting attorney in New Jersey not known for giving quarter to the accused. After only one highly visible term as a county prosecutor, he made a somewhat presumptive attempt to become his party's gubernatorial candidate. Apparently, the party hierarchy in New Jersey was not pleased with his reluctance to get in line. So, they quashed his bid.

Not one to be easily discouraged, he decided to run away and join the circus in Washington. With the support of a few members of Congress, he landed a top post in the Bureau. Most Bureau officials in such lofty positions come up through the ranks. Now, having not learned his lesson in New Jersey, he was getting impatient for a move, not improbably, back into elected office. He could use a high profile case to gain attention. This one had all the markings of a career maker. The media coverage would give him the needed recognition.

For a moment Maggie admired his confidence in aggressively making his play. He had balls. He'd be a formidable poker player, except for one little problem. This case wasn't a good hand. It resembled two/seven off suit, the worst pocket cards you could get. Good poker players would fold it. Unless they were desperate.

Maggie, on the other hand, saw the case as a challenge, an opportunity to do what she was good at. Contrary to Maas, she did *not* want to move up. All the levels above her current position were even deeper political quagmires than she was in now. She'd had enough backstabbing. She hadn't told T.J. yet, but she was going to retire in a couple years also, as soon as she had the minimum twenty five in. He'd have to find someone else to fill Povich's position.

She looked again at the people in the room and did a quick analysis. They were now *her* audience. All eyes and ears were wondering what she might possibly have to offer to resolve such an unreasonable enigma. Naomi had a hopeful look on her face. What was she hoping for? Povich avoided her gaze. Maas met her eyes directly, betting she was out of her league. The guy sitting next to Maas appeared to be in deep thought, or listening to music on invisible ear buds, staring at a spot on the ceiling. His demeanor was that of a disinterested party, not hearing, not seeing, not speaking. T.J., much the opposite, looked at her with a sparkle of hope in his eye, as if saying, *"This is important. Do your thing."*

It definitely was an audition.

A question crossed her mind? Did she want to pass or fail? Her ego provided a quick answer. Of course she wanted to pass. This case would be the test she'd been cramming for her entire career. It would define her professional life. She understood it wasn't going to be a layup, but she had to take the shot.

Her ego also reminded her of something Ted had said to her, "Try not to forget that you're smarter than all of them, and for God sakes, don't ever reveal to any of them that you know it."

So, she warned herself to look serious, but not officious. She gave them her deep thinking look and said, "You can do a probability analysis."

The director said, "How so?" His tone was one of tolerance and a dash of skepticism. He'd hoped for a more practical answer.

Maggie said, "You run simulations using what you know about this case against common characteristics of terrorism and homicide cases. From that you get two probability estimates. Then you simply go with the one that scores the highest."

Maas said, "We don't have time for social science experiments. We need a decision now. It's a matter of risk. Even the president called it a national security matter. If there's any chance of a terrorist plot, we can't dawdle." His sidekick showed no interest in the discussion. He continued to stare at the ceiling.

Maggie responded openly, pretending she didn't perceive Maas's comment as a dismissal. "Won't take any time at all. We can do it right here at the table. We take a list of terrorism factors and another list for plain old homicide, and we stack them both up against what we have. Simple as that."

She consciously avoided calling it a "thumb-nail" approach, which, of course, it was.

Parker's expression took on a hopeful aspect. He leaned forward and said, "OK, let's try it."

CHAPTER 44

I PLAY WELL WITH OTHERS

T*uesday, February 17, 2015.* As they walked out of Parker's conference room, T.J. told Maggie to meet him in ten minutes in his office. He was trying to mask the satisfied look on his face. He liked winning, but didn't want to taint it by looking smug.

He and Maggie were similar in height, about 5'8." The hair remaining on the sides of his smooth scalp was gray. Maggie went to his fiftieth a few years ago, so she knew his age, but she thought his trim shape and agile step showed him younger. She admired him, mostly for his integrity.

He'd come up through the ranks of the Bureau, acquiring what Maggie thought was an insightful view of its future. He saw it as a resource for all the other law enforcement organizations in the country: federal, state, and municipal. He believed that to successfully fulfill that mission, the Bureau had to cure its ego problem. It had to gain the respect of them all, to shed its image of arrogance and self importance. He wanted people in positions of authority who could help make that happen. When Maggie's team in New York brought down a gaggle of big guys on Wall Street, who'd been illegally tilting the playing field, he attached her wagon to his star.

In recruiting her to come to D.C., he told her he was impressed with her style, both her emphasis on getting the job done, no matter who got the credit, and her seeming indifference to the FBI status game. He could have arbitrarily transferred her to his division, without giving her a choice, because the Bureau, like the military, could put you where they wanted. But he gave her the option of staying in New York or coming to Headquarters. She was swayed by his vision and openness and made the move.

After checking phone messages and taking bathroom breaks, they were sitting across from each other at T.J.'s desk. Arnie Povich was absent. Maggie wondered why. Busy with something or not invited? Is T.J. tiring of pretending?

He opened with, "You did good. The broken neck theory is good logical thinking. And your response to Maas was perfect. But I'm curious how you came up with the probability simulation bit? It felt almost like a party game. "

"It's not a bit, T.J.; I do it all the time. In poker it's the first thing you do."

"What. It's a gambling trick?"

"Noooh! Not at all. It's not gambling or a trick. It's life. I learned it years ago in Statistics 101. The prof compared all good decision making to a simple logical process. He said basic life decisions, whether they be financial, career, marriage, kids, house, car, lifestyle, even games; everything comes down to odds. The more often you go *with* the odds, the more you minimize risk and the more often you make the right decision."

"And you establish the odds by going through these probability exercises?"

"Yeah. And it works. In poker it can get more complicated. Sometimes you have to make judgment calls, but life is simpler. You can get more things right. You can do it in your head. Once you know the odds, you go with them. If the odds are 60/40, you'll be right sixty percent of the time. If they're 90/10, you're right ninety percent."

"What about the forty or ten percent of the time you're wrong?"

"You have to roll with them. Better to be wrong forty or ten percent than sixty and ninety."

"But you have to know the true variables. There's so much opportunity to be subjectively wrong in your input."

"There is. You have to be disciplined. If you want something real bad, forget about objectivity. As they say in the ads, just do it. But if you haven't already made up your mind, you have a chance to be objective. If you can be objective, probability simulations are the way to go. Really, it works. It's one of the factors in being consistently successful."

He was still skeptical, "Surprised Maas let you get away with it. You could've tilted that simulation any way you wanted."

Maggie smiled, "I didn't have to tilt anything. It was cut and dried. Everybody at that table, including Maas, knew this case had nothing to do with terrorism. The fact that it even came up was all about Maas's ambition. As it happened, the director didn't have much choice. I gave him an out. He doesn't like to tangle with political animals. He knew he'd have to rule against Maas, but he wanted to have a rational basis, or at least look like he did."

"I'm going to have to remember it. Sure pissed Maas off."

She asked, "By the way, who was the sphinx guy?"

"John Guerlach. Sort of Maas's gofer. Watch out for Guerlach. If he invites himself to sit down at your table in the cafeteria, keep an eye on your dessert."

Maggie shifted in her chair, then leaned forward with her forearms on the desk between them, "T.J., that leads to something else that needs clearing up."

He gave her a raised eyebrow, an unspoken question mark.

She hesitated, looking for the right words. Finally, just saying it, "What's going on? This is a big case; not just any case, but the frigging homicide of the frigging century."

"So?"

"Seems to me a lot of people around here would want this. Well placed, experienced people. People who play the political game better than I do. You're setting yourself up for a lot of shit. Politics is not my long suit."

"Don't you want it?"

"Oh, hell no. It's not a question of whether I want it. Anyone with a little hair on their.....any one would want it. It's the center of the arena. My question is: what's going on? If I'm in the middle of some political conflict or strategy, at least I should know about it."

T.J. was slouched in his chair. He took a deep breath and folded his arms across his chest. "Good that you've asked. It's a perfect lead into a little speech I was planning to give."

He sat up and put his elbows on the desk. He held up his left hand, index and middle fingers pointing upward, "Two reasons it's you."

Folding in the middle finger, he said "First, is leadership. This is a Joint Task Force. Maybe the mother of them all. It's going to need someone who leads by helping everyone else do their job better. You've demonstrated that you already know how to get results out of a diverse group. You don't put on any FBI airs. One of our biggest problems here is most other agencies and law enforcement groups dislike us, or resent us a whole bunch. They don't want to help us. They even make up jokes about us. We have to clean up our act. Your proven strength is to get the locals and other agencies to help get the job done. We need a leader who will set that kind of example for our own people and show the outsiders we're not a bunch of arrogant, conceited, self-serving suits."

He retracted his index finger and raised his middle finger, seemingly unaware that he was, in street parlance, giving her the bird. "Second, you're smart. Very smart. When I vetted you to come to Headquarters, I talked to a lot of people inside and outside the Bureau. They said they respected you for your brains. One guy said 'when you walked into any room full of people, the average IQ in the room went up ten points.' Like the broken neck thing. That was smart thinking. And it just came natural to you. Maybe we all would've gotten there after a while, but you were there fast. You make good decisions. Life is about making good decisions. Maybe it's the simulation bit. Whatever, you use good judgment. Being smart is certainly a factor in making good decisions."

He took down his fingers, apparently still not aware what he'd been signaling.

"Bottom line: we need a smart leader, who makes good decisions, who'll get the job done, and who won't try to hog all the credit. You're a better politician than you know. People trust you. They say they like you and trust you, because you're honest and open. You don't try to take credit for their good work.

"That's my speech. Any questions?"

"Uh, no...guess not." She said it almost as if she was immune to the praise. When she asked, "Why me?" she wasn't fishing for praise, she was trying to get a better handle on her role. She wanted to know exactly what T.J. expected. Now she was ready to move on.

"Good. Let's get started. I've made up a list of all the agencies you'll have access to on the Task Force. Fran will email it to you ASAP, if she hasn't already. I'll lean on them as much as I can to give us good people. Tell me, if you have any favorites. Maggie, you're going to have the best investigative team in the history of investigative teams.

"By the way, the meeting at the White House tomorrow morning has been cancelled. He's decided to take a low profile."

"Good."

He tilted his head, "Why good?"

She said, "This one'll get real sticky. It's a lose/lose for him. He should keep it at arm's length. Unless he had something to do with it. The more he involves himself, the more the opposition will use it against him. When we find the real guys, the conspiracy theorists will say they're just beards."

T.J. smirked, "You're right, they'd say he's doing a Vladimir Putin. If he tried to run it, the radio talk show guys would have orgasms right on the air. Maybe a trusted advisor clued him in."

He paused, "Oh, one more thing, the director is doing a press conference in the morning. 9:30. He'll announce the formation of the Task Force, introduce you, and he might answer questions. Obviously, you need to be there."

She said, "Sure. But just a few more questions. First, anything more on the briefcase and the money?"

Leaning back in his chair, "Nothing. Just very strange. "

"Well, as they say in the movies, we have to 'follow the money.'" I have a special request for a Treasury guy. I worked with him before. He's out of Treasury's New York office."

T.J. raised his eyebrows, "That may be a problem. Nobody's going to want to transfer guys down here, especially with all the talent here in D.C."

Maggie wanted to challenge the quality of the talent in D.C., but she refrained. "Transfer won't be necessary. Anything he needs to do he can do from his desk in Manhattan. He could probably do it from his bedroom. He's a whiz at tracing financial activity around the world. Name's Boddington, Stanley Boddington. Originally from the U.K. Lived over here since college. Talks like a Brit, but he's one of us. Big Giants fan. He was key in bringing down the Wall Street guys. I want him. He's good."

T.J. conceded, "Ok, I'll call in a favor or two. What else."

"I think I'm going to need a computer whiz. A hacker type. Someone who is comfortable with the 'deep web' or the 'dark net' or whatever. All that spooky stuff." She was thinking of how a person not connected with the Mob might find a contract killer. "Maybe somebody from NSA."

T.J. said, "I know the perfect candidate, and he's one of our own. Won't need to go to NSA."

"What's his name?

"Chu, Timothy Chu."

"Ok, last request: I need the world's best homicide investigator. Any thoughts?"

"I'll work on it. You work on it too. Ask around. See what the water cooler gang comes up with."

"Oh, and if it's not a problem, give me that kid, Henley."

"Who?"

"Josh Henley. The guy who picked me up at the airport."

"He's yours."

It was 11:15 pm. Maggie left T.J.'s office and went down two floors to her own. She checked her list and added several items to it, including a personal matter.

She took care of the personal matter first. It was 10:25 in Chicago. Ted answered on the third ring. "Hey, babe, what's up? You winning big?" He didn't know she wasn't still at the tables in Tampa.

"Uh, not exactly. We've had a little change of plans."

"Oh…ok, I'm flexible…usually."

"Ted, first I want you to know I love you."

A pause, then. "You dumping me?"

"Only for our Florida weekend. It's off. They called me back to Oz. I'm back in the saddle."

She heard rustling, as if he was trying to sit up in bed. He must have been reading. He was disciplined in not going to sleep before 11pm.

He said, "I think you just mixed metaphors or whatever."

"You don't want to know what it's about?"

He said, "Ramirez?"

"Ring the bell. You get a prize. How'd you guess?"

"It's the only thing on cable TV and talk radio. They're all convinced the world is coming to an end."

She let herself go off topic, "Honey, why do you listen to talk radio? It's so…déclassé, so intellectually vulgar." She enjoyed being a snob about the more tawdry political discourse in the media. "Gabby says it's been proven to cause brain damage."

"She must be working on a class action." He defended his listening habits, "Maggie, my love, the guy here in Chicago already has Harwell doing a perp walk out of the Oval Office. If I didn't listen, I wouldn't know he did it. Question is, how'd Harwell manage to knock off two people with the Secret Service spooks all around him?"

"That's *President* Harwell, and the Secret Service agents are not spooks. Spooks are spies, like CIA agents."

"You know what I mean."

She brought it back to their lost romantic opportunity. "It's a relief to hear you're not terribly broken up about our belated Valentines' weekend being wiped out. I was worried you might be disappointed."

"Honey, it's all an act. Just covering up my distress with light banter. Don't want you to feel pressured…what with your daunting responsibility to protect our threatened nation."

She smiled at the phone, "I do love you. And before very long I'm going to need you. I'm already starting to feel a little tense, if you get my drift. Can you change your flight to give me a few hours here in D.C. this weekend?"

"Hell, I can do more than a few hours. You can have the whole weekend."

"Well, I suspect I won't be able to take advantage of all of a whole weekend. Should be kind of busy doing my thing, you know, investigating. We might be talking a quickie, if you'll pardon the vernacular."

"Ooh…don't know how to respond. As a rule, macho men like me like quickies, but they have drawbacks, you know. If the foreplay takes less than five minutes, for sure I'll have to fake it."

He shifted to a more serious tone, "Ok, Hon, help me here, and please don't take this the wrong way, but why do *you* have to do this one? You were on vacation. Don't they have thousands of agents in that big old, falling down building?"

"They need me for this one, because I'm special. Haven't I told you I'm the best they've got? Have you not been listening?"

"Oh, I forgot. I'll try not to do it again. Still, what exactly is it you're going to do that only you can do?"

"I think you just did it again. You're not getting it. I'm going to be the best. I'm the only one who can do that."

"But it's a murder thing. That's not exactly your forte. Is it? I mean you're an interrogator or something. And those task forces up in New York were about finances and corruption. What are you going to do on this one?"

"You're not helping my ego. My specific assignment...how do I say this...tomorrow morning at 9:30, FBI Director Nathaniel Parker will be announcing the formation of an FBI Joint Task Force charged with investigating this heinous crime and ultimately bringing the monsters who committed it to justice. It'll be part of a press conference which will no doubt be televised to the nation. Maybe even Chicago. If you're not *too* busy at that time, you may decide to watch, in which case you will see me on the platform being introduced as the head of the fucking Joint Task Force. So there."

"Holy shit! Holy shit! Holy shit!"

"You keep doing it. Or isn't that what 'holy shit' means?"

"C'mon, honey, please. I need a moment to acclimate...whew, such exalted company, I'm just not accustomed...let me catch my breath. Now my mind is wandering. It's going back to that quickie, or whatever. When we're doing that, will you still deem to speak to me?"

"You know I don't talk much at times like that."

"True. Ok, I'm going to risk doing it one more time. So, for real, why you?"

"You've forgotten the first rule of holes. If you're in one, stop digging. Ok, they said it was because I play well with others. Of all people, you should know that to be true."

They agreed Ted should come to D.C. on Saturday for a sleepover.

CHAPTER 45

DAY ONE

W*ednesday, February 18, 2015.* Maggie entered the building at 6:40am on the first full day of her new life. The sky was still dark. A person looking up would see no stars, only a dim vision of charcoal gray clouds. The temperature gauge in her car read 35 degrees. Walking through the lobby, she was stopped by the night security guard, who asked for her ID. His shift ended at 7:30am. He'd never seen her before.

Last night she left the building at 11:40. She got five hours sleep, which to her wasn't enough. She optimistically assumed she would be able to return to her normal life in a couple weeks.

In the kitchenette down the hall from her office she picked up a large cup of black coffee, her second of the morning. The first came from the drive-thru window of the McDonald's near her condo.

On the drive in, while the coffee cooled in the console holder, she started a mental to-do list. The first item was an email to T.J. about a hot line. They were going to need a dedicated line for tips from the general public. The FBI already had an all-purpose call line, but she was concerned about bandwidth. With the media coverage she anticipated, the generic FBI line might not be able to handle the volume.

Now at her desk, she wrote down a new to-call list: Fontaine; the head of the Virginia State Police; the supervisor of U.S. Marshals at the Supreme Court Building; the D.C. police chief; Olen; Boddington; and Maurice Banks, in Albuquerque. None of the calls could be made before the sun came up. She started a separate written to-do list.

The phone rang. She looked at her watch, wondering who would be calling at 6:55am.

She answered, "Foster."

"Special Agent Margaret Foster?"

"Speaking."

"Agent Foster, this is Jenny Waters at CNN. I need to confirm that you're going to be named in this morning's press conference to head the Ramirez/Martindale Task Force."

Maggie was startled. How could they know already? How many of our people even know? Apparently, at least one too many.

She improvised, "Sorry, Miss…Waters, is it? FBI policy is we don't confirm or deny rumors about ongoing investigations."

"That's not really what this is about. It's a staffing question."

"Sorry, hard and fast policy. You know the Bureau."

The CNN caller shifted to a different tack, "What are you doing there so early?"

"Just drinking my coffee. Early bird gets the worm, they say." It was only a little white lie. Her rule was to not outright big, blatant lie to them. In the long run, big lies to the media were bad for business.

Another try, "Agent Foster, where…"

"Sorry, I have to go. Boss is calling." She hung up. Better text T.J. on this one. How'd they get that so early? Media leaks were going to happen, but it would be nice to have a little control.

She decided not to wait to call Josh. He might as well get used to it. He was going to be her administrative assistant for Task Force related activities, which basically meant everything she was doing. It would be a test for him. He answered on the second ring. He was already up, working out at a gym. When she broke the news to him, he was obviously pleased. Like most agents, he relished the idea of being at the center of a big one. He said he'd be there in about forty-five minutes.

At 7:30 she called Fontaine. He was still at home. She asked about the neighbors at the crime scene. Did anyone see or hear anything?

"It's in the report."

Uh oh. Not a good answer. Better tread lightly, "Sam, I'm sorry to be calling this early, but I haven't seen your report. Can you tell me where I might find it? I've got a lot of catching up to do."

"I sent an email copy to Arnie. Is he in yet?"

"I'm not sure, but I can call his office." Still being careful, she didn't ask why he didn't send one to her.

There was an elephant in the phone line. She decided to address it. Get it over with. "Sam, I'm not sure how to say this, but none of this was my idea. I'm as surprised as anyone, and I really, really need your help to get going here. We're already behind schedule, and every hour of new delay puts us farther behind the eight ball. Anything you can do to help us get going, I won't forget it."

No response. She wondered if she'd only succeeded in aggravating his peeve. Did he hang up?

Finally, after what seemed like an hour, but was in fact only five seconds, "There's a printout on my desk. You can go in there and take it. But I'll save you some time. Nobody saw nothin'. The killers came and left without a ripple. No surveillance cameras either, zip, nada."

She thought for a second. "Sam, do you know if anybody contacted the airports or the train stations to get their videos? And the rental car agencies? And the airlines for passenger lists?"

"No, not that I'm aware of. We had no descriptions, nothing to tell them to look for."

Hmmm. Weak excuse. Better let it go. Get Josh to do it today. "Has anyone been to the condo in D.C. yet?"

"Yep. Nothing but a laptop. They took it to Cyber. No report by the time I left last night, which was about 8:15."

She wondered if he said that to impress her. Since she was there herself last night for another three and a half hours, it didn't work. "Ok, thanks, Sam. I'm going to go get that report off your desk. Just for the hell of it."

She went to his office, got the report and read it. Sam was right. She could have saved the time.

At 8:05 she called Olen. He said the safe guy would be arriving at Dulles at 10:40am. She'd have Josh pick him up. She said she'd meet them at the scene.

At 8:20 she called Boddington. He was having breakfast in his Brooklyn Apartment.

"For Christ sake, Maggie, it's rather early, isn't it? This is New York. We don't start charging about around here for at least another hour. I haven't even had my tea yet. What's come over you? Is everything all right?"

"Stanley, old friend, I just called to warn you. For the foreseeable future you may be starting a bit earlier than your usual. I'm doing the Ramirez/Martindale thing, and looks like there's money involved. I've asked for you."

"Is this another one of your bloody FBI task force cock-ups?"

"Cock-up? What a cute expression. You Limeys are really so clever with words."

"You keep forgetting why it's called the English language. We invented it. It's ours. We can do with it as we see fit. So, what the blazes do those two dead chaps have to do with money? You find scads of it under one of their mattresses, did you?"

"Sort of. Not sure exactly how it's going to play out. Just calling to let you know I'm thinking about you."

"Well, isn't that just hunky dory."

"Right. So, Stanley, if they ask if you can handle any extra assignments, just say 'yes.' Pretty please. I expect I'm going to desperately need your special skills. Not to mention, this is a big one. Look great on your resume, when you crack it."

"How will it look if I don't?"

She ignored his response. "We should have a better handle on the money part by tomorrow latest. Nice hearing your lovely voice again, old boy. Ta ta."

At 8:40 she started organizing the Task Force on Excel sheets. She knew her down time for the foreseeable future would be dedicated to organizing and managing the input and conflict from all the disparate sources. Across the top of the columns she put categories of activity. In each column she wrote names of people she wanted or just an assignment title when she didn't have a specific name. When she finished it T.J. would have to approve it and, following approval, Josh would have to notify most of the people and set up a meeting ASAP. Some of them would have to attend via conference call. She wrote a short list of the ones she'd notify herself.

The press conference started on time. Parker fell back on his strength with the press: brevity. He promised the journalists a thorough investigation, assured them the perpetrators of this dreadful crime would be brought to justice, said an elite task force was being formed, introduced Maggie, and turned it over to her.

She said she expected the investigation to be challenging, also promised it would be thorough, gave out the new tip line number, repeated it, implored anyone who thought they had any relevant information whatsoever to call it, gave the number again, indicated it was too early to make any comments on the progress of the investigation, and took no questions. The whole event lasted twelve minutes.

Back in her office at 9:50, she called the Superintendent of the Virginia State Police, Colonel Walker Stanton. He answered his own phone on the second ring.

"Stanton."

"Colonel Stanton, this is Margaret Foster with the FBI. I'm going to be coordinating the Task Force in the double homicide in Fauquier County."

The Colonel interrupted, "Are you the one I just saw on TV?"

"Yes sir, that was me. That's what I'm calling about, the Joint Task Force. Specifically, I'm going to need a lot of help. I'm calling to plead for special participation by someone from your shop. Right off the bat we need an experienced homicide detective, somebody who has a track record on real tough ones. I know it's asking a lot to get one of your best, but this case is already looking like it's not going to be easy. Any chance I can get one of your aces?"

"Excuse me ma'am, but are you sure you're with the FBI?"

"Uh, yes sir. You can call me back at FBI Headquarters, if you like. My number is…"

"No need for your number. I'm just pulling your leg. I can say that, can't I? Pulling your leg? That's not some sort of long distance sexual harassment, is it? Never mind. I thought Parker said you were commander of the Joint Task Force. Didn't you just say coordinator?"

"Colonel, commander is such a presumptive title for these task forces. I've done a couple of them, and my experience is the commander doesn't do that much commanding. More like helping all the talent help each other."

"Damn, you sure don't sound like FBI."

"I've been told that sometimes we're a bit overbearing. But we're trying to do better."

"Well good luck on that. Some think you've got a long way to go. Back to your purpose in calling, Virginia's not exactly the murder capital of the country, but I think we've got somebody who can help you out. He was at the scene in Fauquier, day of the murders. His name's Battinelli, Detective Lou Battinelli. Couple years ago we stole him from New York."

Maggie felt a little tingle run up her spine. She loved New York cops. Both her task force experiences got a lot of help from the NYPD. "How soon can I start picking his brain? Today wouldn't be too soon."

"Right now he's puttering around with some cold cases, so he might need a day or two to clean up what he's doing. I'll have him call you no later than this afternoon. Then you guys work it out. But don't hog him all up. We're certainly not overstaffed. Give me your cell number."

Maggie gave him the number and hung up feeling hopeful and extra aware of T.J.'s concerns about the Bureau's image.

Maurice Banks was the Special Agent-In-Charge (SAC) in Albuquerque. She knew him from meetings and conferences they'd both attended over the years. He was a quiet, tall, dark, heavy set man who everybody called "Mo." Maggie remembered thinking he was mixed race because of the skin tone and wiry hair. But he gave off no other ethnic signals. In fact he had a Pittsburgh accent.

Because of the two-hour time difference, she waited until 10:15 to call. He answered, "Good morning, this is Mo Banks.

"Hi, Mo, it's Maggie."

"I've been expecting your call. Just saw you on TV."

After an exchange of pleasantries, she asked him to contact Ramirez's estranged wife and two ex-wives to request they not talk to the media, at least not till FBI had interviewed them. Banks said there was also a brother. He would call him and give him the same message.

She met Josh, Olen and the safe guy at the country house. Took the guy a half hour to get the basement safe open. They found three long guns – a shot gun, a hunting rifle and an AR-15, semi-automatic, assault rifle – plus three handguns. Stacked behind the guns were several hundred packets of cash, also in twenties and fifties, the same as the packets in the briefcase. Had to be a million bucks there.

Underneath the money, they found a DVD file with forty-nine discs in it, which they sent to the Cyber guys in case the discs had something to do with the computer or the money or both.

Maggie returned to the office while the packets were dusted for fingerprints and counted. Olen called to tell her there were 664 packets totaling $1,651,220. They sent it by armored van to Headquarters, where four junior agents would record the serial numbers for all 63,707 pieces of paper currency. The numbers would be sent to Stanley for his perusal.

Back at the office, Maggie checked her list of messages. There were forty seven, forty-three of which were from reporters. She hoped the hot line would produce a similar response. Thank goodness the outside world didn't have her cell number.

Three were calls from other agents. One was from Detective Lou Battinelli.

She called Naomi Sarrano, Parker's spokesperson. Naomi quickly agreed to handle all media contact regarding the Joint Task Force and its findings. Maggie gushed gratitude. Naomi said, "No problem. That's what I do."

Before hanging up, Naomi couldn't resist a comment, "By the way, you nailed that meeting last night. The cause of death thing was brilliant, so logical, and you got there so fast. You'd only had an hour or so to think about it. Plus that simulation trick. Girlfriend, that was slick. Again, such quick thinking. T.J. was right. He said you were special. Great to have a boss who appreciates you. And I'm pretty sure the director was impressed, too."

Maggie gave a candid response, "Thanks. But I wasn't exactly trying to be slick…I don't think. It's not a trick; it is a real decision-making tool. Granted, I wanted to help the director out of an awkward place. Seemed like he knew this wasn't terrorism, but he felt like he had to give the appearance of objectivity."

"Good read."

Maggie said, "No problem, girlfriend. That's what I do."

Naomi laughed.

As much as Maggie disparaged the political games in Washington, she felt Naomi was going to be a helper, a strategic resource, as they say in our nation's capital.

Her next call was to Battinelli. He'd called from a 703 area code which was encouraging. Most of 703 was close to D.C. He answered, "Battinelli."

"Detective Battinelli, this is Maggie Foster, FBI. Thanks for the prompt call. Did Colonel Stanton fill you in?"

"Yeah, a little bit. Says you want to brain-pick on the big one out in Fauquier. I happened to get the call on it. I'm in Fairfax. Kinda followed your guy, Sam something, around. Tried not to get in the way. Whatta ya' wanna know?"

"Well, I guess I want to know everything." She hoped Fontaine hadn't pissed him off too much with the old FBI stuffed shirt routine. "I'd like to sit down and go over everything we have and get some input from an experienced hand. Murder sleuthing is more of a state and local thing than FBI. I know we've got guys who've done it, but I was hoping for a Sherlock Holmes type who could get me off in the right direction. Just someone to bounce ideas off."

"Hah. You might be disappointed. I don't close 'em all. But I'll do my best. Stan says you're not the typical FBI asshole, excuse my French. When's good for you."

"You said you're in Fairfax?"

"Right."

"We can meet at your place tomorrow about noon. Maybe have a carry-in lunch? I'll buy. That work for you?"

"Perfecto." They decided on pizza, he gave her the address, and they hung up.

She turned her focus to reading and sorting messages coming into the two tip lines. She was right that the generic line would have been swamped with the volume. Within a few hours they'd gotten several hundreds calls, none with earthshaking information. At about four o'clock she recruited an agent to handle the process, then spent an hour training her on how to triage the messages.

She called Mo Banks in New Mexico and gave him a lead from the hotline, a woman who alleged he raped her a long time ago. Mo said the relatives and ex-wives had all been contacted, and they agreed to hold off on talking to the media.

At 7:30pm the lab report on the currency packets in the basement safe were delivered to Maggie's desk. It identified fingerprints from several people, understandably including Ramirez and Martindale. The shocker was the presence of Ken Straight's prints. Ken Straight was a Washington power broker. Indeed, the whole country knew him as a major figure in national politics. He controlled two conservative PACs estimated to be worth a combined half billion dollars. He'd played a major role in five presidential campaigns, and he appeared regularly on conservative cable news shows. Bottom line: he was one of the most influential and powerful men in Washington. Maggie looked up from the report and stared into space, thinking, wondering. *WTF?*

At 8:15pm she got a call from Timothy Chu in Cyber. Cyber was a sister division to Povich's Criminal Investigation Division (CID) to which Maggie was assigned. Both divisions were part of the Criminal, Cyber, Response and Services Branch, all of which reported to T.J. Collins. Chu wanted to make sure she hadn't gone home. He was sending two typed reports to her office: one about the two victim's cell phones and the other about the DVDs. He wouldn't send them, if she wasn't in. He didn't want them to sit on her desk while she wasn't there. She wondered if he was always that careful.

She asked about the computers. He said they were still working on them. He expected that report to be ready in the morning.

Ten minutes later a junior agent delivered the phone and DVD reports to her desk. They were in a sealed envelope. She read each one twice, set them down, thought about them, and picked them up to read again. When she finished, she went into one of her deep thinks. Coming out of it, she thought, *wait'll CNN gets a whiff of this.*

She left the building at 1:15am. The same security guard who asked for her ID coming in this morning was back on duty. He did a double take as she walked past him toward the lobby door.

CHAPTER 46

DAY TWO

T*hursday, February 19, 2015.* She returned at 7:15am. Same security guard. He said, "You got a twin?"

She said, "I could use one."

At 8:05 Chu called and again asked if she would be in her office for the next ten minutes. The computer report was ready. Seven minutes later she was reading it.

At 8:30 she was in T.J.'s office, filling him in on the four reports. His response was to call the director.

At 8:55 they were in Parker's office. Naomi, and Arnie Povich joined them. Maggie was relieved that neither Maas nor Guerlach were there. Parker's office was only slightly more elegant than his conference room. They squeezed in around a medium-sized table away from his desk.

Maggie started with the cell phone report from Cyber.

The cell phones indicated Martindale's last call was with Ken Straight. The two had had repeated phone contact for at least the last year. As likely political allies, it could mean very little. However, both of them had repeated calls to and from Ramirez also. Maybe more than an interesting coincidence, maybe not.

The director leaned forward in his chair, as if he was about to say something, hesitated, a look of concern on his face, then settled back.

Maggie waited to make sure he wasn't going to speak. After an appropriate pause, she took a deep breath and opened the report from the lab about the finger prints. She read the three relevant sentences directly off the page, finishing with the presence of Ramirez's, Martindale's and Straight's finger prints on the money packets in the safe.

The room became silent, the kind of silence that can make other faint sounds, like a central heating fan or a phone ringing in another office, seem very loud. Maggie let the news set in, waiting for comments.

Finally the director asked, "Is there anything else?" The question assumed there wasn't, but Maggie surprised him by saying, "Two more. Actually two in one."

"Can they wait? Perhaps we should deal with what we have first."

Maggie looked at her boss, Collins. He said, "Whatever you prefer, Nate. However, before we finish, you will want to hear what the other reports say. First we'll discuss this one. Maggie has a theory about Mr. Straight's involvement, if you wouldn't mind her going into it."

She could tell T.J. was being careful. They all knew the director was a prudent man. In his world, sticking one's neck out was a distasteful concept. And this case was heading into a highly political and potentially controversial quagmire. A highly partisan conservative Supreme Court justice and an equally conservative and partisan activist for the gun lobby were dead. Murdered. It was already way too politically oriented for him. Now the possible involvement of Straight, the Don Corleone of conservatives, was giving him the worst kind of heartburn.

Parker said, "Alright, let's hear it."

Maggie responded, "Sir, as of this moment, no one from the Task Force has attempted to contact Mr. Straight. I wanted you to know about what we have before we took any action. We're not unaware of the sensitivity there." She paused in hopes that his anxiety level would be diminished by this discretion.

The director nodded.

Maggie said, "Let's start by acknowledging that Ken Straight is not stupid. He's way smarter than the average street criminal."

"Therefore, *if* he knew the murders were going to happen, he wouldn't have left behind obvious evidence pointing to himself. If the killing of the justice was an unplanned, spur of the moment incident, he may have simply panicked and fled. We're almost sure it wasn't that. The murder of Ramirez was premeditated. It was carefully planned. The two-stage lethal injection alone, confirms this was not improvisation."

"So, the logical conclusion, from what we've seen so far, is that Ken Straight had nothing to do with the murders. It just doesn't make sense."

Parker nodded again, this time showing a modicum of relief. Nonetheless, Maggie thought his usual genteel stoicism was fraying a bit. He was becoming an easy read. Too bad they weren't at the poker table.

She couldn't leave him with an unjustified sense that all was well. She had to say the rest, "That's not to say he's not guilty of a crime, a serious crime. He may very well be. Probably is. But it's not murder. When we find out what the money is about, we may have two separate, unconnected crimes. For Straight, the murders may simply be a terribly unfortunate coincidence."

Parker's range of emotions had gone from irritated tension to mild relief then to resignation. The poker term for his state of mind was "on tilt."

"And not to get ahead of myself, but in time you may want to set up a separate investigation. Just give us a couple weeks to straighten it out...pardon the pun…just give us a couple weeks, so we don't have investigators bumping into each other. Then you may want to separate the two."

Maggie saw the frustrated bewilderment in Parker's eyes. He was a company man, known for his devotion to the Bureau and to its reputation as the nation's foremost law enforcement organization. Protecting the FBI's status, both with Congress and in the world of criminal justice, was his purpose in life.

His method, first and foremost, was to ensure that the Bureau not become entangled in political conflicts. Unfortunately, the two murders themselves were showing signs of being a political calamity. One political party or the other was going to be unhappy with the outcome and, therefore, unhappy with the Bureau. When they're unhappy, they always want to mess with budgets. Discovering a second audacious crime, however unrelated, and naming Ken Straight – one of the most powerful and politically connected people in Washington – as a party to it, would be sprinkling hot sauce on the jalapenos.

After what seemed like an interminable silence, Parker said, "What's in the other reports." His tone was flat. His stare was morphing into a glare, no longer the dispassionate administrator.

The caring, southern gentleman inside him was being elbowed out by the Washington bureaucrat.

Maggie pulled the Cyber Division reports from their folder. Once again she read word for word from the reports, with her eyes down at the papers. She started with the second report. It said *the justice had been delving into the "deep web" on his computer. Most activity on the deep web was either illegal or immoral or a combination of the two. Some of it involved terrorism, illegal arms sales and even murder for hire. But much of it had to do with child pornography.* She picked up the first report and read a few lines. *The DVDs found in his safe were made up exclusively of images of very young girls in sexually compromising scenes. Such DVDs are most commonly acquired through purchase from sites on the deep web or while overseas.*

She returned to the second report, about the computers. *Although they had not been able to specifically identify what sites he'd visited, the presence of the DVD's strongly suggested child pornography sites.* The report concluded by stating that *possession of the DVDs plus evidence of web surfing on child porn sites would normally be sufficient to justify arrest and criminal charges in any jurisdiction in the country.*

Maggie looked up from the papers. Naomi and T.J. were looking at the director. His face was turning a gray-green color usually seen on waterborne passengers who are discovering for the first time that they're prone to seasickness. Maggie thought she saw the words "What the fuck?" on his lips, maybe uttered for the first time in his fastidious life. This latest revelation – the murder victim, a conservative and politically charged Supreme Court justice, as a sexual deviate, – was the ultimate trespass into the perilous valley of political controversy.

He rose slowly, ominously, to a standing position, as if standing would add import to what he was about to say. Maggie thought she saw his hands shaking, as he held them out, palms down, to emphasize the need to stay calm, which he clearly was not. "Let's just hold everything right there. We don't want to jump to conclusions. We have to be very careful about something like this. We want to be sure we have all the facts." He ran out of stale expressions advocating caution and stood looking at Maggie, as though she'd been spouting blasphemies in church and could or should somehow be shunned or excommunicated.

Maggie's eyes went to T.J., then Naomi, searching for help. They both were closely watching the director, possibly concerned about his physical well-being.

Parker said, "Who has seen this report?"

Maggie said, "Nobody outside of this meeting and Cyber. I don't know how many people down there know about it. Chu called me before sending it up. He wanted to make sure I was in my office, like he was concerned about who might read it."

He said, "Obviously, we have to treat this with utmost caution." He looked at his watch, gaining a bit of stability. "Let's take a twenty minute break. Naomi, please have Arlene get the Cyber person in charge of this report – Chu, I think you said – and Whitaker to come down here when we resume." Arlene was his administrative assistant. Whitaker was the head of the Cyber Division, Chu's boss.

He started to pick up his pad of paper and walk to the door. He stopped, turned and came over to Maggie's chair. "I would like to read that report while I'm waiting."

Feeling like a school girl being told by the teacher to hand over a clandestine note, Maggie gave it to him. She didn't tell him she had another copy. She thought she was seeing an obvious chink in his armor. It made her wonder if he was up to this investigation. She knew the politics were going to be hairy, even without Ken Straight and packets of money and child pornography.

Naomi asked if 9:45 was ok to resume. Everyone agreed.

They reconvened in the director's conference room. Kate Freeley, an attorney from the Justice Department, joined them along with Whitaker and Chu. Freeley had been briefed by Naomi on the revelations of the earlier meeting.

The director had regained his composure. He handed the Cyber report back to Maggie, thanked her and commented that it was interesting reading. He'd realized (or been told) his reaction was out of character and possibly bothersome to others in the meeting. He was trying to pull it back together.

He opened by reminding everyone that it was Bureau policy not to comment to the media about ongoing investigations. He added, "Since this case is so far out of the ordinary, we might have to take special measures. Let's talk about that."

Naomi spoke up, "Well, we all know the media is going bonkers; this is the mother of all murder cases. And our world, especially inside the beltway, is awash with leakers. As soon as we act on something, it'll be out. For example, when we contact Straight to ask him questions, people will know about it. Reporters might even meet us at the door. The same with the money. Once we start asking questions, it'll be out. We won't be able to contain it."

Director Parker sat forward, literally getting his back up, "Are you suggesting there are leakers inside the Bureau?"

Naomi hesitated, not sure how candidly she should respond. T. J. jumped in, abandoning protocol, "C'mon, Nate. Does the Pope shit in the woods?"

Maggie thought she saw the director's head jerk back slightly, as if he'd been slapped.

T.J. said to Naomi, "So, what's the answer. Where are you going here?"

Naomi said, "We should adapt to the circumstances. Turn them to our benefit."

Parker, trying to recover, said, "We're listening."

"Let's make an exception. *Use* them, instead of trying to *ignore* them. From what Maggie says, we're going to need help from the outside world. So, tell them what we need. Give them something they can use. Get them on our side. Make them think we want to help them. Make a few friends for once. We go to them with information they're going to get anyway."

Maggie said, "You mean intentionally leak our own stuff?"

"No, we don't leak it, we *broadcast* it. We do regular open news conferences and give them a story every day or so. Information we know we're not going to be able to hide. Stay ahead of the curve. Don't let them get it from the leakers. That way when the leakers *do* give them bad info, we can deny it with credibility."

Maggie tensed, watching the director. He looked at T.J. without responding, then settled back in his chair.

Naomi took that as a signal to continue, "For a start, we tell them about the money, that it exists, was found at the scene. That'll keep them busy for at least two days. Then we tell them about the phone calls and that we're interviewing Straight. We don't talk about fingerprints. We just want to know if either victim said anything that might lead us to the killers. We'll be careful not to call him a person of interest."

Freeley, the attorney, nodded.

Naomi said, "We acknowledge only that we'll be interviewing him. Let them chew on that, while we do the homicides. It'll give us a little head start."

The director said, "What about the rest?"

"We hold off on the child porn until we know more." She tipped her head to Whitaker, "Cyber's pretty tight. We should be able to keep that under raps for a while, at least until the body's cold. There's family to think about. We want to wait till after the funeral at a minimum.

"But we give them the other stuff, because they're going to find out anyway. Sooner, more likely than later. If they get it from a leaker, it may come out all wrong. One side or the other may turn it into a completely false story, a false story we may not be able to get back in the barn. The conspiracy theorists will be out of control anyway. And the you-know-what could splatter on the Bureau."

T.J. interjected, seeing an opening to help deal with the Bureau's image issues. "I agree. We need to listen to what Naomi's saying. Being proactive will give us some control. Maggie can dribble stuff out; try to generate some useful hot line calls."

Maggie interrupted, "Should be Naomi. That's what she does."

Naomi was listening to T.J. She gave Maggie a quick glance of acknowledgement. Maggie again got the feeling they'd make a good team. She was looking forward to a strategy session with her, maybe over cocktails. She felt herself being infected with Washingtonitis.

The director said, "The problem is answering their questions. They can wrest control from you and turn it into a disaster."

Naomi said, "It's not my first trip downtown on the bus. I'll know when and how to cut it off."

The director gave in and agreed to try one more press conference. See how it goes.

Maggie interjected one last point, "The child pornography may be a motive for murder; let's not forget that. And if that's what it turns out to be, it's not political, which may help cool everybody's jets; the politicians, I mean. If it's not politics, we won't be on anybody's bad side. Am I making sense? The heat will be off the agency, won't it?"

The director raised his hand to his mouth and stared ahead as if in thought. He raised one eyebrow and gently nodded, as if savoring a pleasant thought, perhaps child pornography had some value, after all.

They adjourned to the next morning.

At 11:05 Maggie left for Fairfax to meet with Lou Battinelli. She took the envelope of crime scene photos and a list of questions. At 12:00 she walked into the lobby of the Virginia State Police office in Fairfax with a large pizza in hand, pepperoni, bacon, onion, fresh tomato and extra cheese.

The young man at the reception desk made a call and thirty seconds later a mob enforcer appeared. He was about fifty, medium height with thick dark-hair, combed straight back. His stature was thick. Not fat, thick. Maggie assumed at some point in his life he'd been a linebacker. He had a neck, but just barely. His head made her think of the front end of a Dodge Ram truck. It was oversized with a flat forehead protruding over thick eyebrows, a broad nose and even thick lips.

He put his hand out and said, "Lou Battinelli." She shook his hand and replied, "Maggie Foster." He gave her a Brooklyn smile that said I can be a nice guy providing you don't fuck with me. Right away she liked him. He was a New York kind of guy.

They went back to a conference room that may have doubled as an interview room. Maggie looked for dark glass windows and saw none. Not an interrogation room. Should be secure. A coffee pot, soft drinks, pitcher of water, cups and glasses, napkins and paper plates sat on a table against the wall. Maggie put the pizza on the table and opened it. Battinelli waited for her to take a slice, then he took two.

They each grabbed a cold drink and walked over to the conference table. Maggie set the envelope full of crime scene photos on the table. They ate their pizza and made small talk.

When she addressed him as Detective Battinelli, he corrected her, "Lou." She replied, "Maggie." So far, so good.

Getting down to business, she pushed the envelope over to his side of the table and cautioned that everything they would be discussing was extremely confidential. He gave her a "what else is new" head tilt.

She'd sent Olin's ERP report over to him after their phone call yesterday. She suggested they start with her taking him through the photos. He shook his head, "I was there when they took 'em."

"You remember everything you saw?"

He took a large bite out of his pizza slice. It was almost gone. After he chewed and swallowed, "I think the relevant stuff, yeah."

Maggie thought, *cocky sonofabitch.*

Reading her mind, he said, "I spent a lotta time thinkin' about it. It's all over everywhere. You can't not think about it. As we go over it, if you think I missed somethin', we can look at the photos."

She let it go, "Ok, I've got a lotta questions and, I think, a few answers. I'm hoping someone with your experience could kind of confirm where I'm at or point me in the right direction."

"Shoot." He started his second slice of pizza, getting at least one third of it into his mouth in one try.

"Why lethal injection?"

He chewed, swallowed, and wiped his fingers on a napkin. Then said, "Not a clue. When you figure that one out, you got it all. It's different. Probably key to the whole thing."

"Why not for Martindale?"

"That's easier. They probably ran out. They were only plannin' to kill one guy. Martindale turnin' up was a surprise. Collateral damage. Fortunately for them, one of 'em was a real killer. He knew what to do and how to do it. Didn't need any more juice."

"Thank you for that. It's encouraging; I came to the same conclusion. Seemed like the only way to make sense out of it."

"Took me a couple days. Last night I woke up and did a head slap. It was so obvious." He finished his second slice of pizza and reached for a third.

"Next question: how'd they get in? There's no sign of a break-in. Did Ramirez know them, let them in?"

"No. Couldn't have. They were already in when he got there." The third slice sat in front of him. "If he let 'em in, he would already have hung his coat in the closet. His overcoat was on the closet floor, kinda rumpled, like it was dropped. The driver said he didn't have the coat on when he went in the house. It was over his arm."

Maggie said, "Why dropped? He didn't intentionally put it on the floor?"

"Number one, nobody *put* it on the floor. It was thrown or dropped, not placed. I looked at the label on the overcoat. Italian I never heard of. I talked to a guy back in the City who knows about stuff like that. Reads GQ and shops uptown. He said that coat cost upwards of five grand. Another guy down here who knows about the Court said Ramirez had a reputation as a clothes horse. Very meticulous about the way he looked. Wore nothin' but the best and wore it with a flourish. Wouldn't be throwin' it on the floor." He still hadn't picked up the third piece.

"What's that have to do with letting them in?"

"It makes me think when Ramirez came in the house, he would'a hung the coat up, unless somethin' happened as he was goin' to hang it up, like a big guy grabbin' him from behind."

Battinelli continued, "Goin' back to the driver, he said Ramirez had his suit coat on when he went in the house. The suit coat was folded on top of the overcoat on the floor. You wouldn't throw a five thousand dollar overcoat on the floor and then fold up your suit coat on top of it. You'd hang 'em both up. You might not even take the suit coat off. But they had to have it off to get to his vein to shoot him up. So they probably took it off and put it on top of the overcoat."

He'd forgotten about the pizza. "The driver also said when he drove away there was no one around outside the house. So, what probably happened was, they were already in there, waitin' for him, probably hidin' behind the archway. As soon as he closed the door, they jumped him. He dropped the overcoat on the foyer floor. Maybe his briefcase, too. It was in the closet on the floor next to the coats. Then they put the first shot in his leg, one guy holdin' his gun hand, the other guy doin' the needle. When they got him down on the floor unconscious, they took off his suit coat, so they could do the second needle in a vein in his arm, folded it and put it on top of the overcoat. Then they gave him the second needle."

"Why'd they fold the suit coat instead of just throwing it somewhere?"

"Not sure. Could be one of 'em was a neatnik. Just a habit." He rediscovered the pizza.

Maggie asked, "Why were they lying on the closet floor? If Ramirez dropped them when they grabbed him, the coats and briefcase would have been on the foyer floor."

Battinelli finished chewing. "When Martindale came to the door, they'd already done Ramirez and carried him into the den. The doorbell rang, and they thought they had to answer it. They couldn't ignore him and leave him out there with his cell phone. He coulda called 911 or somethin'. They know when they answer the door, the guy's gonna see them. So they gotta do him, too. He doesn't know who they are, but they tell him to come on in, the justice is in the john or somethin'. They can't just leave the coats and briefcase on the foyer floor. The guy would see 'em and be suspicious. So before they open the door, they sweep 'em into the closet and close the door. Then they answer the front door, invite the guy in, offer to take his coat, and snap his neck."

"So you're saying the time of death for both was right after Ramirez arrived."

"Right."

Maggie thought about it. "Hmmm. How'd they get in? The place was real secure. The doors and windows were all super heavy duty construction, and none of them were tampered with."

"Not the utility room door into the garage. The lock on that door wasn't the same quality as the rest. It was easy to pick for someone who's got the tools and knows how to use 'em. Easy enough, you might not even leave any scratches. That's what I think they did. They probably hid their car in the garage. You wouldn't see it from the driveway."

Maggie shook her head. "But the garage had an electric door opener. There's no key pad, so it doesn't have a PIN. They needed a remote. We found one in his car, another in a kitchen drawer. Most of those openers only have two remotes. That's what they give you when you buy the opener. You think they had a third remote?"

"No. That's an old garage door opener. There's a device called a code grabber. High tech burglars used to use them. It's an electronic thing that figures out the code on a door opener and zaps it open. Most openers now are programmed to defeat them. But not that one. That's the only way I can figure."

Maggie thought about that for awhile. "It's called a code grabber?"

"Yep."

"Ok, next question. What do you think of the chances it was hired out? A professional?"

"Nah, don't think so. Pros almost always work alone. This had to be two people. And pros wouldn't fuck around with…excuse me… pros wouldn't do a lethal injection. Too much hassle. That lethal injection is the secret to this whole thing."

He seemed to start talking to himself, "Strange. Why would they do that?"

Maggie shrugged, "Let me know when you figure it out. Let's move on. Martindale had a small briefcase, combination lock. When our guys opened it they found money, a hundred grand."

"I know, I was there. In fact I told them to try his initials. That's how they got it open."

"I should have known."

Lou's turn to shrug. "What was in the safe downstairs?"

"More of the same. A lot more. In addition to some guns, there was over a million and a half bucks. All in cash. Mostly twenties and fifties. We haven't let that out to the media yet, but we're going to tomorrow. Any thoughts?"

"Lotta dough. Make a great motive, if it wasn't still there."

"Martindale's prints were on the money packets. So were Ken Straight's."

"No shit! *The* Ken Straight?"

"One and only."

"My, my, my."

"And both their cell phones show recent calls to him. Any more insights?"

He put his head back and stared at the ceiling for a few seconds. "Too easy. He can't be that stupid. You ask him for an alibi yet?"

"No. It's all brand new. They're going to see him this afternoon."

He stared at the ceiling again. "Can't believe he'd plan everythin' so carefully and...."

"I agree. Let me drop this one on you. By the way, this part is the real secret stuff. We're gonna try to keep this under wraps for awhile." She hesitated, making sure he understood.

He said nothing, just nodded.

"There were some DVDs in the safe. Kiddy porn. Forty-nine DVDs of pictures of underage girls committing various sexual acts. On his computer there was evidence, not proof but reasonable indication, he was visiting child porn sites."

Battinelli's casual demeanor collapsed. His big round eyes got bigger, "Ramirez?!"

Maggie nodded, "Yep. Comments?"

"No. Ya gotta give me a minute on that one." After a pause, "You got another big motive possibility there." Talking to himself again, "What would kiddy porn have to do with lethal injection?"

Maggie answered, "Maybe nothing. Might just be another distraction."

Battinelli finished his third slice. Maggie took a bite of her first slice. It was getting cold.

She looked at her watch. She had to get back. "We should wrap up. Would you mind if I just called you every time I got something new, and we talked about it on the phone? Save me a drive. I do appreciate you're thinking on this. You've already been a big help. Maybe we could meet somewhere for a face to face once a week or so. What do you think?"

"Anythin' I can do, be happy to. Boss has already cleared me to work with you. Whenever we can work it out." Then, "Let me ask you one. You're FBI. Has an analyst done anything on this yet? You got any kind of profile?"

"Not yet. Actually I was a profiler once. I've been waiting to get a fuller picture. Hard to come up with something out of thin air. But you've added some interesting stuff. Maybe I can take a go at it now. What about you? If you had to start a profile on the main guy here, what would it look like? Off the top of your head. Any thoughts?"

Battinelli looked at the ceiling again and furrowed his brow. The little adding machine in his head was doing computations. "Lemme think on it. Ask me tomorrow."

When she got back to the office, Josh gave her the latest hotline totals. Through 1:00pm, twenty-seven hours after announcing the tip line, they'd received and triaged over 1,900 calls. They came from all fifty states plus Puerto Rico, Guam and eighteen foreign countries.

Each call was prioritized and would be followed-up by the nearest FBI agent, in person, if possible. Maggie noted that only seven of the tips involved space aliens or UFOs. They'd get the lowest priority.

By mid-day the lists of serial numbers on the currency were forwarded to Boddington in the Manhattan office of the U.S. Treasury Department. The chance he would learn anything from them was close to nil.

At 1:15pm two senior special agents appeared at Straight's office. He wasn't there. The office manager said he hadn't been in all week. He was on a short sailing cruise with his wife. He left about 2:00pm on Friday. The office manager thought they embarked on Saturday. Straight was supposed to be back this morning, but he'd called about nine o'clock saying he wouldn't be in for the day. While they were there, Naomi was reporting it at a news conference.

Straight wasn't at home either. A tipster called the hotline at two p.m. to say Straight was meeting with attorneys at an undisclosed location and was in the process of lawyering up. Maggie wondered if he'd started the process before the Agents went to his office or after. If before, he was guilty as shit. If after, probably still guilty.

When they contacted the attorneys' office, they ran into a stall game. Straight had gone underground. He was completely incognito. There would be no interview today or this weekend, unless they found him and arrested him. He had to be guilty of something.

The director told Maggie that Straight was not to be arrested. It was okay to look for him, just to talk to him. If you find him, don't do anything provocative. He did give in on one thing. Since Straight was playing hard to get, the director told Naomi she could refer to him in future news conferences as "a person of interest." He thought that should be enough to bring him in voluntarily.

CHAPTER 47

DAY THREE

Friday, February 20, 2015. The morning meeting started at 8:30 and was over before 9:00.

Maggie took only fifteen minutes, mostly on the hot line calls and follow-up. She told them the volume was still high – 2,400 calls through 8:00am that morning. She said so far they'd found no surveillance or security cameras that showed anything. She also told them about the tip call from the woman who said he'd raped her as a young girl. She said her man from Treasury was working on the money trail, and it could be weeks before he had anything to report.

She said the relatives, exes, other Court members and close friends of both deceased would be interviewed in depth by FBI Agents, but not until after the funerals, both of which were scheduled for next Monday. Maggie would sit in on as many interviews as physically possible, including those in New Mexico. Everyone to be interviewed had been asked not to talk to the media until after the FBI. So far as she knew, they were all cooperating.

The director was holding fast on no arrest for Straight. No date was set for a next meeting.

She went to her office, closed the door, sat at her desk and began to mentally sketch out a profile. *A reasonably intelligent person. Knows about forensics – what to do and what not to do. Maybe got it from detective novels or TV. Or criminal experience, though not likely. Smart criminals are mostly a myth. A planner. Planned this one thoroughly. May have lots of time on his hands. And resources. Has to pay the rent and the groceries while he's doing all the prep. And he knows about locks and code grabbers. How would he know about code grabbers? A cop? Ooh, I hope not. A retired successful burglar? Nah, no such thing.*

She called Battinelli. He answered on the first ring, and she skipped the usual amenities. "Do the profile yet?"

"Yeah, I been thinkin' about it. Wrote a few things down."

"Whatcha got?"

"Let me see. First off, he's reasonably intelligent. I say 'he', but it could be a she. Probably doesn't have a record. Most ex-cons are not very bright. The movies tend to make 'em look smarter than they are. This guy knew how to do this without leaving any tracks. He planned it carefully.

"Next, he left the money behind. Your run of the mill crook takes the money. Actually, that's the reason he's there. So, maybe he's got plenty already. Fits with the idea he has lots of time to do the planning. Maybe has enough dough he doesn't have to work. Maybe a rich guy who's retired early or a widow who inherited a bunch, but is still pissed about somethin'.

"Third, he knows about pickin' locks and code grabbers. Since he's probably not a reformed burglar, maybe a locksmith or a cop. Maybe a guy who used to be a locksmith. Or an ex-cop. Most cops are not Einsteins either, but some are.

"Then the big guy who did the broken neck. He knew what he was doin'. You don't perfect that in a martial arts class after work. You have to actually do it once in awhile. That makes me think military, probably Special Forces of some kind. They get the training, and then they actually have to do it. They get in some real OJT.

"So, where am I going here? Let's see, the planner, the brains, could be a man or a woman, and an ex-cop or a locksmith. Probably has resources and time on his hands. And a motive. An overwhelming reason that drove him to do this very ambitious crime. The big guy has serious martial arts chops, maybe military, and he's a close friend, even a brother. Sort of a Lenny to George."

"Lenny to George?"

"Yeah, you know, 'Of Mice and Men'."

"Oh, Christ, that was freshman English. So, you're saying an ex-cop or a locksmith with money and time. Could be retired with a nice nest egg and a military guy, possibly related. Like that."

"Yeah, like that. Or it could be nothing like that. You see, Maggie, the key to this whole thing is the needles. Why do it that way? Find out about lethal injections. Then you can do a profile."

Maggie was encouraged by how close they were. Battinelli was good. The locksmith thing was interesting.

At 10:30 Director Parker caved and agreed they had to find Straight and, if worse came to worst, arrest him. Naomi told Maggie the calls coming into his office were two to one in favor of taking action on him. The director's political sensitivities were coming to bear. He could count.

Naomi told the media Straight had become a "person of interest." Within thirty minutes the majority leader of the senate called the director and accused him of botching the whole investigation. Why weren't they calling anyone in the administration a "person of interest?" Clearly they were focusing on the wrong people. It was another Maalox moment for the director.

Six more calls followed from Republican congressional leaders. And Fox News was apoplectic, again.

Maggie spent the rest of the day on the phone with new Task Force members and agents around the country, who were calling in their preliminary reports on follow-up contacts with hot line tipsters. She got off the last call from a California agent at 10:15pm.

The follow-ups had not yet produced a worthwhile lead. Some callers were sure their neighbor, who was a real asshole, had to have something to do with it. For some it was a strange cousin or uncle. They hadn't gotten yet to the callers who thought they should be looking at a specific politician, almost always a liberal.

Banks hadn't reported back yet on the woman claiming rape.

To finish off her night, Maggie started to set up a system for checking out the relatives and close friends of anyone who'd been legally executed via lethal injection in the eight years since Ramirez was appointed to the Supreme Court. At midnight she called it quits and went home.

CHAPTER 48

DAY FOUR

Saturday, February 21, 2015. She was back in the office at 8:30 am, having slept until 6:45 and treated herself to a forty-five minute workout at the gym near her condo. The weekend day-shift security guard in the lobby vaguely recognized her. She'd been in the office on only two weekends since coming down from New York two years ago.

Few people were in that early on Saturday morning. She had to make the coffee. Her desktop was not visible beneath the scattered papers. She spent the first twenty minutes straightening up, putting things in meaningful piles. She opened her computer and reviewed her notes on executions by lethal injection. It occurred to her to look into lethal injections in euthanasia cases, too, but it seemed like a stretch. What could that have to do with Ramirez? She'd put it on a to-do list for later, after they'd played out the hotter options. She hoped this wasn't going to go on that long.

She spent the morning making a computerized "murder book" for each victim. A murder book was a thorough compilation of everything related to the case, from forensics to witness statements of which there were none. She read about murder books in a crime novel. She included her notes from the visit with Battinelli and her latest list of questions:

Why lethal injection?

How does one acquire the necessary drugs for lethal injection?

What was Martindale doing there?

Why did he bring money?

Where did he get it?

What about Straight?

What about the money in the safe?

Little girls?

Why did his wife leave him?

After a quick lunch, she talked to Mo Banks in New Mexico. He said, "We found the woman who claimed Ramirez raped her, down in Las Cruces. Her name is Marlene Descheene. She says it happened over forty years ago on the reservation when she was fourteen years old. She's Navajo, and her story sounds credible.

"We're checking it out with the tribal police, but the woman says we might not get much from them, because they were paid off by Ramirez's dad. On our first pass with them, we got nothing. Nobody knows anything about it. They're checking the old files. We'll stay with it, but I doubt they'll find it. Even if they did, doesn't seem like it will have anything to do with the justice's death. Marlene is one dancer short of a chorus line. Don't see how she could've pulled it off."

Banks was also setting up a tentative schedule of interviews with Ramirez's relatives and ex-wives, beginning on Tuesday. He wanted to start with the brother, Raul. He said Raul gave off some interesting vibes when he called to ask him not to talk to the media.

She made plane reservations for Monday afternoon.

The rest of the day she looked at the notes from the hot-line calls coming in and emails on the follow-ups. Still nothing promising in any of them.

When she got home at 5:20pm, Ted was waiting for her with a freshly made pitcher of martinis. The newly-opened bottle of Plymouth Gin was sitting on the counter, still one-third full. She hadn't had a drink, not even a glass of wine, since Monday in Tampa. He'd cut up some cheese and put it out with a small block of pate and a baguette and some crackers. He planned to cook a light dinner of Alaskan salmon filet and white asparagus.

They tapped glasses before the first sip of martini. Maggie said, "Before your curiosity gets the best of you from that drink, I have to warn you. I cannot discuss the case with you. It's like D-Day over at headquarters. Can't discuss anything about it with anybody. No pillow talk."

Ted said, "Perfectly understandable. I've been there. Top secret projects and all that. So, what'll we talk about? How'd you like that beautiful pre-Spring weather today?"

She said, "We can talk about redecorating this condo. This furniture is getting worn. I think there's a red wine stain on one of the cushions on the couch."

Ted said, "Or we could talk about the Cubs. They have a new manager, Joe Maddon. He's gonna take'em to the World Series."

"The Cubs? Suuure!"

In the middle of the third martini, after a pause in their chat, she looked at her glass and said, "Why lethal injection? What the hell is that about?"

Ted smiled, "You did quite well. It took two and a half martinis, maybe two and three quarters. Ready for a refill?"

"Don't make fun of me. This is hard. The tip line is not giving us much, except we're up to thirteen aliens and seven UFOs. Otherwise we're on our own."

Near the end of the fourth drink, with still no dinner, light or otherwise, Maggie passed out on the couch, the one with the alleged red wine stain.

At 2:30am she woke up, went to the bathroom and brushed her teeth. Now she was ready to celebrate Valentine's Day. She went into the bedroom. Ted was asleep. She sat down in the chair by the window and looked at him, so peaceful, getting his rest. Then she said, "Fuck this." She went over to the bed, sat down not very gently, shook him by the shoulder, and gave him a wet one on the cheek. He roused slowly from what was apparently a deep sleep and she started working on him, making him a wordless offer he couldn't refuse. Thirty five minutes later they were both back asleep, having performed well for their age.

CHAPTER 49

DAYS SEVEN & EIGHT

Tuesday, February 23, 2015. It was one week since Maggie was pulled from the poker table in Tampa. She and Mo were five minutes late for their 10:00am appointment. Raul Ramirez was nervous. The morning sun made him squint as he opened the east facing door. He checked Bank's badge carefully before inviting them in. As they walked past him into the kitchen, he looked over their shoulders at their vehicle, a black Ford Explorer SUV with tinted windows and an oversized aerial pointing at the sky. Clearly a G-ride.

A woman was leaning against the counter next to the sink, arms folded across her chest. Her skin was light brown; her long dark hair gathered in back.

"My wife, Rainey. This is..." He looked at them for help.

Banks held out his hand and said, "Special Agent Banks and," pointing at Maggie, "Commander Foster." He left out the "in-Charge" part of his own title, seeing no reason to mention it in this setting.

Raul said, "OK if Rainey stays?" His tone was hopeful, not wanting to be left alone with them.

Banks looked at Maggie, and she nodded.

He said, "Sure, no problem."

Raul was dressed up for the appointment: clean, wrinkle-free blue jeans; freshly ironed white retro western shirt with black shoulder stitching; string tie; polished cowboy boots. He'd gotten a hair cut and he was clean shaven, clearly hoping to make a good impression. None of the nonchalance and casual confidence of the interview with Rossi, aka Gerald Renfro, almost two years ago. J.D. was dead, murdered, and these two were FBI. Not the same. Not at all.

Raul was their first interview in New Mexico. After him, Maggie and Mo were driving back to Albuquerque to talk to one of the ex-wives, followed by a partner at the justice's old law firm. Maggie had a hotel room in the city.

On Wednesday morning they'd do the niece, then up to Santa Fe for the other ex-wife and an attorney who was on the state supreme court with him, and then up to Taos for the wife. They wouldn't get back to Albuquerque until late Wednesday.

Maggie also wanted to talk to the woman down in Las Cruces from the tip line who claimed she'd been raped by Ramirez forty years ago. That was a long drive, so she made a reservation back to Dulles on the last flight out of Tucson Thursday night. She could always make a change. It was the FBI travel account.

Raul was cautious in the beginning, but eventually he told them what he told Rossi, all of it: guns, rape, Criollo status, sales training, the whole story. When he got to the part about the disagreement they'd had over his wife, Rainey, and her Navajo heritage, he emphatically pointed out that he was in New Mexico when the murder occurred. He had fellow workers who would testify that he was on the job repairing power lines that Friday afternoon. Rainey nodded and confirmed that he was home at six o'clock, impossible if he'd been in Virginia at four-thirty New Mexico time, which they'd been told was the time of death.

Banks, who was asking most of the questions, assured them that Raul was not a suspect. He said they were only there to get a fuller picture of the justice's life in hopes of getting a better understanding of what happened. Raul was doing that. He was giving them plenty to think about.

When they were ready to leave, Raul, starting to relax, said, "You know, you should talk to that guy who's writin' the book. He probably knows more than anybody by now."

Maggie said, "What guy?" She had said little during the interview.

"Can't exactly remember his name. It was Gerald something. Wait a minute. Maybe Kim will remember." He picked up his cell, and then it came to him. "Renfro. That's it. Gerald Renfro. He talked to Kim and Vicky right after he talked to me. Vicky was Kim's mother and our sister, J.D.'s and mine. She died about a year ago."

Maggie pressed, "Who was he?"

"Not really sure. Just a guy writin' a book. Didn't say much about himself."

"Where's he from?"

"Think he said Chicago. Sounded kind of Midwestern. Took a lot of notes. He should be ready to publish pretty soon. It's been awhile. Think he was here in the spring. Musta been almost two years ago. Seems like he's takin' his good old time about it.

"The next day he went to see Vicky. She didn't give him much. Kim was there. Been waitin' to see what the book would say, but haven't seen it yet."

Maggie continued, "What did he look like?"

Raul described Renfro/Rossi as best he could, unaware he was well disguised.

Rainey said, "Looked to me like he was wearing a wig."

Raul said, "What?"

"His hair didn't look like it was his. Something about it. It was too perfect, too much, too thick for a guy his age."

Raul said, "You never mentioned it at the time."

"No need. Seemed like an older guy trying to look younger. Maybe it was really his. I don't know. Just looked a little off." She didn't say Raul was maybe too drunk to remember.

Maggie said, "Do you remember him well enough so you could describe him to a sketch artist for us?"

"Well, it's been awhile, maybe between Rainey and me we might. Then you could show it to Kim. She's pretty sharp. She could tell you if we're close."

Maggie knew it was a long shot. As time passes people lose memory, especially visual memories. It was the basis of the biggest inequity in our criminal justice system, false witness IDs. The sketch might be nothing like the real person. It could even take them in the wrong direction. But if there were others who could verify the likeness, like Kim, it might be worth a try.

Before they left, they arranged for a sketch artist to get out there that afternoon. Maggie wanted to have the sketch to show to the other people they were interviewing.

They recorded the interview with Raul and his wife, and while they drove back to Albuquerque, Maggie put it on speaker, and they both listened. When it came to the end, Banks made a breathy, whistling sound followed by, "How'd he ever get on the Supreme Court?"

Maggie said, "Don't know. Might be interesting to probe into the vetting on that one. Some of what Raul said, we already knew or had indications of. But it keeps getting deeper. He didn't like Mexicans. Ha! More possible motives keep coming up. It's like 'whak-a-mole,' but with murder motives. And Gerald Renfro. Who the f…, who's he?"

They stopped for a quick lunch at one of the I-64 exits. Back in the car, Maggie said little. She stared out the windshield and went into one of her deep-think modes, shutting out the world, as they rolled east across I-64 to US-550, where they turned south toward Albuquerque. It was a clear blue-sky winter day and the ride through mountainous terrain and over the Continental Divide was one spectacular vista after another. Maggie saw little of it.

As they got to I-25, just north of Albuquerque she called Josh at headquarters and told him to find Renfro. She described him as an author about sixty, white, medium build, gray bushy hair, horned rim glasses and a walrus moustache. She'd forward the sketch in the morning.

They had dinner together that night in a good southwestern restaurant. Maggie allowed herself one glass of wine. They discussed their day. They agreed the ex-wife and the old business partner gave them little new information. The ex-wife – his first – named Myrna Jordan, confirmed he was not a very nice person. He was good looking and had a pleasant personality until they got married, then he changed. Still good looking but no fun at all. All he cared about was his guns. Biggest mistake she ever made. Fortunately, he was easy to get over, and she didn't think anyone else would miss him either. "He was a lousy lay," she added without blushing, "seemed to have his mind elsewhere."

The ex-business partner was Derrick Hobson, who, like a lot of people, was not comfortable being interviewed by the FBI. Asked about what he did for a living, he said he was retired, did a little consulting now and then. When pressed, he said, "Marketing." He didn't know anything about Ramirez that would make somebody want to kill him. He said he knew nothing about Gerald Renfro. Maggie noticed his discomfort increasing, but he wouldn't budge on either. She let it go with the thought that it might justify a return visit, depending on where the investigation took them.

Wednesday, February 24, 2015. The next morning they talked to Kim, the late Victoria's daughter and Ramirez's niece. She verified all of what Raul and his wife said including the part about the hair looking a bit strange. She confirmed there was a possible rape issue going back 40 years and told him the alleged victim was a Navajo. She didn't give them the name of the victim or tell them she called the book guy and gave it to him. She apparently assumed that, since they were the FBI, they'd figure it out. She didn't want to get involved anymore, especially since Uncle Jesse was dead.

She looked at the sketch and said there was a resemblance to Renfro, but her memory was a little vague on him. She said they should show it to Father Lopez. He'd spent most of the time just staring at Renfro trying to determine if he was legitimate.

She also was puzzled the book wasn't out yet. She thought that if it came out now, it would probably be a big seller.

They called the priest and he was free to see them, so they squeezed him into their schedule. He looked at the sketch and said it was OK. Maybe the eyebrows were a bit too bushy and the jaw line was a little too lean. He agreed that the hair might've been a wig. He added, "There was an old tattoo on his arm, looked like an eagle. The words under the eagle were 'Semper Fi,' like the Marine motto."

They talked to the second ex-wife and the ex-partner attorney in Santa Fe right after lunch. Nothing new. The ex-wife confirmed what the first one had said and the attorney, Claude Everitt, like the businessman Hobson, had little to add. Couldn't think of any reason why someone would want to kill him.

Up in Taos, Cynthia, his wife, confirmed some of what they already knew. She'd also been interviewed by the writer, Renfro. She told them everything she'd told him. Maggie concluded she had no motive to kill her husband, or at least none was apparent. She did raise a question in Maggie's mind about the justice's travel. It bothered Cynthia, and Maggie made a mental note to look into it. Why did he take all those trips to exotic places, and why did he insist on going alone? Did it have something to do with the money? With the child pornography? Was he having an affair? The case raised so many questions.

When asked about the safe in the basement, she referred to it as his gun safe. She said he had it put in six or seven years ago, when she was on one of her trips back home. Before they were separated, she went home several times a year. She hated Washington. She wasn't into guns, so she didn't pay any attention to the safe, except she thought it was a good idea. She didn't remember him using any of the long guns, but he practiced a lot with handguns. And he often carried a handgun when he went out, even to the Court.

On their way back to Albuquerque Maggie and Mo stopped for dinner in Santa Fe. It was an upscale restaurant with a reddish brown motif highlighted with yellow, pretty much like every other Mexican or southwestern restaurant Maggie'd ever seen. The menu included enchiladas filled with chicken, cheese and green chili peppers. Maggie went for them. Banks had beef tacos. Maggie also broke down and had a margarita. Hernandez stayed basic with a Corona. They compared notes and assignments. Maggie decided to skip the woman in Las Cruces for this trip. If she needed to come back, she might check in on her then. When they got out to the car, she called and changed to a morning flight.

Banks dropped her off at her hotel at 9:15pm, and her first thought after closing the car door was, *who the hell is Gerald Renfro?*

CHAPTER 50

DAY TEN

F*riday, February 27, 2015.* Maggie had spent most of Thursday driving to and from airports, waiting in airports, and sitting on the airplane from Albuquerque to Dulles. She'd made a few phone calls to check on the various balls in the air.

On Friday she walked through the headquarters lobby door at 7:20am, her latest on a weekday since the investigation started. When she left her condo thirty minutes earlier, the morning sun was right at the horizon. Temperatures were expected to climb above fifty degrees in the afternoon, and the clouds were well scattered. The day held promise.

She wished she could say the same for the investigation. All the new information gave off the disturbing odor of smoke screen. Except Renfro. He was a wild card. She'd always avoided games with wild cards, but she had to play this one.

All her phone messages this morning were from the media. Josh had sent the media messages from the previous three days up to Naomi. Maggie did the same with today's, after which she made a to-do list.

1. *Check on report on Gerald Renfro.* (Several agents including the SAC in Chicago had been assigned to find him. That was three days ago.)
2. *Call Battinelli.* (Fill him in on Gerald Renfro.)
3. *Call Banks about the tribal police follow-up.*
4. *Check on the report on Ramirez's travel.* (A senior special agent was working on where he went and why.)
5. *Review tip line report.*
6. *Meet with T.J. and Naomi.* (Update them on everything.)

It was 8:05. She got up and walked to the coffee room for a fresh cup.

Back in her office, she closed the door, sat down and went into her thinking pose, elbows on desk, chin resting in both hands, looking straight ahead, seeing nothing. She laid out all the issues and people, looking for a pattern.

Which of the many possible motives connected with lethal injection?

First, there was money. In spite of the first rule, "follow the money," she'd already relegated that motive to a lower status. The money appeared to take them to Ken Straight, which didn't make sense. He was not a careless person. Plus he was on a cruise ship. He would have had to hire it done. Why would he want to kill a political ally? With a two-stage lethal injection? The money may lead to a crime, but not this crime.

Wife? She didn't need the money. Claims she didn't even know it existed. She thought it was just a gun safe. She didn't like him, but she didn't need him dead. She was already rid of him. Unless it was an ego thing, getting even for the rejection, the scorned lover? Would she know how to hire contract killers? Why would she have them do it by lethal injection? Didn't add up.

Party politics? Do we have people in or close to the White House who are that nutsy? And why would *they* do lethal injection?

Why lethal injection by anyone? The homicide looked professional, but would a professional fool around with two needles? Against an armed adversary? Maybe if it was part of the contract. But why would anyone make it part of the contract? Something to do with capital punishment? Some kind of message?

Could the old rapes be an issue? Bribery? Extortion? Certainly no shortage of motives, but they're all a stretch. And what would any of them have to do with lethal injection?

Did a pro do the injection thing as a red herring?

Why was Martindale there?

How many people are that proficient at breaking someone's neck?

Who is Renfro? Did he just coincidentally show up and go away? Another frigging coincidence?

At 8:35 she stuck her head out the door and asked Josh if he had the Renfro report. Not in yet. He'd called the Agent working on it, and she said they hadn't found him yet, and the full progress report wouldn't be ready today. Hopefully Monday. Maybe not till Tuesday.

At 9:20 Maggie called Battinelli. She told him about the trip to New Mexico, everything from young Indian girls to Criollos to Gerald Renfro.

He said, "Lotta distractin' shit goin' on there."

"Yeah, I Googled Renfro. Whatever he's written should've shown up. Got nothing. The Marines haven't gotten back to us yet. He's the mystery man of the moment. Got people looking for him. Any of the other stuff rattle your cage?"

He paused, then said, "There's just so much. Maybe too much. None of it says lethal injection."

Maggie promised him she'd call when the Renfro report came in.

At 9:25 she picked up that morning's tip line report from her desk. Calls were still coming in, but the volume was down by over half. The good news: none of the callers in the last three days had seen any UFOs. The bad news: people continued to call in who were *sure* the president or one of his key aides had done it.

At 10:20 she told Josh to try to set up a meeting with Naomi and T.J. that afternoon.

At 10:30 she called Banks. He said the tribal police had nothing on alleged rapes of young girls by a white man in 1969 or 1970. Records from before 1988 were archived on micro-fiche. They said it either didn't happen or the record was lost in one of their moves. They didn't mention the possibility that it was destroyed by a bent tribal police chief. The New Mexico State Police had no record of it. The woman in Las Cruces was willing to take a lie detector test, which they could do, if and when her claims became relevant to the murder investigation.

Banks thought he might send one of his senior Agents out to see Hobson and Everitt again. Just to see if they'd remembered anything that might be helpful. Couldn't hurt. Maggie thanked him and said she'd fill him in on the Renfro report as soon as she got it. Might not be till Monday.

At 10:45 she asked Josh to check on Ramirez's travel report. He replied that he had just called on it and was told, as with the Renfro report, it might be ready on Monday.

She spent the rest of the day on paper work and went home at 3:30. She was getting a stress headache. She salved her conscience for leaving early by taking an armful of papers with her. Ted was coming in for the weekend. She wanted to be fresh when he arrived.

CHAPTER 51

DAYS 13 & 14

Monday, March 2, 2015. Maggie got in at 6:45am. As she walked into the lobby, the sun was giving a bronze tint to the eastern sky. She left Ted's place 20 minutes ago when the sky was still dark gray. She was not a morning person and the early hours were already getting stale. The case wasn't moving fast enough for a murder investigation. They should be further along. Her forte, white collar crime, could take months and years. Murders had to be cleared up fast, or they might not be cleared up at all. Her concerns impinged on her weekend; in spite of Ted's presence, he wasn't the usual antidote for what ailed her. He arrived in time for dinner on Friday night. They spent the whole time together, except for a few hours on Saturday, when she went into the office to clean up minutia. She hoped he wasn't aware of how distracted she was. Once she even had to fake it. That was a first with Ted.

Once settled at her desk, she spent the first hour and a half on more clerical work. At 8:15 she started a round of calls to check in with key agents.

At 8:45 Josh informed her she would have both the travel and Renfro reports by 2pm. She wondered how she would fill the time. She went for a walk on the mall. The temperature was 47 degrees, no wind. She walked fast to generate her own warmth. In 45 minutes she walked back through the lobby.

At 10:15 she started making calls. Stanley reported no news yet on the money trail. Naomi was in a meeting. Mo Banks had nothing new to report. T.J. was out. Five agents checking out hot line leads reported they had nothing of value.

At 11:05 she called a nearby nail salon and was able to get right in. After the appointment she had a fast food lunch and was back in the office at 12:35. She sat at her desk, trying to figure out what to do till one of the reports came in.

At 12:45 a knock on her door interrupted her focus. She called for the knocker to come in. It was Josh.

"The travel report is here."

He had a sealed folder in his hand. The travel report was about Ramirez's mysterious and frequent trips out of the country.

He handed the folder to her, she thanked him (translation: you're excused) and he left. The folder contained about ten pages. She read the opening page, and skipped to the end for the summary. It concluded there was little doubt that Ramirez went there for sex with minors.

She went back to the first page and read the whole report. Since coming to Washington eight years ago, he'd made 20 trips out of the country. On the sixth trip he went to Hong Kong and Macao with his wife. They went as Mr. and Mrs. Ramirez, stayed in mid-priced hotels, and flew economy. The other 19 trips he took alone.

The second trip was to Mumbai, the third to Amsterdam, both cities with salacious opportunities for tourists. He didn't return to either place. The other 17 trips were to Bangkok where he went alone. On the 19 solo trips he flew first class out of Atlanta and under an assumed identity. His false ID included a fake passport, which is illegal in itself, even for Supreme Court justices. His alias was Joseph Howell. While in Bangkok Howell, nee Ramirez, stayed in five-star hotels and ate in the best restaurants. On these trips his only apparent concession to thrift was his tipping. He apparently stiffed all the service providers – waiters, porters, concierges, maids, cab drivers and pimps. Big mistake. His stinginess was so extreme as to be well remembered by his victims when questioned by American FBI Agents. They recognized Mr. Howell, the man in the photos and were forthcoming about his exotic habits, and his miserly tipping, once again supporting the adage that what goes around, comes around.

According to these sources, when he left the hotel, he went to a section of the city known for the most lurid debaucheries, where he favored an establishment that specialized in underage girls. He visited that same place every other day during his stay, possibly needing forty-eight hours to replenish his libido or stamina or both. The sources confirmed that, when there, he took full advantage of the establishment's featured service, namely girls who appeared to be about 12- or 13-years old.

The cost of the last trip was estimated to be just under $30,000. Assuming the cost of each of the previous trips was comparable, the total expenditure for the last eight years was about $500,000. His expenses were paid either in cash or with a credit card in Joseph Howell's name.

She called T.J., Naomi and Battinelli and filled them in. None of them were surprised.

Tuesday, March 3. At 11:15am, after a paper work morning, Josh brought the Renfro report into her office.

They found 121 Gerald Renfros in the lower forty-eight. Another 255 with very similar names. Kim, the niece in New Mexico had spelled the name for her. Kim said she remembered seeing it on his business card. She didn't have the card. He gave it to her mother. She assumed it'd been thrown away.

The odds were good that Kim had the spelling right. Maggie usually went with the odds. She put the 255 similars aside and concentrated on the 121 exacts. Not surprisingly, seventy three of them, a majority, were between fifty and seventy years of age. "Gerald" was not a trendy name for boys nowadays. Hadn't been for a long time. Of the seventy three, twenty four were from Midwestern or Plains states, two from the Chicago area. Maggie had asked for special attention to these states and the Chicago area based on what the witnesses in New Mexico said about his accent and his claim to be from Chicago.

The two from Chicago were quickly eliminated; one was African-American, and the other five feet, three inches tall. The report refocused on the remaining twenty two. One of them produced a curious result. He was born in Davenport, Iowa in 1950 but had an Ohio driver's license, first issued in 2006, when he would have been the very mature age of fifty-six. Late for a first driver's license. He also had a Social Security Number first issued in 1963, and a U.S. Passport first issued in 2007. The Social Security account had seen no activity since 1965, which was strange until they discovered a fifteen year old boy named Gerald Renfro who died in Iowa in 1965. The Social Security number belonged to that deceased Gerald Renfro.

Maggie stopped reading. So who got a driver's license in 2006 and a passport in 2007 using the name and SSN of a boy who died in 1965? Gerald Renfro was a fake ID.

She returned to the report. It said the address on the driver's license and the passport application was an apartment building in Cleveland. The building was now vacant, condemned, and under new ownership.

A Visa account and a bank checking account were opened in 2006 for a Gerald Renfro at that address. Both accounts were closed in December, 2013. The credit card had four charges against it in March of 2013: one Southwest Airlines round trip ticket from Chicago to Albuquerque, one rent-a-car in Albuquerque, and two motels in New Mexico. The bank account was opened with $2,000 and within two years carried an $18,000 balance. Rental payments were made monthly from the account. The large balance was maintained until March of 2013 when the various credit card charges were paid out of it. The account was then closed. The closing balance was $14,500.

The report included the pictures on the license and the passport. She compared them to the artist's rendering. Close enough.

Maggie read the report again, then went into her staring pose. Someone stole a young dead boy's identity and went to New Mexico to ask questions about Ramirez. Mother fuck! We have pictures. We've got him.

She gave the pictures to Josh to get copies made.

At 11:40 she was on the phone, talking to Pat Barnes, the SAC in Cleveland about the Renfro address. She wanted them to hunt down the building supervisor and anyone who lived there while he had the apartment.

The SAC said they were already working on it. They were having trouble getting names. The building was recently sold, and nobody had lived there in over a year. They were trying to find the old owners. The new owners knew nothing. Barnes said he'd call back as soon as they had something.

At 12:20pm, copies of the two Renfro pictures came back. She texted one of each to Mo Banks. She told Banks to take them to the priest and have him pick the best one. She told Josh to have both of them enlarged as much as possible short of them becoming distorted and make ten copies. She looked at the photos again and agreed it could be a wig. Maybe the moustache was fake, too.

At 12:45pm she went up to T.J.'s office to discuss the photos. She filled him in on everything to date.

T.J. said, "If you don't locate the guy by tomorrow morning, you should have Naomi put his picture out for everybody to see. I wouldn't wait any longer that that. He finds out we're looking for him, he may disappear."

At 12:55pm she called Battinelli. She told him what they had on Renfro. After a long silence, he said, "The dead kid, Gerald Renfro, would be about 60?"

"64."

More silence. Finally he said, "So the new Renfro is about 64. If he did Ramirez, explains why he needed help."

"Any other thoughts?"

Battinelli hesitated, then said, "Still hung up on the needles. What if our murderer is a milquetoast? What if he did it that way 'cause he didn't want to make the justice suffer any more than he had to? You know, like with euthanasias and executions. They do it that way 'cause it's supposed to be painless. What if our guy is just a nice guy? How you go about findin' a nice guy?"

She said, "How late you stay awake thinking that one up?"

CHAPTER 52

JOURNAL – WHAT HAPPENED

1:00pm, Wednesday, 3-4-2015

It's been over two weeks. I promised a follow-up report. I haven't forgotten. However, I've been procrastinating. I don't like to think about it.

Anyone reading this, however far in the future, will know that events didn't play out exactly as planned. Specifically, Ramirez's associate, Whit Martindale, appeared on the scene unexpectedly, and, to protect ourselves, we had to kill him.

Writing that last sentence is difficult; makes my stomach turn over. One of the conditions of my plan was "no innocent victims" or as the military leaders would say "no collateral damage." I hate that expression, calling innocent victims collateral damage. It's dehumanizing. It makes Keenie a non-person.

Nevertheless, in keeping with the original purpose of this document, here's what happened. The first part, the assassination of Justice Ramirez, went as planned, except after we put the body in the den, I added one element. There was a little electric clock on the desk. It read 6:31. I unplugged it.

Then, as we were about to leave, and contrary to all reasonable assumptions, Martindale showed up. I'd assumed such a thing couldn't happen. My research indicated Ramirez had no friends. He had no social life. While under months of surveillance, he had two visitors at the condo in the city and none at the farmhouse. The two in the city came together, one carrying a briefcase. I think the other guy was Martindale. They stayed about forty minutes. It was not a social call. People simply didn't make social calls on this man.

So, I made what I thought was the logical conclusion that any visitors he had would have something to do with business. And it seemed reasonable to assume that at the beginning of a long weekend, all the way out at the farmhouse, no one would make a business call. So he would be alone for the entire evening.

As the man said, "The best laid schemes…."

When I heard Martindale's car coming up the driveway, and realized we could not escape without him seeing us, my mind virtually shut down. I could not respond. Dylan, on the other hand, could. He was trained to deal with the unexpected. When the doorbell rang, he went to the foyer, moved a few items we'd left on the floor, putting them out of sight, and answered the door. He made an excuse to Martindale for why he was answering the door, saying we were there to exterminate pests, and invited him in. I think the pest thing was a little joke he made for his own amusement. When he told me in the car on the way home, I was too much in dismay to appreciate the humor. I guess I still am.

He offered to help Martindale take his coat off, and when Martindale turned his back, Dylan snapped his neck. Martindale was unconscious immediately and dead within a minute or so. Hell, we could have done that with Ramirez and skipped the needles. Don't know why Dylan didn't suggest it. Anyway, Dylan called me to come out and help him carry the body into the den. When we got him in there, Dylan went back out to the foyer to get Martindale's briefcase. He tried unsuccessfully to open it. I'm not sure why. Out of curiosity, I guess. He quickly gave up. According to news reports, it contained a great deal of money. Was it a bribe?

Starting to come out of the fog, and as a symbolic act, I removed a picture of Ramirez and Martindale from the wall and put it face down on the desk. I did those two things – the little clock and the picture – as a kind of signature against false confessions. Only the investigators and I would know about them. I can't explain it any better than that. Looking back, I wasn't exactly in a clear frame of mind.

Since we drove out of the farmhouse garage, I've been thinking a great deal, trying to better understand everything. Some of those thoughts should be recorded in this document before putting it to bed. But I'm not quite ready. I have to straighten it all out in my head. In a week or so.

CHAPTER 53

WEEK FIVE

M*onday, March 16, 2015.* Maybe Gerald Renfro was a ghost.

They released the photo on Tuesday, the Third of March. It appeared in newspapers and on television throughout western civilization; and on the Internet, which added most of the rest of the world. Thirteen days ago. Nothing. Nobody knows him. A few people claimed to have seen him in a restaurant or gas station, but nobody knows him or where he is.

The last building supervisor at the address in Cleveland can't remember him. The same for his supposed neighbors; at least none the FBI could locate. The building supervisor who rented the apartment to him nine years ago had no recollection either. The photo didn't jog his memory at all. Ditto, the Ohio DOT clerk who took his driver's license application.

Upwards of one hundred eighty Agents in Ohio, Iowa, New Mexico, and Arizona were following up leads. A few people in New Mexico claimed to recognize him. The retired business associate, Hobson, and the ex-legal partner, Everitt were both equivocating on their recollections. They now said somebody may have called them and asked questions about Ramirez. They weren't sure. Somebody may have told them about lying to the FBI.

Kim, the niece in Albuquerque remembered Renfro saying one of his previous jobs was as a locksmith, making Battinelli something of a genius, but not helping Maggie get closer to finding him. Agents throughout the Midwest were showing the photo to people at companies that make or sell locks, but no cigar yet. Must be a very good disguise, or maybe he *is* a ghost.

Battinelli was officially on the Task Force full time now. He and Maggie met and strategized every day. He pursued the capital punishment angle, but found nothing.

Cyber had no more to add. Nor did the group looking into the drugs. Both were common, but not considered street drugs. Most hospitals, doctors and veterinarians used them regularly.

The entire investigation was dragging.

The case of the money and Ken Straight was also in limbo. Straight was not answering questions, supposedly on the advice of his attorneys. Maggie and several prosecuting attorneys with the Justice Department discussed the possibility of threatening him with murder charges in the two deaths. They decided to wait for Boddington's report. He was still slogging through the banking system trying to find a money trail.

Maggie was sitting at her desk, reviewing overtime claims from Barnes, the Cleveland SAC, when she felt a nearby presence. She looked up, and Guerlach, Maas's right hand snake, was standing right in front of her, reading the papers on her desk upside down. How'd he get there?

"May I help you?"

"Oh, no, not at all. Just wondering how it was going. If I could help. You need anything we can do? Anything at all?"

He was downright creepy. She watched his hands, thinking of what T.J. said.

"Not that I can think of. You have something specific in mind?"

"No. Just trying to help. Maybe a fresh set of eyes and ears? A different way of looking at it? Whatever."

Maggie wanted him out of her office, but thought better of telling him to get out. He could turn it into an incident; make it sound like he was the offended party. Say he was just innocently offering assistance, and she got hostile. She didn't want to give him anything to use against her. She said, "Yeah, maybe you've got something there. Have a chair, John. Ok, if I call you John?"

He wasn't expecting her to be open and friendly. He hesitated, then moved to the chair. Sitting down he said, "Sure, that's my name."

"Good. Tell me what you know about the case, so far?"

"Uh, just what I read in the papers, see on TV, you know, talk around the office, like that."

"Oh, what do you hear around the office?"

"Not much. Just…it's a tough case, you know."

"Yeah, it's a tough one. Tell me, from a national security slash terrorism point of view, how would you come at it?"

"I don't know. Guess I'd have to know all the facts first."

"Hmm. Pretty much everything's out there. We're not holding back any secrets. You probably know most of what I know. I suppose you'd have to do it different over in Natsec. You know, keep a lot of it under wraps. National security being what it is. Anyway, I don't know what we could add for you. Already let a lot of cats out of a lot of bags."

She was giving him about the subtlest go fuck yourself she could, and it wasn't getting through to him. He thought he could just keep on schmoozing, and she'd let out something he could use, something he could take to Maas and get a big atta boy.

"John, tell you what, I have to get back to this bureaucratic crap on my desk, but you go and think about everything that's out there, and if you come up with anything, I'll be forever in your debt." She gave him her best "please leave" smile.

He'd been dismissed before, so he knew one when he saw one. He got up from the chair slowly. Maggie thought he might be doing a quick inventory of the papers on her desk hoping to find one he could pilfer. She watched his hands, almost laughing at herself for doing so. He could take any stack he wanted, if he'd follow through on whatever processing it needed.

He turned and walked to the door of her office, said, "Ok, talk to you later," and was gone.

Maggie got up from the desk, walked to the door and said, "Josh." He looked up and she gave him a "come here" wag with her index finger. He got up and walked over to her.

Almost whispering, she said, "don't ever let that guy come into my office again without warning me."

Josh said, "What guy?"

"The guy who was just in here. Guerlach from Natsec."

"He was in there? I never saw him go in or come out. He must have…I don't know how he did it. I didn't see anything."

"Shit, I didn't see or hear him come up to my desk either. He..." She didn't know what to say about him. Maybe he and Renfro are both ghosts.

"Ok, try to look out for him and warn me. By the way, do you lock your desk at night?"

"Yeah, but there's nothing in it, except a stapler I don't want to lose."

"If you ever get hold of anything you want to keep secret, don't leave it in your desk. I'll get a safe. We'll both use it. Do you know anybody in Natsec?"

"A few guys who work out."

"You trust them?"

"I hardly know them."

Maggie shook her head. What's happening to the world? "Me neither. Maybe I'm just seeing monsters under the bed. Anyway, I'll get a safe."

The child pornography story was still a secret, or so she hoped. It would have to go in the safe.

CHAPTER 54

JOURNAL – CLOSING COMMENTS

11:00am, Thursday, 3-19-2015

This is my last entry, my final words on the course of events leading up to and immediately following the two deaths in Virginia. When I finish this final chapter, we'll put it all in safekeeping where it will stay until Dylan and I are both gone.

Here goes.

In the aftermath of the two killings, I ran an emotional gauntlet, from stunned, almost catatonic – when Martindale arrived, and Dylan responded – to angry, to frustrated, to dismayed. It was like an escalator down to the cellar of depression.

The focus of my despair was quite narrow, specifically, Martindale's appearance at the scene. I fretted over that single aspect of the whole affair. It was in my mind that if he hadn't shown up, the assassination would have come off without incident, and the "suitable redress" for Keenie's death would have been achieved. My Goliath would have been slain, and I would be able to sleep again.

However, Martindale did show up, and an unnecessary death occurred, namely his, and it was my fault, because I'd made the incorrect assumption that no one would visit Ramirez at the country house. That incorrect assumption, I believed, was the issue. I berated myself on why I'd made such a mistake. What was I thinking? Why didn't I take into account the consequences of such a thing happening? After so much careful planning, how could I have been so careless as to cost an innocent man his life? I couldn't get beyond that isolated part of it. It was blocking my way to reconsidering the ultimate wisdom and logic of the whole concept.

With that offense – the death of Martindale – now added to my stockpile of guilt over Keenie's death and Donna's suicide, my mental state regressed. The insomnia continued unabated, even worsened. I was as impaired as I'd ever been. The prospect of endless sleep deprivation loomed, a prospect I just couldn't accept. I was at the point of considering Donna's ultimate solution for myself.

In desperation I started taking a more powerful sedative, the kind of potentially addictive medication I'd been avoiding all these years. These drugs are big in the news lately, called opioids. Heavy duty stuff. Used by doctors for pain relief, they can also knock you out. Literally. The one I use comes in time release capsules, spreads the effect over several hours; enough to get a full night's sleep.

I knew about opioids but stayed away, not only because of the addiction issue, but because I thought doing Ramirez would be my cure. Not using them was an incentive to keep going with the plan. Well, now I'm taking one of those capsules every night. And it does the job. The first night, three weeks ago, I slept for seven straight hours. That hadn't happened in over fourteen years. It was wonderful. So maybe a clear conscience isn't the only soft pillow. When my current supply is depleted, I'll have to make a decision. I doubt the doctor here will renew the prescription without asking a lot of questions. I may have to make a quick run to Mexico. There's always the street here, but I don't trust it.

Of course, there's still the matter of potential addiction. But who cares. I want sleep, and now I have it. Whatever else happens, maybe it'll be for the best; for all intents and purposes, my life is over. I've completed my mission. There's nothing left to do.

The other good side effect is getting my brain back. After three weeks of deep, mind-nourishing rest, I'm sharper, mentally and physically. It's like de-toxing, not from drugs, but from the poison of sleeplessness. Clearing out the cobwebs does take a few hours each morning, but by noon, I'm fairly sharp, more so than at any time I can remember since before that day at Keenie's school. I can function again as a normal person. So what if it's only part of the day? It's better than where I've been.

This recovered state of awareness has made me re-look at the process, ask questions about the journey. Was it born of a clean logical progression, or did I wander off the path somewhere? How exactly did I get from the old Pete Rossi to the Lone Ranger destiny? Why such a leap?

To re-trace my thinking, I went back to this journal, to its beginning. With a somewhat clearer head and a questioning attitude, I reread it. The first time all the way through without stopping. Then, more meticulously, making notes as I read. After the second read-through, I felt an inkling of dissonance, a sense that the chain of reason, of basic premises and assumptions to conclusions, may have been flawed. I read it a third time, looking for those jumping-off points, junctures where I went from the old Pete Rossi to what I am now, intersections that led me to decide to kill a man.

Summarizing, it went like this: I'd concluded that Lester, the shooter, was a victim himself. Ramirez, on the other hand, through his fundraising acumen, was the primary actor on behalf of the firearms industry, the linchpin blocking necessary legislation, the one individual most responsible for preventing reasonable screening of gun buyers and prohibiting unrestricted private sales of handguns. His position on the Supreme Court only exacerbated his potential to do harm. On top of that he was an evil, disgusting human being. Based on these findings, his elimination, his killing, was easily justified, and he would be the most suitable candidate to die to offset the tragic loss of Keenie. And, of course, as the Lone Ranger designate, or surrogate, I should be the instrument of his death.

I arrived at that last conclusion by drawing a correlation between my Grandfather's experience and my own. His unusual influence on me, particularly the Lone Ranger metaphor, and what happened with Bella and Signore Pavoni, all gave it an aura of personal destiny, not to mention the financial windfall from the business, which provided the time and resources to pursue such a destiny.

It started with Grampa. He was a good man on every level. He was my mentor and life guide, the best possible example to follow. His moral and ethical imprint on me was indelible. His goodness was a beguiling lure, which I took. But in my sleep-deprived state, did I blindly pervert it? Did I lose perspective?

In my mind the story of Signore Pavoni and Bella created a connection – or at least a solid correlation – with what happened to Keenie. Those two tragedies had similarities, but were they analogous? Perhaps, perhaps not. A bothersome detail is that I had to look for a Signore Pavoni to fill my matrix. My bad guy was not readily apparent. I refused to pin ultimate responsibility on Lester; he just didn't fit. So it took me years to find, some might say *create*, an acceptable candidate. Was I doggedly persistent, or was I irrationally driven?

Another matter is that Grampa did not intend to kill Signore Pavoni. His aggression led to what might be better described as a preventable accident. In the eyes of the law, manslaughter at worst. I, on the other hand, not only intended to kill Ramirez, I planned it for years. It's called premeditated murder. The outcome's the same; both men are dead. But is the distinction meaningful in this case?

Third, Pavoni was directly responsible for what happened to Bella. He raped her. Is there that kind of direct connection between Ramirez and Keenie? Of course not. How indirect is the connection? Is it so indirect as to be meaningless? Did helping the NRA raise PAC money indirectly contribute to Lester's brain-damaged attempt to kill his wife? Certainly, Ramirez was a bad guy, but was he *the* bad guy? Did he even *share* responsibility for Keenie's death? The NRA probably thinks not. Others might say he does.

Most interesting is the role of Grampa's Lone Ranger parable. Did I take it too seriously? I was trying to emulate a fictional character, the equivalent of a comic book super hero. Is that sensible? Should we be seriously guided by such role models?

The old Pete Rossi may have concluded that none of these factors justified what I did. The new Pete Rossi is not sure.

Certainly the controlling driver was guilt. It picked me out of the herd in the same way a wolf pack goes after a vulnerable elk. I was damaged – emotionally crippled. As a grieving father and husband, I felt responsibility; somehow it was my fault. But maybe Curlew, the shrink was right; I should have gotten over it. I didn't. Was I too disabled by lack of sleep to help myself? Curlew tried to provide a cure for my feeling of guilt, when all I wanted from him was a pill to help me sleep.

I admit I was in a self-perpetuating cycle. The guilt caused the insomnia which caused the fuzzy thinking which supported the guilt. If I'd opened up to Curlew about everything, he may have helped me, helped me understand it wasn't my fault. But I wasn't able to. Like Lester, I was obsessed. I wanted to do something, the right thing, to follow Grampa's example. But were my moral and rational compasses spinning out of control? My paternal instincts, the memory of the family meeting where I voted against Donna to let Keenie go to that school, Donna's accusing behavior; they all contributed to my sense of guilt. And the guilt fed my insomnia, and the insomnia addled my brain, which made the Lone Ranger destiny seem plausible.

The ultimate question is: did I do right or wrong? The outcome – the death of *two* worthless men, instead of one – clouds the answer. The old Pete Rossi would answer, "Wrong." But he's dead. He died a long time ago. When something happens that makes us fundamentally change, it's the same as dying. The person who was in there is gone, never to return. The new person takes over, makes all the decisions. The new Pete Rossi wouldn't necessarily agree with the "wrong" verdict. The new Pete's experiences are different. For one thing he experienced what made him change, what made the old person go away. So he makes different decisions, decisions the old person would not have made. It's circumstantial. There it is again. If a different person makes a different decision based on different circumstances, can the other person be held responsible?

Of course not.

It seems that responsibility is an elusive concept, perhaps an illusion altogether. It can be multi-faceted in that outcomes often have multiple causes. Little that happens is caused by only one thing or action or person. When do we truly understand who is responsible for what? Who can take credit, or accept blame? Some say no one. Others say everyone. In Keenie's case, was it the owner of the company that marketed the gun, or the employees who actually made it, or the gun show organizer, or the seller at the gun show who sold it to Lester, or the NRA, or the politicians who are afraid of the NRA, or Lester, or the driver of the truck Lester ran into, or Ramirez, or me, or all of the above?

I've come to believe I did the right thing with Keenie. It made sense for her to go to her local public high school with all her friends and all of its extracurricular opportunities. There was no reasonable threat of danger. It shouldn't have been a source of guilt. Nevertheless, it was. I saw the very long thread between my judgment call and her death as causal. It wasn't. The effects of acute, chronic insomnia made me forget what they taught in the college Logic class, that what happens before an event does not necessarily cause the event. Nor in my fog was I able to understand that parents cannot protect their children from every possible consequence, especially an irrational consequence.

In my final analysis, it's a coin flip. Different people might come to different conclusions. The assumption that no one would show up at the farmhouse was reasonable. But, as reality proved, incorrect. Other issues are less clear, less absolute. Maybe it was not my destiny to compensate for Keenie's tragic accidental death by committing murder; and even more painful to acknowledge, maybe the assassination of Justice Ramirez does not offset the loss of Keenie. As for Martindale, maybe he was just collateral damage, as awful as that term is, incidental to a greater purpose. The new Pete Rossi is not sure, except for one thing – I'm not going to feel guilty about it. I've suffered enough.

Whatever the ultimate truth, now I'm forced to pursue a new purpose. Now I must avoid capture for however long remains for me. No matter the verdict, I cannot accept incarceration. I'd be better off dead. Nor can

I jeopardize the rest of Dylan's life. So we continue, for whatever time we have left, as fugitives. When you read this, whoever you are, we will be dead, which may be the ultimate answer to all the questions.

On a more practical note, I have four post scripts:

1. A photo of me, taken several years ago has been released by the FBI and is appearing everywhere. It shows me in full disguise. It's the Gerald Renfro Passport photo. They're also looking for him by name and have published the Cleveland address I set up for him. Dylan, who never saw me as Renfro, says the photo has no resemblance to me at all. Nevertheless, it's out there. They also are showing around a second image, a rendition of what some forensic artist thinks I would look like without the disguise. It's not that close.
2. Dylan refused the payment I offered. He said he would only help out as a friend. This troubles me, because I suspect his financial situation is not good. So, he's in the will. If the drugs have the predicted effect, he'll be collecting in the not too distant future.
3. Dylan may be having a problem with alcohol. Twice now I've detected unusual behavior, the kind usually related to drinking. I hope it's not because of what he did for me.
4. To keep the FBI honest, there will be two copies of the thumb drive instead of one. The second will go to the Detroit Free Press. It will be sent two days later. The Bureau will have forty eight hours.

CHAPTER 55

AFTER THREE MONTHS

M*onday, May 18, 2015.* Maggie walked into her office at 8:45am. She hadn't been in earlier than 8:30 in the last month. No need. The investigation was at a crawl, if there was any movement at all.

Josh was already at his desk, drinking coffee, reading the Post. Most of the Task Force had been reassigned to other cases. The tip line was down to less than two calls a day. The belated callers insisted that the FBI should round up prominent Democrats and shake them down. Probably political activists trying to keep the pressure on. Fox News still mentioned the assassination and lamented the Bureau's incompetence, but it was no longer the featured topic. CNN and most of the others had lost interest completely.

Battinelli was back to working cold cases in Virginia. Maggie talked to him about once a week. He would call to cheer her up.

She checked in periodically with Banks in New Mexico and Barnes in Cleveland. Neither had anything new to report. Six weeks ago Naomi announced that the regular press conferences were being discontinued.

A separate investigative team had been assigned to the money issue, and Straight was still not talking. An indictment was in the works, but Parker was moving slowly. Maggie stayed interested in that side of it only for the slight possibility it might shed light on the killings.

The big news came late that morning. At 11:15 Fox reported the Chairman of the Senate Crime & Terrorism Committee was scheduling a hearing on the investigation of the assassination. Within an hour the chairman of the equivalent House committee proposed the same for his side of Congress. They were both Republicans. Both said the American people believed the killings were part of a larger political conspiracy. Maggie felt that if the shoe were on the other foot, the Democrats would be doing and saying the same things.

Through some miracle of bureaucratic restraint, or maybe just disinterest, the child pornography evidence had not been leaked. In the Congressional hearings, it would get out. Not in the best interest of the Republicans. They truly believed their side had been victimized by the killings, but the evidence did not make them appear to be deserving of sympathy. They were not happy. Wags joked that Director Parker was taking Xanax regularly.

The next day a rumor surfaced that the anti-terrorism branch of the FBI would become involved in the investigation. That afternoon Assistant Deputy Maas met behind closed doors with Director Parker for over thirty minutes. After he left, the director called T.J. Collins and told him he'd thought about it but decided the investigation should remain with the crime branch. Maggie conjectured that Maas now saw it as a losing hand and had talked the director out of it.

She hadn't played poker since that frantic day in Tampa. She was having trouble concentrating on anything. She thought it might be because she couldn't sleep.

CHAPTER 56

THE THUMB DRIVE

Tuesday, January 19, 2016. It was eleven months and two days since they found the bodies. The ten by thirteen padded envelope came addressed to Joint Task Force Commander Margaret A. Foster at FBI Headquarters. The return address was a law firm in Troy, Michigan. She went down to the lobby to sign for it at 11:00 am.

The letter said the enclosed USB flash drive was being forwarded to her per the instructions of the firm's client, Peter Rossi. They'd been directed to do so upon notification of Mr. Rossi's death and that of another man, Dylan Armstrong. Mr. Armstrong had perished in a boating accident in July, and in December, Mr. Rossi had suffered a drug-related death in Mexico. They received official confirmation of Mr. Rossi's death last week.

She stared at the small, black electronic device, sitting in the middle of her desk pad. Why would a dead man want to send a thumb drive to the Task Force commander? Her very logical mind told her that the long search was over; all the answers were inside the little electronic storage device.

She felt lonely. She wanted to be with someone when she viewed the contents, someone who would know what she was feeling, someone who had been through this losing battle, someone who would be a supportive presence. She couldn't easily call on a member of the Task Force. It was disbanded. Even Josh was gone. He was the last to go, save for Maggie herself. He'd been reassigned to regular duties in August. She called him to see if he was free. He wasn't in. His voice mail said he was at Quantico for the week attending a training class.

She called Naomi in Public Affairs. Naomi was at a media confab in New York. Director Parker was with her. She called T.J. Collins. Fran said he was in Florida with his wife. Povich came to mind. She was reporting to him again, since the Task Force investigation came to a halt. The two of them were not a contented couple. He seemed to get too much pleasure out of the lack of progress. She elected not to include him in this unveiling. Battinelli was at least two hours away. He'd received a promotion and was now located in the VSP headquarters in Richmond. They hadn't talked since before Christmas when she called him with holiday greetings. The last time before that was back in late summer.

Boddington was in New York, so he'd have to hear about it second hand. He'd tracked the Ramirez money trail to Ken Straight and a cartel of firearms manufacturers. Eight people, including Straight, were indicted in July. Straight's legal team had effectively delayed the trial, but word was that several of the co-conspirators were ready to cave. He could be in serious trouble. But would his political influence keep him from seeing the inside of a real prison?

Timothy Chu was in Europe working on something to do with Russians and WikiLeaks.

Olen Richards was transferred to Seattle at his own request. He had a parent out there who needed him nearby. The Bureau was normally stingy with such transfers, but there was an opening in Seattle, and he got it. He joked to Maggie that they gave it to him based on time served and good behavior.

Maas left the Bureau in September to join a hedge fund. Could it be that money was more important than power? Had to be a tough decision for him. Or was it just a political staging move? She had no idea what happened to Guerlach, though he and Josh had a run-in when Josh caught him nosing around back in May. Maggie reported it to T.J. Collins, and Guerlach disappeared after that.

Maggie's own career was in a bit of a hiatus. She'd told T.J. she was retiring within a couple years, not mentioning Povich. T.J. didn't mention him either. If he was disappointed, he covered it well. She was still officially Joint Task Force commander, but it was an empty place; the investigation had made no progress in over six months. Boredom was her biggest enemy. That and a hit to her self-esteem. Since August she'd been temporarily assigned to a few cases as an interrogation consultant. She was fifty-one years old with over a year left to qualify for a full pension. She envisioned the prospect of a long, slow year of trying to stay busy. Fortunately, the insomnia last spring didn't last. She credited intense daily workouts along with Ted's weekly treatments.

With the thumb drive in front of her, she continued to resist plugging it into her computer. She wanted to have solved the case, not have it given to her, as if she'd conceded defeat. She felt a blasphemous tug of hope that it didn't hold the answers to the big case. But the envelope was addressed to her in her official capacity.

What else could it be?

As a last resort, she called Ted in Chicago. He answered, "Howe here." It sounded like the punch line to an ethnic joke. She'd heard him say it hundreds of times. Even on this day in her melancholy state, it made her smile.

She said, "I'm calling for therapeutic counsel…again."

He replied with an officious tone, "Well now, Ms. Foster, how can I help?"

"Are you in a meeting?"

"Nope, you have my full attention."

"Are you getting tired of these calls?"

"No again. They make me feel important and useful. Plus I love you and, as such, I'm obligated to help you, when you need it, which is rare, so, out with it. What's up?"

"I think my life as I've known it for the last eleven months…it feels a lot longer than that…it feels like a long, long time; I think it's over, and the ending's not going to…what's the expression…it's not going to provide meaningful closure."

She sounded weary. He was standing by his desk and moved over to the chair to sit down. No more light banter. "Maggie, what is it?"

"I just received a thumb drive in the mail. Special Delivery. It was addressed to me as Commander of the Task Force. Nobody has called me that in months." A sharp intake of breath indicated she was having trouble. Maggie didn't cry easily.

"It's from a law firm in Troy, Michigan, near Detroit, I think." Another deep breath, followed by a pause. "The letter says their client told them to send it to me when he died. The client's name is Peter Rossi. It mentions another guy named Dylan Armstrong, who apparently is also dead. I didn't know either one of them." Starting to lose it again, a deep breath, almost a sob.

Confused, "Well...what's on it?"

"I haven't looked yet. But I think I know. It's gonna be about Ramirez and Martindale. It's over...I think. I just feel...I don't know how I feel. I didn't catch them. I didn't get it done. Now they're both dead."

He gave no helpful response.

She said, "I'm down. I'm alone here. Everybody's gone somewhere. I'm going to have to look at it alone. I almost hope it's nothing...just another hoax. I need human contact...maybe a pep talk. One of your specials."

He hesitated, as a doctor would, pondering a range of remedies. After a moment he said, "Hon, you did everything right. It's not you. Think of it as a *systems* failure...like on an airplane. You're the pilot of the plane, but you didn't create the systems that make it work. You just operate them. If one of the systems doesn't work, the plane may not fly right, but it's not your fault. What you have to do now is save as many passengers as possible.

"Go plug the thumb drive in and look at it right now. Don't delay. There may be a time issue...though it doesn't sound like it. Maybe not...but you have to look. As you say, might be nothing, just another hoax. I'll stay on the line, or you can call me as soon as you've seen it. We can talk about what it says. What do you say?"

"OK, OK...I'll try to be a big girl. But hang on while I give it a look."

Four minutes later she picked up the phone, and sounding recovered, said, "Gonna have to call you back. It's long. Might be real. Call you when I'm done."

At 1:15pm she called Troy, Michigan. "Yes, thank you for taking my call. My name is Margaret Foster…with the FBI. You sent me a letter yesterday with a UBS flash drive on behalf of your client, Peter Rossi. I have a few questions."

The managing director of the law firm, a Mr. Doner said, "Yes, of course. I'll try to answer them."

Maggie was interested in the proof of death. Mr. Doner said they had a death certificate signed by a physician in Mexico City. They checked on its legitimacy before forwarding the material to her. They also had an urn full of ashes. Mr. Rossi had been cremated.

"You're confident the document is authentic?"

"Certainly." A pause, "Uh, well, it *is* Mexico." He said it with an uncomfortable chuckle. "I'd say we're as confident as possible under the circumstances. We did confirm with his landlord in Mexico that he'd passed. So, we had independent verification, a pretty high degree of certainty…as much as we're going to get, I should think. May I ask, what is this about?"

Avoiding the question, "Did you check the ashes for DNA?"

"As a rule, cremated ashes don't retain DNA traces. Or so I'm told. Apparently, the very high temperature at which the body is cremated destroys the DNA."

"Did you send the other flash drive to The Free Press yet?"

"No. Tomorrow morning. Our instructions were to hold it for forty eight hours after yours went out."

"Mr. Doner, you need to hold it for a bit longer than that…and don't look at it. May I have your assurance on both of those matters?"

"Uh…I…of course we won't look at it, but we have very precise instructions from our client about when to send it…I need to consult with the partners regarding our legal obligations."

"Mr. Doner, don't send it. Is that clear? Or should I get a restraining order? This is a matter of national consequence." She didn't say "national security," knowing it was an overreach and assuming this guy was a big time attorney. "Once we've confirmed the deaths of those two men, you'll be free to do as you think best."

"Ms. Foster, I have to ask again, what is this about? My associates will require some reasonable justification for such an unusual request."

"You haven't looked at the thumb drive?"

"Absolutely not. We have to respect our client's privacy. We can't just poke into things." He sounded appropriately offended.

"If I tell you what this is about, can you maintain silence, on behalf of your apparently deceased client, not even tell your associates?"

"If it has to do with a client confidence, we're all sworn to silence, as you say. They can be counted on to be discreet. It would be inappropriate for me not to share it with them."

"How many are they?"

"About fifteen."

"No, Mr. Doner, you can't tell *fifteen* goddamned people. I don't care if they're cloistered monks. You're going to have to keep it to yourself. If you assure me of that, I'll tell you what we're about. Otherwise, about twenty-five FBI agents will be in your office in less than three hours – that'll be around 4:00 this afternoon – and they'll have the authority to go through all of your Rossi files. Your choice."

"I've been doing this for a long time, Ms. Foster, and I don't like being threatened."

"I've been doing this for a long time, too, Mr. Doner, and I don't like threatening. Rest assured, you don't want to call my bluff on this one. I'm holding Aces. Again, your choice."

After a few seconds, "I'll hold it till Monday. If you want longer, you'll need the restraining order."

She hung up without telling him anything. Her next call was to Director Parker in New York. She told him what she had. He congratulated her on "solving the case" and thanked her for her dedication. She wanted to gag. He suggested she get the restraining order ready as a just-in-case. If she needed clerical support, his administrative assistant, Arlene, was available. The relief in his voice was of a man who had just learned his budget would get approved.

CHAPTER 57

NO MORE REGRETTING

F*riday, January 22, 2016.* The two men sat on the balcony of the sixth floor apartment, watching the surf in the ocean gain intensity as the Atlantic breeze stiffened. The early afternoon sun had passed behind them and was blocked by the roof of their high rise, leaving them in a comfortable shade. Each had a lemon flavored soft drink on the small glass-topped table between them.

After a period of silence, the older man said, "They should have it by now. Don't know how much we'll hear down here." Down here was Punta Del Este, a resort city just east of Montevideo, Uruguay.

The younger man, who was taller and slightly heavier said, "You can always check the Internet."

"Don't have a computer yet. Thought I'd give myself a month or so of independence."

"You want real independence, come out with me on the boat. It's a beaut. Amazing what you can get down here for half a mil. We can slip up to Rio next month for Carnival. Hear it's a pretty exciting time. Always wanted to go. Or come on over and visit us in Buenos Aires. Stay at our place for a few nights. See the big city."

"You're inviting me without consulting Javier?"

"He'll be ok with it. He's pretty laid-back."

"Does he know?"

"No. Don't want to burden him."

They didn't use names when addressing each other, for fear of saying the real name and someone overhearing.

The younger man asked, "How you sleeping?"

"Better. The shrink in Mexico City helped wean me off the heavy stuff. He also tried hypnosis for the nightmares. It may have helped. Haven't had one in a while."

"You tell him anything?"

"Only they'll come looking for me. When it hits the Internet, he'll know."

"Is he under any kind of professional ethics requirement to keep your secrets?"

"The best kind – he's on retainer, five thousand a month until they arrest me or I die. That's mucho dinero in Mexico. More than enough to pay for the "amiga" he keeps on the side. He also took care of the death certificate and the ashes. So, it behooves him to stick with the story. Could get himself in trouble. Plus, it's Mexico. The line there between what's true and what's false is kind of wavy." He pointed out at the ocean and said, "It's like that line out there separating the blue water and the blue sky. Some places it's hard to see. Like a lotta things." He added, "Not to worry, anyway. He doesn't know where we are."

The big man was reminded of his friend's loss of innocence. In the old days it would never have occurred to him to bribe a doctor.

He changed the subject, "So what are you going to do with the rest of your life?"

"Try to relax, I guess. No more regretting. According to the alcoholic's prayer, it doesn't do any good. Planning to read more, like you. A good book takes your mind off things. And I'll take you up on the boat ride. Take a long cruise, if we may. Go up through the locks in Panama. Visit some of our money. Go down to Peru. Food's the best there. Patricia showed me some places. And there's the ruins. Maybe the Galapagos, see what Darwin got so worked up about."

"Sounds like you've been making a bucket list."

"Yeah, been thinking about things to do, places to see, before it's all over. Like to find me another Patricia. She was good for me. Too bad I can't go back to her. What about you? You thinking about the future?" "

"I'm still wondering if I have one. Think they'll ever find us?"

"Depends on whether they keep looking. I put some false leads in the journal; about you drinking and not taking the money and me and the drugs. Tried to reinforce the idea we could be dead. We'll see. The money's the problem. I used some pretty sharp people to try to create a dead-end trail, but…"

It was good to see him so taciturn. "You don't seem to care."

"I may have worn out my caring muscles. I try to care, but sometimes nothing comes out. I remember in Vietnam, starting not to care. Over there I thought it was about circumstances. People made decisions depending on the circumstances. And the circumstances were pretty bad over there. Good people did some bad things. Things they might not have done otherwise. It happens a lot of places, I guess. Like we're all guilty and innocent at the same time. Might be where they got the idea of original sin."

"Original sin? What the hell you been reading?"

The older man smiled, "Don't know where that came from. Just a thought."

"So you're ok with everything?"

"Everything? I suppose. There's so much...a long line of victims: Bella, Signore Pavoni, Grampa, Keenie, Donna, Lester, Ramirez, Martindale...you and me. Some of us innocent, some of us guilty, some of us both. It's just hard to tell...maybe not even important. Yeah, I'm ok with it.

"I can sleep with it."

CHAPTER 58

LOOSE ENDS

Saturday, January 23, 2016. Maggie sat in the oversized chair near the fireplace in Ted's condo in D.C., taking a first sip from the martini he'd started mixing when she came through the door.

She said, "Naomi's doing a press conference Monday morning on the whole thing. The Free Press won't get their copy till Monday afternoon. It'll be on their website right away, but nothing in print till Tuesday morning."

Ted stood near the mantel opposite Maggie's chair. The artificial gas fire combined with the martini gave off the right amount of warmth to remind them it was January outside. He wasn't sure how much Maggie wanted to talk about, but his curiosity got the best of him, "How's Naomi going to play it?"

"Just as the document lays it out. Nobody could have made that all up and gotten it so right, even the part about the little clock. We never let that out. Battinelli agrees with me; it's the real deal."

"So, it's all over?" He let himself down into the fireplace chair opposite Maggie's, careful not to spill his drink.

No response from Maggie as she went into her deep thinking mode. Ted had seen it often enough not to interrupt. After a moment she said, "Just a couple loose ends."

"Like?"

"Like maybe they're still alive...still out there." She took more than a sip on her drink.

"Didn't you say Naomi was going to...?"

"She's going to give everybody the version on the thumb drive. The director directed it, in a manner of speaking."

They both sipped again. After an appropriate silence, Ted said, "S'plain."

"He wants the case closed. So we're closing it."

"What's Battinelli say?"

"He says he's a homicide cop, and homicide cops are paid to close cases. He says as far as he's concerned, it's closeable." She took another sip. "I think he suspects they're still out there. But he moved on months ago. Don't think he likes long, drawn-out cases."

"So, what has you staring into space again?"

"It has an odor, a 'something is rotten in Denmark' kind of odor. The odds that these guys would both get their tickets punched that soon, like ten months, the odds are against it. It can happen, but I wouldn't normally play those cards. The Coast Guard in Michigan didn't recover a body on Armstrong, the accomplice. Supposedly had a drinking problem. Rossi mentioned it in his document. They found the empty boat out in the middle of Lake Huron near one of the deep shipping channels. Couple empty gin bottles rolling around on the deck. They say he couldn't have swum that far...all the way to shore in Lake Huron; he was apparently drunk, and it's huge and real cold, even in July. They say he probably got turned into fish food. I suppose it's possible, but it doesn't usually happen that way. They usually find a body. Again, it's against the odds. And the guy was a champion swimmer in his youth, and a fitness freak and an ex-SEAL.

"As for Rossi, you never know about Mexico; anything goes down there. Another thing is his money. He was loaded – over fifty mil at one time. Stanley thinks some of it's gone missing. Only about twenty-five left, according to the will. You know, there's taxes, and he could've lost a bunch in the Great Recession, but Stanley is skeptical. Plus the odds of two healthy guys….and no bodies."

Ted got up to refill their glasses. "You're taking it rather well."

"Remember the little speech you gave me on the phone about systems, airplane systems? You didn't just make that up on the spot, did you? You aeronautics guys probably use it all the time. Anyway, it was good. Really settled me down."

"What are you going to do?"

"Keep an eye out, I guess. Have to be in my down time, though. As far as the Bureau is concerned, the case is closed. Stanley might be an ally. It's gotten under his skin. He's the key. They may be out there. Be good for my ego if we find them."

"And then what?"

"Not sure. Problem is, after reading Rossi's journal, I feel sorry for him. He went through hell, and the other one, Armstrong, according to the DOD, he was a fucking war hero. They kicked him out because he was gay. They both suffered more than people should have to. They were both good guys. I'm not supposed to think this way, but the truth is, they did the world a favor. Ramirez was a complete waste of skin and Martindale was his enabler. This case has changed me."

"So, if you find them, are you going to be a human being or an FBI Agent?"

"Don't know. Have to figure out which way saves the most passengers."

ACKNOWLEDGMENTS

Two guys, Bob McGowan and Charlie Weaver, made me write this book. Otherwise it never would have happened. They also helped throughout the process. I can't thank them (or blame them) enough.

Norm Davis told me about MPs in Vietnam. He was one. I'm grateful for his service and for sharing his expertise on the subject.

Roger Goralski, a one-time Detroit police officer, provided useful comments on the DPD.

My daughter, Becca, an experienced Fed, provided insights on federal law enforcement matters and D.C. politics. She also was my first beta reader and made comments that improved the book.

Pauline Druschel and my wife, Marilynn, were both beta readers who contributed valuable feedback. Marilynn also proof read the whole manuscript.

Bill Haney counseled me on several publishing issues.

Tom Ferguson edited portions of the book. His efforts, both literary and structural, along with his encouragement, were invaluable.

Several others kept me going by continually asking, "How you doing with the book?" I had to keep at it, because I couldn't face them if I gave up. Thanks to all of you. You know who you are.